GIDEON'S WAR

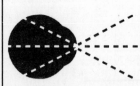

This Large Print Book carries the
Seal of Approval of N.A.V.H.

GIDEON'S WAR

A THRILLER

HOWARD GORDON

THORNDIKE PRESS
A part of Gale, Cengage Learning

GALE
CENGAGE Learning

Detroit • New York • San Francisco • New Haven, Conn • Waterville, Maine • London

GALE
CENGAGE Learning

Copyright © 2011 by Teakwood Lane Productions, Inc.
Thorndike Press, a part of Gale, Cengage Learning.

LIBRARY OF CONGRESS CATALOGING-IN-PUBLICATION DATA

Gordon, Howard, 1961–
  Gideon's war / by Howard Gordon.
    p. cm. — (Thorndike Press large print thriller)
  ISBN-13: 978-1-4104-3714-3 (hardcover)
  ISBN-10: 1-4104-3714-0 (hardcover)
    1. Intelligence service—Fiction. 2. Brothers—Fiction. 3. Terrorism—Prevention—Fiction. 4. Washington (D.C.)—Fiction. 5. Large type books. I. Title.
PS3607.O5937G53 2011b
813'.6—dc22   2011004430

Published in 2011 by arrangement with Simon & Schuster, Inc.

Printed in the United States of America
1 2 3 4 5 6 7 15 14 13 12 11

For Cambria

Those who can win a war well can rarely make a good peace, and those who could make a good peace would never have won the war.

— WINSTON CHURCHILL

PROLOGUE

Cole Ransom was tired from the long flight, though not too tired to admire the functional design of the airport. Passing easily through customs, he followed the bilingual signs that led him outside to the area for ground transportation. He didn't lose a step as the glass doors slid open and he walked outside, where he was hit by a whoosh of blazing tropical air. Squinting against the impossibly bright sun, he could see the glass and steel spires of the capital city of the Sultanate of Mohan rising in the distance.

A man — unmistakably American — stood next to a black Suburban parked by the curb. He wore dark wraparound sunglasses, a camo baseball cap, and a heavy beard. An ID badge hung from his belt. The sign in his hand said DR. COLE RANSOM. If not for the beard, he would have looked like a soldier or a cop.

"Dr. Ransom," the man said, lowering his

sign and holding out his hand. Ransom reached out to shake it, but the man smiled. "I'll take your bags, sir," the man said.

"Right. Sorry," Ransom said, handing him his suitcase.

"I can take the other one if you want," the bearded man said, nodding toward Ransom's laptop.

"That's okay," Ransom said. "I'll hold on to it." He had come to Mohan on the biggest job of his career. The last thing he needed was his laptop getting smashed or stolen.

The driver put Ransom's suitcase into the back of the Suburban and closed the gate, then opened the rear passenger door for Ransom, who climbed inside.

The driver settled behind the wheel, then glanced at Ransom in the rearview. "Dr. Ransom, before we get going, you might want to double-check that you've got everything. Bags, passport, computer?"

Ransom took a quick inventory. "Yeah, that's everything. And you can call me Cole. I'm just a structural engineer."

The driver smiled as he started the ignition. "I know who you are, sir."

Ransom was, in fact, one of the finest structural engineers in the world. He was here in the Sultanate of Mohan to test the structural integrity of the Obelisk — a newly built deep-sea oil rig, the largest and most expensive in the history of man's quest for crude. There had been problems with the motion-damping system, and he was here to sort them out.

The Suburban exited the airport through a security gate, then turned onto a service road. To the right stretched a long swath of deserted beach and beyond it, the glittering blue surface of the South China Sea. Ransom would be spending the next few weeks somewhere out there. As the Obelisk was being phased into service, it had begun to exhibit some troubling sway characteristics in rough seas. Kate Murphy, the manager of the rig, suspected a design flaw. The rig's designers insisted that she was being paranoid, or at the very least, that she was trying to cover her ass to cover her production shortfall. Ransom had talked extensively with Kate before flying out, and she didn't sound even remotely like an alarmist. But you never really knew. Ransom had come here to run some tests and see who was right.

The Suburban suddenly lifted and fell on its suspension, pulling Ransom from his thoughts. The driver had turned off the service road onto a short gravel track that led down to the beach. He stopped the Suburban in what looked like an abandoned quarry. Ransom was puzzled.

"Why are we stopping here?"

"I need to make sure you've got your passport," the driver said.

Ransom gave the driver a curious look. That was the second time he'd asked about the passport.

"I told you before. I've got it."

"I should probably hold on to it up here."

"Why?"

"We've had some civil unrest these last few weeks. We'll be passing through some checkpoints the government's put up, and I'll need to show the soldiers your passport." The bearded man held out his hand, palm up.

Ransom wondered why the driver hadn't asked for it back at the airport as he dipped into his breast pocket for his passport and handed it to the driver. The bearded man scrutinized the little blue booklet. Ransom felt his heart rate speed up slightly, felt a tickle of concern in the back of his neck.

"This civil unrest . . . how serious is it?" Ransom asked.

The bearded man lowered the passport and looked up at Ransom. "Ever hear of the terrorist Abu Nasir?"

Ransom frowned and shook his head. "No, I haven't."

"Now you have."

Ransom saw the big black circle pointing at him before he realized the driver was holding a large automatic pistol in his hand. Then the driver shot him in the face.

CHAPTER ONE

Until he tried putting on his tuxedo, Gideon Davis didn't realize how much weight he'd gained. The extra pounds were hardly noticeable on his muscular six-foot-one frame, but Gideon had felt the tug across his shoulders when he buttoned his jacket earlier that afternoon. Now, it felt even tighter, and he tried to keep himself from squirming in his chair as the president of the United States addressed the General Assembly of the United Nations.

". . . ten thousand lives have been lost in the bloody civil war between the Guaviare militia and the armed forces of the Colombian government, most of them innocent civilians. For years, both sides repeatedly rejected calls for a cease-fire, until the prospect of a peaceful resolution to the conflict seemed unattainable to everyone in the international community. Everyone . . . except for one man." President Alton Diggs nodded toward Gideon, who smiled a smile that felt as tight as his tuxedo. Being in the spotlight was something he still hadn't grown accustomed to.

Seventeen hours earlier, Gideon had been sitting in a jungle hut in Colombia, while armed men prowled around, waiting for an excuse to start shooting one another. The cease-fire he'd negotiated was the culmination of a three-month-long series of marathon sessions during which he'd spent day and night shuttling between government and rebel forces, usually eating the same meal twice — once with each faction — which accounted for the extra ten pounds he'd put on. In order to keep the warring sides at the table, he'd partaken of huge heaping portions of *ajiaco,* the traditional stew made of chicken, corn, potatoes, avocado, and *guascas,* a local herb, and *chunchullo,* fried cow intestines. As effective a diplomatic strategy as it was, Gideon knew that no amount of food would make the cease-fire hold. Chances were slim that it would last through the month. But the president had told him the best way to maintain the cease-fire was to get the international community invested, and the best way to get them invested was through a major media event. And the media loved

Gideon Davis.

President Diggs continued reciting for the audience some highlights of Gideon's career as a Special Presidential Envoy. He credited Gideon with defusing crises from the Balkans to Waziristan, and for being among the first public figures with the courage to argue that the United States needed to rethink its approach to the war on terror. To his detractors, Gideon was dangerous — a pie-in-the-sky slave to political correctness who thought the enemies of Western civilization could be jawboned into holding hands and singing "Kumbaya." But anyone who'd ever spent any time with Gideon knew how far from the truth that was. They knew he was a straight talker with zero tolerance for bullshit. They knew he listened to people. Simple enough virtues, but ones rarely found in Washington — which was why some insiders had tagged Gideon as the fastest rising star in American politics. Before Gideon had left for Colombia, President Diggs had let slip that some party bigwigs were considering him for one of several upcoming races. One rumor even had Gideon on the president's short list of potential running mates. This caught Gideon by surprise, since he'd never had any real political ambitions. Exposing his private

17

life to that kind of scrutiny, and having to make the inevitable compromises that come with holding public office, had no interest for him. But the prospect of wielding enough power to make a real difference in world affairs had caused Gideon to rethink his position. It was one of the reasons he'd agreed to squeeze into his tuxedo to accept this award from the president, who was now winding up his introduction.

". . . more than simply building bridges, this man has dedicated himself to that ancient and most sacred cornerstone of our moral code: Thou Shalt Not Kill. And so, it is my great privilege to present the United Nations Medal of Peace to one of the great peacemakers of our time, Gideon Davis."

Gideon approached the podium to a generous stream of applause. He shook the president's hand, then bowed his head to allow him to place the ribboned medallion around his neck.

"Thank you, Mr. President," Gideon said, before acknowledging several other heads of state whom protocol deemed worthy of acknowledgment. "This is a great honor, and I accept it with gratitude and humility. All of us in this room know that peace is more than just the absence of war . . . it's also the absence of poverty and injustice.

The real work still lies ahead of us, and its ultimate success depends on the diplomatic and economic support of every country represented in this room tonight." As Gideon continued to talk about the necessity of international solidarity, he saw a woman in a red dress stifle a yawn. He was losing them. But that didn't stop him from making the point he wanted to make — that the real heroes were the men and women in Colombia who had found the courage to compromise and to break the cycle of violence that had claimed the lives of so many of their countrymen. "With your support, their goodwill and hard work might actually make this a just and lasting peace. They're the ones we should be honoring tonight. And so I share this award with them." He took off the medal, held it in the air over his head.

But his gesture was met with silence.

I blew it, Gideon thought to himself. These people hadn't come here to be reminded of their moral and economic obligations. They'd come to feel good. They'd come expecting Gideon to shovel out the kind of self-congratulatory rhetoric that keeps the United Nations in business. Gideon scolded himself for ever thinking otherwise and wished he'd found an excuse to stay home and get some sleep.

But then the applause started. Sudden and decisive, like a thunderclap followed by a great rain that just kept going until it flooded the room with the collective approval of every person in the audience. Even the woman in the red dress was clapping. And for a moment, Gideon allowed himself to feel a flicker of hope that the cease-fire he'd worked so hard to make happen just might last. At least for a little while.

A few minutes later, Gideon was ushered into a large adjoining room. As successful as his speech had been, he had no illusions that it would have any real impact on the cease-fire. Making speeches was the easy part. Turning the enthusiasm of politicians and diplomats into real action was a much taller order. Most of the people here couldn't be counted on to follow through on any of the wine-inspired promises they'd made. Some of them were powerless; others were simply full of shit.

An embassy official from the Netherlands introduced himself to Gideon, who remembered that the man had been his country's foreign minister before being sidelined to an embassy post because of an ongoing relationship with a call girl. "You are a visionary," the embassy official said, his small hand clamping around Gideon's bicep.

Gideon did his best to smile. "I appreciate the compliment, but I just did what the president sent me to do."

"Your modesty is attractive, of course," the man said, "but you do yourself an injustice when —"

"Mr. Davis? I'm sorry to interrupt . . ."

Gideon turned toward the speaker. Unlike the people around him — all of them wearing tuxedos or evening gowns — the man who was addressing him wore a crisp military uniform. Dress blues with a white web belt. His hair was trimmed high and tight, with the sidewalls rarely seen outside the United States Marine Corps.

"The president would like to see you."

"Excuse me," Gideon said to the embassy official, grateful for an excuse to end their conversation before it had a chance to start.

The embassy official glared at the marine, clearly unaccustomed to being interrupted by some lowly soldier, as he parted the crowd for Gideon.

The marine led Gideon to a door. Posted on either side was a pair of Secret Service agents. One of them opened the door for Gideon, who entered a large conference room, where President Diggs was talking quietly to a plain but pleasant-faced man in his sixties with the jowly, careworn expression of a hound dog. It was Earl Parker, Gideon's friend and mentor, and as close to a father as anyone in his life.

"Uncle Earl . . ."

"You were good in there," Parker said. "Truly inspiring."

"I didn't know you were here."

"I was standing in back," Parker said, smiling. "I'm proud of you, son."

Gideon returned Parker's smile, surprised at how eager he still was for the older man's approval.

He had known Earl Parker most of his life. Parker was not actually his uncle, but he had been a friend of his father's, and after Gideon's parents died twenty years ago, Earl Parker had stepped in, becoming almost a father figure to him — and to his older brother, Tillman. After their parents' deaths they had gone to live with a foster family. But Parker had come to visit them every weekend or two, playing football in the yard with them, checking on their progress in school, and generally acting as though they were related by blood. They had wondered enough about his constant attention to eventually ask him why he spent so much time with them. He explained simply that he had served in the Marines with their father and owed him a debt so great that caring for his sons would not even begin to repay it.

Beyond the fact that he'd never married, the boys knew precious little about Uncle Earl's personal life. Which didn't stop Gideon from trying to assemble some rough biography based on his observation of certain details. Like Parker's teeth. They weren't good, indicating an upbringing in the sort of family where dentistry was considered a great extravagance. When he spoke, his accent had the marble-swallowing quality found only in the highest, most desperate hills of east Tennessee.

But the public record had also yielded some choice facts, which is how Gideon first learned that beneath that modest exterior was an extraordinary man. Parker had been the first and only Rhodes scholar to come from East Tennessee State University. After his stint at Oxford, he enlisted in the army and served for eight years in the Marine Corps, before going on to hold a string of increasingly powerful jobs in various departments and agencies of the United States government whose functions were rarely clear to the average American. His current job was deputy national security advisor, and his was generally considered to be one of the most important voices on foreign policy in the White House. Some said even more important than that of the secretary of state.

It was Uncle Earl who'd brought Gideon into the State Department, convincing him to leave his position at the United Nations. But after the Twin Towers fell, the apprentice found himself challenging his mentor. Gideon started supporting the position that the United States needed to engage more fully with the Islamic world, using the tools of soft power, like diplomacy and economic aid, while Parker argued that overwhelming military force was the only thing our enemies understood. Gideon and Parker had always engaged in good-natured debates over their political differences. There had been a time when the vigor of those debates had been part of the bond that connected them. But in recent years, their policy differences had begun to strain their personal relationship — especially as Gideon's influence with the president grew. Both men were pained by the widening rift between them, but neither knew quite what to do about it.

Gideon looked from Uncle Earl back to

the president, who was now speaking. "How familiar are you with the Sultanate of Mohan?"

"Just what I've read in the State Department briefs." Gideon proceeded to tell them everything he knew about the small island nation — that it was equidistant between Malaysia and the Philippines, with a population of somewhere between five and six million people, 90 percent of them Malay-speaking Muslims, 5 percent ethnic Chinese and Indians, and a smattering of off-the-census tribes living in the uplands. Gideon also knew that Mohan was more or less the personal possession of the Sultan, who had ruthlessly put down an Islamist insurgency a few years earlier. With some back-channel military assistance from the United States, the Sultan's armed forces had managed to contain the jihadis to a few remote provinces.

The president nodded tightly. "Except it turns out the jihadis were down but not out. Once they realized how much oil was buried beneath those coastal waters, they started recruiting and rearming. And while you were in Colombia, they came out of hiding. They're moving against several of the inland provinces, and our friend the Sultan is in some serious trouble."

None of this had even been on Gideon's radar when he headed down to South America.

"I need you and Earl to get over there."

"When?"

"Right away."

Gideon ran his hands across his tuxedo. "In this monkey suit? I don't even have a toothbrush."

The president's eyes glittered with amusement. "I hear they have toothbrushes in Mohan."

"With respect, sir, I just got back a few hours ago. I haven't even been briefed on Mohan, I don't know the conflict points or the key players on either side —"

Uncle Earl interrupted, "This isn't about negotiating a truce."

"Then what's it about?"

"Your brother," he said.

Although Uncle Earl's face rarely betrayed emotion of any kind, it was as troubled as Gideon had ever seen him. "Tillman needs our help."

"Our help with what?"

Parker wrestled with the question before he finally answered. "We've got forty-eight hours to save his life." He glanced down at his watch. "I take that back. Make it forty-seven."

CHAPTER TWO

It was an ambush, pure and simple. Kate Murphy had been told that she would be testifying at the Senate Subcommittee on Foreign Policy as a technical expert on offshore drilling. Deepwater fields had been discovered in the South China Sea, a few miles off the coast of Mohan. As manager of the Obelisk — the largest and most sophisticated rig in those waters — she had come prepared to talk about the trends and technology of offshore drilling.

But now that she was here, she saw the truth. She hadn't been subpoenaed to talk about horizontal drilling or steam injection or how she calculated the production of an underwater field. She had been brought here to get clobbered.

It had started pleasantly enough. The six men and one woman sitting at the horseshoe-shaped table facing her looked so much more human than they did on TV.

Smaller, older, more rumpled, shoulders flecked with dandruff, teeth stained with coffee. They looked like a bunch of retirees, sitting around the old folks' home in their Sunday clothes.

The first questions had been disinterested softballs. What were the estimated reserves of oil and gas in the South China Sea? How many rigs were located there? How many oil tankers moved through the Strait of Malacca?

Then the questioning shifted to Senator McClatchy, the chairman of the subcommittee. He was a doddering-looking old fellow, with a thin comb-over and a slight tremor in his left hand. His watery eyes were magnified by his thick glasses, giving him a slightly idiotic look. He smiled uncertainly, as though not entirely sure where he was.

"Miz Murphy, it's so kind of you to fly all the way over from Mohan, just to talk to us."

"It's my pleasure, Senator," Kate Murphy said.

"We do appreciate it. I know you're a busy person, got all kinds of important things to tend to. I bet running an oil rig, a young gal like you, you must be a heck of a . . . a heck of a . . ." He seemed to lose his train of thought.

"Well, thank you, Senator," she said after the moment of silence had begun to stretch to an embarrassing length.

Then the senator's vapid smile faded and his eyes seemed to clear. "Now having gotten all the necessary formalities out of the way — could I prevail on you to tell me why you and the last four witnesses from Trojan Energy have all lied to me, to this subcommittee, and to the American people?"

She felt a flush rise to her cheeks. "Ex*cuse* me?"

"Let me rephrase the question. Isn't it true that your company, Trojan Energy, has on numerous occasions paid out ransom money to pirates over the past year?"

She stuttered, "Pirates?"

"Islamists. Jihadis. Insurgents. Call them whatever you want, but please answer my question."

"Honestly, I'm not all that sure what —"

"And isn't it true that these pirates are closely allied with Islamic terrorists in the Philippines, in Malaysia, and in the Sultanate of Mohan?"

"Sir, I was under the impression I was brought here to testify about oil drilling technology."

Senator McClatchy spread his hands widely and gave her a broad smile. "You were, were you?" Senator McClatchy's smile faded just the slightest bit. "See, and I was under the impression that you were here to truthfully and completely answer the questions I directed to you. *Whatever* questions I directed to you."

"I just —"

"You just what? You just wanted to avail yourself of your constitutional right to hold your tongue so as not to incriminate yourself?"

"I didn't say that."

"Then why don't you just tell this committee the truth? That Trojan Energy is funding terrorism."

Kate Murphy could feel the red spots forming on her high cheekbones, the ones that always popped up right before she said something she shouldn't. So she kept her mouth shut.

Senator McClatchy looked down at his notes. "How much do you know about a man named Abu Nasir?"

"Only that he's some sort of terrorist in Mohan. I mean, if the guy actually exists. Some people seem to think he's just a myth."

"Oh, he's not myth. I guarantee you that." McClatchy fixed his eyes on her for a long time. "Are you aware that Trojan Energy has paid over forty-seven million dollars in ransom to Abu Nasir in the past twelve months?"

She swallowed. "If that's true, I was not aware of it."

"Really?"

"Those decisions are above my pay grade." Kate Murphy had of course heard rumors that various ships owned by Trojan affiliates had been seized by pirates, and that substantial ransoms had been paid. But her bosses at Trojan had kept those details private.

"Above your pay grade. I see. Except it is a matter of the public record that Trojan Energy continues to receive U.S. government loans and loan guarantees to encourage its participation in the Obelisk project. Which means either you're ignorant or you're lying."

"You're free to draw whatever conclusions you like."

"So you refuse to comment on whether or not American taxpayer funds have been funneled into the coffers of Islamic terrorists and pirates."

Kate had an urge to stand up and shout that she knew nothing about any of this. But instead she kept her voice low and cool. "Refuse? No, Senator, I'm not refusing. I keep telling you, my job is to run a rig and make sure that when my bosses pull the handle, oil comes out. I just don't have the answers to your questions."

Senator McClatchy's eyes narrowed. "Don't you think that a bunch of ducking and dodging is out of place when our national security is being threatened by a bunch of fanatical terrorists?"

"I'm not dodging —"

The senator cut her off. "Don't you think it's time to start taking action? To stand shoulder to shoulder with our friends like the Sultan and fight our enemies instead of subsidizing them?"

Kate Murphy sighed. She knew none of this had anything to do with her personally, but it made her angry that she'd been brought here to get made a fool of on national television just so Senator Mc-Clatchy could rattle his saber and score some political points.

"Do you really think the United States of America should just sit around helplessly while these criminals and thugs take off with millions of dollars' worth of oil revenue *we* pulled from the ground with *our* technology and expertise?"

"I keep telling you, I don't know enough about the situation to answer that question." Then, without thinking, she added, "But if what you're saying is true, I damn sure hope we won't."

For a moment Senator McClatchy glared at her. Then a loud bleat of laughter escaped his lips. "Bless your heart," he said. "Young lady, you make me want to stand up and salute the flag."

When she was finally dismissed, Kate was still hot with anger. Her bosses at Trojan Energy had sent her to Washington because she knew enough about the Obelisk to be a credible witness but not enough to cause any real damage. She couldn't decide if she was angrier at them for making her their sacrificial goat, or at these smug politicians who spent their lives gaining and maintaining power by tearing down other people. So she decided to let it go and checked her BlackBerry. For some reason she couldn't access her email or her phone messages. Her display window read SYSTEMS ERROR. Being out of touch with her rig, even for a day, left her feeling uneasy and incomplete, the same way she imagined other women her age felt about being away from their husbands and children. Kate thought to herself that if Ben were still alive, she might have been one of those women. His face with the crooked smile appeared to her, then vanished just as quickly — along with the expectation of a life she knew would never be hers.

As she made her way down the corridor, she saw the subcommittee members emerging from the hearing room. They'd apparently adjourned after her testimony for a break. McClatchy was heading in her direction with another senator. She tried to avoid him, pretending to make a call on her broken BlackBerry. But he abruptly excused himself from his colleague and waited for her to disconnect from her imaginary call. "Sorry if I was a bit rough on you in there, Miss Murphy. Nothing personal, you understand."

"Right. Nothing personal," Kate said, trying to keep her voice flat.

Kate expected him to move past her, but instead he moved closer. Close enough that Kate could smell his sour breath. He lowered his voice to an intimate tone that made her skin crawl. "Listen, if you've got some time tonight, I was hoping you could join me for dinner. I'd like to show you around town, have a little fun."

Kate blinked, stunned. She felt like saying, *Are you out of your fucking mind, old man?* But instead she heard herself thanking the senator for the invitation, politely declining, and telling him she had to catch an early morning flight. Which was true. And once she brushed past the sour-smelling senator, the thought of getting back to the Obelisk eased her mind. The anger drained from her body, replaced by the comforting knowledge that tomorrow she'd be back on her rig, the only home she'd known in nearly two years.

A chopper was idling on the roof waiting to take Gideon and Earl Parker to McGuire Air Force Base. It was a white Sikorsky bearing unobtrusive air force markings. No sooner had they strapped in than the bird was aloft. It was a stunning view, the chopper sailing below the tops of the tallest buildings.

As they scudded over the massive construction site where the Twin Towers had once stood, Gideon had to restrain himself from asking Parker what the hell was going on. Back at the UN, President Diggs had preempted Gideon's questions, telling him it was a long and complicated story, and since they were working against time, Parker would brief him during their flight to Mohan.

Even if Gideon had tried to speak during the chopper flight, the noise inside the cabin would have made conversation impossible.

So Gideon found himself thinking about his older brother. How they had fought for as long as he could remember — first over childhood treasures like candy and toys, later over sports and girls, and later still, over politics — and how all their years of fighting had come to a head one night seven years earlier. They'd exchanged some ugly words, too ugly for even the most sincere apology to erase. Not that either of them had even tried. But since then, they hadn't seen or even spoken to each other.

At Teterboro Airport in New Jersey, Gideon and Parker were escorted from the Sikorsky to a waiting Gulfstream G5. They boarded the jet and settled into a pair of leather seats that faced each other over a gleaming teak table. Before the engines had even spooled up, Gideon pressed Earl. "Okay, Uncle Earl. Tell me what this is about."

"You heard the president. There's not a simple answer —"

"Just tell me what's going on," Gideon insisted.

Earl Parker fixed Gideon with a look, then sighed. "I hate to do this to you, son, but you need some context to understand the trouble that Tillman's gotten himself into." From his briefcase, he pulled a thick, bound folder. "This briefing book has up-to-the-minute intel on Mohan. It'll help explain what's happened to your brother. Get through as much of it as you can, and I'll fill in the rest." Before Gideon could speak, Uncle Earl preempted him with a reassuring smile. "I promise."

"Forty-eight hours to save his life? That sounds a little melodramatic."

Parker regarded Gideon compassionately. "I'm not being coy, son, but I do need you to read the briefing. Especially the sections about Abu Nasir."

Gideon felt his body being pressed back into his seat as the Gulfstream acclerated down the runway. He looked out the window as they lifted into the air, climbing quickly before banking away from the Manhattan skyline. Then Gideon turned his attention to the heavy book Uncle Earl had handed him.

Abu Nasir? Gideon remembered seeing the name in the State Department briefs he'd read, but he couldn't recall anything more. *Who was Abu Nasir?*

CHAPTER THREE

Gideon had left Bogotá on the red-eye, so he'd only gotten a few hours of sleep. But Uncle Earl's cryptic words kept his fatigue at bay as he propped the briefing book on the table in front of him and tried to absorb as much as he could.

Mohan had been an independent state for nearly four hundred years. The State Department described the current Sultan as a decent and tolerant-enough leader who'd grown the economy tenfold by tapping the oil reserves beneath Mohan's coastal waters. The latest drilling project was a billion-dollar state-of-the-art rig owned by Trojan Energy and christened the Obelisk. If the geology was correct, it would be the most productive rig in history. Three other major energy companies had already closed agreements with the Sultan and were drawing up plans for a dozen more rigs just like the Obelisk.

But the Sultan's government also suffered from the typical problems found in most modern nations where one royal family runs the show: nepotism, corruption, and the lack of a broad power base. These weaknesses had created conditions that were now being exploited by the jihadis. No longer content to govern themselves under Sharia law within the boundaries the Sultan allowed them, they were agitating for another insurgency. The Sultan had requested military assistance from the United States to help suppress the jihadis, and a core congressional group, led by Senator McClatchy, wanted to comply. But President Diggs had refused, reluctant to get our troops stuck in the middle of another civil quagmire halfway across the world.

Of the several insurgent factions in Mohan, one was headed by the man Parker had mentioned, Abu Nasir. What Gideon found most interesting was that Nasir was not Mohanese. He was an unidentified Westerner wanted by the Sultan for smuggling drugs and dealing arms. He'd also developed a reputation for piracy and kidnapping, holding Western oil executives hostage for impossibly large ransoms, which he used to fund the insurgency.

Gideon spent another hour wading

through the briefing book until the words started to blur. He read the same section over and over until he finally gave up, leaning back in his comfortable leather chair, and sinking into a fitful sleep.

When the G5 was descending through a scattering of puffy clouds many hours later, Parker was drinking coffee from a mug with the presidential seal on the side and working on his laptop. He looked up over his reading glasses at Gideon rubbing his eyes and said, "Sleeping Beauty awakes!"

Gideon took a moment to orient himself. According to the bulkhead monitor, their estimated time of arrival was in twenty minutes.

Parker glanced down at the briefing book, which was splayed open, spine up, on Gideon's lap. "I see you didn't get very far," he said, smiling with uncharacteristic affection. "You needed that sleep pretty bad."

"Yeah. But since we're landing soon, what I really need is for you to tell me what's going on."

"How much did you read about Abu Nasir?"

"No more questions, Uncle Earl. Just tell me what's happening with my brother."

"All right." Parker nodded but hesitated a good ten seconds before he spoke again.

"We have good intelligence that Abu Nasir is your brother."

Gideon blinked. Unable to make sense of the words he'd just heard.

Parker dropped his shoulders, as if finally unburdening some great weight he'd been carrying. "He's dug himself into a hole, and now he needs you and me to pull him out before he gets himself killed."

Parker allowed Gideon to absorb this before continuing. "I know it sounds insane. I'm still trying to get my own head around it."

"How good is this intelligence?"

"Very," Parker said, then handed Gideon a photo from the pocket of his briefing book. Behind the CLASSIFIED stencil was a grainy surveillance photo of a bearded man who was clearly unaware that he was being photographed, focused instead on someone or something out of the frame. The features behind the beard resembled Tillman's, yet it was not him at all. The hot anger that had once animated his eyes was now extinguished, replaced by an icy and far more lethal indifference.

"This is Tillman?"

Parker nodded. "It was taken a little over a month ago."

Studying the face of the stranger reminded

Gideon of why he'd decided not to follow Tillman into the army and had gone to college instead. Gideon knew that his brother's reasons were more pragmatic than patriotic. He'd enlisted in order to avoid serving time for a street brawl during which he'd almost killed a man five inches taller and a hundred pounds heavier than he was. The man was left in such rough shape that the D.A. tried to bump the charges from assault and battery to attempted murder. Because of Uncle Earl's well-connected intervention, Tillman managed to avoid prison, and found himself in the army. He thrived as a soldier and was quickly promoted to the most elite ranks of the Special Forces. He'd finally found a way to channel the anger and the violence that had always run through him like a live wire. As angry as Tillman had once been, though, Gideon couldn't bring himself to believe Parker's story.

"The last time you spoke to him, where was Tillman working?" Parker asked.

"Afghanistan."

"After that, he was sent to South America, then Indonesia. But Mohan was his first long-term assignment. Al Qaeda and its offshoots had been making inroads with the local population, and Tillman was sent to infiltrate their ranks. And he did. Posing as a Chechen arms dealer, he fed crucial information to the Sultan's intelligence service. With Tillman's help, the Sultan was able to beat back the insurgency." Parker sighed heavily. "But that's when things started going wrong." Parker tapped the seat beside him. "Come over here so I can show you."

Gideon switched seats, watching as Parker moved his blinking cursor and clicked one of his desktop icons. A map of the South China Sea appeared on-screen. Parker traced his finger along the southern edge. "See this skinny little strip of ocean here, from the Strait of Malacca just below Singapore, up to the coast off Vietnam? Sixty thousand ships, billions of tons of goods, over a trillion dollars' worth of commerce, pass through this corridor every year. It's one of the most heavily trafficked shipping lanes in the world, and the one most vulnerable to piracy.

"Last year, off the Somalia coast, we saw just how vulnerable. The jurisdictional issues are messy, the money is huge, and the shipping companies view piracy as a cost of doing business. A write-off. A ship gets seized, they don't call the navy, they reach for their checkbooks. Spending a few million bucks now and then is easier than jeopardizing the safety of their crews and cargoes."

Gideon held up his hand. "Hold on. What's this got to do with Tillman?"

"It was his cover story. Disaffected American soldier turned independent contractor. To prove himself, he seized an oil tanker bound for Mohan. It was all playacting, of course, with a local crew he'd put together and a cooperative vessel he'd hired to go along with the setup.

"Problem was, it worked too well. The jihadis wanted Tillman to do it again. He tried to stall, but they kept pushing. Next thing we knew, he and his men had seized a second ship. This time, it was a real one. Tillman claimed he had to do it in order to avoid blowing his cover. Said it was worth doing a few bad things to stop some much worse things from happening, and the Agency went along with it. Nobody gets hurt, a couple of big companies lose a negligible amount of money, all for the greater good. But after a couple more seizures, he broke off contact with his handler and started doing this stuff for real."

"What is that supposed to mean?"

"It means he started identifying with the people he was sent to destroy. He changed his name, became a Muslim. Or, I should say, a follower of the violent extremists who've perverted and co-opted that religion."

Gideon shook his head. "I don't believe you."

Earl blew out his breath. "That doesn't make it any less true."

"How long have you known about this?"

"Almost a year."

"*A year?* And you're only telling me now?"

Parker's eyes flashed. "Do not play the guilt card with me, son. The last time I asked you to reach out to Tillman, you told me to mind my own damn business." Parker was right. Gideon had traveled the world brokering peace between warring parties, but he'd been unwilling to reach out to his own brother. A dozen times he'd picked up the phone to call him. Each time, he'd hung up before the connection even went through.

Parker lowered his voice to a wistful register. "Besides, I knew there wasn't anything you could do about it. I tried contacting Tillman myself through an intermediary, begged him to come in. But he never even responded. For him to lose himself like that . . . I can't even begin to imagine the twisted logic that must have gotten into his head."

"Bullshit." It was the only word that fit. "Tillman may have changed, but he's not someone who changes sides. Not like this."

"You need to understand, he's not the same person anymore. Last year, in this shipping lane, over a hundred ships were seized. We've got multiple intelligence sources saying your brother was behind at least thirty of those."

Gideon kept shaking his head as Parker continued. "Problem was he got so good at it, he became a target himself. He pissed off the insurance and shipping companies. He pissed off some of the more radical jihadists in Mohan, who saw him as an outsider. Even worse, he pissed off the Sultan, the man he'd been sent over to help out in the first place. And now that the insurgency is gaining momentum —"

Gideon finished his sentence. "The Sultan wants him dead."

Parker nodded. "He ordered his top operatives to hunt down Tillman. They've been spreading around lots of money, squeezing some captured insurgents pretty hard. Two days ago, they located him."

"How did you find out about this?"

"From Tillman."

"You spoke to my brother?"

"Not directly, no. He contacted me

46

through a man named Prang. He's a general in the Sultan's army who Tillman worked with. Apparently, your brother kept a back channel open with Prang, even after he went dark. Prang warned Tillman about the hit, and he's the one who's brokering this whole deal."

"What deal?"

"Tillman's agreed to surrender himself and provide intelligence about the insurgency if the Sultan calls off his hit. He's holding some big cards — safe houses, weapons caches, organizational structure, leadership, money flow, the whole nine yards."

"Then the Sultan agreed to call off the hit."

"Only temporarily. He's giving us until tomorrow to bring him in. After that, it's open season."

"And President Diggs signed off on this?"

"Absolutely. He's already getting pressure to send troops to Mohan. If this insurgency gets any bigger, he may not have a choice. He'd much rather let Tillman disappear into witness protection than be forced to put our troops in harm's way."

Gideon's head was spinning.

"All right. So bring him in. I don't understand why you need me."

"Because Tillman only agreed to come in under one condition. If he could choose who President Diggs sends."

"And Tillman chose *me?*"

"You're the only one he trusts."

Below the descending plane, the lush green canopy of the jungle was receding, giving way to the tar paper rooftops and steel containers of the sprawling shantytown adjacent to the airport. "How exactly is this supposed to happen?" Gideon asked.

"General Prang is still working out the operational details. He's meeting us at the airport."

Gideon sat motionless, turning over in his head what he'd just heard. As impossible as it sounded, he knew he had no choice but to see it through. At least until he'd heard more.

"Tillman's a grown man," Parker said. "He made his own bed, I realize that . . . but I still feel responsible for him. I feel that way about both of you." Parker's eyes welled, and his voice had more gravel in it than usual. He cleared his throat, as if trying to break through the delta of emotions that had collected there.

The plane hit the tarmac with a jolt and a screech of tires. As the aircraft decelerated, Gideon stared down at the photograph and realized that his brother, his only blood relative, had become a complete stranger to him.

"You need to bring him home," Parker said.

Despite the sick feeling rising from the deepest part of himself, Gideon found himself nodding his head.

CHAPTER FOUR

"Couldn't you at least have wiped off the poor guy's blood first?" The artist frowned as he studied the passport.

The bearded man in the camouflage baseball cap didn't speak. The crown of his hat bore the prominent outline of some kind of pistol. The artist — his name was Barry Wine — had never met anyone he liked who wore a hat with a picture of a gun on it. Or a gun logo. Or a gun joke. Or a gun anything.

Gun people were morons. Barry Wine detested morons.

Wine was a freelance document forger. In the trade, document forgers are called "artists." Once upon a time he'd been with the Company. But there had been a minor misunderstanding about some receipts for supplies, and now he had to take whatever work he could get. Even for guys like this troglodyte creep in the baseball cap. Barry

Wine had operated out of Singapore for a while, but the tax situation was better here in Mohan. And now he was holding the bloodstained passport for some poor bastard named Cole Ransom. The humorless guy in the baseball cap wanted him to replace the photo of the real guy with a photo of himself. Artists referred to this as a "face pull."

Barry Wine was a perfectionist, so he didn't like face pulling. It offended his dignity and professionalism. Face pulling was a crude and thuggish procedure that any high school art student could do. If you were a serious professional, you did a "fab" — a complete fabrication of the passport. But a perfect fab took two to three weeks. And that was only if you could get your hands on the right kind of paper.

"Did I ever tell you about that Bulgarian passport I did for our mutual friend?" Barry Wine said. "The Bulgarian passport — it's the one and only artistic achievement of any note in the entire history of the Bulgarian people. Absolute work of art. The flash page is intaglio printed if you can believe that. All the paper is manufactured at this very small factory near the Turkish border. Seven unique colors of hand-dyed security threads. *Silk* threads. They even have a security feature that's unique to the Bulgarians. An integral magstripe made from powdered magnetite that's literally impregnated into the paper. Impregnated! No plastic film involved. None whatsoever. I had to paint it in with this tiny hog-bristle paintbrush —"

The bearded man looked at Barry Wine with his empty black eyes.

"Sorry," Barry Wine said. "Sorry. I just need to get your picture inserted in the passport. It'll take awhile. Feel free to grab some lunch and come back."

The bearded man didn't move.

The artist was eager to do anything that would get the man's eyes off of him. He pushed the Gucci bag with the rest of the documents in it across the table toward the man in the camouflage hat. "It's all there. Feel free to review them. Company IDs, Social Security card, credit cards, you name it. I even threw in a library card from the Baton Rouge Central Library. Which I thought was a nice touch."

Barry Wine waited for some kind of approval or appreciation for his extra effort. But all he got was a tight nod. So he returned his attention to the passport.

He sharpened his X-Acto knife on a 1200-grit diamond stone using a small jig of his own design and then carefully slit the plastic that sealed Cole Ransom's picture into the passport. It took about twenty minutes to affix the new image. He used a special solvent he'd developed himself to make the line between the new overseal and the old overseal fade away. You could never make it completely disappear of course. It would get his client past most customs agents and border patrol checkpoints, but Wine still scowled at the passport. Hackwork. This was absolute hackwork and butchery. Nobody cared about quality anymore. Back when he'd started you actually had to learn your craft. Engraving, printing, dye work, the list went on and on. But now all these assholes wanted you to do was slap something in a copy machine. You might as well just go to Kinkos!

He slid the face-pulled passport across the table to his customer. "Here. Notice what I did with the —"

The bearded man swept it up and stuck it in his pocket.

"You're not even gonna look at it?"

The man reached across the table, picked up the X-Acto knife.

"Careful," Barry Wine said. "That's very sharp."

"I know," the bearded man said, before he plunged it deep into Barry Wine's left eye.

■ ■ ■ ■

Two hours later Detective Senior Grade Wafiq Kalil walked into a small office in central Kota Mohan with a sign that said B. WINE DESIGN on the door. A handful of blue-clad state policemen were milling around the room aimlessly. Wafiq knew the older of the two men, a sergeant named Mustaffa.

"What have we got, Sergeant?"

"An American named Barry Wine," Sergeant Mustaffa said. He beckoned Wafiq over and said, "You'll want to see this."

Wafiq peeked over the counter in the front of the room. A dead white man lay in a pool of blood. Some kind of thin metal cylinder was sticking out of his eye. Before he had died, though, he had apparently managed to write something on the floor in his own blood.

Wafiq squinted, trying to make out the bloody letters. It was not easy. The dead man's handwriting left a little to be desired.

The sergeant said, "I think it says 'Abu Nasir.' "

Now that the sergeant had said it, he could see the letters, too. "Clear this room," Wafiq shouted. "Now!"

CHAPTER FIVE

When Gideon and Parker deplaned, they were greeted by a furnace blast of muggy air and a phalanx of heavily armed soldiers who had formed two parallel lines, creating a corridor between the plane and the gleaming modern air terminal. They wore tropical tan uniforms and olive drab berets. They faced outward, their eyes scanning for potential threats.

"These guys look serious," Gideon said.

"They are," Parker muttered.

A small Mohanese man in a military uniform burst out of a doorway from the terminal, trailed by four more uniformed men. Gideon counted four stars on his epaulets. Clamped between his teeth was a corncob pipe, canted at the same angle favored by General MacArthur, which he removed as he shook Parker's hand.

"Mr. Parker," the military man said. "A pleasure as always."

"General Prang, this is Gideon Davis."

Prang studied Gideon's face as they shook hands.

"This way, please." The general indicated a Range Rover parked near the jet. Flanking the Range Rover were two Chevy Suburbans and a Lincoln Town Car. Next to each Suburban stood more uniformed men. They all carried MP5s and wore small earpieces and throat mikes. These were elite commandos, not the ceremonial window dressing typically sent to impress visiting dignitaries.

Parker turned and said to Gideon, "General Prang will brief you on the operational details, and we'll meet after you've picked up your brother."

"Where are you going?"

"I'm picking up our ambassador, then heading out to the Obelisk."

"What for?"

"That's where we'll meet once you've got Tillman. I set up an official state visit as a cover for the exfil operation. I'll be making a public statement to the media about our solidarity with the Sultan and our pledge of continued economic support — all the usual bullshit. Your brother will be safer on the rig than on the mainland, until we transport him to a U.S. naval vessel."

"Fine. Except I still haven't heard how this is going to happen."

"I told you, General Prang will explain everything." He leaned toward Gideon and lowered his voice. "Prang's a good man. Tillman trusts him — as much as he trusts anybody right now. Do what he says, and he'll get you to Tillman."

Gideon studied Parker for a moment before he nodded his okay.

"Good luck," Parker said. Gideon watched him get into the waiting Lincoln Town Car, which sped away.

"This way, Mr. Davis. Please." General Prang was gesturing impatiently toward the Range Rover. His accent was more English public school than Southeast Asia. "Not to rush you, but the longer we stay here the more exposed we are."

"Exposed?"

Prang took his pipe out of his teeth and swept the horizon with it. "Snipers."

"Is it really that bad here?"

"Just precautions, Mr. Davis. Just precautions."

As soon as Gideon climbed into the idling Range Rover, the door slammed, and the motorcade leapt forward.

Gideon turned to Prang. "Tell me where I'm meeting my brother."

The general took off his sunglasses and wiped each lens carefully with a small handkerchief before placing the glasses in his breast pocket. His eyes never left Gideon's.

"I hope you have not been misled, Mr. Davis, but what you are about to embark on is not, as they say, a walk in the park."

The motorcade was speeding down the empty two-lane road. Not a single other vehicle was in sight. Given the size of the city in the near distance, the complete absence of traffic could only mean that the road had been closed off so their motorcade could travel on it unmolested. Normally this was the sort of accommodation made for visiting heads of state. Gideon took it as a measure of how important this mission must be to the Sultan.

"It has not been widely reported, but the Sultan's government is losing ground quickly. The jihadis and their proxies control four of the nine provinces in the Sultanate."

"The briefing book I just read said they controlled only two provinces."

"That was last week," General Prang said drily. "Now the insurgents are gathering on the outskirts of KM —"

"KM?"

"Kota Mohan, our capital. The city proper

is secure, as are the provinces to the west of KM. How long this will last . . . no one can say."

"So where are we going? Where *exactly?*"

Prang drew deeply on his pipe. Smoke filtered from his mouth as he spoke. "You look different than him. Except for the eyes." Gideon squirmed under the general's scrutiny. "I considered your brother a friend, you know. He is an extraordinary man. Great force of will. But there was always a darkness inside him that kept him distant from his true friends. His betrayal was painful to me, but it was not surprising."

Gideon bristled. Whatever truth there might be to what Prang was saying, Gideon resented hearing it from a stranger. It was something he'd never admitted to anyone, not even to himself, but Gideon understood the source of his brother's darkness better than anyone. Even though their paths had diverged, their lives had been stained by the same tragedy. Gideon didn't need a psychiatrist to tell him that the seeds of his work as a peacemaker were sown in the anger between his parents. Although their anger would erupt into violence only occasionally, during one of those eruptions, everything had changed forever. Had the pull of that ancient ugliness finally dragged Tillman down some dark hole that he couldn't return from? Gideon still couldn't bring himself to believe it.

"Watch your back," General Prang said. "That's what I'm trying to tell you."

"Tillman would never turn on me."

"I thought the same thing," said Prang wistfully. Clearly, he still carried with him the pain of Tillman's betrayal. Then, suddenly, he snapped his fingers, and an aide in the front seat handed the general a plastic map and red marker.

Prang spread the map on his knees. "We are traveling along National Road 7. Here. Next we will turn onto Provincial Road 91. Then we'll cut across on a smaller rural road. At a town called Alun Jong we will turn you over to a river pilot." The general circled a dot on the map with the red marker. "He will take you upriver. Local security has been arranged. You'll be safe . . . at least until you get to the upper reaches of the river."

"And then?"

"Things could get a bit spicy for a kilometer or two. Once you hit the fall line, though, you'll reach territory controlled by your brother. His base of support is in the uplands."

"So we'll be going through rebel territory before we reach him."

"Just a brief stretch."

As General Prang spoke, their convoy turned onto a new road. There was traffic now, but it was all going in the opposite direction. Trucks piled high with personal belongings, cars stuffed with extra passengers. Alongside the road, people were walking or riding in carts pulled by water buffalo. Occasional herds of goats scattered as the convoy blasted through. Gideon recognized the look on these people's faces, their grim determination barely covering their uncertainty and fear. It was the face of the refugee.

The Range Rover was tearing along at nearly a hundred miles an hour, the driver pressing his horn repeatedly as Prang continued. "At the headwaters of the river, you'll have to go by foot. A guide will lead you through the mountains, to a place called Kampung Naga. That's where you'll find your brother." He made another circle, then wrote the name of the town. Nothing printed on the map itself indicated the location of Kampung Naga. "Ideally you'll both return by river. If that becomes impossible for any reason, your government has a chopper crew standing by. The contact code and frequency are on the back of your map." He turned the map over. A seven-digit sequence was printed on the reverse. "We'll give you a radio transmitter when we reach Alun Jong."

Gideon frowned at the map. "Are there no roads leading to Kampung Naga? Why aren't we going by land?"

"There is some . . . uncertainty regarding the roads right now. The river, on the other hand, is still patrolled by boats from the national police."

"Why not go by air?"

"Because the insurgents have shoulder-fired missiles. Thanks to your brother, I might add. Not many, but some. And there are more extremist sympathizers inside our government than the Sultan will admit. All it would take is for one of them to give away your flight plan. No, the river is the safest route."

Gideon's success had been built on his willingness to take personal risks, to step outside the comfort zone of resort hotels and government compounds. Only by ignoring diplomatic protocols and going it alone in the Colombian jungle had Gideon been able to negotiate an agreement between the rebels and the government. Still, a voice in the back of his head was whispering that he was being sent on a fool's errand, that he should tell the general to turn around and take him back to the airport.

If Tillman weren't his brother, he might have done just that. Despite their estrangement, Gideon had always told himself that he would be there for his brother no matter what. And viewed in that light, he had no choice except to see this through.

"We'll be traveling into the backcountry now. The road may get a little rough, but my people tell me this is the safest route to Kampung Naga."

As he spoke, the vehicles screeched off the road onto a narrow, unpaved track. They barely slowed down, though. They were well past the city limits, tearing past rice paddies and houses roofed with corrugated iron and plastic tarps. Chickens pecked at the ground, and pigs rooted here and there. Water buffalo aimed their dull eyes at the passing motorcade.

Gideon felt a pinprick of concern. "Excuse me for speaking so bluntly, General Prang. But if Tillman betrayed you, tell me why I should trust you with his safety. Or mine for that matter?"

The left corner of General Prang's lip curled upward, an unconvincing attempt to cover his anger at Gideon's question with a smile. "I carry the Sultan's personal guarantee."

"With all due respect, I don't know the Sultan."

"With all due respect to *you,* Mr. Davis, you don't have a choice in the matter. Not if you wish to see your brother again."

Gideon locked eyes with the general, who held his look. Sensing no duplicity, just a matter-of-fact appraisal of the situation, Gideon said, "Fair enough."

General Prang nodded.

"We're close. A few kilometers before we reach the river. I'm sure you have many questions. I'll answer as many as I can before we get there."

"I got dragged straight from a function at the UN," Gideon said, waggling the corners of his black bow tie. "I feel just a hair overdressed. You think I might be able to change somewhere along the way?"

General Prang laughed. "I'm sure we can find something for you when we reach —"

The explosion that interrupted the general's sentence lifted the lead car in the motorcade into the air and tossed it into a nearby rice paddy like a Tonka truck flung by an angry child. The shock wave blew the entire windshield back into the Range Rover, shattering the safety glass, which sprayed over the two men in the front seat.

Before the lead vehicle had even come to rest, bullets began thumping into the general's vehicle, each one making a sharp thud, like the blow of a small hammer. Prang began shouting orders in a language Gideon didn't understand.

But whatever the general was telling his driver quickly became irrelevant. Blinded by the shattered windshield, the driver struggled wildly to control the wheel. The Range Rover cut sharply to the right, the left front wheel digging into the soft dirt at the edge of the road. The vehicle shuddered, listed hard to the left, and began to flip end over end.

On a few occasions of particular stress in his life, Gideon had noticed that time seemed to slow down, to stretch like taffy. This was one of those occasions. The crash unfolded at a strange, leisurely pace, the Rover rotating as slow as a Ferris wheel. Once, twice, three times — the bullets whacking into the car as it bounced and flipped.

When it finally stopped, the car lying upside down, the bullets continued to thud against the steel body. They blew out windows, bits of seat cushions, the television screen on the back of the passenger seat, and several pieces of the general's rib cage. Miraculously, nothing hit Gideon.

Just as suddenly as the onslaught had started, it stopped. Dead silence. Gideon's vehicle had landed on its roof in a flooded rice paddy. Brown water leaked rapidly into the cabin.

Gideon was hanging upside down, retained by his seat belt. He tried unbuckling the belt, but it was jammed. He shifted his weight until he managed to open the buckle, then fell into the stinking brown water that was quickly flooding the inverted roof.

The general was also hanging upside down, blood dripping down his face and into the quickly collecting water. The corncob pipe was still clamped between his teeth. Gideon took the Benchmark knife the general had clipped on his pocket, cut his seat belt, and eased the man down into the water. Red circles bloomed where the shrapnel had sliced through his uniform and into his torso. From one of the frag wounds, blood was spilling in powerful pulsing surges, which meant the shrapnel had hit an artery.

Prang's rheumy eyes locked on Gideon's. "Alun Jong," he whispered, his voice hollow and cracked. "Go to Alun Jong. A boat pilot named Daryl Eng . . . he'll get you to your brother."

Then General Prang's face went slack, and the pipe slipped from his lips and tumbled into the water with a soft splash. It hissed, then went silent.

Gideon heard men shouting commands and the sound of their feet sloshing through the rice paddy. How close were they? He couldn't tell, but he could hear them getting closer.

Gideon's eyes fell on the general's holstered pistol, a chromed Colt 1911 autoloader with ivory grips, cocked and locked. He grabbed the pistol, freed it from the holster, checked the chamber. A brass cartridge gleamed in the throat of the gun.

It was the oddest sensation, how easily it all came back. The sensation of the pistol, the sound, the feel. The 1911 felt — as it always had to him — like an extension of his own hand. For a moment, he froze. It had been almost twenty years since he'd touched a gun — any gun. A complex mix of feelings flooded through him. The first sensation was of pleasure, of the rightness of the thing, the purity of it in his hand.

Until his hand began to tremble.

I can't, he thought. *Not even now.*

He let the gun slip from his grip and watched as it dropped into the water, leaving only a ripple, which quickly went still. Although the water couldn't have been more than a few feet deep, he couldn't see the gun in the muddy darkness.

The noise was getting louder, the shouts more intense.

What was he waiting for? *Time to get out of here.* Floating listlessly on the brown water was the map Prang had shown him only a few minutes ago. On it was the location of the town where he was supposed to meet his brother. *Kampung Naga.* He grabbed the map, shoved it into his back pocket.

Tiny cubes of glass raked his body and fell away as he shimmied through the jagged remains of the window. All the sloshing sounds and shouting were coming from the driver's side. For a moment he hunkered behind the car, wondering if they'd seen him yet, although he didn't think they had.

Gideon's first impulse was to run. But the little computer in his brain — the one that took over when time slowed down — told him that he'd never make it. There were too many of them. And it was a good hundred yards to the edge of the paddy.

As if to confirm his thought, he watched as one of Prang's soldiers struggled from the wrecked front seat of the car. He was covered in blood. But he still carried his MP5. He fired two quick bursts over the underside of the car, then made a break for the berm at the edge of the paddy.

Before he'd gone five steps, he was hit three times and went down like a marionette that had its strings cut.

One part of Gideon's mind watched calmly, almost pleased at the confirmation of his earlier analysis, while the other part stared in horror.

What now?

And then he knew. The pipe. The general's pipe was floating nearby, like a buoy marking a channel. Gideon snatched it from the water. The bowl was still warm from its recent load of burning tobacco as he tore it off, then put the stem in his mouth and slowly, calmly, lay back into the murky water. He pushed himself away from the car, splaying out his arms and sinking his fingers into the slimy mud. He closed his eyes, and pulled himself under the surface of the water.

It was a trick right out of the silly adventure books he'd read when he was a kid — the Indian hiding underwater and breathing through a reed as he hid from the enemy. Was it really possible? Could he get enough air through the tiny hole? Would whoever had just ambushed them be able to see him?

He had no answer to these questions.

He simply concentrated on calming his heart, slowing his breathing. He could hear a soft whistle through the pipe stem as he drew his breath in and out. It took some effort, but he was able to draw just enough air through the pipe stem to breathe.

He could hear the splashing of the assailants. Nearer and nearer. Then a gunshot. Then another. Muffled voices shouting. Another shot.

Then silence.

In. Out. In. Out.

His hands started losing their grip on the mud. If he lost his grip, his body would float up when he took a deep breath and they'd see him. He tried to move his hands as slowly as possible, worming them deeper into the muck.

More splashing. The killers were moving slowly around the car. It was obvious they hadn't spotted him. Yet. He tried to calm his quickening heart.

In. Out. In. Out.

If his heart beat too fast, he wouldn't be able to take in enough air and he'd have to break the surface in order to breathe.

In. Out. In. Out.

He began counting. One, in. Two, out.

Three, in. Four, out.

The splashing continued. Sometimes moving closer, sometimes farther away.

Sixty-one, in. Sixty-two, out. Sixty-three, in . . .

The splashing continued for a long time. Maybe they were looting the car, taking the weapons. Maybe searching for intelligence material. It was impossible to know.

Gideon reached a count of 2,440 before he realized that the splashing had stopped. He had been concentrating so hard on his breathing that he hadn't even noticed them moving away.

He was tempted to surface now, but he knew that was a bad idea. The fetid water burned his eyes as he opened them. The sun burned brightly above him, visible even through the opaque, eye-stinging water. He closed his eyes and continued counting.

CHAPTER SIX

At twelve thousand, Gideon opened his eyes again. Pale light still filtered through the murky water, but the sun was getting lower. He closed his eyes and kept breathing and counting.

At fifteen thousand, he forced his eyes open long enough to see that night had finally fallen. He sat up slowly, concentrating on not making any sound. As his face broke the surface, he looked around. The only light came from a hut at the far side of the paddy. He rose and walked as slowly as he could toward what he believed to be the road.

He was shivering as he climbed onto the berm. He lay gasping on the dry earth for a few minutes before finally rising to his knees. The air was probably close to ninety degrees, but the water had been cold enough to lower his core temperature several degrees. He was shaking so violently he felt as if he might fall over if he stood. But he knew he had to start moving — both to distance himself from the ambush site and to get warm.

Gideon began walking slowly down the side of the road. His tuxedo was soaked and stinking. Manure appeared to be the fertilizer of choice here. Gideon smiled ruefully. Fifteen hours earlier, he'd been sitting on top of the world, at the center of its attention. And now, here he was, creeping around some forgotten part of the world, absurdly dressed and smelling of shit.

What surprised him most was how good he felt. Not just good, but vibrantly, gloriously alive. *Why?* he thought. *Was it just a natural reaction, endorphins running wild after nearly getting killed? Or was it something else?* Gideon didn't have much time to consider the question. Before he'd gone more than a few yards, he heard something moving toward him. A rustling in the tall grass. He sank to his haunches. The sound grew closer. A sentry? A farmer? Suddenly the rustling sound gave way to a ferocious bark. A dog. His heart began to race. The dog sounded like some kind of monster.

He knew that if he ran, it would catch him. Better to prepare to fight. He picked up a fallen branch from a nearby tree and braced himself for confrontation.

From the volume and pitch of its bark, he had pictured some giant slobbering beast, a mastiff or a Doberman. So when he saw the little mutt bursting into the clearing, he laughed. Still, he feared the dog's furious barking would draw the unwanted attention of some villager.

He crouched down and held out his hand.

The dog stopped, hurled a few more tentative barks at him, then approached him cautiously. Finally it sniffed his hand. One quick sniff, then it quivered all over, as if it was trying to shake off the stink.

"I know . . ." Gideon patted the dog on the head. "I smell like a goat fart."

The dog ran a quick lap around him.

Gideon decided he'd better keep moving. Although the dog had quieted down to a breathless pant, someone might still come out to investigate. He moved as quickly down the road as he could without making noise. The dog trotted after him. The berm on which the road was situated ran as far as he could see. Which wasn't very far. But he remembered a tree line in the distance, maybe half a mile down the road. If he could get into the jungle, he felt confident he could avoid being discovered.

Twice on the way down the road, cars

passed by. Each time he was forced to slip off the side of the berm and back into the foul-smelling mud of the adjoining rice paddy. The first vehicle just barreled past him. But the second slowed, then stopped. He heard the sound of harsh voices, then someone jumped out of the vehicle.

Click.

The sound of a rifle being cocked. Probably an AK. Jihadis? Probably. Gideon shivered. He still wasn't close to being warm yet.

Footsteps, moving toward him. Gideon flattened himself against the berm. He considered slithering back into the water again, but he was afraid he might be heard. So he stayed pressed against the warm earth, which stilled his shivering body.

Suddenly the footsteps stopped, replaced by a chorus of raucous laughter. Then a thump and yelp.

It took Gideon a moment to figure out what it was. One of the men had apparently kicked the poor animal. As much as Gideon wanted to kick the man back, he stayed put.

Doors slammed and the vehicle skidded away, throwing up a shower of gravel.

Gideon waited until the engine noise had faded before he climbed over the berm. The dog lay on the ground, whimpering.

75

"You okay, boy?" He bent over and stroked the dog's flank. It slowly rose to its feet, licked his hand, then began limping toward the tree line. "You and me both," Gideon said softly.

The tree line was visible now, the tops of the trees frosted with silver. The moon was starting to rise. That was good. He'd be able to make better progress with some light.

By the time he reached the trees, the moon was visible. A full moon. Bright enough that he could see every leaf on the trees, every stone and blade of grass on the ground.

As he moved into the jungle, the dog followed, limping gamely along after him. He turned, dropped to the ground, and patted its head. "Okay, gimpy, time to head home."

The dog didn't budge, looking up at him with pleading black eyes.

"Go home!" He snapped his finger, pointed back toward the village. "Go!"

The dog cocked its head and blinked, still staring at him. Gideon stood and began walking deeper into the forest. The dog followed, wagging its tail.

They walked together, man and dog, for several hours.

Then, as quickly as he'd appeared, the dog trotted off into the woods. It was a silly thing, but the moment he realized the dog wasn't coming back Gideon felt afraid.

CHAPTER SEVEN

Kate Murphy heaved a sigh of relief as the Sikorsky Sea King hit the deck of the Obelisk. She hadn't slept well on the plane, frazzled from the stress of testifying in Washington and anticipating the major problem she'd been having with her rig. Its motion-damping system was in desperate need of repair. To top it all off, her Black-Berry was still on the fritz.

But the air calmed her nerves. Jet fuel and seawater. Back in Washington, she'd felt frightened and out of place. Here, in the middle of the South China Sea, at least she knew what she was up against.

As soon as she stepped onto the deck of the Obelisk, she spotted the tool pusher, Big Al Prejean, her number two on the rig. He was a bear of a man about twenty years her senior, and right now he didn't look very happy.

"Did you get my messages, *chérie?*" he

shouted, shielding his face from flying debris with a clipboard. Even with the roar of the chopper, Big Al's Cajun accent was unmistakable.

The world Kate worked in was an intensely macho one. In all the years she'd worked on oil rigs, she'd never allowed anyone to call her *babe* or *hon.* Except for Big Al. He was an exception. He wasn't just a legend in the drilling business, he was her best friend. So even though she was his boss, she let him call her *chérie* — the French word for "dear."

"My BlackBerry died," she said. "I didn't get any messages."

Kate had flown in with some welders who were now descending the stairs with their equipment. Prejean waited until the last one disappeared below deck before he spoke. "I was wondering why you didn't call me back."

"Call you about what?" Kate said.

"Don't you feel it?"

She squinted at him curiously, about to ask him what he was talking about, when she felt the vibration through the soles of her boots. A tremor so subtle that you wouldn't notice it unless you spent a lot of time on oil rigs. Then it stopped. Then there it was again. Not too strong, but still troubling.

"Yeah. I feel it."

Prejean pointed at the blue waves rolling slowly beneath the platform. "There's a typhoon east of the Philippines. Right now, the waves are running eighteen, twenty feet."

Her face creased with concern. "I need the latest weather report."

"Forecast says the typhoon's heading north. The chance of it hitting us is less than five percent, so we should be okay."

Al's assurance left her oddly unsatisfied. Underscoring this was her creeping realization that something else was wrong. Once the chopper was gone, she realized what it was.

The noise. Rather, the absence of it. There was never a time when an oil rig didn't have noise, the relentless cacophony of generators and compressors, flame-offs and crane motors. She surveyed the drill deck. One forty-foot string of pipe hung listlessly from a chain, swaying in the wind. The drill deck was deserted.

This was a billion-dollar oil rig with a complement of nearly a hundred personnel. Labor and interest on investment ran forty thousand bucks an hour. Every minute you weren't drilling, you were hemorrhaging money into the ocean.

"What the hell's going on?" she said sharply.

"You didn't get *any* of my messages?"

She shook her head.

Big Al shifted uneasily. "Visitors," he said. "Some bureaucrat from the White House is hitting the deck in an hour with an official delegation."

"They're coming here?"

"Yeah. For some kind of press conference."

"I didn't authorize this."

"It came straight from the top. From Mr. MacLesh himself."

Kate winced. Gil MacLesh was the CEO of Trojan Energy. "This rig's been operating for over a year," she protested. "We're already pumping twenty-five thousand gallons a day. Why do they need a media event now?"

"Because of what's happening on the mainland. Since you've been away, the situation's gotten worse. They're afraid it could turn into a full-blown civil war. Mr. MacLesh says the president wants to demonstrate his support for the Sultan."

"By staging a PR stunt on our rig."

"Something like that."

Kate made a face of disgust. She'd had

her fill of politicians and their reckless manipulation.

Big Al spread his hands apologetically. "I sent you a dozen e-mails."

She exhaled, resigning herself to the fact that she had no choice in the matter. She ran her hands through her hair and realized how desperately she needed a shower. "Follow me," she said. "I want you to brief me about this media event while I'm in the shower."

Big Al smiled. "Let me shower with you, *chérie.* You'll be able to hear me better."

"If I catch you even trying to peek, I'm gonna smite you with great vengeance."

"You and whose army?"

She punched him in the shoulder. Hard.

"I've missed you, too," he said, massaging his bruised muscle.

All the tension Kate had been carrying drained from her as the scalding water cascaded over her head and down her naked body.

"First things first," she said. "How's the damper housing holding up?"

Where most oil rigs operated in fairly shallow water, the Obelisk towered eight hundred feet above the ocean floor. Stabilizing a structure as tall as a skyscraper had been a major challenge for the engineering team behind the Obelisk. They'd come up with a novel and ingenious solution — a *semi*compliant tower designed to sway like a reed in a river, but which also contained active and passive damping systems designed to counteract that sway when currents and waves reached a certain magnitude. Which was great in theory. Except somewhere along the way from theory to practice, something had gone wrong.

"The passive damping system is shit," Big Al said. "Every time I send a diver down there, they come back with more bad news."

"I'm tired of hearing thirdhand reports on this thing," Kate said. "As soon as these VIPs leave, I'm going down there to inspect it myself."

"Can you spell *delegation, chérie?* Let the pros dive."

After her father went bankrupt for the fourth time, Kate had spent two years working as a diver and welder in the Gulf, until she'd saved enough money to pay her way through Stanford. "I am a pro, Al."

"Not anymore you're not. You're the company man on this rig. You need to start acting like one. Stand in the control room and shout obscenities at people."

She laughed until she suddenly remembered what Big Al had told her. "You said there's a five percent chance this typhoon comes our way —"

"It won't," Big Al interrupted.

"What happens if it does?"

Big Al took a moment to answer. "If these seas get much higher before we reinforce the housing, the whole goddamn thing's gonna crater."

As if on cue, another tremor shook the rig. She felt it through the steel bottom of the shower. A year into operation, and the rig was in danger of shaking itself apart.

"One piece of good news is that Cole Ransom is coming out on the same chopper as the media suits."

Kate had corresponded extensively with the engineer, who was confident that he could come up with a retrofit to fix the passive damper. Ransom told her he had a rough plan, but he needed to scout the location first and run some tests before nailing down the final details. In the meantime, he would direct the welders to make some temporary fixes that would shore up the system until the full retrofit was complete.

Kate lathered her hair and tried to focus. But in her fatigued state, her mind wandered, and she laughed, realizing this was the closest her naked body had been to a man in nearly two years.

"What's so funny about a retrofit?" Big Al asked innocently.

"Nothing," she lied, before quickly covering, "I'm just thinking about how ridiculous my time was in Washington."

"Did you watch the news while you were there?"

"You know me, Al. I never watch the news."

"Your hearing got a lot of play. Trojan got bashed. Some guy on CNN basically called Mr. MacLesh a liar. Maybe MacLesh thinks we'll get some good publicity from this visit."

"It's a waste of time and money." She turned off the water. "Hand me my towel, would you?"

A hairy arm appeared through the gap in the shower curtain, holding her towel. She wrapped herself, then stepped out.

"On a more positive note, though, Bill O'Reilly said you were hot. Although personally, I don't approve of that kind of sexist remark."

"Who's Bill O'Reilly?"

"You really don't watch the news, do you?"

She smiled at Big Al in the mirror, then started combing her wet hair. "So who's coming from the White House?"

"Some old boy by the name of Earl Parker. He's the national security advisor, or something like that."

"This is an oil rig, not a freaking battleship. Why is the president sending some national security guy here?"

"I told you why. Because of what's happening on the mainland."

"Who else is he coming with?"

"You've met the ambassador. The Honorable J. Randall Stearns. Didn't he ask you out a few months ago?"

"Yes."

"And you said 'no.' "

"He's not my type."

"No one is ever your type."

"Let's not talk about this now, all right? I'll meet you in the control room in a few minutes."

"You can't be alone forever, *chérie*."

"*Out.*"

Big Al grinned, then closed the door behind him.

Kate wrapped herself with a fresh towel. Al was right. She had kept at arm's length every man who showed any interest in her. She hadn't been with a man since Ben died. Not even a casual date. She still loved Ben, she always would. But Ben was dead, and if she didn't let a man into her life soon, regret would be her only companion in old age. For the first time in a long time, Kate considered what it might feel like to be with someone else . . . until another tremor shook her cabin, scattering any thoughts she had about trying to rekindle her love life. Now wasn't the time to think about that. A chopper would be disgorging a bunch of bureaucrats onto her rig within the hour. Kate began to put on her clothes as the floor shuddered again beneath her feet, trying to absorb the rising waves of the gathering storm.

Chapter Eight

Around dawn Gideon had reached his destination, a small river town called Alun Jong. The center included a few large, modern buildings and a large mosque with an ornate gold dome. The rest of the town was composed of single-story cinder block structures. For its size, though, the town seemed oddly abandoned.

The few people who were on the street looked at him strangely and gave him a wide berth. He supposed that was natural when you saw a muddy, tuxedoed white guy who smelled like a cesspool.

He spotted the broad expanse of the river from a low hill at the edge of town. Getting there was just a matter of following the main road straight through town.

The closer he got, though, the stranger everything seemed. The sun was well above the horizon now. And there were still only a few furtive people on the street. No cars, no buses, no trucks.

He was close enough now to the river that he could see boats moored along a quay. As he passed before a storefront, a voice hissed at him from somewhere in its dark recesses.

"Are you insane?"

A young Asian man was standing behind the counter of the open-fronted shop. He wore a black shirt and an Indiana Pacers cap, canted low over his taut, anxious face.

His nose wrinkled at the smell of the stranger. "What the hell happened to you?" The young man had a perfect American accent.

Gideon considered how to answer. "Long story."

"Get in here."

Gideon looked around, then walked inside.

"Dude, this town's crawling with those jihadi assholes."

"What do you mean?"

"What do I *mean?* Did you just get dropped off a spaceship?"

"Something like that," Gideon said.

"Are you not aware that the insurgents took over like half the province yesterday? Look at them the wrong way, they'll drag your ass off the street and shoot you."

"Good to know," Gideon said, peering out

the door before turning back to the young man. "Do you have a phone I could use?"

The guy shook his head. "They cut the lines. And cell coverage has always been shit around here. But listen, my family's heading to KM as soon as it gets dark. You can come with us. If my grandfather wasn't sick, we'd have been gone already."

"Kota Mohan's downriver. I'm going upriver."

"*Up*river?" The young Chinese guy stared at him. "What the hell for?"

"I've got someone waiting for me with a boat. His name's Daryl Eng."

"I don't think so, dude. Daryl headed for KM like eight hours ago. Took his whole family."

Gideon felt a spike of dread. "How do you know this?"

"Daryl's Chinese, same as me. We pretty much stick together around here. My people have been here for like three hundred years, but the Muslims still consider us outsiders and infidels and all that shit."

For a moment, Gideon considered taking the young man up on his offer. But only for a moment. "I need to get upriver. Do you know *anyone* who might be able to help me?"

The young man laughed. "Maybe a psychiatrist." When Gideon didn't laugh, the young man shrugged. "Your funeral, bro."

Gideon smiled. "You sound like you're from Ohio."

"Indiana. Lived in Fort Wayne for ten years, then went to college at IU in Bloomington." He held up his hand, showing off a heavy gold college ring. "Bachelor's degree in chemical engineering. Came back here temporarily to help out with a family business situation and —"

His words were cut short by a burst of machine-gun fire somewhere in the distance. A truck engine raced, getting closer and closer.

"Get down!" the young man said.

Gideon was barely able to conceal himself behind the counter when a Toyota pickup packed with heavily armed young men, some of them only boys, cruised down the street. Gideon waited for the truck to pass before he stood.

"You wanna buy an AK?" the young man said. "Four-seventy-five, U.S. If you want something cheaper, I got a nice Mossberg pump with a pistol grip and —"

Gideon shook his head. "I have to go."

The young man cocked his head and studied Gideon's face. "You're serious. You're really gonna head upriver . . . *un-*

armed. What are you, a missionary?"

Gideon felt compelled to tell him his story but decided to keep it simple. "There's some family business I need to take care of."

The young man nodded sympathetically. "Same reason I'm here. Family's family, right?" Then he wrote something on a piece of paper, handed it to Gideon. "You got enough money, this guy'll take you any-where."

Before Gideon could look at the paper, he heard tires screeching outside. The Toyota pickup was doing a U-turn somewhere down the street.

"They're coming back. Someone ratted you out."

"Is there a back way out of here?"

The young man ushered Gideon toward the rear of the shop, into a small room that smelled of fried food. Eight people were crammed inside, staring fearfully at him as he moved past them and out the back door, which deposited him in a squalid alley. Beyond its narrow mouth the river was vis-ible. Gideon thanked the young man and started working his way toward the river.

He'd gone about a block when he heard automatic gunfire in the near distance. Hid-ing behind barrels and boxes in the narrow alleys that paralleled the main road, he made it to the river within ten minutes.

Almost.

Only a broad avenue separated him from the long wooden quay running alongside the river. A jumble of boats was moored there, from tiny rowboats to large flat-bottomed river barges.

Gideon paused behind a pile of rubbish.

Three young men wearing turbans and carrying AK-47s lounged by one of the boats. This was not turban country. If someone wore one around here, it was because they were consciously adopting the uniform of their Middle Eastern confederates.

For the first time, Gideon glanced at the piece of paper. He cursed at the young man from Indiana whose name he didn't even know for playing such a cruel joke on him. On the paper was scrawled

screaming monkey

Screaming monkey? Before Gideon could think any more about it, bullets started slamming into the wall next to his head.

CHAPTER NINE

Omar Haqq was late for work. He hurried toward the helipad for Trojan Energy's storage and logistics facility, which took up several square blocks of the industrial zone on the outskirts of Kota Mohan. Being a security officer here had once been considered a plum job. But over the past few months, several oil depots and processing plants in Mohan had been sabotaged by insurgents. At least a dozen of his colleagues had been killed, and twice as many wounded. Because of this, a day didn't pass without some new security procedure being instituted.

Before, company employees only had to show their badges at the facility's main gate and that was the end of it. Now every badge was embedded with a microchip that only gave you access to those parts of the facility for which you were specifically cleared. People were always walking into the wrong areas and setting off the alarm. When that happened, Omar was supposed to run to the site of the breach with his gun drawn. No walking. He had to *run.* If you didn't run, you were subject to a fine of at least five rupiahs.

And now Omar's heart sank when he saw his boss, Abdul Momat, standing at the counter of the security office by the chopper pad. He expected his boss to give him grief for being four minutes late. He would probably fine him for that, too. Oddly, his boss didn't even seem to notice that Omar was late. In fact, he was surprisingly cheerful.

"Biometrics!" Abdul said, smiling with paternal pride as Omar rushed to his station behind the security desk and logged on to his computer. "Biometrics will stop the terrorists."

"Biometrics," Omar repeated, although he had no idea what the word meant.

Abdul patted a wall-mounted panel beside the door to the helipad. In the center of the panel was a glass circle, like an unblinking eye. Next to the eye was a green button. Omar had never seen anything like it.

"They installed it last night," Omar's boss said, brushing some invisible dust from the surface of the panel. "Starting today, we will be identifying every employee and visitor by scanning their retinas. Their biometric information will be digitized and stored. If the retinal scan doesn't match? Boom!"

Omar was not quite sure what a retina was, much less how you scanned one, but he smiled broadly anyway. "Excellent, sir!" he said. Omar always made a point of agreeing with whoever his boss was, and for the last year, it was Abdul Momat. Omar hoped to be the boss himself one day. He knew the only way to become a boss was to agree with everything your current boss said.

"A lot of my people just complain," Abdul said. "But you? You see the big picture."

"I try, sir."

Their conversation was cut short by the sound of a fist rapping impatiently against the counter. The man standing there was white, his face covered by a heavy but neatly trimmed beard. He wore a baseball cap and mirrored sunglasses. "Sorry to interrupt your important conversation," he said in a tone that didn't sound the least bit sorry, "but I'm supposed to be on that chopper out to the Obelisk." He pointed toward the idling chopper outside. "Dr. Cole Ransom."

The white people who worked at Trojan Energy generally talked to Mohanese people as if they were children. But this man was different, more than simply dismissive or patronizing. This man seemed to be looking *through* Omar, as if his face were made of glass.

"Name, please?" Omar said.

The bearded man raised his sunglasses and looked at Omar, who preferred it when the man had been looking *through* him. The man smacked his knuckles against the counter again, once for each syllable he spoke. "Cole. Ran. Some. Same name as I had when I told you thirteen seconds ago." He waved his passport in Omar's face.

"Thank you, sir," Omar said, smiling as he took the passport and swiped it over the reader. Scrolling through the passenger manifest on his monitor, Omar's fake smile began to hurt his face.

The bearded man glanced out the tall windows that faced the helipad. The chopper that was about to head to the Obelisk was spooling up its engine. The other passengers were already on board.

Omar found the man's name. Normally he would have simply waved him through. But Abdul was watching him now, so he made sure to follow procedure to the letter. He typed the man's name into the log, then slid a clipboard across the counter. "Signature, please."

The man signed his name, picked up his bags, and started walking toward the door. Omar traded a look with Abdul, who rolled his eyes. Even a man like Abdul got tired of kowtowing to pompous white people. Suddenly Omar noticed something on the manifest.

"Sir?" Omar called.

The white man stopped and turned. Omar had noticed on the manifest that the man's retinal signature had been recorded yesterday and he thought this was a great opportunity to impress his boss. "I need to scan your retina."

"Huh?" the man demanded, narrowing his eyes.

Omar pointed at the box on the wall. "Retinal scan, sir. For identification."

For a moment the man didn't move. His jaw worked. "Jesus H. Christ," he said. But then he walked over, stood before the box, and pressed his eye to the round glass panel. He thumbed the green button. A line of light ran back and forth across his eye.

Oh, Omar thought. *It's one of those things.* He'd seen them in movies before, but he never knew what they were called.

Suddenly, a high-pitched alarm filled the room. The same irritating beeping sound that went off when somebody swiped their

ID card in an area they weren't cleared to enter.

Omar instantly regretted that he had tried to impress his boss. He looked to Abdul, who was looking at the bearded man. "Sir, I'm sure this is just a computer glitch, but I need to call my supervisor. So if you'll please step away from the scanner —"

But the man stood his ground, as if *he* were the boss. "I don't have time for this shit," he said.

Abdul eyed Omar, whose chest tightened. Something about the bearded man scared him. Maybe they should just let him go through. Whoever he was, he obviously wasn't a terrorist. White people were many things, but they weren't terrorists.

"Sir, please step away while I call my supervisor." Abdul picked up the phone.

What happened next happened so fast that Omar couldn't quite make sense of it until it was too late. The white man somehow pulled Omar's Glock from its holster and fired twice. The side of Abdul's head exploded in a spray of blood and bone.

Omar stared as Abdul collapsed in a heap, his legs twisted at impossible angles beneath him. The phone receiver he'd been holding a second ago now dangled from its cord, bouncing, until the white man caught it and shoved it at Omar.

"Call dispatch and tell them it was a false alarm," the white man said.

Omar did as he was told, hoping they would hear the fear in his voice and come anyway.

"Drag his body into that closet," the man said calmly, indicating a storage locker.

Omar felt sick. But he couldn't move. His brain still couldn't quite process what was happening.

"Now," the man said, lowering his voice.

Omar didn't want to die. So he lifted Abdul's feet and dragged his dead boss toward the closet. Abdul had somehow broken his left leg as he fell, and the bones made a grinding noise as Omar dragged him. Stuffing the dead man into the tiny closet was a messy, horrible, and slow process. After Omar was finished, he turned to find the bearded man setting an object beside the computer. It was gray, roughly the size and shape of an egg. The bearded man stuck the twin prongs of some small mechanism into the soft material.

"Come here, Omar," the bearded man said. "Put your finger on this."

He pointed to the device he'd stuck into the egg, which was ovular and concave.

"How do you know my name?"

"Don't make me ask you twice."

Omar did as he was told.

"Now, Omar, from the retinal scanner over there, I can see that you know something about biometrics. Facial recognition, retinal scans, fingerprints, blah blah blah — turning biology into data. You understand what I'm saying, right?"

Omar nodded.

"Outstanding," he said. "This device you've got your finger on? It's a biometric trigger. If it senses any interruption in your pulse, say from taking your finger off the device and breaking contact, it will detonate this." He pointed to the egg-shaped object. "It's a military-grade explosive called Semtex," the man said. "Enough to make your entire body look like your friend's head. Do you want that to happen to you?"

Omar shook his head.

The bearded man pressed a button on the device, and a small red light started blinking.

"So I have a mission for you. It's called Operation Omar-Doesn't-Blow-His-Own-Ass-Up. The way it works is this: you sit here for the rest of your shift, keep your finger on the button, and smile at every asshole who walks through that door. Anybody asks you about Cole Ransom, you just shrug and act stupid. If anybody asks where your buddy went, you shrug and act stupid. I imagine you'll be good at that."

Omar was tempted to explain how a lack of finances was all that had prevented him from going to university, but he realized it was pointless at this particular moment.

"If you complete your mission, I'll call you later and tell you how to disconnect the bomb. But if I get arrested or shot or the chopper gets called back or if I get spooked for any reason — obviously, I won't be coming back. And whatever bomb squad you're thinking of getting over here? Trust me, they'll never figure out how to disarm this bomb."

Omar felt a drop of sweat trickling down his neck.

"Operation Omar-Doesn't-Blow-His-Own-Ass-Up." The bearded man gave him a cynical smile. "You and me. We're on the same team now, right?"

Omar nodded.

"You gonna screw up your mission?"

"No, sir. I want to live."

"Outstanding!" The bearded man pulled out his cell phone, dialed a number, and spoke to someone on the other end of the line as he walked back out the door toward the waiting chopper, in no particular hurry.

His voice was too low to hear, but Omar had managed to hear the man on the other side of the line greet the bearded man. *Abu Nasir.*

As soon as the bearded man boarded the chopper, it lifted off. Omar watched the chopper until it disappeared from view. Was it possible that he was really Abu Nasir?

Omar sat trembling for what seemed like an hour. He looked at the clock. Barely a minute had passed. Was the bomb really rigged the way the bearded man had said it was? Probably. Would Abu Nasir ever tell him how to defuse the bomb? Probably not.

Omar's hand was already beginning to hurt. He began thinking about his three-year-old son. He remembered how he felt in those first few minutes after Hakim was born. The sun was just about to rise, and the sky was glowing a deep ruby color. *This is the color of happiness,* he remembered thinking. Another drop of sweat trickled down Omar's neck, and he wondered if he'd ever see his son again. Probably not, Omar thought miserably. Probably not.

CHAPTER TEN

Gideon's father had kept his guns in a windowless room with two deadbolt locks. Whenever his father went inside that windowless room, he'd secure both locks. And when he left, he'd lock the door again, first the top lock, then the bottom, in unvarying succession.

No one was allowed inside, not even the few men his father counted as friends. But Gideon was always standing nearby, waiting for his father to enter or exit, in order to glimpse the mysterious interior for the brief moment when the door was open. Day after day, Gideon inhaled the sharp smell of Hoppe's No. 9 bore solvent that wafted through the open door and peered inside until he'd memorized every inch of the room. Its walls were mahogany paneled, decorated with the mounted heads of deer and elk and even a brown bear. The guns were lined up in a long glass-fronted cabinet

— shotguns first, then rifles, oldest to the left, newest to the right, starting with a twenty-bore Holland & Holland hammer gun, and ending with an AR-15 chambered in .223. A wooden rifle cleaning rest, worn with age, sat on the spotless workbench next to a reloading press.

Other than the occasional addition of a new firearm, nothing ever changed in the room. Gideon's father was a man of rigid habits and fixed ideas. A place for everything, and everything in its place. Any variation from routine drove him into an immediate and merciless fury. You didn't knock on the door — or even make loud noises — when Father was in the gun room.

Gideon was given his first firearm, a Marlin .22, when he was five years old. He learned early that one thing, and one thing only, could ensure his father's affection. That one thing was good shooting. When you went to the range with Father, you didn't mess around, you didn't talk, you didn't smile, you didn't shuffle your feet. You simply loaded and fired. With precision and accuracy.

From the moment he touched the Marlin .22, Gideon knew he had a gift. Trap, skeet, air pistol, bench rest, offhand, prone, practical handgun shooting — no matter. He had *it* — that magical trick of eye and brain and finger that allowed him to aim a gun and hit what he wanted to hit. *Kill* was the word that Father used.

For the first three years, his father taught him. After that, all his father had to do was man the spotting scope and let the boy work. "Good kill, son," he'd whisper. "Good kill."

Tillman, on the other hand, struggled to keep up on the range. Compared to any other kid, he was excellent and could drive tacks with a rifle or run clays set after set. But he did it through gritted teeth, flinching under his father's perpetual scrutiny. Every near miss, every stray shot earned him an ear-ringing slap on the back of the head, a pinch on the inside of his upper arm, or — worst of all — a few cutting words. These ranged from "useless fool" to "you're no son of mine, boy." Always whispered softly. Even at his most violent, Father never raised his voice.

But the violence was always there. When the dark rage came on him, he struck out at anyone within reach. Anyone except Gideon. While their mother sometimes absorbed his wrath, Tillman was always their father's main target. It had taken a long time for Gideon to see it, but Tillman hadn't absorbed the belittling and the beating and the abuse by accident. As the older of the two, Tillman had routinely stood between their father and Gideon — deflecting his anger, absorbing his blows, protecting the younger boy. In fact, Tillman had been his protector throughout his childhood — whether it was from bullies at school or opposing linemen on the football field. Thanks to Tillman, nobody messed with Gideon Davis. People came to understand that if you put a late hit on Gideon Davis, when the next play rolled around, Tillman Davis was going to cut you off at the knees.

It was only as he grew older — and increasingly estranged from his brother — that he began to understand what that protection had cost Tillman, how much pain he had absorbed on Gideon's behalf. The realization came only slowly and grudgingly. But eventually Gideon realized that only through Tillman's self-sacrifice had Gideon been given the space to grow into the man he had become.

It was a debt that Gideon knew he had never adequately repaid.

There had been a time when Gideon's forebears owned half of Yancey County, Virginia, a rural county to the west of

Washington. But a succession of poor business decisions had stripped the family of their land, until Gideon's father had been left with nothing but their house and the small plot of land around it that he hadn't sold off. In the early 1970s, Gideon's father sold what was left and invested the proceeds in a final speculative venture, which quickly failed.

The week before Gideon's fourteenth birthday, the entire thing had caved in.

The day the bank seized Father's office, Father came home, parked his Cadillac outside the house, unlocked the gun room, took out the old Remington 10, walked into the bedroom, and shot Gideon's mother in the chest. She was a beautiful woman, and being a vain man who prized her face as one might prize a good setter or a matched pair of Purdeys, he had not wanted her spoiled. Then he went into the gun room and ended his own life.

Gideon came running after he heard the first shot and found his mother lying in a blooming pool of blood. His desperate attempt to keep her alive was interrupted by the familiar sound of the door slamming shut on his father's secret room. Then Gideon heard another shot.

When Sheriff Wright came, he found the

gunroom unlocked. He just turned the knob and walked in. Gideon's father lay dead on the floor, the back half of his head gone. There had been no investigation, no securing the crime scene, no bits of evidence collected and stuck in numbered plastic bags. After all, it was obvious what had happened. So the sheriff had simply called the funeral home and had the bodies carted away.

A few weeks later, when he and Tillman finally returned to the house to gather their personal possessions, Gideon found himself piling his father's guns on a blanket, dragging them down to the pond behind the house, and throwing them into the water, one by one. The Holland & Holland, the matched pair of Purdeys, the Weatherby double rifle, the Kimber 1911, the Luger, the K-frame Smith, the Model 70 — the only things his father had ever really loved. And now all Gideon cared about was knowing that none of those guns could ever be fired again.

After he was finished, he walked to the front porch steps and sat down next to Tillman and said, "Why do you think he did it?"

Tillman snorted but said nothing.

That was it. Since that day, neither of them had ever said another word about what happened. And since that day, Gideon Davis had never touched a firearm.

The AK-47 is not an especially precise rifle. But in the right hands it can cut a man in half, and Gideon could tell that the man shooting at him knew how to handle his weapon. The next burst would take his head off. So he did the only thing he could, bounding from his hiding place and sprinting for the river, hoping that his movement would throw off the shooter's aim.

In front of him were three turbaned young men on the quay. One held his gun by the barrel, the butt hanging over his shoulder. The other two had leaned their guns against creosote-smeared mooring posts.

Gideon had no choice except to keep going.

Hearing the gunfire, the men whipped around and saw him, before noticing the man from the alley pursuing him and firing at him. None of the bullets found Gideon, but a stray slug hit one of the three jihadis, opening his neck in a spray of blood and gristle. Before the two surviving jihadis even had a chance to level their weapons, Gideon blasted between them and rocketed off the quay and into the brown water. He swam underwater as far from the quay as his lungs would allow until finally he had to come up for air.

The moment he cleared the surface, he heard sharp snapping noises all around him. Bullets, slapping into the water. Some of them ricocheted off into the air and some tore down into the water.

He turned and looked back. He was about forty yards out. Gideon counted seven turbaned men gathering at the edge of the water, blasting away, as he sucked in as much air as his lungs would hold and dove again, this time heading for cover behind an ancient teak river barge.

Surfacing slowly, he pressed his cheek flush against the algae-slick hull of the wooden barge. There was no gunfire. Just shouting and the slap of cheap plastic flip-flops and running feet coming toward him. He panted as quietly as he could, trying to get oxygen back in his bloodstream.

He felt a soft thudding against his cheek, footfalls on the barge deck.

If he could only talk to them, make them understand that he was no threat to them. Of course, he understood, that was a ridiculous thought. Right now, escape was his only chance to survive.

He looked down the row of boats for shelter. About forty yards down, a modern twin-hulled catamaran lay among the many old-fashioned wooden boats. If he could swim the full distance under water, he could hide between the two hulls of the cat. He was skeptical about making it, though. A ten-yard gap yawned between the cat and the next boat. If he came up in that gap, they'd have a good chance of blowing his head off.

Gideon took a couple of deep breaths, then dove again. He could scarcely see anything in the brown water, just dark shapes floating above him. He passed one boat, then a second, then a third. *Don't push too hard,* he told himself, trying not to burn up all his air.

How many boats had there been between the barge and the cat? He couldn't remember. Then he saw the pale wobbly sky above him. He was in the gap now. Ten yards from the cat. Well, it had looked like ten yards from where he'd been before. Now that he was here, he was afraid it might be more. His lungs were already burning.

Stroke, kick. Stroke, kick. Stroke, kick.

His vision narrowed as he felt the oxygen deficit shutting down his brain. *Just a few more yards.*

But the urge to breathe was getting hard to suppress. His arms and legs felt like rubber. He could see the wavering dark shape of the cat, two long dark streaks of shadow running down into the water.

Stroke, kick. Stroke, kick.

Everything was getting gray now. He wasn't going to make it.

Stroke, kick.

Then . . . something dark.

Forcing the cobwebs from his mind, he kicked once more before surfacing. A gasp broke from his lips. He hoped it wouldn't be audible from the quay. Air rushed into his lungs as he panted again, so weak that he could barely hold on to the nylon rope that trailed into the water near his hand.

But he had made it.

Above him was the fiberglass deck of the cat. He took two weak strokes, repositioning himself underneath the center of the deck. He couldn't see the quay. Nothing was visible except the lower hulls of the nearest boats. If he couldn't see them, they couldn't see him.

There was some more shouting. Obviously the men who'd been after him were getting frustrated. Occasionally they fired into the water, shooting at nothing.

Then, after a while, it all stopped. No shouting, no shooting. Just silence.

Now that the excitement was over and he

had time to think, he also had more time to get worried. How was he going to get out of here? He supposed he could work his way from boat to boat until he reached the end of the quay. But what then?

The jihadis would be on the lookout for him now. He had no friends here, no money, no contacts, no phone or radio. Gideon hung on to the nylon rope, treading water with as much physical economy as he could manage.

He waited for what seemed an endless amount of time, then worked his way down to the end of the cat and looked out. A row of boats bobbed gently in the water. The quay was deserted.

Then he saw it. At the far end of the dock was a large modern speedboat. Crudely painted on the stern was some sort of large monkey. It had wild eyes and its mouth was wide open in what was either hysterical laughter or a threatening grimace. Gideon whispered a silent apology to the kid from Indiana for having doubted him, as he worked his way silently through the water toward the speedboat bearing the image of a screaming monkey.

Sometimes the jihadis reappeared on the quay or on the boats. They seemed to be looking for him — but not that hard. They must have assumed that he had drowned or been shot, because they didn't seem to be breaking their necks to find him.

Finally, he was getting close. Another forty yards and he'd reach the speedboat. As he swam slowly and silently past an old wreck of a fishing boat, a face appeared over the side. Two black eyes stared right at him. He froze. It was an old woman, toothless and wrinkled, her head covered with a black scarf. For a moment neither of them moved. She was caught as much off guard as he was. His heart hammered in his chest.

Finally, he lifted one finger to his lips. The old woman continued to stare. Then her head disappeared.

He waited for a cry, a noise, an alarm. But he heard nothing.

The old woman hadn't given him away. Maybe she was no more a fan of the jihadis than he was. He took a few last strokes, found himself alongside the boat with the monkey painted on its hull. He worked his way to the front, found a mooring line, grabbed it, and swung himself up onto the deck. For a river speedboat, it was a sizable craft, well over twenty-five feet. In the front was a sort of wheelhouse. Behind that, a deck lined with tie-downs and sturdy alloy cargo rails, which were clearly designed to carry some kind of freight.

Housed in the aft were a pair of massive inboard engines. Gideon wondered what kind of freight required being carried at forty or fifty knots. Probably not anything legal, Gideon reflected, when he smelled cigarette smoke.

Before he had a chance to see where it was coming from, the door of the wheelhouse opened and a small man stepped out. A thin brown cigarette protruded from his mouth. His face was horribly disfigured, lipless, so that he had to clench the cigarette between the few rotting teeth still in his mouth. Had the man been burned or was it some kind of congenital deformity? Gideon couldn't tell, but the guy looked a lot like a screaming monkey.

The man's face was so arresting, in fact, that it took Gideon a moment to notice the automatic pistol he was holding, an ancient Colt 1911.

He was barking at Gideon in a sharp, raspy voice. Although Gideon didn't understand the words, he didn't need a translator to understand their meaning. *Don't move, asshole!* Or some less polite equivalent. So he didn't move.

CHAPTER ELEVEN

Kate slipped into the control room, brushing her still-damp auburn hair. "What's their ETA?"

Big Al set down the radio handset. "Just talked to the pilot. He's two minutes out. He's got the ambassador on board, along with the State Department press attaché, plus this Earl Parker guy, two marine bodyguards, and a Secret Service agent. And he's got that engineer, Cole Ransom."

"Where are the news crews?"

"On a second chopper, right behind the first one."

"How's that supposed to work? They can't both fit on the deck."

"The news chopper will hover."

The last thing she wanted was a bunch of newshounds wandering around her rig. "After it's over, I want the news crews restricted to the mess or the rec room. Tell them it's a safety issue."

"I got you." Big Al nodded.

The radio crackled. "Obelisk, this is State four-seven-one, request clearance to land."

Kate looked at the security camera monitors. The chopper deck was visible on one of the small windows. Big Al keyed the handset. "Clearance granted, State four-seven-one."

"I better get up there," she said.

As she prepared to move, she felt it again — a slight tremor coming up through the steel deck. In her last conversation with Ransom, the engineer had said that he was confident that the passive damping system would hold as long as the seas stayed below thirty-five feet. Waves that high occurred rarely in the South China Sea, and even then, only during the harshest typhoon conditions.

She scanned the control room equipment, checking the gauges, dials, and readouts. It was a habit with her. From the moment she accepted this job, she had felt compelled to know every last detail about what was happening on her rig at all times. And she knew that she wouldn't have a chance to check anything again until after her VIP guests were gone. Her eyes settled on the wave height monitor. The moving average graph was inching slowly upward. A large red number gauged the height of the latest wave.

32.

Thirty-two feet. That was worrisome.

The monitor blinked and a new number popped up.

33.

"Let's go," she said. "We need to get this thing over with as fast as possible."

Gideon stood motionless, hands chest high. "Do you speak English?"

The boat captain's eyes twitched to the side, briefly scanning the quay. "Down!" he said in strongly accented English. *"Now!"*

But Gideon didn't move. The captain leaned closer, whispering conspiratorially, "Before they see you."

Gideon knelt, ducking below the gunwales of the speedboat.

"Who are you?" the boat captain said.

"My name is Gideon Davis. I was sent here by the American president."

The man ran his eyes over Gideon and cackled, forcing smoke through his broken teeth. Gideon realized how absurd his story sounded and tried to explain himself.

"My motorcade was ambushed. Someone in town gave me your name. He said I could hire you to take me upriver."

The man narrowed his eyes. "Upriver? You crazy."

"A thousand dollars."

The man laughed.

"*Two* thousand."

The boat captain stopped laughing. Despite his better judgment, he actually seemed to be considering the offer, when a noise on the quay drew his attention. Someone was shouting at him. The boat captain tried to hide his pistol as he shouted back at the person on the quay.

Gideon heard footsteps coming toward them. Then the unmistakable sound of a gun being racked.

"Shit," the captain whispered. Then he dove into the cabin. The huge Mercuries roared to life. "Get the mooring line!" the captain shouted.

Bullets started thwacking into the sides of the boat. Gideon could see he'd be shot if he jumped onto the quay to take the mooring line off the cleat. So he grabbed the pocketknife he'd taken from General Prang, flicked it open, and severed the yellow nylon cord in a single quick motion.

The boat surged away from the quay, throwing up a massive rooster tail and showering the three jihadis on the quay with water. Gideon ducked behind the gunwale, still gripping the knife tightly in his hand.

As he crouched behind the gunwale, he studied the blade of the Benchmade liner-lock. It had a pocket clip for easy access, and you could open it one-handed with the flick of a wrist. His father had always carried a knife. Always. He used to say, "A man who doesn't carry a knife is like a woman who doesn't carry a pocketbook."

The captain looked over his shoulder at him, his gaze resting briefly on the knife.

"Which way are you going?" Gideon said.

"Downriver to KM."

Gideon shook his head. "Turn the boat around. We're going *up*river."

"You want to die, find somebody else to take you."

"I told you, I'll give you two thousand dollars," Gideon said.

"Show me," the captain said.

"I don't have it now. I'll get it." But the captain held his course. "Please trust me, I really am an envoy for President Diggs. You'll be paid."

Still, the captain didn't turn the boat around.

Gideon extended his arm, pointing at the captain's face. "Up! River! Now!"

Gideon realized that he was not pointing with his finger but with the knife. He had intended not to threaten the man, just to make a strong point. But it was too late. The deed was done. He also knew that if he showed any weakness, he would never reach his brother.

The captain's eyes flicked around the boat, and Gideon followed his look to the Colt on the floor. He had apparently set it down when he started the boat, but when he pulled away from the quay, the centrifugal force had caused it to slide away from him, and it was now out of reach.

For a moment, their eyes locked. Finally the man spun the wheel hard, and the boat headed back upriver.

Gideon scooped up the Colt and instinctively worked the slide, checking the chamber. He held the weapon over the side, hit the magazine release, dropping the clip into the water, then racked the gun and ejected the round in the chamber.

"What the hell?" the captain said. "Why you doing that?"

"I don't like guns," Gideon said, tossing the empty weapon on a bench seat in the aft of the boat.

The man scowled in disgust. "We get where you want to go, you gonna wish you never did that."

■ ■ ■ ■

The steady roar of the Mercuries was not quite deafening, but it was loud enough to discourage conversation. Eventually Gideon closed the knife blade against his thigh and slid it back into his pocket.

Noticing that the threatening blade had been stowed, the captain of the boat finally spoke again. "You really work for President Diggs?"

Gideon took out his soaked wallet, peeled out a wet business card, and set it on the wheelhouse. "That's me."

The captain stared at the card for a moment, raised one eyebrow, then said, "My name is Monyet. But people call me Monkey."

Gideon pulled out General Pang's map of Mohan, indicating the spot deep in the island's interior. "There's a city right here called Kampung Naga. That's where I want to go."

"City?" Monkey laughed derisively. "There ain't no city there. That's the end of the earth."

"End of the earth?"

"You know what *Kampung Naga* means? It means 'Town That Doesn't Exist.'"

Monkey dragged a dirty thumb across the middle of the map, leaving a smudge. "See this? That's where you hit the waterfalls. No boats past that line."

"Then get me as close as you can. I'll go the rest of the way on foot."

The captain lit a cigarette. "They'll kill you before you get there."

"Jihadis?"

"Jihadis?" The man looked at Gideon like he was a fool. "You been listening to me or not? There's no jihadis up there! How you have jihad, you don't have no God?"

"Then who lives up there?"

"Tribesmen. Jungle people. Stick you with arrows, eat your ass." Gideon heard fear in the man's voice. "Why you want to go to this place anyway?"

"To find my brother. You might have heard of him. His name's Tillman Davis."

Monkey shrugged.

"He calls himself Abu Nasir."

Monkey's face went stiff. He studied Gideon's face, as if noticing him for the first time. "I should have known. You look like him."

"We don't look a damn bit like each other," Gideon said. The words came out stronger than he'd intended. As someone who generally thought before he spoke, he was a little surprised at the vehemence of his response. Gideon didn't look a thing like his brother. Gideon was tall and muscular, like his father, while his brother favored his mother's side of the family — short and wiry.

"The eyes," Monkey said, staring hard into Gideon's face. "You both got them scary green eyes."

Scary eyes. It was something he'd heard once from a girlfriend. He'd been taken aback by her observation, since he'd never thought of himself as a scary-eyed kind of guy. But now the one physical trait he shared with his brother seemed to confirm Uncle Earl's claim that Tillman was in fact Abu Nasir. "So you've actually met him."

"Once." The air whistled loudly through Monkey's teeth as he drew on his cigarette. "But he's not someone you forget."

"Why is that?"

"Wherever he goes, people die."

A sick feeling washed over Gideon. But before he could ask anything more, Monkey narrowed his eyes and pointed toward a bend where the river snaked around a low island, barely more than a sandbar covered by a few miserable-looking trees. A power-boat was making a sweeping curve toward them.

"They must have radioed ahead," Monkey said. The distant silhouettes of the men in the boat became clear enough to see that they were carrying AK-47s.

"Can they catch us?"

"We find out soon enough." Monkey firewalled the throttle and the big Mercuries howled in response. "Hold on."

The noise was deafening as the speedboat slammed into the chop. It was obvious Monkey meant it literally when he said hold on. Gideon's fingers whitened as they clenched the gunwale. Every tiny wave jarred his teeth.

Monkey pointed at the pistol Gideon had taken from him. "You gotta shoot. There's more clips in the storage compartment under the seat back there."

Gideon eyed the pistol but didn't move from the gunwale as Monkey steered toward a small channel on the far side of the island. The boat was getting closer. In his mind, Gideon could feel the Colt's grip on his fingers, its texture, weight, and heft. He could feel the dance of his hands on the slide, the safety, the magazine release. His father's favorite pistol was a Kimber 1911, pretty much the same model as this one, and Gideon had shot endless piles of ammo through it.

"Take the gun!" Monkey was sweating, his face a mask of concentration. "I saw how you handled that gun. I know you know how to shoot. *Shoot.*"

They weren't going to make it. Gideon could see the intersection of the two arcs. Monkey's was the more powerful boat, but the jihadis were tracing the interior arc of the circle, and there was nothing Monkey could do to avoid being intercepted.

"Shoot!"

Gideon took a tentative step toward the rear of the boat where the pistol lay. It would be so easy. All he had to do was —

The boat shuddered and slammed into the air. They must have hit something — a submerged log, a sandbar — Gideon wasn't sure. But whatever it was, the whole boat went airborne for a moment, the Mercuries jumping up in pitch for a moment as they clawed for purchase in the air.

Gideon lost his balance, grabbing for the railing as the boat slammed back into the water. When he looked toward the back of the boat, the Colt was tumbling in a high slow arc through the air. And then it was gone, swallowed by the boiling wake of the speedboat.

Gideon surveyed the deck, looking for something he could use to fend off the attackers. Within seconds a plan was forming in his mind. Grabbing a life ring attached to a yellow nylon rope, he flicked open the Benchmade he'd taken from the Prang and sliced the ring free. Then he grabbed an axe that was duct-taped to the bulkhead, and wrapped two loops around the axe head, securing it with a quick square knot.

"Turn toward them!" he shouted, jabbing his finger at the pursuing speedboat.

"What?" Monkey said.

"We're not gonna make it. Head straight for them."

Monkey gripped the wheel, his teeth gritted. For a moment he kept barreling straight toward the inlet. But then, he yanked the wheel in the direction Gideon was pointing.

Suddenly the two boats were heading toward each other at a combined speed that probably exceeded a hundred miles an hour. The eyes of the jihadis went wide with surprise. The distance had closed to only a matter of a few hundred feet by the time the first of them managed to shoulder his AK and start shooting.

"Straight for them!" Gideon shouted. "*Straight* for them."

Gideon heard the bullets snapping in the air around him and thudding into the hull.

"Hold steady . . ." Gideon was swinging

the axe over his head in a slow circle.

Monkey held his bearing, turning what had moments ago been a chase into a game of high-speed chicken. As the distance closed, Gideon saw it register on the face of the jihadi boat's pilot. Seeing that a collision was inevitable, he suddenly swerved. The shooters lost their balance and, for a moment, stopped firing.

That was all the time Gideon needed.

When the boats flew past each other, missing by inches, Gideon let the axe fly. It sailed through the air, trailing yellow rope in its wake. The bow of the jihadis' boat passed under the rope, which caught on the edge of the windscreen. The axe whirled around in a short arc, snapping like a whip and embedding its blade in the driver's chest.

A heavy thump jarred Monkey's boat as it caught the weight of the man's body. The contest between man and boat was no contest at all. With the axe still buried in his ribs, the jihadi was hurled fifteen feet into the air. For a moment he was pulled behind the boat, flailing like a fallen skier caught in a tow rope, before the axe blade tore free from his chest. He sank immediately.

The remaining jihadis scrambled toward the wheel of their driverless boat, but not before the boat slammed onto the little island and flipped. The men pinwheeled in the air before falling in heaps on the sandbar or splashing down into the water. One landed in a small tree and was impaled by the sharp end of a leafless limb. His body convulsed for a brief violent moment, then hung lifeless, like some horrible twisted fruit.

And then Monkey's boat was around the bend, and the jihadis were gone.

Monkey shook his head, eyes big as shot glasses. "You messed them people *up*," he said, his expression a mixture of fear, gratitude, and amazement.

The entire episode had taken less than a minute. Gideon expected to feel some kind of remorse over the horrific deaths he'd caused. And yet he didn't. He realized, too, that he hadn't felt any fear, just a sense of total absorption in the moment, of utter commitment to the fight.

Then, when the emotion finally came, he was surprised by what he recognized was an almost giddy sense of well-being, even a kind of elation. Men had tried to kill him, and he had survived by killing them. Simple as that.

He felt his teeth bare in a brief, feral smile.

My God, Gideon thought. *What's wrong*

with me?

He tried to square himself with the man who had just killed other men with such instinctive efficiency. He'd been in the moment and he'd reacted and . . . he hadn't meant to kill them, just to mess up their boat enough to stop them.

Gideon turned to Monkey and started to talk, but his mouth had gone dry. He licked his lips and tried again. "How long before we reach my brother?" he asked, his voice cracked and hollow.

Monkey reached inside his shirt and scratched himself nervously. "Soon," he said. "Very soon."

CHAPTER TWELVE

The wind had stiffened by the time Kate came up onto the chopper deck. Beneath her hard hat, her hair whipped at her neck. The State Department chopper was struggling to get onto the deck. Pilots who weren't used to it didn't like landing on rigs. She didn't blame them — especially not in this kind of wind. Anything above thirty knots and they shut down chopper landings. It wasn't thirty knots yet — but the gusts were probably getting close to that.

After a minute of tilting and bouncing, the chopper finally settled onto the deck and its rotors wound down.

Kate moved toward Big Al, who was staring toward the eastern horizon. She knew what he was looking for. If the typhoon changed direction, it would come from the east. The sky was still clear and blue, but a thin dark smudge had appeared threateningly along the horizon.

Big Al turned toward her, covering his concern with an admiring smile. "You clean up nice, *chérie*."

"Thanks."

"While you were getting all pretty, we got a call . . ."

"From?"

"The White House. The president wants Mr. Parker to call him."

Kate raised an eyebrow, then followed Big Al's nod toward the idling Sikorsky. A small man with a face that reminded her of a bloodhound was now emerging from the chopper, followed by a Secret Service agent. Behind him was the U.S. ambassador, Randy Stearns, a large, red-faced man wearing a bespoke suit. Stearns was nearly as big as Big Al. He'd played pro football for the Vikings, Kate knew, because on all three occasions that she'd met him, he had made a point of telling her. He was talking to a slim woman with hair that was dyed one shade too blond, whom Kate recognized as his press attaché. Her name was Tina. Or Tara. She couldn't remember which.

Two more bodyguards followed, and as soon as they cleared the rotors, the chopper rose into the air again, as though the pilot had had enough of sitting on a tiny platform a hundred feet above the sea.

Kate extended her hand to the man with the bloodhound face. "Mr. Parker, I'm Kate Murphy, the rig manager."

"Call me Earl." If not for the bodyguard who shadowed him, you'd never have known he was a man of any importance.

Ambassador Stearns leaned in to kiss her cheek without her offering it. "How you doing, hon?" he said. "Good to see you again. You remember Tina."

Kate gave the ambassador a noncommital nod, then turned back to Parker. "Sir, the president wants you to call him right away. If you need privacy, you can use the observation room."

"Thank you," Parker said. "Soon as I'm done, I hope you can show us around."

"Of course," Kate said, before leading Parker to the glass-walled observation room. She remained outside with Parker's security man, watching through the window as Parker raised his satellite phone to his ear. But the disapproving glare of the Secret Service agent prompted her to turn away. Before she did, though, she could see Earl Parker's expression darken and his ramrod-straight posture give way to what she could only imagine was some kind of bad news.

Following the reception at the UN, President Diggs had spent the night at the Park Avenue apartment of Cameron Stack, an investment banker who'd been one of the leading fund-raisers during his campaign. Stack had declined a cabinet position, preferring to remain an unofficial economic advisor. They had talked well into the night, discussing the sobering economic challenges facing the nation, from rising unemployment to price competition from China, all of which caused the president to sleep fitfully. He'd returned early the next morning to Washington, when he learned what had happened to Gideon's convoy. It took another hour before he was finally able to reach Earl Parker, who'd just landed on the Obelisk. The president's chief of staff, Elliot Hammershaw, held out the encrypted satellite phone.

"I have him, sir."

Diggs pressed the phone to his ear and proceeded to tell Parker that General Prang and his men had all been killed during an ambush, but that Gideon's body hadn't been found yet.

"Then he may still be alive," Parker said.

"The Sultan's troops are sweeping the area, but they're not optimistic. I'm sorry, Earl, I know how much Gideon means to you. And you know how much he means to me."

Parker leaned heavily against the communications console. "Mr. President," he said, hesitating before finishing his thought. "Tillman may have been behind this."

"Based on what?"

"Tillman and General Prang were the only people who knew Gideon's itinerary."

"I realize Tillman's capable of betraying his country . . . but do you really think he'd try to kill his own brother?"

"Who else could it have been?"

Kate stole another furtive glance into the observation room. Parker was pinching his forehead as he talked to the president. When Parker finally ended the call, he lowered the phone into his lap and remained as still as a statue. Then, suddenly, he turned toward Kate, who averted her gaze, hoping he hadn't caught her watching him. A few seconds later, he emerged from the room, clearly shaken by whatever news he'd just gotten from the president.

"Is there anything I can do, sir?" Kate asked.

Parker hesitated before he spoke. "You said you'd give us a tour of the rig before the camera crews come."

"Yes, sir."

"Lead on."

Kate was keenly aware of Parker's lingering distraction as he waved for the ambassador and the rest of his entourage to join them. She led the group to a place at the edge of the chopper deck that gave them the best view of the rig. "As you can see, the Obelisk is composed of two structures linked by a small bridge."

They stood nearly a hundred feet above the surface of the ocean. Only the steel skeletons of the drilling derricks and cranes were higher. Even after all these years working on rigs, being on the deck was still thrilling to her.

"The unit we're standing on is the Wellhead Service Platform. It includes not only the drilling apparatus, but also the mess, bunk quarters, rec room, laundry, and control room."

"Why is the rig split into two parts?" Stearns asked.

"There are some structural considerations — but primarily safety. As soon as the oil comes out, we pipe it over to the Bridge Linked Platform. Over there we have the power-generation equipment, storage, and preprocessing. Normally an FPSO — that's a factory processing and storage ship — is moored a few hundred yards away. It stores and processes the oil and gas prior to transshipment to our onshore facility. Because it's so far out at sea, the Obelisk was designed to warehouse larger quantities of oil so production can continue if the factory ship needs to return to port in the event of a storm or some other emergency. That allows us to continue pumping while the ship isn't here. At full production, our operating budget is around a hundred thousand dollars a day. Needless to say, we make every effort to keep production going at all times."

Except when Washington bigwigs show up to stage some pointless exercise in political theater, she thought.

"Of course, the downside to storing that much oil and gas is the potential for fire. If that happens, we can delink the pipes until the fire is controlled. The idea here is to make even a catastrophic event survivable by the crew."

She led Parker's entourage down the stairwell and through a door.

"One of the most interesting things about this rig is that it's a semicompliant tower, which means that it sways with the movement of the ocean. Most of the time it's pretty imperceptible. But in the kind of heavy seas we have today, you can actually feel it. We have systems in place that can both actively and passively dampen those potentially destructive forces."

Kate pointed to a pair of large pumps in the middle of the room. "These pumps can move water at a rate of over eight thousand cfm — sorry, for you nonengineers, that's cubic feet of water per minute. Several large nozzles beneath the rig are constantly steadying the structure by automatically countering currents and compensating for other forces, like wind or tectonic movement."

"What about the passive system?" Parker said. "How does that work?"

Kate was surprised that Parker had been paying attention, considering his earlier distraction. "Good question. There's a four-hundred-ton weight situated about seventy feet below the surface of the ocean. It's mounted on a sort of gimbal that allows the weight to shift with respect to the rig. Skyscrapers along the Pacific rim are being built with similar systems to counterbalance the forces of an earthquake." She didn't see the need to tell the visitors that the passive system was in serious danger of failing, and she quickly led the group out the door and up the next flight of stairs.

"This is the heart of the rig," she said.

"The drill deck." In the center of the slippery steel floor was a hole, through which the now-idle drill pipe ran down into the sea.

"As state-of-the-art as the Obelisk is, it still works pretty much the way Anthony Lucas's drill did when he first tapped Spindletop back in 1901. At a certain point, there's only so much you can automate. The drilling operation itself is just as dirty and noisy and hands-on as it was a hundred years ago. As you can see, the characteristic derrick structure of an oil rig is right there above us. It's about sixty-five feet from here to the top of the tower. Hanging from the derrick, that big complicated claw-looking thing is the traveling block." She pointed to the massive steel claw hanging from chains in the middle of the deck. "It clamps around the drill pipe, screws the pipe into the preceding section. Then that big ram up there drives the pipe through the kelly deeper into the hole."

Parker stepped up to the edge of the hole and peered down at the ocean.

"Sir, I'd prefer you stayed away from there. One misstep . . ."

Parker straightened. "Is there anything on this rig that *isn't* dangerous?"

Kate laughed. She realized that as she had

140

taken them around the rig, she had pointed out one thing after another that was capable of catching fire, blowing up, or collapsing onto someone or chopping them in half. "Honestly? Not much."

Parker looked up at the derrick. "Ever work on the drill deck yourself?"

She nodded. "My father was an independent oil man. He made and squandered a couple or three fortunes drilling in Texas. While I was in college, he went broke for the fourth time, so I had to get a job as a roustabout and then as a diver to pay for my final two years of college."

"That must have been an adventure."

"I like to think I pulled my weight."

"I bet you did," he said.

She led the group through the innards of the Wellhead Service Platform, showing them the sleeping quarters, the chem lab, and the rec room.

"We've got a crew of sixty-eight," she said as they entered the mess. It was a small room, six long tables crowded together like in an elementary school cafeteria. "Everybody works ten-day stretches, twelve hours on, twelve off. In addition to the drilling crew, we've got electricians, welders, a mud engineer, various equipment technicians. We've also got two fulltime chefs, a two-person laundry staff, a maid, a medic . . ."

"It must feel a little claustrophobic sometimes," Parker offered.

"You get used to it," she said. She felt a slight tremor beneath her feet, smaller than the ones she'd felt earlier, then realized with some small relief that it was Big Al tromping toward them on the gridded steel floor. "Sorry to interrupt, Kate, but the news crews are arriving."

"Let's head back up," Kate said. "Not to be unfriendly, but the sooner we get this over with, the sooner I can get back to pumping oil."

The chopper that landed on deck was at least twice as large as the State Department Sikorsky that was still hovering overhead. Kate was a little surprised at the number of newspeople that had come. She counted twenty of them. Mohan only had one national television station. Some Indonesian and Malaysian crews had arrived, too. *They must really be starved for news to attend something as trivial as this,* she thought.

Several crews were busy dragging steel equipment cases across the deck. They were all dressed as you'd expect news professionals to dress — blue jeans, clean tennis shoes, polo shirts emblazoned with the logos of well-known Western brands. Because they worked for the government news channel, they wore skullcaps, which identified them as Muslims.

But something about them seemed odd. They were all fairly young — twenties and early thirties — which was not odd in itself — but each one of them seemed unusually fit. Professional men in Mohan generally didn't work out the way Americans did. If one of them had looked like an athlete, it wouldn't have seemed so unusual. But twenty of them?

One cameraman was setting up on the far end of the chopper deck. Another pair were rolling a steel case the size and shape of a coffin across the deck. She couldn't imagine what kind of camera equipment required a box that big. Before she could think much more about it, she noticed one more man who'd emerged from the chopper and was now beelining toward her, conspicuous because he was the only Caucasian. He wore a dark suit, a laptop computer case slung over one shoulder.

"Miss Murphy?" he asked, although his inflection didn't sound like a question. "I'm Cole Ransom."

Kate was a little surprised by his appearance. The several times they had talked, she had imagined him as kind of a geek, but he moved with the fluid grace of an athlete. And behind the neatly trimmed beard of an academic, he had the face of a cop or a soldier — hard and impassive.

"I really want to get started on the retrofit, but I need to take care of this nonsense first," she said apologetically, indicating the surrounding crews. "Frankly, I was blindsided by all this. Hopefully it won't take long."

Ransom nodded curtly. He sure didn't give off a friendly vibe. Their phone conversations and e-mail correspondence had been lively and animated, but in person the guy had about as much personality as a fireplug.

She was puzzling over this when she noticed the embassy press attaché, Tina, directing several of the cameramen to set up on the deck.

"Dr. Ransom, one of my people will show you to your cabin down on B Deck. Will you excuse me?"

Without waiting for an answer from Ransom, Kate rushed over to the press attaché, shouting over the roar of the State Department chopper, which was circling slowly past the rig a few hundred yards away. "Wait a minute, wait a minute. You can't film your news conference here."

"Why not?" the press attaché said.

"Because it's not safe," Kate said, flashing her eyes angrily.

The attaché gave her a bright, slightly condescending smile. "Oh no, we have to do it here." She formed a rectangle with her thumbs and forefingers, framing the derrick rising above the deck. "See? It's *perfect.*"

Kate shook her head. "Wait a minute —"

But Tina was already looking past her, at a reporter who was calling over to her. "Sorry, I have to get this," the attaché said, offering another calculated smile before rushing off to the other side of the deck.

Safety regs were nonnegotiable on an oil rig. You stepped foot on a rig, you put on a hard hat. Period. Too many things could go wrong when you started bending the rules. This was quickly turning into a highly unsafe situation. And to make matters worse, the chopper deck had no railings along its perimeter to prevent some careless reporter from falling eighty feet into the sea.

Kate waved sharply at one of her roughnecks, who was standing near the stairs. "Eddie!" she shouted. "Come here, please."

Seeing her urgency, Eddie trotted over. "Get these people off this deck *now.* And I want hard hats on every damn one of them."

"Yes, ma'am!" he said.

"Starting with those guys right over there." She pointed at the camera crew on the far end of the rig.

"Sorry, Tina," Kate said, catching up to the press attaché. "I know this is a great photo op, but I cannot and I will not permit this to happen up here. It's too dangerous."

"Don't force me to go over your head, Miss Murphy."

"Listen to me carefully, Tina." Kate gripped the press attaché with a firm hand, her voice low and intense and nonnegotiable. "On this rig, my head is the only one that counts. Now get your damn news crews below deck —" Kate stopped suddenly when she saw what was happening.

How it happened, she wasn't sure. She didn't see the event itself. All she saw was the roughneck, Eddie, falling backward over the edge of the deck, away from the camera crew, his face a mask of horror and surprise. He clawed at the air as he toppled backward, screaming. Kate saw him through the steel mesh deck, tumbling toward the surging sea below, his arms and legs circling. There was a strange, dreamlike quality to his fall. For a moment she couldn't believe it was happening. Then he disappeared, her vision cut off by a section of the rig below the chopper deck.

Kate started to move, but by then it was too late.

At the far end of the chopper deck, one of the cameramen had opened a case, pulled out a short, stubby tube, and flipped up some kind of eyepiece. The State Department chopper was still circling overhead when a rush of flame erupted from the stubby tube. Something belching white smoke shot from the tube and tore through the air toward the chopper.

A missile.

The trail of the missile stretched out like white taffy. Then there was a loud *whump,* and what had been a helicopter was now a ball of flame, spewing randomly shaped black debris that slammed into the steel superstructure of the Obelisk. Within moments the chopper hit the water, rolled once, then disappeared, swallowed by a twenty-foot wave.

"Oh my God," the press attaché whispered.

Kate turned to see the cameramen and journalists all stooping simultaneously, throwing open their cases with the precise coordination of dancers in some lethal ballet.

There was no camera equipment in the cases. As the camera crews stood, they were all holding guns. Kate recognized them as AK-47s, the kind with the big curved ammunition clips.

The two marine bodyguards and the Secret Service man were raising their weapons when the counterfeit news crews opened fire. The noise was deafening.

The two marines and the Secret Service man dropped like bags of meat, blood erupting from their necks, faces, and bodies.

One group of terrorists started roughly rounding up the rest of Kate's on-deck crew, as a second group broke off, quickly descending the stairs toward the lower decks, sweeping and taking ground as they did. Using the chaos as cover, Kate started moving toward the second stairwell to try and warn Parker's group, when she found herself face-to-face with Ransom. She gestured for him to come with her, when she noticed he was holding an automatic pistol. And it was leveled point-blank at her head.

Kate's brain went into overdrive, trying to absorb what was happening. It became apparent to her that Ransom — or the man who'd claimed to be Ransom — was actually in charge when he addressed everyone on deck. "Listen to me carefully, because

I'm only going to say this once," he said. He wasn't shouting, but his voice carried. "No one else needs to die." He prodded one of the dead men contemptuously with his toe. "This was stupid and unnecessary. Cooperate and you'll be home soon, playing with your kids."

"Please don't kill me, please don't kill me —" Tina whimpered.

"Shut up, Tina," Kate snapped.

Tina stopped talking. Kate confronted the lead terrorist. "What do you want?"

"You'll find out soon enough," he said.

"You're not Cole Ransom. So who are you?"

"You can call me Abu Nasir."

Kate felt a cold fear rising inside her. The man Senator McClatchy claimed had bled Trojan Energy for almost fifty million dollars over the last year was now seizing her rig. Her fear suddenly gave way to a primal anger when she heard a burst of gunfire nearby, followed by the desperate screams of men whose voices she recognized as members of her crew. "Leave my people alone, you son of a bitch —"

She lunged toward Abu Nasir, her fingers reaching for his eyes, but he sidestepped her easily and swung his gun-weighted fist across the side of her head, and she went down like a steer in a slaughterhouse.

Kate blinked hard, trying to squeeze the stars from her eyes as she was pulled to her feet by a large Asian man whom Abu Nasir called Chun. She felt her head. A tender knot was already rising under her hairline, where she'd been struck.

"Take Ms. Murphy to B Deck with Stearns and Prejean. Place Deputy National Security Advisor Parker in the stateroom. And after you finish rounding up the rest of the crew, put them in the mess hall."

Kate saw four of Abu Nasir's men down on the drill deck, wrestling with the large steel box that she'd seen them rolling across the chopper deck just a few minutes earlier. They were attaching it to the crane used to move drill pipe, winching it down through the drill shaft to some lower point on the rig. The men seemed completely comfortable and familiar with the equipment on the drill deck.

It was quite clear to Kate that whoever these people were, they had extremely good intelligence. They knew the design of the rig, and they knew who was on board.

Earl Parker eyed Abu Nasir. Then he spoke, his voice quiet but full of a calm authority. "I would prefer that you put me with everyone else. As the senior United

States government official on this rig, I have a responsibility to take care of these people."

Abu Nasir turned and eyeballed him with amusement. "You'd *prefer?*"

The bearded American slapped the older man across the face so hard that his glasses flew off. A thin trickle of blood ran from the corner of his lip.

Earl Parker continued to meet Abu Nasir's gaze.

"All right then, Tillman. I *insist,*" Earl Parker said. Again, his voice was not loud. But it carried.

Abu Nasir laughed.

Earl Parker said, "All that I've done for you, Tillman . . . and you repay me like this?"

The American slapped him again, even harder this time. Earl Parker staggered backward, and his eyes lost focus. "Take this old bastard down to the control room, Chun," Abu Nasir said, "while I decide whether or not to shoot his ass."

The big man whom Abu Nasir had referred to as Chun quickly cuffed Earl Parker's hands behind him with flexible plastic cuffs, then steered the now compliant deputy national security advisor away.

Abu Nasir surveyed the remaining people on the deck and said, "Anybody else feel

151

the need to share any questions or concerns with me?"

Nobody spoke. Kate's stomach churned.

"Good." He turned to one of his men and said, "Round up any strays and get them to the mess hall. In the meantime, take Stearns, Murphy, and Prejean down to my cabin on B Deck."

Heads nodded.

Tina raised her hand, ducking her head obsequiously. "Um, sir? What about me?"

Abu Nasir blinked. "What *about* you?"

"Don't I go with the VIPs?"

Abu Nasir looked at her curiously. "Don't you go with the VIPs? Hm. Would it reflect badly on you if you had to rub shoulders with the hoi polloi? Is that the point of your question?"

Tina smiled weakly. "I just meant . . ." Her words died in her throat as Abu Nasir drew his pistol and shot the young woman in the head, then pushed her with his foot. She rolled once, then flopped over the side and fell into the ocean. The wind gusted, died, gusted again.

"Folks, I want you to understand something," Abu Nasir said, smiling genially. "Any questions you might have, you're going to get the same answer. This." He waggled the pistol in front of them. "Do what I tell you, and don't ask questions. We clear?"

Everyone nodded. Kate wanted to rage at him, wanted at least to raise her eyes from the deck. But she knew that it wouldn't do any good. Right now she needed to focus on protecting her crew. And she couldn't do that from the bottom of the ocean.

"Good." Abu Nasir motioned with his head toward the stairs. Kate followed Stearns on rubbery legs as they headed back across the chopper deck.

Chun steered Earl Parker to the control room down on the drill deck, pointed silently to a chair, then stood by the door. Parker stared sullenly at the big man, who looked off at the ocean. The skies were low and dark, and the waves were so huge that you couldn't quite make sense of just how big they were.

According to the last weather forecast Parker had seen, the typhoon off the Philippines wasn't supposed to hit the rig. But it sure looked nasty out there. Maybe the forecast was wrong.

After three or four minutes, the muscular bearded American walked through the door, a pistol thrust into his belt.

"Can anyone see us?" Parker said.

Abu Nasir shook his head. "They're all locked up in the cabins now."

"Then get these goddamn cuffs off me . . . *Abu Nasir.*" Parker gave the nom de guerre a sarcastic twist.

"Yes, sir."

The bearded American pulled a knife from his pocket and quickly cut the cuffs off Earl Parker's wrists.

"Sorry about the face, Mr. Parker," he said. "You told me to make it look real."

Earl Parker eyed him expressionlessly, touched the corner of his mouth, then studied the blood on his fingers.

"You want me to get you something for that, sir?"

Earl Parker spit blood onto the deck. "Your people screwed the pooch. Gideon Davis is still alive."

The bearded American nodded. "I know, sir. My team is still on it, though. They'll find him. Trust me. He's a dead man walking."

"He damn well better be." Parker stood. "I trust you didn't blow it at Kampung Naga, too?"

"Clockwork. No survivors."

"Good. Anything else I need to know? Any more screwups?"

"No, sir. Other than the ambush, everything's right on schedule."

"Good. Then put me back in with Kate Murphy and that fool Stearns. We've still got a long way to go before we cross the goal line, so I want to keep an eye on things from the hostage perspective. But if anything comes up, any decisions that need to be made, any wrinkles in the plan, anything whatsoever that's above your pay grade — you bring me out. And I mean double-time quick."

"Absolutely, sir."

Suddenly Earl Parker's hand shot out. He grabbed the younger man by the collar and jerked him forward so that their eyes were only inches apart. "And if you ever hit me like that again, Timken, it'll be the last fucking thing you do."

If you had managed to locate the passport for the leader of the group that had seized the Obelisk, you would have found that his real name was neither Cole Ransom nor Abu Nasir. And it certainly wasn't Tillman Davis.

Sitting in a safe-deposit box in a discreet bank in Geneva, Switzerland — along with ten passports with ten other bogus names on them — was his genuine passport, the one imprinted with his real name: Orville

155

Timken. The last person to call him Orville, though, was a kid in junior high. After Timken beat the kid to the ground for calling him "ORRRRRRRville," nobody else had wanted a piece of *that,* thanks, and it had become understood that he preferred Tim or Timmer or just plain Timken.

Later Timken found out that he shared his name with a company that made ball bearings. He had been sent by his military unit to a convention for weapons manufacturers, where he stumbled across a booth with his name on it. The people who ran the booth had a glass bowl full of ball bearings on the table at the front of the booth. Each ball bearing had his name laser etched on it.

"Half-inch, ultrahigh precision 62100 steel, hardened to Rockwell 59," the helpful salesman had said. "Every single one of them will mike at plus or minus three ten-thousandths of nominal, guaranteed."

Timken looked into the bowl, saw his face reflected in hundreds of tiny fun-house mirrors. Something about the ball bearings — their featurelessness and hardness and regularity — gave him a momentary stab of pleasure. He reached into the bowl, grabbed a handful.

"Sir, if you wouldn't mind limiting your-

self to just one or two?" the helpful salesman had said.

Timken had given him The Look.

"Well, I suppose it's okay," the salesman
said with a tight smile. "What application
did you have in mind for them?"

"Putting them in a sock and hitting some
nosy faggot in the face until he shuts the
fuck up."

The salesman's tight smile didn't go away.
But after that he had just looked over
Timken's shoulder, as though Timken
weren't standing there at all.

Since then, Timken's name had worn off
the tiny, shiny ball bearings, and he suspected they probably would no longer mike
at three ten-thousandths of nominal anymore. But they suited his needs just fine.
He could put them in a pocket or a briefcase. He could take them on a plane without
the TSA morons confiscating them. He
could take them anywhere. Then when he
needed them, he put them in a bag or a sock
or a wadded-up shirt. And when he hit you
with them you fell down and didn't move.

Timken had carried the ball bearings in
his pocket since that day. Except for the six
months he'd served in Leavenworth after
punching out General Rowbothom — the
minor lapse in judgment that had ended his

promising military career.

His life would have been pretty much over with if he hadn't been rescued from the wastelands by a man who understood the peculiar nature of his talents. A man who understood that a great nation sometimes had to do dark and ugly things, and that when those things had to be done, Orville Timken could be counted on to come through.

A man named Earl Parker.

CHAPTER THIRTEEN

Water cascaded in a thunderous rush over the high U-shaped cliff that rose before Monkey's boat. Sunlight caught the spray from the waterfall, refracting a brilliantly colored rainbow. If not for the circumstances, Gideon reflected silently, this could have been a postcard for some idyllic tropical retreat.

Monkey throttled the engine back. To one side of the waterfall was a tiny strip of beach from which extended a bamboo pier. Behind it was a small cluster of grass huts.

"Is this where my brother is?" Gideon asked.

Monkey shook his head and pointed. "Up there." The cliff face ran in an unbroken line of white rock as far in both directions as Gideon could see. It was as though the entire surface of the earth had cracked in half, one piece sliding down below the other. The cliff must have been nearly a thousand feet high and was topped by a thin green rim of jungle.

"How do I get up there?"

"Climb," he said.

"Climb?"

Monkey shrugged, nudged the boat against the rickety bamboo pier, and killed the engine.

"Do you at least know the trail?"

"No," he said, quickly adding, "And I'm not about to find out."

Gideon knew that Monkey wasn't to blame here. This wasn't *his* fault. But still, he felt a flash of anger. "You took me all this way and you're just going to abandon me?"

Monkey gave him a sideways look. "What you expect? You gonna get me killed." He waved vaguely at the green line of jungle that capped the cliff. "We have a saying . . . Where the river ends, Allah has no power."

"Meaning what exactly?"

Monkey stared up at the high cliff. "The people up there? They're not people. Not like you and me. They got no rules, no laws, no right and wrong. No God."

"Do you at least know someone who can guide me up?"

"Maybe if you had money . . ."

"My brother has money."

"I don't see your brother here." Monkey seemed moderately pleased with the fix that Gideon was in.

"Come on," Gideon said. "Help me out here. You're in my shoes, what would you do?"

Monkey continued to stare up at the jungle. "Do what I'm gonna do. Get down-river, hope you reach KM without getting killed."

Gideon's eyes narrowed. "I've come this far, I'm not about to turn around now."

Monkey shook his head, as if to say he was done trying to talk Gideon out of his suicidal scheme, then pointed at a cleat on the pier. "Tie us to the pier. Maybe I translate, help you find somebody."

Gideon had cut one of the mooring lines back in Alun Jong, but there was another one coiled on the bow. He grabbed the end and stepped onto the pier, which felt spongy under his feet, as if it was rotting from within. As Gideon stepped carefully on the bamboo deck, afraid that he might fall through, he heard a roar. He turned in time to see Monkey slamming the throttle into reverse. Before Gideon could leap back onto the boat, it had already pulled away from the pier. Monkey was laughing as he backed the boat up.

Gideon tried holding on to the rope, but the boat was too powerful, and the rope slid through his hands, burning his fingers and palms as it slipped into the water.

"Next time you hold a knife to my neck —" The rest of Monkey's threat was drowned by the sound of the Mercuries. He spun the wheel, slammed the throttle back into forward gear, and the boat tore a circular hole in the water, accelerating downriver. Within half a minute, the boat was gone, the engine noise lost in the thunder of the waterfall.

Gideon turned and looked at the village. He'd need to hire somebody to guide him to Kampung Naga. Just *how* he was going to manage that with no money, he wasn't quite sure. But he'd figure out a way. He had no choice.

He walked through the tiny village, which was strangely empty. "Hello!" he called. "Is anybody here?"

But there was no answer. In fact there was no sound at all. The place was deserted. The roofs of the houses sagged. Several had been burned to the ground.

Gideon realized that he was very hungry. Almost a day had passed since he'd eaten. He searched the houses and finally found a tin of fruit sitting on a rotting shelf. He tore the tin open and gobbled the peaches hungrily. But instead of satisfying his appetite, it only made him hungrier.

He looked for more food but didn't find any. He reflected wryly that he could think of better ways than this of taking off the ten pounds he'd gained in Colombia.

When he reached the far end of the village, he saw a small trail heading toward the cliffs, overgrown with vines and fast-growing tropical plants. He pushed his way through vegetation, then began to climb. As he walked, he looked at the map General Prang had given him. Staring up at him was the red circle. Kampung Naga, the city that doesn't exist.

From a distance, the cliffs looked white. Closer, and Gideon found they were composed of a grayish limestone. Foliage seemed to have a hard time growing on the winding trail. There were only a few gnarled trees and occasional clumps of grass sprouting from the rock. At first the cliffs were not really cliffs at all, just very steep hills, eroded into sharp gulleys and ravines.

But the higher he climbed, the steeper the trail became. The limestone was loose and crumbly, and the path narrowed as the face of the limestone grew steeper. Eventually the path was no more than a foot wide, sometimes dropping off for hundreds of feet on either side.

Halfway up, Gideon paused to rest his burning thighs. He ran thirty miles a week — but running on flat ground was not the same as climbing hills. Resting his back against the cool rock, he surveyed the view that spread for miles below him. In the distance he could just make out another small village on a crook in the river. When he and Monkey blasted past the village, it had seemed normal. Now it was on fire, a thick column of smoke rising into the sky.

In the distance he saw a tiny V-shaped wake rippling on the surface of the river. A boat was approaching. Gideon felt a stab of fear. Coincidence? Or was someone following him?

He stood and started up the trail again.

The going was slower now. The higher he went, the more it became like mountain climbing rather than hiking. He could see the lip of the jungle above him. But there were still probably five hundred sheer vertical feet to go. Gideon had drastically underestimated the height of the cliffs. And the steepest part of the climb was yet to come.

Soon he found that he had to keep both hands on the rock face at all times. The rock slid away below him. The only good news was that the temperature had dropped. It was still warm — but it wasn't the oppressive tropical furnace that it had been.

Occasionally a toehold or handhold crumbled beneath him, the loose rock falling and bouncing and tumbling down the slope. Each time it happened, he momentarily lost his balance and had to claw for purchase to keep himself from following the dislodged rocks down the rubble-strewn face of the cliff.

Gideon tried pushing away the persistent doubts and fears that flitted through his mind — that this mission was foolish and pointless and that he should turn around and go back. If he wanted to find Tillman, he would have to face whatever lay ahead in the place that Monkey feared so much.

He paused again to massage his trembling thighs. The sun was lowering on the horizon and he still had a few hundred feet to go. He looked down. The boat he'd seen earlier was pulling up to the pier. A man leapt out and secured the boat, then several more men followed him ashore. They swept through the abandoned village. Even at this distance, unable to see faces or expressions, Gideon could tell they were moving with purpose, searching for something or someone. He wondered if the surviving jihadis from downriver had followed him all the way up here. But why would they bother going to all that trouble over some muddy, bedraggled foreigner? It seemed odd. Except for the fact that he'd been responsible for the death of several of them. Maybe they just wanted to make an example of him. Or maybe they were looking for someone else entirely.

As he was mulling over the questions and massaging his legs, one of the men pointed up toward the cliff. Gideon heard a distant, barely audible shout. Then the men began running up the trail that led up the cliff. *Well,* he thought, *that was clear enough.* They were definitely following him. As they got closer he could see that they were carrying guns.

Gideon gave his aching calf a last hard squeeze, then headed upward. Speculating about why they were chasing him wouldn't help him escape.

Gideon's pursuers quickly closed the gap between them. He estimated that when he first spotted them, they had been more than a thousand yards away. But because they were on the flatter part of the trail, they were moving much faster than he was. Soon they would be within three or four hundred yards. And when they were —

The first bullet pinged off the rock and ricocheted with a noise that sounded like something out of an old cowboy movie. But the shot was nowhere close. Gideon guessed that his pursuers were carrying AK-47s with iron sights. Unless they were serious marksmen, he was in little danger at this distance. But once they were within two hundred yards, he'd be in trouble.

Gideon waited for the second shot. It didn't come. He figured they were being smart, conserving their ammo until they'd closed the gap a little more. Once they got close enough, they didn't have to be great marksmen to hit him. Gideon started climbing faster, in rhythm with his own quickening heartbeat. He realized that his legs no longer hurt. The fight-or-flight endorphins were powerful painkillers, better than aspirin any day.

He glanced back over his shoulder. The lower portion of the trail wound back and forth across the face of the cliff, passing directly beneath him. When his pursuers reached that point, he would be inside their kill zone. He had to think of something. Fast.

He scanned the steepening face of the

cliff. An outcropping of rock about twenty yards ahead would give him cover until his pursuers passed directly below him. He scrambled upward as fast as his body would take him, until one of his footholds gave way under his weight and he only managed to keep from falling by catching his weight with his right hand. The broken rock fell away below him and disappeared. He held on with his one hand, spread-eagled on the rock face. The slightest motion might cause his grip to fail. He froze. He felt himself breathing steadily, his heartbeat slowing, and his mind clearing — and felt an acute focus he'd never experienced before. In front of his eyes a tiny sprig of lichen clutched onto the limestone.

Be the lichen.

He heard the words in his head. Literally: *be the lichen.* He almost had to laugh. It was as if his own personal Yoda was whispering to him from some unseen perch. But it made sense. Lichen had no hands or feet, rooting itself to the rock with its entire structure. Gideon relaxed, allowing his own body to mold to the irregular contours of the rock face. When he felt his center of gravity balanced, he began snaking his left hand upward, then his knees, his feet, and even his chest — trying to find another hold so he could relieve the strain on his right hand.

A bullet smacked the rock three yards to his left, and a little below him. The report of the AK followed, a sharp crack.

Another bullet struck the rock just below him. A third to his right.

He moved spiderlike, finding one foothold, then another, until he'd clambered up the last ten or twelve feet and over the outcropping. A steady rattle of gunfire chased him, then ceased.

Gideon lay with his face pressed against the rock. Several small boulders scattered on the escarpment left just enough room for his body. He took a few deep breaths, then rolled over and looked up. He was no more than fifty yards from the top. There was a definite rim where the cliff ended and the jungle began. *Serious* jungle. Full-on triple-canopy rain forest. If he could make it to the trees, he could find cover. Two hundred yards from the trail and he might as well be two hundred miles. They would never find him. Never.

But right now he was pinned down.

If the jihadis were smart, they'd send half their guys up the cliff and keep the other half in position below. If he tried to make the last fifty yards, they would pick him off.

And if he stayed where he was, they'd cover and advance for one another until one of them could kill him at close range.

Gideon peered over the ledge. The pursuers *were* smart. Two men were already working their way up along the narrow path while the remaining four stayed behind, their weapons pointed right at him. Seeing this, Gideon ducked just as a volley of gunfire smacked against the downslope side of the outcropping.

He made a quick assessment of his worsening situation. The rock behind which he had found cover was no more than three feet wide and ten feet long. Enough to protect him as he lay on it, but not enough to shield him once he started climbing. The rubble on top of the outcropping consisted of two boulders as large around as his body and several smaller rocks that were roughly the size of bowling balls.

An idea came to him, born of that purest and most primitive animal instinct — survival.

He shifted his weight behind one of the bowling ball–size rocks and pushed it toward the edge. It rolled with a grinding noise until its own weight carried it down the slope. Gideon heard some warning cries as he peered over the edge and watched one of the men below dodging the boulder, which narrowly missed him as it crashed at the base of the cliff.

Gideon pulled his head back, registering a strange disappointment that he hadn't hit at least one of them. But at least he'd confirmed his theory: his attackers had been so concerned with the falling rock that they hadn't shot at him.

He looked up at the cliff again. The next fifty yards weren't too bad. He couldn't exactly sprint up. But he figured he could make it in twenty or thirty seconds.

He set to work on the other rocks, pushing them all to the edge. As he was pushing the largest one, he noticed a large rust-colored smear on its surface. Blood. He held up his hand, turned it around. A jagged wound ran across his palm. He must have cut himself during his near fall. It wasn't until he saw it that he noticed how much it hurt. Blood ran down his arm, dripping off his elbow in fat drops onto the limestone. Realizing that he couldn't afford to think about it right now, he tore a strip from his shirttail and wrapped his bleeding hand, then finished moving the rocks.

It took him only a few minutes to line up the remaining rocks along the ledge. His plan was to push them over the edge in fast sequence, from smallest to largest. His foot lingered on the rock for a suspended moment. *Now,* he realized. *It had to be now.* And he pushed the rocks over the edge — one, two, three, four, five — one after the other.

A volley of frantic shouts echoed from below, as he launched himself up the cliff.

The last of the rocks were still clattering down the hill as he scaled the rock face. It was steeper than he'd thought, and his legs were weak. Up and up he climbed, realizing halfway that he'd underestimated the time it would take him to reach the summit.

He would need at least another twenty seconds. And twenty seconds may as well have been a year in this exposed position. He wanted to look back but knew he couldn't. He waited for the gunfire to start. But it didn't come. His pursuers were shouting. He could make out their voices now.

"Run!" one of them yelled.

And then there was a sound, like the crack of thunder.

He charged upward, from handhold to foothold, his legs shaking violently from the buildup of lactic acid. *Faster,* he scolded himself. *Go faster.*

The thunder grew louder, building on itself. Gideon pounded upward, waiting for the gunfire, which still didn't come, as he threw himself over the lip and collapsed onto the ground, his body heaving as he tried to fill his lungs.

Below him, the thunder subsided until the only sound Gideon heard was his own ragged breathing. The air was thinner up here. A soft breeze cooled his face.

Finally he peeked over the side, just a quick glance, to see where his pursuers were.

No one was there. Only a massive, roiling cloud of dust. For a moment, he couldn't make sense of what he was looking at, but then he realized what had happened. He'd started a landslide. And not a small one. The boulders he dropped had caused some kind of seismic chain reaction that had sheared off a large part of the mountainside. Tons and tons of rock had cascaded down and buried the six men who had been trying to kill him.

He found himself remembering every detail of the pursuit up the cliff, every feeling, every thought — none of which, he realized, included a moment of moral equivocation. All the pacifist ideals he had invoked only yesterday during his speech at the UN? Not one of them had even crossed his mind. In fact, he felt the same exhilaration now as he had felt on the river, when he had confronted and beaten the men who'd been pursuing him by boat. He held his hands in front of his face, stretching his fingers. They weren't shaking. A sense of well-being settled over him like a warm blanket, which he quickly shrugged off. This was not the time to reflect. It was time to act. If he had any moral reckoning to do, he would do it later.

As he surveyed the scene below, he reflected that the rock slide hadn't just wiped away his would-be killers. It had wiped away the trail.

He had passed the point of no return. Either he would make it to Kampung Naga or he would die trying.

Beyond the rubble, the river wound into the distance, a brilliant red serpent, glowing with the reflected light of the setting sun. He only had another hour of daylight before he'd need to find a place to sleep. He stood, dusted himself off, and turned to enter the jungle. But something was nagging at him, tugging at the back of his brain. Whatever it was, he couldn't put his finger on it. And he stopped trying to figure it out when he entered the jungle and found that he wasn't alone.

A group of men stood before him in a half

circle. Their complexions were darker than the Mohanese he'd seen before, and their hair was curlier and thicker. One of the men, the oldest, wore a pair of battered tennis shoes. The others wore only nylon soccer shorts, their feet bare. They all carried spears, which they pointed at his chest.

The man with the shoes screamed something at him.

"It's okay, guys," Gideon said evenly, slowly holding up his hands. "I'm not armed."

The man kept barking at him and was soon joined by several other men. Although Gideon couldn't understand their words, he suddenly understood what had been bugging him earlier. The voice that had risen up from below when he'd started the landslide. The voice that had screamed, "Run!"

One of the men who had tried to kill him had spoken English.

But the men who were now surrounding Gideon and brandishing their spears couldn't have cared less about his epiphany.

CHAPTER FOURTEEN

Kate sat on the floor, her hands tied behind her. The hostages had been thrust into the guest cabin on B Deck, the one that had been assigned to Cole Ransom. In the corner sat a bag and a notebook computer. Both wore scuffed aluminum nameplates with Cole Ransom's name etched onto them. Kate realized, with a sinking feeling, that if they were the real Cole Ransom's belongings, then something bad had happened to Ransom.

Ambassador Stearns was sitting stiffly on the floor next to Big Al Prejean. They hadn't been in the room for more than ten minutes when the door opened and Earl Parker was thrust into the room.

After the door slammed shut, Kate said, "Are you okay? We were worried."

Parker sat heavily on the bed and said, "I'm fine. He just stunned me for a minute."

"Did you see any of my crew?"

Parker nodded. "They were herding them into the mess hall. A couple of your people tried to resist." His lips curled. "They shot them like dogs."

Kate swallowed. "How many?"

"Five, maybe six. Everybody else settled down. I think they'll be okay for now." He shook his head sadly. "I know that's not much consolation."

"You're right," she said. "It's not."

Parker didn't reply.

"The guy who's in charge says he's Abu Nasir," Kate said. "It seemed like you knew him."

Parker nodded. But Kate detected something else behind his silent confirmation, something he was leaving out.

"Do you know what he wants?"

"He hasn't told us yet." Parker hesitated, as if deciding whether or not to continue; then, deciding that he would, he lowered his voice to a whisper that only she could hear. "But it's my fault this is happening."

"Your fault?"

"The man who calls himself Abu Nasir . . . his real name is Tillman Davis. He used to work for me." Parker looked away in apparent shame as he went on to tell her about the secret mission he had initiated. He told her about Tillman's transformation from covert operative to unrepentant terrorist, and about how he had enlisted Gideon Davis, who had come to Mohan with Parker to retrieve his brother. "Trusting Tillman was the biggest mistake of my life. And now Gideon . . ." His voice cracked with regret. "I should have left him out of this."

Suddenly the steel door slid open, and an Asian man wearing a Sky TV T-shirt walked into the room, pointed at Kate, and barked in heavily accented English, "You! Come with me."

Kate didn't move.

"Just do what they tell you," Parker said softly.

"Come!" the guard yelled. He yanked her toward the door, and she saw Big Al coiling to spring at him, but she shook her head sharply, stopping him before he did anything stupid.

"It's okay, Al. I'll be fine." The sentry pulled a black cloth hood over her head, tying it loosely at her neck. Kate's heart began beating faster, and her mouth felt dry as sandpaper. Were they going to hurt her, beat her, chop off her head?

The sentry guided her out the door and into the passageway. She couldn't see through the blindfold, but the man exerted just enough pressure on her arm to steer her down the hallway without her tripping or banging into anything.

Her footsteps echoed as they moved slowly through the passageways. She tried to figure out where they were heading, but after winding around inside the rig for a while, she lost track. Eventually the man stopped.

She stood silently for what seemed like minutes. Finally another man spoke. He was behind her. "Knees," the man said. She recognized his voice. It belonged to Abu Nasir, the man who had boarded her rig by impersonating Cole Ransom. "Knees," he said again.

Before she could respond, someone kicked the back of her right leg, buckling the joint and forcing her to land on her knees.

"We have clear and simple objectives here, Ms. Murphy. We will not waver in those objectives. Harming you is not one of them, but if you try to get in the way, I will not hesitate to kill you."

Only yesterday Senator McClatchy had been questioning her about Abu Nasir, a man who had seemed to her more mythical than real, the stuff of urban legend. And now she not only knew his real name and what he looked like . . . but he was on her rig, threatening her life.

"Please indicate that you understand me, ma'am."

"I understand English," she said, "if that's what you mean."

Someone punched her in the stomach. She gagged, almost falling on her face, but managed to remain upright.

"You may think that being flippant does not interfere with our objectives," Abu Nasir said. "You would be wrong in that assessment. Are we on the same page now?"

She nodded.

"Outstanding."

The blindfold came off. She blinked. She was in the mess hall, a trio of halogen work lamps blazing in her face. Squinting to better see the silhouetted terrorists, she made out an approaching figure whose features came into relief as he drew closer. He was carrying a crisply folded square of bright yellow material, which he tossed toward her, the momentum of his throw causing it to unfurl partially. It was some kind of jumpsuit.

"Put this on."

Kate offered no response.

"If you don't do it, I'll do it for you." His voice was flat, nonnegotiable.

She picked up the jumpsuit and said, "I need somewhere to change."

"You have a place. Right here."

She held his look for a long, defiant moment, then kicked off her shoes, unfastened her skirt, and let it fall to the ground. She unbuttoned her shirt and peeled it off, until she was left wearing only her bra and panties. She held Abu Nasir's look the entire time. Not once did his eyes leave hers, not even for a flickering moment of voyeuristic curiosity about what her seminaked body looked like. She pulled on the jumpsuit, shrugging her arms into the sleeves, then stepping back into her shoes.

As she zippered the jumpsuit, Abu Nasir nodded toward the man just behind him, who now adjusted a tripod-mounted monitor toward her. Displayed on the screen in large capital letters were the words: MY NAME IS KATE MURPHY. A video camera was mounted on another branch of the tripod. "All you have to do is read the teleprompter, like those phony politicians in Washington."

"No."

"Fine. We'll shoot you in the head. I'm sure Ambassador Stearns will be happy to read the statement."

Kate tried navigating through her swirling emotions. Anger, fear, humiliation. Whatever message he wanted her to read — was it really worth dying for? She didn't think so. Especially since whoever saw it would certainly understand that she'd read it under duress. "Okay," she finally said, her voice soft as a whisper.

"See how easy that was?" Abu Nasir pointed toward the man holding the cue cards. "When he points at you, start reading."

The man operating the monitor pointed at Kate, who began to read in as flat a tone as she could muster.

"My name is Kate Murphy," she read. "I am the executive in charge of the Obelisk, which is now under the control of Abu Nasir." When she read the next sentence on the scrolling text, Kate stopped and her mouth went dry.

"Just read what's on the screen, Ms. Murphy. Please don't make me shoot you in the head. I'm trying to save ammo."

She didn't want to continue, but short of dying on the spot, she had no choice. Her voice sounded thin and shaky in her ears as she started over, reading the statement from the beginning, then continuing where she left off.

When Gideon was ten years old, he and Tillman had whittled spears out of hickory, sharpening the points with Case knives and playing a game of their own invention called Spartan. The rules were simple. You stood about thirty yards apart and threw your spears at each other. If you had to move to get out of the way of the other person's spear, you lost.

Since he was Tillman's junior by two years, Gideon couldn't throw quite as hard or quite as accurately. So he usually lost.

One crisp fall day, he hurled the spear, and before it even left his hand, he knew that he had done everything right. The spear was heading straight for Tillman.

But Gideon's euphoria vanished as quickly as it had appeared when he realized that Tillman wasn't going to move. The spear arced gracefully through the air, seemingly as slow as a feather carried on a soft breeze. Gideon had watched his brother's face. Tillman knew the spear was coming, too, knew it was going to hit him. But he didn't so much as flinch — he just clamped his mouth shut and let it come.

The tip of the spear hit him just above the collarbone, passing through his right shoulder and out his back, clean as a knife through butter. He grimaced slightly, then turned a quarter turn, fell on his side and began, improbably, to snore.

Eighteen inches of bloody, sharpened wood stuck out of his back.

According to the doctor, a half inch lower and it would have hit the subclavian artery, killing him in under five minutes.

It was the only time Gideon's father ever laid a hand on him. He doled out his son's punishment as methodically as a tennis player practicing his forehand before a match.

The image of his snoring brother and the searing pain of his father's hand on his backside came back to Gideon now, as he stood looking at the ring of spears pointing at him. They were tipped with sharpened scraps of iron that looked as if they might have been ripped from car hoods or forged from cook pots. Crude as they were, Gideon knew how easily they could slice through muscle and bone.

The men were still bombarding him with angry questions and accusations in a language he couldn't understand, so he just kept talking in as soothing a tone as he could muster. "I'm just here to find my brother." Gideon hoped that even if they couldn't understand his words, they would understand his intent, but he might as well have been reciting the Pledge of Allegiance.

"His name is Tillman. Tillman Davis."

More shouting and spear waving, so he decided to try another tack. "Abu Nasir." he said. "He calls himself Abu Nasir."

The commotion suddenly stopped. "Abu Nasir?" one of them said softly.

"Yes. Abu Nasir."

Two of the older men exchanged glances, their hostile suspicion giving way to curiosity.

Suddenly remembering that Uncle Earl had given him a recent photo of his bearded brother, Gideon reached slowly into his pocket and pulled it out.

The oldest man snatched it from him, studying the photo, then looked up at Gideon. The others crowded around, setting off a raucous debate. Several of the men pantomimed stabbing Gideon with their spears. Did these men work for Abu Nasir, or were they rivals? Did they love him, hate him, what? He wasn't sure.

Abruptly, they came to a decision and settled down.

The old man pointed his spear at Gideon's chest and then nodded once, as if bestowing some seal of approval on him. "You. Abu Nasir. Come."

"Okay." Gideon smiled and nodded vigorously. *Keep smiling,* he thought. *Keep smiling.*

The men — there were seven of them — turned and began to walk silently back into the jungle. Gideon followed. They walked for several hours, stopping several times to listen carefully before moving on. Although their faces betrayed no emotion, it was clear that they were nervous. Gideon got the impression they were worried about being ambushed.

They followed a hardpacked trail, which was only sporadically overgrown. Several of the men carried machetes, but they used them only once to clear the trail.

Late in the afternoon they came to a ruined patch of land where a village had stood until recently. Black soot and cinders were all that remained of its grass-and-bamboo huts. The air smelled of rotting meat. The carcasses of a sow with her litter of piglets lay in a heap, thick with buzzing flies. Since pork had to be a prized food here in the jungle, Gideon couldn't imagine several hundred pounds of meat being left to rot by local tribesmen.

Then he saw a body, a woman, lying tangled in the underbrush. And then it was as though some key had turned in his vision. Suddenly he could see more dead people — women, old men, children — lying around the periphery of the clearing.

The highlanders kept their eyes straight ahead of them, not remarking or even looking at the evidence of tragedy around them. *Who did this?* Gideon thought. But no one was there to answer him.

Soon they were back in the jungle, the light waning. Gideon realized that other than the tin of peaches, he hadn't eaten all day. With all the physical activity he'd been engaged in, he was starving. As the light began to die, the highlanders finally stopped. They sat in a circle, silently eating dried meat and some kind of smelly goo wrapped in broad leaves. The men never offered him anything, and he didn't ask.

As night fell the sounds of the jungle filled the darkness. Hoots and howls, growls and buzzing noises. Except Gideon saw no animals, no monkeys or snakes, nothing but mosquitoes and moths nearly as big as his hand, which thudded around in the trees above him. The highlanders never spoke. One of them moved away from the group — presumably to serve as sentry. The others simply lay down on the cold, hard dirt and fell asleep.

The night brought on a damp cold. Gideon's stomach knotted with hunger as he stared up into the darkness. The canopy of trees blotted out most of the sky. Where it was visible, the sky was full of stars brighter than he'd ever seen them.

The ground was hard, and every part of his body was sore. Insects skittered around in the leaves. Gideon felt as alone as he'd ever felt in his life. Even on the night when his father and mother had died, he had not felt quite so alone. At least he'd had Tillman.

Tillman. He was here because of Tillman. The thought of seeing his brother again comforted him.

And then he slept.

CHAPTER FIFTEEN

President Diggs entered the secure Situation Room deep beneath the White House, trailed by Elliot Hammershaw. Everyone stood, all nine members of the ad hoc working group that the president and Earl Parker had assembled only a few days earlier to plan and support their covert operation to retrieve Tillman Davis. The group included Admiral Dirkson Reed, chairman of the Joint Chiefs of Staff, a compact man with silvered hair and piercing forest green eyes, who had earned his reputation for courage under fire as commander of the nuclear sub the USS *Reagan* — a reputation he had burnished many times over in combat and in the halls of power. In the nearly twenty years that Diggs had known the admiral, he'd never seen the man as rattled as he looked right now. Diggs had come here to discuss the implications of Gideon Davis's ambush, fully expecting that it would mean the end of their covert attempt to shore up the sultan in his escalating civil war. But seeing Admiral Reed's eyes, he braced himself for even worse news. Which is exactly what he got.

"Admiral, give me the sitrep on Gideon Davis."

"His status is unchanged, Mr. President."

"Then you still haven't heard from Tillman Davis."

"Actually, sir, we have." The admiral's jaw clenched, trying to curtail his rising anger. "He's apparently seized the Obelisk."

Diggs blinked, trying to get his head around the words. "Earl Parker is on that rig. I just talked to him an hour ago."

"We only learned about this ourselves a few minutes ago."

"From what source?"

"YouTube, sir."

"YouTube?"

Admiral Reed nodded at the air force sergeant who ran the communications equipment in the Situation Room.

The president watched as the oversize LED screen at the front of the room lit up, revealing a grainy video framed by the ubiquitous YouTube player. An attractive woman in her early thirties, wearing a neon yellow jumpsuit, was on her knees, addressing the camera. She appeared calm, but her eyes betrayed her terror. Behind her were several masked men holding AK-47s.

"Turn up the volume," Diggs said.

The terrified woman's voice sounded strangely quiet, even as it boomed out over the speakers: "My name is Kate Murphy," she read. "I am the executive in charge of the Obelisk, which is now under the control of Abu Nasir. Because of U.S. support for the corrupt CIA puppet, the so-called Sultan of Mohan, Abu Nasir's men have seized the rig and are holding hostage the surviving members of my crew along with Ambassador Randall Stearns and Deputy National Security Advisor Earl Parker." She paused, letting out the tight breath she'd been holding, then resumed. "A bomb of sufficient power to destroy both the rig and all its occupants has been planted on the Obelisk. Our demand is simple: in exchange for the lives of the hostages, the president of the United States must recall all U.S. military forces from Mohan, including all CIA operatives, all contractors, and all so-called military advisors. If this demand is not met by eight o'clock a.m. tomorrow, Abu Nasir will kill the hostages and destroy the Obelisk. There will be no negotiation and no further contact."

The woman looked past the camera, glaring defiantly at some off-screen presence, as if to say, *Are you satisfied?* Then the image froze and a superimposed window appeared, giving the viewer the choice to replay the video or to share it with a friend.

President Diggs jabbed his finger toward the monitor. "I want that taken down now before the media gets hold of this. Get those YouTube sonsuvbitches to take that down."

"It's too late, sir." Hammershaw looked up from his cell phone, then turned the screen toward the president to illustrate his point. "At least a dozen news agencies are already running the story."

"Eight a.m. local time tomorrow. How long does that give us?"

Hammershaw looked expectantly at a representative of the CIA.

"Twenty-three hours, sixteen minutes."

Diggs exhaled sharply, but his anger burned off quickly, giving way to confusion. "I don't understand . . . Tillman Davis knows better than anyone that our national policy is never to negotiate with terrorists. He knows damn well we'll never agree to what he's asking. So what the hell is he thinking?"

Diggs scanned the room, but no one spoke, so he went ahead and answered his own question.

"Whatever his endgame is, this confirms that Tillman Davis has cast his lot with the insurgency and needs to be defeated. If we don't stop him before his deadline . . ." The president trailed off, turning inward as he realized the implications of failure. "If Abu Nasir kills those hostages, we will have no other choice except to respond with force. Their deaths would constitute nothing less than an act of war, and the American people will demand reprisal against the insurgents."

Admiral Reed said, "As you requested, sir, the Joint Chiefs have been wargaming several scenarios with the Sultan's military staff. There's not a single option that uses less than an entire division of American troops."

"A division!" Elliot Hammershaw said. "The president is talking about reprisal, Admiral, and you're talking about a straight-up *war!*"

"War? That's your word, Mr. Hammershaw," the admiral said. "I'm just a military man giving you military —"

The president interrupted, "Bottom line is, we need to take back that rig."

Admiral Reed spoke. "Sir, I've already ordered Special Forces Operational Detachment Delta to deploy. Both units can be in

Mohan within ten hours, well before Tillman Davis's deadline. But I'll let General Ferry address the tactical specifics."

General Ferry, commander of SOCOM, stood. He had the tall, rail-thin frame of a competitive long-distance runner and the combative eyes of a cage fighter. "We're repositioning a satellite so we'll have aerial recon in a few minutes. But at this point we have very little intel as to the disposition of the folks on the rig. In the YouTube video at least four enemy can be identified. In all likelihood he's got significantly more men than that. Tillman Davis has seized a large number of maritime targets in the recent past. In every case, his forces were not only well equipped and highly trained, but they were also more than sufficient in size for the task at hand."

"So how do you plan to take the rig, General?" the president said.

"Before we can give you a definitive operational assessment, we need some answers. Beyond the leverage he's got with the hostages, what other measures has he taken to defend the rig? Does he have any antiaircraft or antiship capability? Will he use his hostages as human shields? Until we answer those questions, there is no way to predict the probability of success, or to assess how many hostages might be killed if we do succeed in reacquiring the rig."

President Diggs was not happy with this answer. He stared at the general, waiting for something more definitive.

The tense silence was broken by Dave Posner, a young, nervous-looking CIA analyst in an ill-fitting suit, who raised his hand tentatively as he spoke. "And then there's the weather issue, sir."

"Weather?" the president said.

General Ferry shot Posner an irritated glance. "There's a typhoon off the Philippines. If it hit the rig, it would obviously bottle up the rig until the storm passed."

"Bottle up?" the president said.

Ferry explained. "Right now the seas are running at close to thirty feet, so an assault by sea would have a high likelihood of failure. The best option for attack is aerial insertion — what we call a HALO jump — high altitude, low open parachuting. Preferably with fire support from helicopter gunships. Obviously even that would be impossible if the rig was in the middle of a typhoon. But it's only a five percent chance."

"That seems a fairly negligible risk," President Diggs said hopefully.

"Actually, Mr. President . . ." Posner

cleared his throat. "I've just received an update. The typhoon appears to be heading west." An image of Southeast Asia appeared on the big screen at the front of the Situation Room. A vast white swirl had enveloped all of the southern Philippines. It looked perilously close to a red triangle indicating the location of the Obelisk. "If it keeps turning, it might hit the Obelisk."

Diggs felt like he'd been punched in the gut. "Can you quantify that?"

"Hong Kong says there's a sixty percent chance now."

The president's eyes didn't leave the screen. "How much time before it hits?"

Posner squinted briefly at his monitor. The only sound in the room was the clicking of keys on his keyboard. Finally he looked up. "*If* it hits? — the outskirts of the storm could be there within four hours."

The president turned and looked at General Ferry. "Tom? We need a Plan B here in case this storm keeps turning. Can you get your men on that rig inside of four hours?"

"There's a Delta Force in Hawaii."

"I take it that's a no."

General Ferry's jaw clenched. "Flight time to Mohan is six hours minimum. And once the storm hits, it would severely impede their insertion."

"Sixty percent, that's pretty high," the president said. "Have we got any other options?"

Ferry swallowed but didn't answer.

"Give me options, dammit!"

Ferry looked briefly at the floor and said, "There's a platoon of SEALs from SEAL Team One in Mohan. Sixteen men."

"Can they take the rig in the next four hours?"

"Possibly. With enough support and the right equipment."

"And luck," added Admiral Reed.

The strain of the moment was starting to fray the president's nerves. "I need that rig, General. I can't take a chance of that storm hitting before the deadline runs out."

It was obvious that Ferry was reluctant. The odds would be heavily stacked against such a hastily organized mission. But President Diggs had to weigh the lives of sixteen SEALs against all the lives that would be lost if this turned into an all-out war.

The yawning silence was broken by the sound of a vibrating cell phone. Elliot Hammershaw scowled as he read the number on the display window. "Excuse me for interrupting, Mr. President, but I have Senator McClatchy."

President Diggs's expression darkened.

He knew what McClatchy was calling about. The seizure of the Obelisk by the insurgents had given the senator the excuse he'd been looking for. He'd be clamoring for war.

"I'll take it in the Oval Office." Before heading to the door, the president turned to General Ferry and said quietly, "Do whatever you have to do to take back that rig."

General Ferry nodded once. "I'll give the order, sir."

CHAPTER SIXTEEN

It was only after their parents died that Gideon and Tillman learned that their father had gone bankrupt following a series of poor investments. They were literally left with nothing.

The day after the funeral, Uncle Earl had driven them up to the portico of their stately old family home and said, "Your aunt has asked me to bring you out here. The house and the property are all going to be sold. You can take whatever you can fit in the back of the car. Your aunt tells me that everything else will be sold. I'm sorry, but there's no other way."

In the end, they hadn't taken much. Their clothes, a few toys, some family pictures. As they looked through the house, Tillman had found a metal container inside the open safe where some of their father's guns were stored. Written neatly in black Magic Marker was a legend: FOR MY BOYS.

"You want to take it?" Gideon had said.

"Hell no," Tillman growled.

Tillman hadn't wanted to talk about their father, or to keep any material reminders of the man. Not even something their father had deemed worthy of placing in a separate box inside his safe and designating for his sons. So Gideon had taken the metal container with him, placing it inside one of the few cartons of books, photographs, and other small personal items. But for reasons he had only dimly understood, Gideon didn't open the container. Not until many years later.

Gideon woke to a sharp crack. He sat up, heart pounding. For a moment he was disoriented. He had been dreaming about the box, the one with FOR MY BOYS written on the side. It was the only tangible legacy left to Gideon and Tillman by their father. And he'd awakened with a question in his mind, a question that he'd never resolved about what their father's true legacy to his sons really was. Gideon was beginning to think that he might be on the verge of finding out here, in this remote part of the world, what that legacy had been — and that maybe it had been hiding inside him all these years.

It took another cracking sound before he realized the noise was gunfire. He tore his mind away from the dream. Now was not the time for gloomy speculation.

The first light of dawn was slipping through the thick jungle canopy. As his eyes adjusted, he saw the highlander who'd been acting as a sentry lying facedown about thirty feet away, blood pouring from his chest. The other highlanders were leaping to their feet, yelling at one another and scrambling for cover.

One of the men caught a burst in the leg and fell, his face twisted with shock and agony.

Gideon grabbed the fallen man's spear and jumped behind the broad trunk of a tree. He could tell from the intensity of the sound that the shooters were no more than a hundred feet away. He peeked out from behind the tree. There was a fair amount of broad-leafed foliage between him and the shooters. But he managed to catch a glimpse of them.

They weren't highlanders. So he figured they must belong to the same group of jihadis who had followed him up the river and up the cliff. He was astonished. What could possibly have motivated them to track him all the way up the river from Alun Jong, climb a thousand-foot cliff, and then pursue him half a day's hike into the jungle?

His mind quickly moved from the speculative to the practical. How many of them were there? He was sure he'd killed all six of them during the landslide back on the cliff. There must have been others he hadn't seen. He closed his eyes and listened.

Two. There were two guns firing at once.

The firing ceased. He looked around. The highlanders were all flattened against the trees. Including him, there were six men with spears. Against two with AK-47s. Gideon could hear them moving slowly forward, rustling in the underbrush.

A plan formed in his mind. He motioned to the other men, trying to communicate his plan with hand signals. He looked questioningly at the old highlander, wondering if his men understood. The older man nodded.

Gideon dropped to his belly and began wriggling forward under the cover of the underbrush, trying hard not to make a sound.

His idea was simple enough. There was a tree in front of him, right next to the trail. One of the highlanders needed to make a break for it down the trail, drawing the jihadis toward him. If Gideon stationed himself behind it and waited for the jihadis to pass by it, he could spear one of them.

Then it would be six on one. Six spears versus one AK. That was *if* the highlanders understood the plan and played their part.

He reached the tree, turned to look behind him. He could still see the old highlander. Gideon signaled that he was ready.

For a moment, nothing happened. Then, suddenly, one of the highlanders leapt out from behind the tree and raced down the trail.

Gideon could hear the jihadis now. Footsteps pounding toward him. He watched one pass by, then the next. As he was preparing to step out and hurl the spear, another jihadi flashed by.

There were three of them.

He cursed himself for miscalculating, but it was too late to do anything about it. He stepped forward and hurled the spear. The third jihadi was no more than five feet from him when he released the missile. It was just like the game of Spartan that he'd played with Tillman all those years ago, the spear passing cleanly into the man's body. Only this time he hit the jihadi dead center in the back. The spear must have severed his spinal cord, because he fell like a bag of wet sand.

Hearing the noise, the second jihadi turned. His eyes widened as he saw his comrade fall. He swiveled to fire at Gideon, who realized he had no choice except to dive straight at the man. Reacting to Gideon's forward motion, the jihadi backed away and stumbled slightly.

It wasn't enough to make him fall — just enough to keep him from bringing his gun around in time. Gideon grabbed the barrel with one hand, clamping the other on the stock just behind the receiver. The jihadi was a typical Mohanese — barely more than five foot three, probably a buck and a quarter soaking wet. He didn't have much chance against a six-foot-one, two-hundred-pound American.

Gideon wrenched the gun out of the man's hand in a sweeping motion, then reversed direction, swinging the stock backhanded. It connected with the man's face. He staggered backward. Gideon hit him again, and the man crumpled.

He heard a scream, turned in time to see the third jihadi clawing at a spear. Three of the highlanders had thrown spears at him. One had missed, but two had found their target — one in the groin and one in the thigh. The man dropped his gun and tried to pull the spear out of his thigh.

The old man stepped calmly out from behind the tree, kicked the jihadi in the stomach, then jammed a third spear into him as the man doubled up. It entered the side of his neck and drove deep into his body.

The man fell to the ground, gurgling and moaning. The highlander who had missed his throw picked up his spear and stabbed the man in the back until he stopped moving.

The highlanders whooped loudly over the dead men, then began rifling through their clothing and packs. They collected a Swiss Army knife, several ammo clips, three wads of Mohanese currency, and three cardboard rectangles the size and shape of a passport. Each of the jihadis had been carrying one.

The old man's eyes narrowed as he laid them on the ground and studied them. He looked up at Gideon, repeating a single word in an accusatory voice. *"Look!"* he seemed to be saying.

Gideon saw that they were photographs. He moved closer, and a chill ran up his spine.

The photos were of a smiling man wearing a white shirt, a necktie, a pinstriped suit coat with an American flag pin in the lapel. Printed in English at the bottom of each picture: SPECIAL U.S. ENVOY GIDEON DAVIS.

This confirmed Gideon's fear. It was no accident. These men had pursued him into the bush. They weren't just chasing down random Americans — they were hunting for *him.*

But who had sent them? Islamist sympathizers within the Mohanese military working under General Prang? Unlikely. They would have sent locals who spoke Malay, and Gideon had heard these men speaking English. Plus, how could they even have known Gideon was in the country? The answer came to Gideon in the form of two chilling questions: *Could it be Tillman? If it wasn't him, who else could it be?*

CHAPTER SEVENTEEN

Captain Avery Taylor had been waiting for three hours in the anteroom of the opulent offices of the commanding general of the Mohan Defense Forces when his phone rang. Captain Taylor was not an easy man to rattle. But when he found himself talking directly to General Ferry, the commander of SOCOM, he broke into a sweat.

The general did not engage in pleasantries. "Where is your platoon, Captain?" he demanded.

"Here in KM, sir, making arrangements for the SEALs and Delta to —"

"Negative, son. Not anymore. You have new orders. By direction of the president of the United States I'm now ordering you to lead your platoon in an assault on the Obelisk. You need to seize the rig on or before twelve hundred hours your time."

Captain Taylor's mind briefly went blank. Back in Coronado he'd had access to the finest equipment available in the world. But here in Mohan, his men had arrived with nothing but sidearms, M4 carbines, and a paltry amount of ammunition. Political considerations made it impossible for them to bring any materiel that was deemed to have "offensive capability," as they were here solely in a training capacity. They had no boats, no chutes, no scuba gear, no comms equipment, no grenades, no night vision . . . The list of what they didn't have that they ought to have for a night assault on a well-defended naval target could have gone on for pages. "Twelve hundred hours *today,* sir," Taylor said in confirmation. "Local time?"

"Today. Twelve hundred hours, Mohan time."

The room Captain Taylor stood in was a huge, echoing marble chamber with the air of a mausoleum.

"Sir, we don't have much in the way of gear."

"The president is speaking to the Sultan right now. Anything you need, he will supply."

"Twelve hundred hours."

"Captain, I am fully aware of the difficulty of this mission. Therefore I will not detain you any longer. If you get one iota of shit about anything from the Mohanese, you call me direct on this number. Clear?"

"Yes, sir."

"Captain, this is how humble soldiers like you and me get into the history books."

As Captain Taylor thumbed the *off* button on his phone, a Mohanese soldier, an immaculately groomed adjutant whose coat dripped with gold braid, opened the massive teak door and said, "Captain, the general can spare five minutes for you."

Captain Taylor said, "Sorry, but I can't spare five for him." Before the gawking adjutant could reply, Taylor was sprinting down the long marble hallway. *Praise the Lord!* he thought. *This was the real shit!*

After they found the pictures of Gideon, the surviving highlanders had a heated argument. It didn't take them long to come to a decision.

Gideon didn't need to speak their language to understand what they'd concluded: being in proximity to Gideon Davis was hazardous to their health. They shouted angrily at him, pointed at the trail leading deeper into the jungle, and threatened him with their spears.

"Okay, okay," he said softly, backing away from them. "I'm going. I'm sorry. I didn't know anyone was chasing me. I'm sorry about your friends."

Once he was comfortably beyond spearing range, he turned and jogged down the trail a couple of hundred yards, then stopped and hid behind a tree. The shouts faded after a few moments. Oddly, the tribesmen walked back in the direction from which they had come, toward the river, silently carrying their dead comrades. Gideon waited until they were gone before he returned to the scene of the battle.

The three jihadis lay on the ground, arms splayed, mouths open. It made him a little queasy looking at them. They seemed half like men, half like sacks of meat. Who were they? They were all small-statured Asians. Mohanese? Maybe. But why did they speak English? Were they led by someone who spoke English? Or were they Americans who just looked Mohanese? Were they Asians — jihadis possibly — from various countries who spoke English because it was their only common language?

Gideon steeled himself for an unpleasant task. Each of the dead men carried a small backpack. Gideon unzipped each pack in turn and went through it systematically, looking for food, water, and information. The highlanders had already ransacked their gear . . . but they might have left something that would give him a clue as to who had sent these people after him.

He found precious little.

There were a few pieces of spicy beef jerky tucked into an inside pocket. Another had an unfinished candy bar hidden in his shirt, the silver foil carefully folded over the crescent of bite marks. A half-full canteen lay in the weeds near the third man. Gideon wolfed down the jerky and the chocolate, then chased it with a few mouthfuls of water. He knew he had to ration his water. There was plenty of water in the rain forest, but it wasn't potable. In all likelihood it would give him dysentery — uncomfortable in a civilized area, but potentially deadly up here.

Everything else that might have been of any use to him — cell phones, radios, tools, weapons — was gone, taken by the highlanders.

The men carried no IDs, no wallets, no credit cards. The highlanders might have taken currency. But credit cards? IDs? They'd have left them. And yet there was nothing here. These men had been sanitized before they had been dispatched.

After he finished his modest meal, Gideon crouched in the dim light and tried to think what to do next. Whoever these men were, there would be more of them waiting if he went back the way he'd come. Getting to Kampung Naga was still the only way he'd find his brother.

He and the highland tribesmen had hiked at a pretty good clip for most of the previous afternoon. They might have made ten miles. He pulled out the map. If he was reading the scale correctly, he still had at least fifteen miles to go. Maybe more. And that was assuming he was even heading in the right direction. The town was due south. He could orient himself based on the direction of the rising sun, of course. But that wasn't like navigating by compass. If he veered east or west by a few degrees, he might miss his destination entirely.

He looked around. Daylight was beginning to filter down through the heavy canopy of foliage. Everything was strange to his eye — the broad-leaved bushes, the gnarled trunks of the tall trees, the curious-looking fruit hanging here and there, the vines that twined upward into the green distance.

When he was a kid, he and Tillman had spent hours and hours wandering in the woods and fields around his house. By the time he was in junior high, he knew every plant and bush and berry — which were good to eat, which weren't, which berries gave you the runs, which plants made you itch or break out, which ones cut you or stung you. Here he was like a baby — completely at the mercy of the jungle. Even the hoots and cries of the animals rising up around him meant nothing to him.

He had to move. Every minute he spent here was a minute closer to death. He figured the faster he got to wherever he was going, the faster he'd know if he was in the wrong place or the right place.

Gideon stood, feeling more acutely the blisters that had formed on his feet. He measured the dead men with his eyes, removed the boots and socks from the tallest one, and put them on. They were tight, but still better than his soggy wingtips.

He began trotting down the trail — just a slow jog, enough for him to make ten miles in a matter of a little over ninety minutes. The pace would force him to use up his water a little faster. But he determined it was still his best course of action. If he'd been at home, lost in a national park, then a conservative, hunker-down-and-wait-for-help strategy would probably be the smart play. But help wasn't coming here. And the only people looking for him wanted to kill him.

As he ran, he counted his strides. He figured he had a stride of about four feet. That was roughly fifteen hundred strides to the mile. Back home, he ran regularly — four miles, most days. Sometimes five. He hadn't run more than seven miles at a stretch since college. Could he run fifteen?

Probably. It was no good thinking about it, though.

So he just kept running and counting, counting and running.

He came to the first village at just past the two thousand mark. Unlike the village he'd passed through with the tribesmen on the previous day, this one hadn't been burned. But it was abandoned. Food was rotting in the houses. Whoever had left here had bailed out so quickly they didn't have time to take their food with him.

There were several small trails leading out of the village, but only one large trail heading south. He took a few sips of water, chose the large trail, and plunged on.

At the eight thousand mark, he reached another village. This one was larger than the last and seemed closer to civilization. There was no electricity, but there were lamps, gallon cans of kerosene, tire tracks in the ground. The tracks weren't for a car, though. Something smaller, like an ATV. Gideon estimated that a couple hundred people had lived in the town, but the surrounding fields and houses had been burned to the ground.

What was going on around here? This was starting to look like a full-fledged war — a war accompanied by something resembling ethnic cleansing.

As he paused, he saw something red lying on the ground. A flower. A red flower. He reached down and picked it up.

It was a poppy. He surveyed the field. And then he saw it. Much of the field was burned. But not all. Opium poppies. Someone was growing opium up here.

There was no time to think about what this meant — if it meant anything at all. He ran.

The trail had widened as it left the burned village and had parallel ruts — presumably formed by the wheels of regular ATV traffic. Though it was wider than the trail he'd been running on earlier, it was covered in weeds, as though it hadn't been used much lately.

By the time he passed ten thousand, Gideon's body started rebelling. At home, with a good pair of running shoes, a good night's sleep, and plenty of food, a five-mile jog would have been routine. But he'd only eaten a few morsels in the last twenty-four hours and hadn't slept worth a damn in forty-eight. So there was nothing routine about this run. He kept running, but his limbs felt leaden, his head throbbed, and his lungs ached. Every stride seemed to be an act of will.

But he didn't stop. The heat was not too bad here in the highlands — but he knew he was operating on a water deficit. He wouldn't last much longer without water. When he reached fifteen thousand, he finally stopped to drain the canteen. He leaned against a tree. Next thing he knew, he was sitting, staring blearily up into the dark canopy of the jungle. For a moment he couldn't remember where he was. A monkey appeared, stared curiously down at him, then leapt to another branch, screamed once, disappeared back into the dim distance. Gideon tried to force himself to his feet, but his body kept coming up with reasons not to.

He closed his eyes and thought back to the day when his father and mother had died. *That's who I'm here for,* he thought. *Whoever my brother has become, whatever he's become, I'm here for him.* He pictured his brother sitting on the front steps of the house, that terrible empty expression in his eyes.

And then Gideon was on his feet, pressing on into the jungle. Occasionally he passed through a stream. It was all he could do not to stop, lie down in the stream, and suck the water into his mouth.

He knew there was a point where dysentery was less of a danger than immediate dehydration. But he kept telling himself that he hadn't reached that point quite yet.

The sun was higher in the trees now. He felt himself getting more and more light-headed, less and less clear in his thinking.

The trail he'd been on had been going due south for a while. There was no trick to navigating it. It simply headed south. But suddenly the trail split.

He stopped. Which way? He looked up, trying to determine by using the sun which way was south. But the sun was high in the sky now, and it was harder to tell east from west. Both trails were equally rutted. There were no signs, no marks, nothing to indicate where they were heading.

He realized after a while that he had been standing, staring up in the air for a long time. How long, he wasn't sure. His mouth felt like a bag of sand.

Somewhere in the back of his mind a voice

said, *Okay, this is it. Time to find water.*

But where?

Earlier it seemed like he'd been splashing through a stream every five minutes. He looked around. No streams were visible anywhere. He knew that if he just pressed on, he'd find one. And yet . . .

And yet neither his mind nor his body seemed capable of moving. He couldn't make up his mind. Which way? The trail on the left or the trail on the right? He stared up at the sun. A shaft of light pierced the leaf and plunged into his eyes, blinding him momentarily. He realized vaguely he'd pushed himself too far, let his body dry out too much. He closed his eyes.

How far had he come? Gideon wondered. *Was he even close to Kampung Naga?* He realized he had stopped counting strides a long time ago. How long was a long time? Five minutes? Five hours? He really wasn't sure.

Gideon stood, swaying, eyes closed, waiting to fall.

It was just a matter of time before his legs gave out, he thought. *Just a matter of time.*

But he didn't fall. Instead, he smelled something.

Smoke.

A vague signal penetrated his consciousness. Smoke. Smoke equaled people. People equaled water.

Opening his eyes, he saw the leaves stirring in a bush near his face. The wind was pushing them to the right. Which meant the smoke was coming from the east. If he took the trail on the left, that would lead him to the fire.

He swayed, almost losing his balance, before he was running again. It might not have been *actual* running. In reality it might have been a slow, painful, tottering walk. But it felt like a sprint.

As he stumbled forward, Gideon's mind drifted, going back to the last time he'd seen his brother. Politics. That's what they'd fought over.

What could be more absurd than a fight over politics? A discussion — even a heated one? — sure, nothing wrong with a couple of brothers having a few sharp words over political differences. But for a pair of grown men, brothers, to sever their relationship over a difference of political opinions? It was crazy. And if Gideon faced the issue honestly, it was his fault.

It had happened a little more than seven years ago. At the time Gideon was still on the Princeton faculty, teaching at the Woodrow Wilson School of International Relations. But he was frequently in New York for work he did with the UN. Tillman had called late one afternoon saying that he was passing through New York before heading off on what he implied was some sort of covert operation. He said he wanted to talk.

Gideon had recently been offered a permanent fellowship at the UN, a dream job that allowed him to stay on the Princeton faculty while being dispatched as a special mediator to various conflict areas throughout the world. At the time it seemed as if he had reached the pinnacle of his life's work. He wanted to share the news about the appointment with his brother. In his excitement about the job, he had made the mistake of inviting Tillman to meet him at the Princeton Club in Midtown.

Gideon had joined the Princeton Club on a whim and rarely ever attended the wood-paneled Forty-third Street clubhouse. But when the call had come from Tillman, Gideon had wanted to show that all the years of penny-pinching through grad school, all the years of shacking up in the library, all the years of sacrifice and hard work had added up to something. *Here I am,* he wanted to say. *Look what I've achieved.*

Gideon had arrived late — his meeting at the UN had run long — and Tillman was waiting in the lobby with a scowl on his face. "That asshole over there has come up to me at least five times to ask if he can help me," Tillman said acidly, pointing at a supercilious man behind the reception desk. "Do I have a sign on my back that says 'Not Princeton Material' or something?"

Tillman had left the military several years earlier, but everything about him shouted army noncom. He still cut his hair as if he was ready for the parade ground — closely shaved sidewalls topped by a bold stripe of dark, crew-cut hair. Or maybe it was his carriage — the coiled anger that looked as if it might erupt at any moment. Whatever it was, something about him seemed out of place here.

"You're fine," Gideon said. "It's probably just because they don't know you."

While they were speaking, a floppy-haired twenty-something breezed in the door with a squash racket under his arm. He gave Tillman a brief look like he was something from the zoo.

"What?" Tillman said softly, giving the young man a glare of sleepy-eyed malice. "Something wrong?"

The young man gave him a wincing smile: "I don't know *what* your problem is but . . ."

He gave Tillman a slow, condescending shrug.

Tillman rose to a half crouch, ready to pounce on the young man. Gideon put his hand on Tillman's thigh. The young man backed away nervously, clutching his squash racquet, as if he might have to use it as a shield.

Gideon managed to steer Tillman up to the Tiger Bar before anything happened. But he could see things were already heading in the wrong direction.

Tillman had always claimed allegiance to the blue-collar world, professing a dislike that ranged from mistrust to outright hatred of anybody who had occasion to wear a necktie at anything other than a wedding or a funeral — bureaucrats, bankers, lawyers, doctors, college professors. Bringing Tillman to the Princeton Club was pretty much like waving a red flag in front of a bull.

Tillman finished his first glass of single malt in a single swallow as he started in on one of his standard diatribes. Pointy-headed liberals and media pundits were destroying the country by refusing to support our troops, while the UN kept sucking up to terrorists and Third World dictators. It went on and on. He quoted Earl Parker liberally. "You know Uncle Earl always says . . ." or

"Just last week Uncle Earl told me . . ." Not that there wasn't some truth to what he was saying. But Tillman never allowed even the possibility that sometimes it took more courage to talk than to fight. He seemed to think there was no human problem that couldn't be solved by force.

Gideon had intended to start the conversation by telling Tillman about his upcoming appointment at the UN. But Tillman wouldn't let his brother get a word in edgewise.

By the time he started working on his fourth Glenfiddich, Tillman's voice had gotten loud and ugly. People were eyeing him, wondering who this loudmouthed jerk with the military haircut was. It only seemed to make Tillman louder and angrier and more insulting.

Finally Gideon had had enough. It was time to change the direction of their conversation. "Wait a second," Gideon said, holding his hands up. "Take a break from your lecture and let me talk for a minute. I have some good news."

"I already know your good news," Tillman said, giving the final words a sarcastic twist. "You got a job working for those pansies at the UN."

Gideon felt his eyebrows rise in surprise.

"How did you know that?"

Tillman hesitated before answering, "I heard about it."

Which is when it dawned on him: Uncle Earl. It had to be. Only Uncle Earl was well connected enough to have known about the job offer before Gideon had even had a chance to tell anybody about it.

Gideon had known for several years that there was some kind of professional connection between Tillman and Uncle Earl. He knew that Uncle Earl had been instrumental in recruiting him from the military to covert operations. But he couldn't quite bring himself to believe that Uncle Earl would actually send him to talk Gideon out of a job he'd created for himself, the culmination of his life's work.

"Uncle Earl sent you," Gideon said incredulously.

"He didn't send me," Tillman insisted.

"Yes, he did. He sent you to talk me out of taking this job."

Tillman held his brother's accusatory glare before he finally spoke. "He thought maybe I could talk some sense into you, make you see that you're about to become —" Tillman broke off suddenly, as if stopping himself from crossing some red line that he knew he could never step back from.

But it was too late.

"What?" Gideon said, feeling a flush of molten anger rising into his cheeks. "That I'm about to become a traitor to my country? A dupe? A tool of terrorists? Go ahead. Say it."

Tillman locked eyes on Gideon. His eyes slowly narrowed.

"Seriously, Tillman," Gideon said. "Did he honestly think sending you here was going to change my mind? You two are so profoundly wrong about —"

"You don't know *anything,* Gideon," Tillman interrupted. "And what you think you know is more dangerous than you can even imagine. All this high-minded talk of yours? It's all bullshit. Six days ago a friend of mine bled to death while I held him, trying to keep his guts from falling out in his lap. For what? To protect you and the rest of these Princeton phonies? We're fighting the same bunch of thugs and monsters that drove airplanes into the Twin Towers, while you and your friends are selling out this country by making excuses for evil and trying to figure out why they hate us."

The manager beelined toward Gideon and Tillman, a tight smile on his face. "Perhaps the gentlemen would be more comfortable if —"

Gideon stood, blocking the manager from getting any closer, knowing full well that if he did, Tillman would put him in the hospital. "We're okay here." The manager nodded tightly and retreated.

Gideon turned toward Tillman, who eyed him for a hard moment, then bumped past him as he half-stumbled toward the door. Gideon followed him outside onto Forty-third Street, where his brother wheeled around in a silent challenge, as if to say, *We're past words, so let's just settle this man to man.* Which was when Gideon realized that he wanted to tear out Tillman's throat, wanted to tear the flesh and muscle from his neck with his bare hands. And that urge to kill his own brother had sobered him instantly.

"You're not the only person who's taken risks in his life," Gideon shouted in Tillman's face. "You can disagree with me all you want. But I'm not gonna stand here and let you lecture me like I'm some kind of fool. You've taken your stand. Fine. So have I. It's a principled stand, something I believe in. And if you can't respect that, then go back to your jungles and your deserts and watch your buddies die to your heart's content. But don't put their deaths on me. Because I believe there's another way."

With that he turned his back on his brother and walked away.

It was the last time they'd spoken.

What Gideon hadn't gotten the chance to tell Tillman was that he was about to put his own life on the line, embarking on his first major political mediation in his new capacity. It was a program he'd developed from his doctoral thesis and had been refining ever since. He was going into a mountainous and war-torn province where he would have little or no personal security — no gun, no air force, no navy, no world power at his back — armed only with the trust he'd developed with members of the warring parties. If he succeeded, he'd save the lives of countless innocent civilians. If he failed, he might look like a fool to his peers and maybe derail what had once been a promising career. Or worse, he could end up beheaded, his wallet and watch stripped, and his teeth pulled out for the gold fillings — another hapless do-gooder left dead in an unmarked ditch.

But Gideon never got to tell Tillman any of that because of the widening abyss defined by their political differences — which Gideon had since come to realize weren't nearly as important as the fact that they were brothers. Tillman had sacrificed a lot in his life, had chosen for himself a path that was arduous, dangerous, and frequently unrewarding. The lesson Tillman had taken from their rough childhood had been that you had to confront, to battle, to fight. And Gideon had benefitted from his brother's protection, no question about it, and he should have cut his brother a little more slack.

But he hadn't. And that had been that.

And now it was time to make peace.

The first thing Gideon saw was the smoke. He tottered weakly up the small ridge, and there it was, nestled in the valley below him. A village. And the village was on fire, a huge column of black smoke rising high into the air. Whatever this place was, though, it was different from the earlier villages he'd come through.

There were concrete block buildings with corrugated iron roofs, and something approximating a road ran through the middle of the town. It was like the other villages, though, in that he saw no people. No living people anyway. There were human-shaped figures lying here and there in the streets and alleys, a few more scattered across the field of poppies that climbed up the far side of the mountain.

But other than the smoke, nothing moved. Some of the buildings were not simply burning, they had been flattened.

Gideon stumbled down the path until he reached the burning village. The path meandered through a waving crimson sea of poppies.

At the edge of the town he saw something glinting on the ground. A metal sign lay smashed into the dirt. It appeared to have been run over by a vehicle. He walked slowly to the sign, looked down. Written in English were two words.

KAMPUNG NAGA

I'm here, Tillman, he thought. *I'm here.*
Then his legs gave out and he collapsed onto the ground and closed his eyes.

CHAPTER EIGHTEEN

Captain Avery Taylor assembled his team
on the Sultan's boat dock, their backs to
the Pacific Ocean. The Sultan had loaned
his personal speedboat to the team. It lay in
the water behind them, bobbing up and
down on the waves so violently that it
threatened to tear the gangway from its
mounts.

Because Mohan had briefly been a possession of the British Empire, its military
continued to use British weapons. As a
result Taylor's men had been forced to buy
.223 ammo for their M4s directly from a
gun shop on the outskirts of Mohan. From
the Mohanese Defense Forces they'd scared
up some grenades, a 1960s-era British
rocket launcher, three rockets, some scuba
gear commandeered from a dive shop on
the beach, and a set of blurry blueprints of
the Obelisk faxed from Trojan Energy's
headquarters in Houston. None of the men

said so, but they all knew they were under-armed and ill-equipped for an ill-conceived mission that had been planned too quickly with too little intel.

"Everybody knows our mission," Captain Taylor said. "We'll complete the briefing on the boat. All I have to say is that I'm proud as hell of you guys. You're the finest soldiers I've had the privilege to command. Which is why I know we *will* succeed."

"Hoo-ah!" shouted the men.

He turned to Chief Petty Officer Ricardo Green. "Chief? Any words of wisdom?"

"You bastards don't need no goddamn words of goddamn wisdom because you already know your goddamn jobs better than any sixteen other sons of bitches on planet earth!" Green shouted. The standing joke in the unit was that the last time the Chief had uttered a complete sentence that did not contain a curse word was when he'd said "I do" to Mrs. Chief Petty Officer Green eighteen years earlier. "Now get your goddamn shit and get on the goddamn boat."

The men began struggling up the gangway with their heavy gear. The boat pitched and rolled in the heavy surf. The fourth man onto the boat slipped on the polished teak gangway and plunged into the punishing surf between the boat and the pier.

By the time they managed to haul him out of the water, blood was pouring from his left arm. A needle sharp length of bone protruded through the fabric of his sleeve.

"Motherfucker," Green muttered as the injured man was ushered away by one of the Sultan's smartly dressed boating staff.

Green's black eyes briefly met those of his commanding officer. The two men didn't speak. But they didn't need to. This mission was a cluster fuck from the get-go.

Four minutes later, the Sultan's boat was battering its way through the heavy surf toward the Obelisk. As they rounded the protective jetty at the tip of the Bay of Mohan, the waves immediately reared up to even greater heights. In nearly ten years in the navy, Captain Taylor had never seen waves like this — great black foam-capped wedges of darkness, coming at them like skyscrapers rolling sideways down a giant hill.

Captain Taylor saw Green's lips moving, but this time he couldn't hear him. For a moment Captain Taylor thought he was cursing. But then he realized he was wrong. *Oh, my!* Taylor thought. *The Chief is praying.*

That was not good.

■ ■ ■ ■

When Gideon regained consciousness, he felt someone cradling his head and pouring water onto his face. He choked and sputtered.

For a moment he had no recollection of where he was or how he'd gotten here.

It was a man, a white guy, muttering something Gideon didn't understand but recognized as Russian. The guy was speaking Russian.

Gideon sucked down the water, then tried to sit up.

"Don't move yet," the man said, this time in heavily accented English.

But Gideon sat up anyway. Not that he didn't appreciate the help. But sitting with his head in a strange man's lap felt a little awkward. He winced as he sat up. His head was pounding.

"Is clean water," the Russian said. "Don't worry. You won't get sick."

Gideon took the cup of water and drank until it was gone.

"Slow. You gonna puke, you drink too much."

Gideon nodded, then handed the empty cup back to the Russian. "My name is —"

"I know who you are," the Russian said. "The one who got medal at UN. Abu Nasir's brother."

Gideon looked around at the burning village. "Is he here?"

"Does it look like he is here?"

"You're here."

The Russian shrugged and stood up. For the first time Gideon saw how strangely the man was dressed. His clothes had been military uniforms at one time. Not one uniform, but many of them. They had been cut into strips and squares and triangles, crudely reassembled into a sort of ragged camouflage harlequin costume. He was also painfully thin and sick-looking. He wore a long beard and a small skullcap. His eyes had a lunatic glint.

"Who are you?" Gideon said.

"Chadeev." He patted the center of his chest with a bony hand.

"You're Russian?"

"Fock no." The man spit on the ground. "Kabardian."

"Kabardian?"

"We live Georgia, Chechnya, Russia, Turkey. Focked on by everybody."

"Ah," Gideon said. "First I heard of Kabardians."

"You and everybody else."

"So where is Abu Nasir?"

Chadeev shrugged. "Gone. Everybody dead."

"Who's responsible for this?"

Chadeev looked around. "You Americans, you always looking for responsibility. This is nature of universe, man. Is one long focking war. Everybody against everybody."

Gideon stood. His legs felt wobbly. But the water had helped. "Do you have any food?"

Chadeev laughed. "Food." He looked over and spoke as though to an invisible third person. "He talk about responsibility. God see it and make it so."

"Where did Abu Nasir go?"

"Abu Nasir don't talk to Chadeev," he said. "Chadeev live out there." He pointed at the endless green forest. "God wills it to burn down this place, Chadeev come."

"Did the jihadis do this? The government? Who?"

Chadeev pointed at the sky. "Is the eye in the sky."

Was he talking about Predator drones or satellites? Or was the guy just nuts? Whatever the case, there seemed little likelihood of getting a straight answer from him. He decided to start foraging for food.

There was one concrete block building

that seemed to have incurred less damage than the others. Other than the half-collapsed roof there was little damage. He decided to check there first.

As he walked toward the building, Chadeev followed. He began speaking — apparently to himself — in Russian. Or maybe it was Kabardian — if there even was such a thing. Gideon had earned his doctoral degree in international relations and he'd never heard of Kabardians.

Gideon surveyed the town as he walked. Whatever had happened here was different from what had happened in the other villages, which had clearly been attacked and burned by foot soldiers. This place had been bombed from the air. Straight-up, good-old-fashioned aerial bombing. Numerous craters dotted the rocky soil. He'd been around enough of them when he was mediating the Waziristan crisis to know what he was seeing.

Dead men were everywhere. And pieces of dead men — hands, arms, a foot still wearing a boot, a hank of hair still rooted to a clump of clotted scalp. Some had been shot or hit by frags, but others were intact, having been killed by the concussion of the bomb blast. The men all wore uniforms, jungle camo. The uniforms looked American, but the men wearing them were obviously locals, with the same distinctive features as the highlanders who had escorted him earlier.

Blowflies and flesh flies were buzzing around the bloating bodies. Gideon looked for the small maggots from these flies that appear within the first few days of death but saw none. Which meant this massacre had happened recently.

The closer he got to the one remaining building, the sicker he felt.

Could Tillman have survived this? And who was responsible? It could only have been the Mohanese government. Gideon was beginning to think that maybe this whole thing had been orchestrated, that he had been sent as some kind of stalking horse, drawing Tillman out so that the Mohanese Air Force could get a fix on him in order to level the village that had provided sanctuary to him and to his followers. But that scenario meant that General Prang and his men had been set up as well. The puzzle still had too many missing pieces.

Chadeev danced after Gideon, grinning and talking to himself.

Gideon entered the ruined building. There he found more corpses, all of them men, all wearing the same uniforms as the men outside. Unlike them, these men had been shot.

Sickened as he was by the carnage, Gideon could barely think about anything but food. At the far end of the building stood a makeshift stove composed of two gas cook rings welded to the top of a rickety table. On each cook ring was a wok. A refrigerator sat next to them.

Gideon opened the door. To his astonishment, a light came on. The refrigerator was still working. He heard it then, the hum of a small generator over in the still-intact corner of the building.

The refrigerator was crammed completely full of Budweiser. But not a scrap of food.

He shook his head.

Chadeev saw the beer, scurried over and started grabbing as many bottles as he could fit in his arms. "Beer! Is totally prohibit in my focking religion. Is Allah's joke on Muslims. He make beautiful beer and then he only give it to focking infidels." He twisted off the cap, tipped it up, and drank until he'd drained it completely.

Gideon looked around, saw a bowl full of food on the ledge of a low wall. Flies buzzed around it. He moved toward the food, waving the flies away, when he saw behind the low wall the body of the man who had probably been preparing the meal for himself when he'd been shot. Gideon picked up the bowl, respectfully turning away from the man who'd been deprived of his last meal, and took a sniff. It smelled fantastic. Curried vegetables and a few bits of chicken over rice. The town had obviously been attacked so recently that the food hadn't had time to rot.

Gideon virtually inhaled the entire bowl of food.

Chadeev opened another beer and began drinking. "Your brother is genius," he said. "I come to this place after fight in Chechnya, Afghanistan, Pakistan, all kind of place. Now I gonna put it to the focking infidel here in Mohan. But your brother, he open my eyes. He reveal to me real nature of God."

"He did, huh?" Gideon said. He looked around the room at all the dead men. Now that his belly was full, he was able to see them more clearly. Before the food it had been almost as if they were just obstacles in the way of his eating. Now . . .

"This." Chadeev made a sweeping motion with his hands. "This is nature of God."

"Is my brother dead?"

Chadeev winked and pointed surreptitiously above them. The roof had been blown off, so the building was open to the clear blue sky.

"What's that mean?"

"Eye in the sky!" Chadeev whispered. "Eye in the sky!" He motioned with his thumb to the one corner of the building where the roof still stood. "Over there."

"What?"

"Over there. We talk over there." Chadeev's voice had dropped to a whisper.

Gideon followed the crazy man to the far side of the building where they were shadowed by the roof.

"Eye in the sky can read lips. Don't never talk in open."

"Did Abu Nasir teach you that?"

"Don't be ridiculous!" Chadeev laughed. "Is al Qaeda doctrine."

"You're al Qaeda."

"Labels! Responsibility!" Chadeev laughed again, then put his hand gently on Gideon's arm. "Your brother, when he see you, he always make a toast and say, 'Here's to my naive brother The Peacemaker . . . and to all his kind.' "

"What do you mean, whenever he saw me? How could he see me?"

Chadeev shrugged. "CNN! Your face on CNN all the time. They love you, love your cute little dimples." He reached out and rubbed the side of Gideon's face.

Gideon swatted his hand away. "Is my brother here?"

Chadeev offered a cryptic shrug.

Gideon took a threatening step toward him. "Do you know where he is or not?"

"You don't want to see Abu Nasir, my friend. Trust me. You will not like what you find."

"Then you know where he is."

The Kabardian nodded in sad resignation. "Come. I show you his room."

Chadeev led Gideon into an adjacent concrete building, half of which had been leveled. They climbed over the rubble and entered through a jagged hole in the wall. Inside were more dead bodies, and some folding chairs arranged around a stove. Gideon checked the bodies to see if any of them were Tillman.

Beside a neatly made cot stood a makeshift nightstand made from an ammunition crate. It held a book, its binding no longer stiff and its pages well thumbed. Other than a thin skin of dust, the room had been left untouched by the bombing.

"He sleep here," Chadeev said.

Gideon idly picked up the book on the nightstand and was fairly shocked when he brushed the dust from the cover.

The Way to Peace by Gideon Davis.

It was a book he'd written a decade earlier, an expansion of his doctoral thesis, which had led to his job at the UN. He opened it, saw a paragraph underlined. Then another. Tillman had gone through the book carefully and thoroughly.

Gideon flipped back to the title page, read the simple dedication: "To Tillman, who has fought too many wars." Gideon had sent his brother the book when it was published and had never heard a word of response. He had nursed a minor grudge about it all these years, imagining that Tillman had never even bothered to crack it open and had probably thrown it in the trash. Yet here it was, the pages worn soft as if from repeated readings.

Gideon curbed his rising anger when he noticed a flickering light coming from a flat-screen television lying facedown on the floor, having been blown off its mount by the bomb blast. Not only was it still working, but it was tuned to CNN.

Chadeev mumbled to himself in Russian as he lifted the top edge of the television and set it down against the base of the stove while Gideon stared down at the screen. Wolf Blitzer was moving his lips silently.

Behind him was a file photo of an oil rig. The words crawling across the bottom of the screen stopped Gideon cold. OBELISK SEIZED . . . He recognized it as the rig where Uncle Earl was waiting for him to bring Tillman. But Gideon felt a wave of cold realization when he read the rest of the crawl: . . . PIRATES LED BY ABU NASIR DEMANDING COMPLETE WITHDRAWAL OF U.S. FORCES FROM THE REGION.

"See?" Chadeev looked down sadly at the television. "There is your brother."

Gideon found the remote control and thumbed up the volume. "Remote control — another great blessing of Allah, praise be unto him."

Wolf Blitzer's voice echoed in the empty room. "President Diggs is expected to comment shortly on the seizure of the rig and its connection to the unfolding civil war in Mohan. But we do have information from the video put up on YouTube by the terrorists showing one of the hostages —"

Chadeev grabbed the remote. "All right. You see enough."

Chadeev changed the channel. A woman with lots of blond hair and a bright red dress that looked like 1980 came on the screen.

"Look!" Chadeev crowed. "*Dallas!* Is excellent show. You know who is big fan of

Dallas TV show? Osama bin Laden. Seriously. He *love Dallas.* He got whole series on DVD."

"Wait! Go back!"

"Go back? No way. Is *Dallas!* You know how long since I watch *Dallas?*" Chadeev held the remote protectively against his chest.

"Go back!"

"Fock you, man," Chadeev said. "Look. Is 'Who Shot JR?' episode. Most famous episode in history of —"

"Give me the remote," Gideon said.

"No."

Gideon snatched the remote from the crazy Kabardian, changed the channel back to CNN. A grainy video now filled the screen. Standing before a group of masked and armed men was a woman wearing a brilliant yellow jumpsuit. She was in her early thirties, her long auburn hair framing a face that was beautiful even without makeup. She looked frightened but defiant as she read from the terrorists' script.

"My name is Kate Murphy. I am the executive in charge of the Obelisk, which is now under the control of Abu Nasir . . ."

Gideon couldn't quite process what he was hearing, some part of him still clinging to the possibility that there had to be another explanation. But then he saw one of the masked gunmen lift his arm to adjust his mask, and the denial he'd been clinging to fell away. On the back of the gunman's wrist was a small tattoo. Gideon had seen that tattoo before. It was two numbers: an 8 and a 2. His brother had tattooed an 82 on his wrist the day he'd finished jump school with the 82nd Airborne Division. Gideon felt the truth twist and writhe in his gut. Tillman had betrayed him. He'd been behind the ambush and the subsequent attacks along the river. And now he had taken the rig and was threatening to kill dozens of hostages, including Uncle Earl.

"I want *Dallas!*" Chadeev said, grabbing feebly at the remote.

If the situation weren't so bizarrely horrific, it would have been funny — two grown men fighting over a remote control in the middle of the jungle.

"Give me a minute," Gideon said. "Then you can watch all the *Dallas* you want."

Chadeev knelt next to a dead man. Draped over the dead man's shoulder was an AK-47, held on by a worn leather strap. Chadeev yanked on the gun, but the strap caught on the dead man's belt. Chadeev put his foot on the dead man's neck and heaved.

On the television, Wolf Blitzer had replaced the beautiful hostage. "The South China Sea has seen a sharp increase in piracy over the past year, but this latest situation clearly has broader geopolitical implications. The consensus among foreign policy experts is that any capitulation to Abu Nasir would be seen as a victory for the insurgency —"

"Give me remote." Chadeev had finally freed the AK-47 from the dead man and was pointing the barrel at Gideon's head.

"You're gonna shoot me over *Dallas*?" Gideon said.

"Remote!" Chadeev screamed, a tiny bead of spit flying from his mouth. "Give me focking remote!"

"Fine." Gideon slid the remote across the floor then backed away with his hands in the air.

Chadeev smiled broadly and changed the channel to *Dallas*. Chadeev set the gun down on the floor, then squatted in the middle of the room full of bodies, a placid grin on his face, and began to drink another beer.

Gideon walked out into the ruined camp, reeling from what he'd just seen and heard, yet still unable to completely shake the hope that there had to be some other explanation, some missing piece of information.

Whatever that might be, he knew there was only one place he would find it. On the Obelisk.

CHAPTER NINETEEN

Gideon scoured the smoldering village until he found a military-grade shortwave radio in what had until recently been a communications room. The casing was scorched and cracked, but when he turned the switch, it crackled to life. He thought briefly about General Prang, who was supposed to have given him a radio but had only managed to give him a map before he'd been killed. Written in grease pencil on the reverse of the map was the emergency frequency Gideon was supposed to hail if he needed to order an emergency evacuation.

Gideon dialed the frequency on the radio, then spoke into the microphone.

"This is Gideon Davis. Can you read me?" he said.

"Clear this frequency," a man's voice said, followed by a long silence. Finally the voice came back. "Please give us the confirmation code."

Gideon squinted at the code Prang had scrawled on the back of the map. "Circuit Alpha Nine Zero One Zero Seven. I repeat. Circuit Alpha Nine Zero One Zero Seven."

Another pause. "Confirmed," the voice said.

A second voice came on. "Mr. Davis. We thought you might be dead."

"Who am I speaking to?"

"I'm with the home team."

"Tell me what's happening on the rig."

"We'll brief you in person. Please give us your location."

"Dammit, just give me the sitrep —"

"Your location, sir," the voice insisted.

"I'm in Kampung Naga."

"Are you injured? Do you require medical attention?"

Gideon realized he'd have to wait for any answers about the status of the rig. "I'm fine."

"Are you under fire?"

"No."

"Are you aware of any hostiles in the vicinity?"

Gideon's mind went to Chadeev. "Negative."

"Please stand by, sir. We'll have a chopper to you in one hour, sir."

The voice was replaced by white noise.

Gideon listened to the static as he released a deep breath he'd been holding in his chest. The moment he sat down, he felt himself being swallowed by fatigue. Adrenaline had been masking the physical toll the last twenty hours had taken on his body, but even more draining for Gideon was his increasing disorientation. Rather than finding answers, he'd only gathered more questions.

The chopper hit the ground fifty-six minutes later. It didn't bear military markings, but Gideon recognized it as a military model. A tall black man wearing a tropical suit stood in the doorway, an MP5 submachine gun in his hand. He beckoned furiously with his hand for Gideon to come toward him, but Gideon needed no prompting.

"We were afraid we'd lost you, sir," the man with the MP5 shouted over the whine of the twin turbojet engines. "I'm Gary Simpson, cultural attaché from the embassy." *Cultural attaché* being an obvious CIA cover.

They shook hands, but before they exchanged any more pleasantries, Gideon wanted some answers. "Who hit this place?"

Gary Simpson frowned, but didn't answer.

Gideon pointed his finger at the CIA man.

"And don't give me any shit about how you don't know."

Simpson relaxed his defiant posture. "It was the Mohanese air force."

"Did this happen after my brother made his deal with the Sultan?"

"No, sir. Before. Your brother contacted us after the air strike. We thought it was the thing that finally turned him around. Apparently we were wrong."

Gideon studied the man, measuring his sincerity. Satisfied that the man was telling the truth, he said, "Tell me what's happening on the rig."

Simpson hesitated. "How much do you know?"

"Just what I saw on CNN. That my brother seized the rig and now he's threatening to kill hostages. What's the time frame?"

"Eighteen hours, twenty-five minutes."

"What's the President doing about it?"

"He's deployed Deltas from Hawaii to take back the rig, but they may not be able to get in under the weather."

"What weather?"

Simpson told Gideon about the typhoon, which had changed course and was limiting the possibility of an aerial assault.

"The president must be doing something."

Simpson nodded. "He's ordered a SEAL team to take back the rig. They've already launched." Gideon heard the uncertainty in Simpson's voice. But before he could ask anything more, Simpson said, "We need to get going, sir. The situation on the ground is not good right now. The rebels are making a big push. We nearly got pegged by a Stinger on the way up here, so we're going to be hugging the trees, keeping a profile for evasive action."

Gideon climbed into the chopper, which rose into the air over the ruined village of Kampung Naga. Through one of the roofless buildings, Gideon could see Chadeev sitting cross-legged on the ground, still watching *Dallas,* surrounded by a litter of beer bottles.

CHAPTER TWENTY

The trouble started before the boat had even launched.

On paper the boat that the Sultan had loaned to Captain Taylor's SEAL platoon was an ideal fit for the mission. At 41 feet it was large enough to accommodate the platoon and powerful enough to fight through the massive seas — driven by a pair of intercooled, supercharged MerCruiser V-8s that put out over 750 horsepower apiece.

The problem was that it was a poser — a rich guy's pleasure craft masquerading as a high performance boat. The decks and superstructure were heavy teak. Every cleat and hitch and light fixture was fashioned from brass. To make matters worse, the innards were protectively shielded by 3/8-inch hardened steel plate. It was made for going fast in a straight line, but its weight made the craft ponderous to handle and more than a little top heavy.

As long as they were blasting straight into a wave, they were fine. They powered up the face of one wave, throttled back at the top, surfed down the face of the next wave, and submarined into the next wave. Each trough brought a momentary heart-stopping thud as the wave broke over the bow and engulfed the craft, which shuddered before bursting up from the water like a breaching submarine.

The Obelisk was due northeast from their launching point, but the waves were rolling in from the east. For a while Taylor was able to head directly into the waves. Once he adjusted to a true north course, though, the waves began hitting the hull broadside. And that's where the weakness of the Sultan's boat began to show.

Every time the craft crested a wave, it heeled over to port, then rolled rapidly starboard as the wave passed underneath. The momentum of the wave and the weight of the armored hull made the boat just want to keep rolling.

Taylor stood in the wheelhouse at the shoulder of Petty Officer Derrick Winters, who concentrated as he silently piloted the craft. He faced a computerized helm rivaling the cockpit of a jet aircraft. Manifold pressure, oil pressure, boost, coolant temperature, bearing, depth, wind speed and direction, radar, sonar. But the one digital readout that kept drawing the captain's attention was the pitch indicator, which showed how much the craft was rolling.

They crested a wave and the boat rolled to starboard. Eleven degrees. Twelve degrees. Fifteen. Sixteen. Finally the boat settled and began to roll back.

"Can she handle it?" Taylor asked.

"Yes, sir."

But Taylor heard the uncertainty in Winters's voice. "As much as I appreciate your optimism, I'd rather have your honesty."

Winters didn't answer right away. "We'll find out soon enough, sir."

A voice suddenly interrupted. "She's taking on water, sir."

An inch or two of water had been sloshing from one side of the wheelhouse to the other for at least ten minutes.

The boat's wheelhouse was enclosed, but water was getting in from somewhere. "Mr. Kennedy, find a pump," Taylor called back.

"Gaylord's on it already, sir," Kennedy shouted. "There's only one, and he's got it going full blast."

"Very well," Taylor said.

The water was washing over his boots

now. He didn't have to tell the men what they knew already: the more water they took on, the worse they'd roll. Enough water, or a big enough wave, and they would capsize.

"What's our ETA to the rig?" Taylor said.

"Five minutes," Winters said. "Seven tops."

Taylor nodded.

They crested the next wave. The boat rolled again. Nine degrees. Twelve. Fifteen. Eighteen. Something fell over and crashed behind Taylor. The boat was still rolling. Nineteen degrees.

"Come on, baby. Come on." Winters was riding the throttle and carving to starboard, making micro adjustments to keep the boat from rolling any farther.

Finally the boat began to settle. Taylor exhaled, but his relief was short-lived.

"Oh, Jesus!" someone said.

Taylor didn't see it at first. In the dim light it was hard to make out exactly what was going on outside the craft. But then he saw what his men were pointing at. A gathering blackness was swelling, rising up before them. Suddenly, Taylor felt himself falling, as if he were on an elevator that had its cables cut. The boat let out a horrible, rending groan.

And then it was upon them.

The news that Gideon Davis was alive had boosted the president's mood, but it didn't diminish the helplessness or the anxiety he felt as he sat in the Situation Room, monitoring the SEAL operation. Because the cloud cover was so thick, the satellite could only send thermal images onto the wall-mounted monitor. The Sultan's boat appeared as an orange triangle as it sliced through the blue-black space of the sea toward the Obelisk. Periodically a wave would crash over the boat and much of the orange triangle would disappear for a while. But it always came back.

"How close are they?" President Diggs said softly.

"Four kilometers." The man from the National Reconnaissance Office didn't glance up from his screen. His fingers flew as he kept the satellite tracking the fast-moving boat.

The president realized he'd been sitting there with his fist clenched in front of his mouth for five or ten minutes. It wasn't a very presidential posture, he thought. His hand was getting sore, he'd been squeezing so hard. He looked at his hand, flexing his fingers a couple of times. When he looked back up at the monitor, there was nothing on the screen but a field of blue. The NRO man kept stabbing at his keyboard.

"Bring them back," the president said. "Where are they?"

The NRO man shook his head like a boxer shaking off a hard right hook.

"Find them!" General Ferry echoed the president. "Find my boat!"

The NRO man shook his head a second time.

"Don't shake your head at me, young man!" General Ferry shouted. "Find my boat."

The NRO man didn't look up from the screen. "I can't, sir."

"Why not?" President Diggs said.

"Because it's gone, sir," a voice said from the back of the room. It was an admiral Diggs didn't recognize, although he was clearly the oldest man in the room. His was the creased and rugged face of a man who'd spent most of his life at sea, and now it wore a somber expression.

President Diggs stared at the admiral for a moment. "I'm sorry, Admiral, what did you say?"

"They're gone, Mr. President," the admiral said. "Captain Taylor knew the specs on that boat were far from ideal in this weather, but he and his men believed it was worth the risk. Waves were just too high for that boat."

Diggs looked over at Elliot Hammershaw. The chief of staff's face had gone white. Neither of them needed to say anything because they both understood the math. The terrorists' deadline was in fewer than twelve hours, and the storm wouldn't pass for seventy-two hours. Their last chance to take back the rig depended on the Delta team threading the eye of needle.

Gideon glanced at Simpson every time he heard the sound. They were flying so low that the limbs of the tallest trees occasionally whacked against the undercarriage of the helicopter. Suddenly, the chopper pitched forward and went into a dive. Gideon's stomach went up into his throat.

"Don't worry, sir," Simpson called. "We just hit the fall line."

And out the window Gideon could see it. They were thundering down the face of the cliff, the entire airframe pitched over at what felt like an aerodynamically impossible angle. Just when Gideon was sure they would slam into the ground, the chopper steadied, pulled its nose up, and began barreling cross-country again.

Below them was an entirely new terrain, the thick rolling jungle uplands replaced by flat rice paddies and small villages.

Gideon waited for his equilibrium to return before he spoke again. "Simpson, you need to get me onto that rig."

"Sir, there's a jet waiting to fly you home."

"I'm not going back to Washington."

"And I'm under orders from Langley. The uplands are a no-fly zone now. We have to get out —"

Before he could finish his sentence the pilot called from the cockpit with a calm but urgent voice. "We've got a bird in the air."

"Flares away!" the copilot said, as the chopper banked into a hard turn. Through the window, Gideon could see the airport several miles in the distance, the blue sea glinting just beyond it.

The chopper continued its turn, tipping over sideways. The airport disappeared until all Gideon could see was a rice paddy below them. Snaking up through the air with frightening speed was a flaming object trailing white smoke.

Then it was out of view again.

A sudden thud came from the back of the chopper. Gideon felt the impact in his chest.

"We're hit," the pilot yelled.

The helicopter began to make a terrible rattling sound, like a pair of bowling balls in an oil drum.

"Brace for impact," the copilot yelled. "We're going down!"

The chopper may have been going down, but it wasn't quite the crash that Gideon had anticipated. Instead the chopper bounced up and down and continued to fly. It was losing airspeed and slowly rotating. But the pilot was obviously extraordinarily skilled: he managed to keep the aircraft limping onward.

"Just get us to the airport!" Simpson shouted. "The Sultan's got two regiments stationed there."

The pilot nodded curtly.

The ground below them rotated, like the view from a slow merry-go-round. They were away from the rice paddy now, moving over a commercial district of warehouses and industrial buildings. Each time they rotated so that Gideon could see in the direction they'd come, he could see a jeep full of jihadis driving after them. It had a large Soviet-era machine gun mounted on the back.

When the chopper's rotation showed the

view of their intended destination, Gideon could tell they weren't going to make it to the airport. The corkscrewing of the copter was forcing them relentlessly northeast. The airport was due north, still a good five miles away.

Now they were facing the jihadis again, who were driving at a breakneck pace through the deserted streets below. They were getting closer.

The airport appeared again, then the sea, then the jihadis again. Now the insurgents were firing the machine gun.

Bullets thudded into the helicopter.

The jihadis disappeared. Airport, ocean, commercial buildings, jihadis. Closer still.

"You gotta go faster!" the CIA man shouted.

"I can't," the pilot shouted. "The hydraulics are leaking. We won't make it much farther!"

And indeed the chopper was spinning faster and faster, causing its forward progress to slow.

The jihadis were still firing.

Gideon saw the gunner reloading a new belt of ammo from a full can. One more rotation of the aircraft and the gunner would tear them to ribbons. He couldn't have been more than a hundred yards away.

All the jihadis on the jeep were blasting away now. The machine gunner worked the feed handle, chambering a round from the new belt.

As the jihadis disappeared from view, Gideon braced himself, then he felt a huge thud. Gideon's first thought was that the machine gunner had hit the chopper — the fuel tanks or the fusilage. But the chopper seemed unaffected and was still spinning . . . ocean, airport, industrial buildings.

This time, though, the view of the jihadis had changed. Smoke spewed from the hood of their jeep, which swerved sideways and slammed into a wall.

"The Sultan's troops!" Simpson shouted, pointing out the window as their view scrolled past an eight-wheeled armored personnel carrier, trailed by SMDF soldiers. Mounted on the top was a heavy gun which continued firing toward the jihadis.

Simpson allowed himself a tight smile reflecting his relief and satisfaction. *We're going to make it,* he thought.

And with that, the chopper hit something — a palm tree? A billboard? Gideon was never quite sure, as the chopper nosed over and dropped like a giant brick, fifty feet to the ground.

■ ■ ■ ■

For a moment there was no sound at all. Gideon sat, stunned. The entire helicopter had smashed nose first into the ground. The cockpit was a twisted mass of metal. Gideon and Simpson were now hanging facedown about ten feet above the wreckage.

Finally he regained enough presence of mind to unstrap himself. Next to him, Simpson was unstrapping, too.

"You all right, Mr. Davis?"

"Fine, fine."

"We need to get out of here."

Gideon thought that was a somewhat unnecessary comment. But he kept his thoughts to himself. He grabbed the back of his seat, his feet dangling just above the ruined cockpit. He dropped, landing on the twisted bulkhead. "You guys, okay?" he called toward the cockpit.

There was no answer. He leaned in through what had been the cockpit door and saw that neither the pilot nor the copilot had survived.

Gideon looked at Simpson and shook his head.

"Shit," Simpson said. Then, apparently thinking he might have offended Gideon, he quickly added, "Sorry, sir."

"Hey, the same word crossed my mind," Gideon said drily.

Simpson freed himself from the seat, dropped down next to Gideon. He grimaced as he landed.

"Let's go," Gideon said.

"I think I caught one in the leg," the CIA man said. "I'm sorry, sir."

"No more apologizing," Gideon said. "Lean on me and let's get out of here."

They struggled out of the cabin and surveyed the wreckage. No longer recognizable as an aircraft, the helicopter was teetering on the edge of a road running alongside a small canal about two hundred feet wide. If it had fallen even a few feet closer to the airport, they would have drowned.

Gideon looked at Simpson, clearly sharing the same thought.

"We need to get to the airport," Simpson said.

"Yeah. Except it's over there," Gideon said, pointing across the unbroken strip of brown water, which fed out into the bay, and beyond it, the ocean.

"The good news is we didn't fall into the canal, but the bad news is, we landed on the wrong side." The armored SMDF vehicle was grinding toward them, from about half a mile away.

"How's your swimming, sir?"

"Probably better than yours right now," Gideon said.

"Then you need to get across. If the jihadis send reinforcements, I'll hold them off till you make it over to the SMDF." Simpson pulled forward the MP5, which was still strapped around him in a tactical sling.

"We're both getting over there."

"No, Mr. Davis, you need to go. Please."

Gideon pointed toward the bay, which was only a few hundred yards away. "There's a dock down there. We'll take a boat across."

"Our plan was to exfil you and your brother by boat and take you to a naval vessel. The boat's still on standby." Simpson pulled out a satellite phone and punched in a number. "I'm calling him so he can meet you there. I'll follow in a bit."

"I'm sure you're familiar with the wall in Langley that has a star for every agent who's sacrificed his life serving this country —"

"Of course, Mr. Davis, but —"

"News flash, Simpson. Your star is not going up on that wall."

Simpson looked nervously back to the south.

"Are we clear?"

"Yes, sir," he said, before speaking into

the phone. "Sandpiper Seven this is Uncle Bob. Our air asset is down, but our primary is uninjured. Hostiles are in pursuit. There's a quay about three klicks west of KM International. I need our water asset there for immediate exfil. Prepare to exit hard. Out." He folded the phone and shoved it into his pocket.

Gideon draped Simpson's arm around his shoulder, supporting him as he hobbled down the deserted highway. Blood had soaked through Simpson's pants and was leaking onto the road, leaving a trail. Gideon didn't want to say anything, but if Simpson didn't get to a hospital within the hour, he was going to bleed out.

They had about fifty yards to go when the jihadis appeared on the highway behind them. Turbaned men armed with AKs were jammed in the back of a white pickup. Some hung over the side.

"Make a break for it, Mr. Davis," Simpson said.

"Shut up, Simpson," Gideon said. "I told you, your star's not going up on that wall. At least not today."

Simpson was in no shape to argue. The jihadi vehicle was accelerating toward them.

From the far side of the canal, the gun boomed from the turret of the SMDF vehicle. But the pickup truck was going too fast to make an easy target, and the armored vehicle's shells were landing short of it.

"Hustle up, Simpson," Gideon urged. "We're almost there."

Simpson was trying, but the bullet that hit his leg had hit bone. With every footfall, he grimaced in agony until Gideon was forced to support nearly all of his weight.

Behind them, the jihadis in the pickup truck began shooting.

"Hang on," Gideon shouted. He crouched and planted his shoulder in the pit of the CIA man's stomach, lifting him off the ground.

"My God, Simpson, how much do you weigh?" Gideon said as he staggered toward the boat. He was trying to keep Simpson distracted, afraid if he didn't then Simpson would get all heroic and try to get off Gideon's shoulder — making it impossible for either of them to make it to the docks.

Out in the bay Gideon saw a boat tearing toward them.

"That's our boat!" Simpson grunted.

It was a large, powerful boat — something like a cigarette boat — and it spewed a rooster tail a good twenty feet in the air behind it. The seas looked unusually heavy, and it went airborne occasionally, clearing one wave before slamming into the next.

"Put me down," Simpson said feebly. "You won't make it if you —"

"Two forty? Two forty-five?"

"Two fifty-five," Simpson said.

The speedboat was getting closer now, decelerating as it drew toward the quay. Gideon could make out three figures in the boat, all of them armed. He waved at the boat and it steered toward him, still carrying enough speed that it looked as if it would slam into the dock. At the last moment it nosed around sharply, digging into the water and throwing up a wave that sloshed up onto the deck.

Gideon crossed the final strip of concrete, pounded across the last few feet of wooden decking, and eased Simpson over the gunwale.

The captain of the boat had a cigarette in his mouth and a Sig Sauer on his hip. The other two men stood in the bow, MP5s at the ready.

Behind him, Gideon could hear the *thump-thump-thump* of the heavy machine gun mounted in the back of the jihadi pickup truck. Gideon vaulted himself over the the gunwale and landed on his feet next to Simpson.

"Get Mr. Davis to the airport," Simpson

shouted to the boat captain.

The captain slammed the dual throttles forward, and the boat tore away from the quay as the CIA men kept up a continuous barrage with the MP5s. Before they had made it more than fifty feet, the white pickup truck accelerated straight toward them. They were close enough that Gideon could see the driver, slumped over the wheel, half his head blown off. The truck blasted off the end of the dock and plummeted into the ocean.

As they crossed the canal, Gideon spoke to the captain of the boat: "Drop Simpson off over there so he can get medical treatment." He pointed to the armored SMDF vehicle.

"Yes, sir."

As the powerful boat accelerated forward, Gideon verbalized the plan he had been forming since the chopper went down. "Could this boat make it to the Obelisk in this kind of weather?"

"She'll take you to the gates of hell, sir," he said laconically. "But without authorization . . ." The captain trailed off, looking questioningly at Simpson.

"Absolutely not," Simpson said. "Mr. Davis is going straight to the airport and flying directly back to Washington, D.C."

"Give me your SAT phone," Gideon said to Simpson.

"Excuse me?"

"Dial the embassy, then give me your phone."

Simpson grudgingly complied. Gideon identified himself to the operator at the embassy and asked to be patched through to the president.

Within a minute, he was speaking to Alton Diggs.

"Gideon," the president said, "I am glad to be talking to you."

"Thank you, sir. Can you give me an update on the Obelisk?" Gideon said.

"Then you already know about your brother. And about Earl."

"Yes, sir." Both men shared their personal concern for Earl Parker's life, then Gideon repeated what he'd seen on CNN, and what he'd been told by Simpson.

"I'm afraid it's gotten worse." The president continued after a tentative silence. "I ordered a SEAL team to take back the rig, but the mission failed. And now we've got twelve hours left to meet demands that we can never accommodate. To make matters even more difficult, there's a typhoon about to hit the rig. Our meteorologists are saying the Obelisk will be socked in for the next fifteen hours."

Gideon did the math. By the time the typhoon passed, the hostages would be dead.

The president quickly added, "But there may be a brief window for us to act."

"How?"

"Assuming the eye of the storm passes directly over the rig, we are going to drop a Delta Force team directly onto the deck of the rig. They're getting ready to take off from Hawaii."

Gideon took a moment to process the president's report. If Tillman was on that rig, the Delta Force guys wouldn't be there to take him prisoner. They'd be there to take him out.

"Mr. President, there may be another option," Gideon said.

"Another option?" the president said dubiously.

"Let me go out there myself."

"Go out where? To the rig?"

"Yes, sir. Let me talk to him."

"Your brother has made it very clear he's not negotiating."

"Not to me he hasn't. Once I'm face-to-face with him, maybe I can talk some sense into him."

"For God's sake, Gideon, your brother

tried to kill you."

Gideon said nothing, silenced by the stark truth of this. "Besides," the president continued, "even if I authorize this, you'll never make it out there. I told you, the rig's about to get swallowed by a category five typhoon."

"At least let me try to make it out there. With respect, sir, I think I've earned that chance."

This time it was the president who remained silent. "Whatever's going on with my brother, there's something we're missing, some reason behind what's happening that we can't see yet. I haven't figured out what it is, but I will."

Still, the president offered no response. So Gideon laid the rest of his argument on the line. "As I understand it, Mr. President, unless we take back that rig, you're going to be put in an impossible situation by McClatchy and his congressional cronies, and frankly by most of the people who put you in office. You'll be forced into a war you don't want to fight. There is zero downside to you letting me try this."

When the president finally spoke, his voice sounded weary and frayed. "Fine. If your brother is willing to talk to you, you have my blessing."

Gideon stared out at the sea, above which hung a low and leaden sky. Huge waves were pounding the jetty at the edge of the bay. But there was no rain, and the wind was not too bad. "Thank you, sir."

"Good luck," the president said, and disconnected.

Gideon clapped the phone shut, handed it back to Simpson. Then he turned to the boat captain. "The president has authorized me to go to the Obelisk," Gideon said. "You don't need me to explain how risky this is, so I don't expect you to put yourself in harm's way. I can pilot the boat myself."

"This boat?" The captain tossed his cigarette into the ocean. "Wherever she goes, I go." He was already pulling up to the dock on the far side of the canal. Several SMDF soldiers jumped aboard. One of them was a medic, and he began compressing Simpson's leg.

As the soldiers carried him out of the boat onto the SMDF vehicle, Simpson nodded weakly to Gideon, bidding him Godspeed. Before Gideon could reciprocate, the captain firewalled the throttle and the boat tore away from the pier.

CHAPTER TWENTY-ONE

The noise of the engines was deafening as the big boat barreled out of the bay and into the mountainous waves of the South China Sea.

The captain drove with one hand and dialed a knob on the radio with the other, a freshly lit cigarette perched on his lower lip. "Put the headphones on, sir," he said.

Gideon pulled on a pair of green headphones.

"Transmitting now."

Gideon thumbed the button on the edge of the microphone. "This is Gideon Davis hailing the Obelisk. Do you copy?"

Gideon released the button. He could barely make out the sound of static over the roar of the engines and the rush of the wind over the cockpit.

"Obelisk, do you copy?"

This time a voice came over the speaker, barely penetrating the static. "This is the

Obelisk."

"This is Gideon Davis. My brother is Tillman Davis. Who am I speaking with?"

The unidentified speaker answered with his own question. "Gideon Davis?"

Gideon heard the surprise in his voice. Whoever he was talking to probably assumed he was dead. "That's right."

"What do you want?"

"I've been authorized by the president of the United States to negotiate directly with my brother. I'm requesting permission to board the Obelisk."

The long subsequent pause was filled with static.

"Do you copy?" Gideon repeated.

"Permission granted," the voice said.

"Who am I speaking with?"

"You'll have safe passage to board the rig. Over." Again, the voice had avoided answering Gideon's question. But before Gideon could ask anything more, the transmission was cut off.

Gideon took off the headphones. The boat captain was regarding him expectantly. "Okay," Gideon said. "My brother says I can board the Obelisk."

Timken smiled as he set the radio microphone back in its cradle. He turned to Chun and said, "Bring up Mr. Parker. I need to talk to him."

Two minutes later, Parker entered the room.

"Well, I've got good news and bad news," Timken said.

"Stop smiling like a Cheshire cat and tell me the bad news first."

"My men never got to Gideon Davis. I don't know how, but he's still alive."

Earl Parker's gaze was stony. "What's the good news?"

"Guess who the president is sending to the oil rig to negotiate with Abu Nasir?"

Earl Parker's left eyebrow rose slightly.

"Sir, Gideon Davis is heading out here on a speedboat as we speak. He's been given . . ." Here Timken couldn't stifle an ironic grin. "He's been given Tillman Davis's personal guarantee of safe passage."

Earl Parker nodded. "Well done, Timken."

"I assume you want —"

"Of course I want him dead. The moment he's in range, take him out."

"Understood."

"You said that before, Timken. And here we are." Parker turned to Chun and said, "Take me back to the cabin."

"Sir, there's something else. That typhoon's about to hit us."

"That's good news," Parker said. "It means we don't have to worry about another assault dropping on our heads."

"Yeah, except that engineer I took out, Cole Ransom? He was coming here to check on the damping system that keeps the waves from tearing this rig apart."

Parker waited for more.

"Haven't you been hearing that noise? It's gotten worse since the storm picked up, and it may have something to do with the problems Ransom was coming here to fix." Timken pointed at the horizon. "Look at those waves. Soon we'll be in the middle of a cat five typhoon. I don't want to find out the hard way that this rig can't take the strain."

"This is a billion-dollar rig. It's not going to fall apart." But Parker saw that Timken wasn't mollified.

As if on cue, the floor shook, and deep noise welled up through the rig.

Parker conceded with a grudging nod. "Get the rig manager up here and talk to her about it."

"Yes, sir."

Parker started to leave but paused in the doorway. "Just make sure you don't screw up this time with Gideon Davis. He was supposed to be dead before this operation started."

CHAPTER TWENTY-TWO

An hour had passed since she'd been returned to the cabin, and Kate once again
found herself being escorted to the upper
deck by masked men. She felt the same
nauseating buzz of fear. Although her wrists
were cuffed behind her, she felt some small
consolation that they hadn't covered her
face with a hood this time. It wasn't much,
but she was grateful to have her bearings
and to be spared the indignity of bumping
into rails and pipes she couldn't see.

The jihadis prodded her forward, into the
control room, and her chest tightened at
what she saw through the windows. Yesterday, when the rig had been seized, the sky
had been a bright cheerful blue. Now it was
low and leaden, and a heavy rain pounded
the windows of the control room. To the
left of the stairs was the weather station —
rain gauge, digital thermometer, barometer,
and a wind speed gauge. Its propellors were

a blur, spinning so fast she couldn't see the individual blades.

Below the rig, the waves were looking nastier. She couldn't tell if they were actually higher than they had been — but the wind was shredding the tops, capping them with crests of white foam. It was a steady, hard wind now, blowing west-southwest without the slightest deviation. Just the sort of wind that made for big waves. Night had not yet fallen, and there was enough light that she could see darker clouds and a heavier sheet of rain bearing down on the rig.

She heard footsteps ringing on the metal deck. Striding toward her, the wind snatching at his uniform, was the American jihadi — Abu Nasir or Tillman Davis, or whatever his name was. The anger and frustration and fear that had been building for hours suddenly erupted from her.

"What did you do with my people?" Kate shouted at him. "I want to see them!"

One of the jihadis slammed her in the kidney with a rifle butt. The pain ran up her side, so sharp it made her nauseated. She lost her balance and fell to one knee. The American said something in a language she didn't understand, and the jihadi who'd hit her hoisted her to her feet.

"That's not going to happen, Ms. Murphy. The reason I brought you up here, I've got a couple questions about the damping system. I keep hearing that clunking noise, and I want to know if I should be concerned."

Kate looked at him point-blank and said, "Yeah. You should be."

"How concerned?"

"Very." Kate gave him a brief history of the problems with the damping system. She nodded out the window toward the horizon. "That typhoon may take down the rig if we don't fix it first."

She was hoping to rattle him, and she could see that she had. But before he could ask her anything more, Abu Nasir was interrupted by a big Asian guy who looked more Korean than Mohanese. "Gideon Davis is hailing us again."

"What does he want now?"

"Confirmation that you're giving him safe passage."

Abu Nasir nodded. "Tell him what he wants to hear," he said.

The Asian guy ran back down the stairs toward the drill deck. The Obelisk's radio, Kate knew, was located in the control room on the drill deck.

Abu Nasir turned back to Kate. "Ever

hear of Gideon Davis?"

Kate didn't answer. She had, of course, heard of Gideon Davis. You couldn't read a newspaper or turn on the TV without seeing Gideon Davis's face.

"We're brothers." The bearded American smiled. "Ironic, huh?"

Kate sighed.

"Am I boring you? Maybe if one of my men tuned you up a little, you'd be more interested in my witty observations." Abu Nasir laughed. "Well, anyway, the president of the United States has just sent him out to negotiate with us."

"Good," Kate said.

"The thing about my brother, we never got along. Every time we talk, we end up in a fight. So I'm wondering if talking to him would be . . . what's the word I'm looking for? Unproductive?"

As Abu Nasir was talking, several of his men came up on the deck and began setting up a large machine gun on a tripod near the edge of the chopper deck.

The American turned back toward Kate with a shrug. "Honestly, at this point, what would we gain by a bunch of chitchat? Once I'm done here, we're going to sit down and you're going to tell me how to fix that damping system."

A cry from one of his men drew his attention to the far side of the chopper deck. Several other calls followed. The jihadis were pointing out into the sea.

Blasting toward them out of the white-capped seas was a boat. Given the crazy size of the waves, it seemed a very small and vulnerable craft. But the boat was obviously powerful and was banging through the turbulent waves toward them at a high speed. Kate could make out two people on board. One was piloting the boat and the other was crouched in the bow. The man in the bow was waving at the rig, his hands moving deliberately, unhurried.

"I'll be right back," he told her as he started toward the far side of the platform where the jihadis had just finished setting up the heavy machine gun, oblivious to the driving rain.

As the boat got closer, the American leaned over the machine gunner. "On my signal, light him up."

Kate was sickened. This monster was going to murder his own brother.

The machine gunner leaned forward.

"Not yet." Abu Nasir yanked the gunner's shoulder. "Wait." Abu Nasir lifted his finger in the air, keeping it suspended for another thirty seconds, then dropping it decisively.

"Now."

The noise of the machine gun was astonishing. The cartridges were the size of small bananas, and the concussion rattled her ribs.

The boat veered away from the trail of bullet splashes in the water and disappeared behind the face of a huge wave.

The noise resumed, shell casings cascading onto the deck as the mouth of the big gun spit fire at a thousand feet per second.

The boat swerved again. The burst of gunfire missed the boat, but just barely, and then the boat wheeled, heading up the face of the next wave. As powerful as it was, the vessel had to strain to make it up the wave. Its speed dropped precipitously. The big engines howled as it raced the track of bullets chasing after it.

In the end, the race was no contest. The bullets caught up to the boat, chewed through the stern, set one of its engines on fire, then hit the boat pilot. One moment he was a human being, and the next he was a scrambled mass of blood and tissue, sliding across the deck along with a wash of seawater. It was the most horrific thing Kate had ever seen. Her entire body was trembling.

The crippled boat heeled to the right and headed straight toward the rig, the bullets still smashing it to pieces. The man in the prow was still alive though, crouching like a swimmer about to dive off a cliff. To Kate's shock, he leapt straight from the boat into the ocean. The boat disappeared from view, obscured by the bulk of the rig. She heard a terrible rending crunch, and the entire rig shook. The boat must have hit one of the massive concrete piers holding it up. A fireball appeared briefly, replaced by a cloud of inky smoke, which was immediately ripped apart by the wind.

"Shoot him!" Abu Nasir shouted.

Every jihadi on the chopper platform leaned over the edge and began firing down into the water.

Kate looked around. Her two guards had moved to the side and were blasting away with their AK-47s.

Nobody was paying her the slightest attention.

Now was her chance. Now or never.

She sat down on the wet deck and wriggled her hips until the rain-slick wrist cuffs passed under her butt. From there it was a simple matter of pulling her heels in and passing her arms in front of her.

Then she stood and sprinted to the door, down the stairs to the D Deck as the guns continued firing.

There was no one between her and the

bridge leading to the other section of the rig. She glanced back, saw a man in the water, bullets splashing all around him. The remains of the shattered boat were pressed up against one of the massive concrete piers. Without flagging, she sprinted — as best she could with her arms cuffed — across the metal bridge toward the Bridge Linked Platform. Someone shouted. Bullets thudded into the metal behind her. She reached the other side, diving for cover behind a steel beam.

As she considered what to do next, her eyes fell toward the sea. She scanned the rolling waves for a sign that anyone on the boat had survived.

The boat was gone, every shred of it. And so was Gideon Davis.

CHAPTER TWENTY-THREE

Gideon loved to swim. Always had. He loved water, loved the beach, loved lakes and pools and the ocean.

But this was like being in the foothills of some strange mountain range, where every hill was alive, moving.

When you were caught in surf this heavy, there was only one strategy that would keep you from getting crushed. You had to dive. Get underneath the wave, where its motion wasn't quite so violent. So that's what he needed to do here. He knew that he'd have one chance. The current wasn't all that fast, but if he missed the rig, got carried past it, he'd drift on to the west . . . and that would be that. The South China Sea was fairly warm, so it would take a while to die.

Well, best not to think of it. He bobbed to the top of the wave, its ragged crest washing over his head, nearly choking him. And as the wave rolled away, he slid down the back side, where a bullet pierced the water a few inches from his face.

He took a bead on the big concrete leg of the rig and dove into the water, swimming down and down further still, until his ears popped.

The saltwater burned his eyes. But he had to force them open or he'd swim past the oil rig's leg.

The sun had just set, but there was still some light left in the leaden sky. Once he was underwater, though, everything went dark. He stroked on and on in the direction he believed that he'd find the rig. But he couldn't see it.

Why had they shot at him? The man Gideon had spoken to on the radio had said that Tillman had given him safe passage. The sting of betrayal Gideon felt was even worse when he pictured the bullet-chewed body of the intrepid boat pilot. It didn't make sense. Had some of Tillman's men taken matters into their own hands and fired on him despite Tillman's orders? Had something prevented Tillman from giving the orders to his men? Or had Tillman ordered his men to finish the job they'd failed to complete in the jungle? Maybe the president was right after all, and Gideon had finally overplayed his hand.

Now wasn't the time to try to figure out what had happened.

His lungs were burning. A tiny worm of panic began to burrow up from the back of his brain.

Stay calm. Keep stroking. All around him, a murky darkness.

Where was it? Where was the rig?

CHAPTER TWENTY-FOUR

Two jihadis were racing across the bridge from the drilling platform toward Kate on the BLP when the fireball erupted.

One of the bullets they'd fired at her as she ran across the bridge had hit a gas line. The first jihadi onto the bridge was blown off the span and into the ocean. The other backed up screaming, his hair and shirt on fire.

There were twenty-six main pipes, eight-inch and four-inch schedule 40 steel, running across the bridge from the BLP to the Wellhead Service Unit. Half were for drilling mud, the carefully engineered goo that was used to lubricate and cool the drill bit as it ground its way down through the rock beneath the surface of the ocean. The other pipes conducted oil and gas to the various receptacles and processing facilities on the rig. If the bullets had hit oil or mud, nothing would have happened. But gas was combustible.

The big ball of fire had subsided, but a steady gout of flame eight or ten feet long was shooting across the walkway. The sun had set now, and so the fire threw a weird, shifting light across the rig that barely managed to pierce the driving rain. Nobody was going to be crossing there for a while. Eventually the terrorists would figure out how to shut off the valve, or — if enough time passed — the holding tank would run out. Either way the jihadis would cross over and come after her.

The good news was that until that time, she was free.

The jihadis had stopped firing. But right now she was stuck behind a steel I beam, her hands still cuffed together with plastic flex cuffs. If she stood there until the gas leak burned out, they'd eventually nail her. There was no knowing how much gas was in the holding tank. Total capacity was around twenty thousand cubic feet, but generally they just pumped it directly to the A reservoir on the BLP. So it might have no more than a few hundred cubic feet. The flame was probably burning a hundred cubic feet a minute. At best, she had thirty minutes before the jet of flame petered out.

Over on the other side she heard voices

speaking English. She couldn't make out everything they were saying. But she heard the words *transfer valve*. Apparently the jihadis had brought somebody who had experience on a rig. They were obviously going to track down the valve and shut it off.

She looked to her left. The doorway into the BLP's main stairs was about four yards away. She knew the jihadis would be waiting for her to make a move so they could pick her off. For a moment she froze, her entire body gripped by a straitjacket of fear. She really didn't want to die.

But she had to do something. Her people were over there, and right now she was the only person who had a chance of helping them. But she couldn't do them any good if she was dead. She had to seek cover so she could rally and come up with a plan.

Could they see her in the deepening darkness? She wasn't sure. As she dove for the door, her question was answered: gunshots erupted from the drilling platform, spanging off the bulkhead. It sounded like somebody was throwing wrenches at her.

And then she was through the bulkhead, falling, rolling painfully into a heap.

The shooting stopped.

She charged down the stairs to D Deck,

then pushed open the green door with the giant *D* stenciled on it. All the walls on D Deck were painted green. Pipes snaked everywhere. Unlike the other decks, D had no solid floor. Instead the "floor" was a tight grid of welded steel through which you could see straight down into the water.

Kate had spent much of her adult life on oil rigs, so big seas didn't generally bother her. But these waves were like nothing she'd ever seen. From her view, she couldn't see the horizon, couldn't see the water with normal perspective. Looking straight down, you couldn't really make out the waves as such. Instead, it was like some vast, dark elevator made of water, rising and falling below her.

Normal distance between rig bottom and sea level was fifty-eight feet. So she knew that she was well out of range of the waves. And yet each time the water began rising toward her, she felt as though it would just keep coming, rising and rising until it came boiling through the floor.

As she looked up something in the corner of her view caught her attention. For a moment she wasn't sure what it was. A dark flash in the white foam.

By the time she looked at it, it was gone. She scanned the water. Had it been her imagination? Then, there it was: as the water fell away, she spotted a man. In the gathering gloom she could only barely make him out. He was clinging to the barnacle-encrusted pier — the third giant leg of the rig.

It was the man from the boat, the one who'd jumped over the side — Gideon Davis.

The concrete pier was about fifteen feet in circumference. Way too big around to encircle with your arms. How he was holding on, she couldn't imagine. He must have literally been holding on with his fingernails. The wave continued to sink farther and farther from the man's feet. If he fell now, he'd surely be washed away on the next wave.

A flicker of light from the burning gas on the bridge illuminated him briefly. The muscles in his shoulders were corded with effort as he struggled to maintain his grip. He was a powerfully built man, obviously in good shape. Still, she could see he wouldn't be able to hold on much longer.

The waves must have been running over a hundred feet from peak to peak. Maybe ten seconds between troughs. Could he hold on for that long? Suddenly some frothy chop hit him, and he disappeared from view. She looked frantically for the man.

The water started rising again. *Where was he?*

Just as she was about to give up hope, his head broke water. If she had been in his situation, she would have been thrashing wildly. But Gideon Davis showed no sign of desperation or fear. He moved carefully, almost methodically — bracing himself, letting the current press him against the concrete, and push him slowly upward. It was then that she realized his dilemma.

In his current position, he was invisible to the jihadis on the other platform. But once he came around to the other side of the F strut, they could shoot him. Plus, with nothing to hold on to, he'd be in danger of being swept away by the current. He'd have to time things perfectly, make it all the way around while the wave was in the trough, if he was to have any hope of reaching the ladder. And even then, he'd be in serious danger of being shot.

"Hey!" she called — hoping that the jihadis on the other platform wouldn't be able to hear her voice over the howl of the wind and the thunder of the waves.

The man looked up, when a small crosswave hit him, bounced him off the barnacled concrete. She knew from her experience as a diver that those barnacles were like a pile of razor blades. He grimaced.

"Hold on!" she shouted.

She ran back to the bulkhead near the stairs, where an emergency kit hung from the wall. Fire extinguisher, axe, pry bar . . . and a life ring with a couple hundred feet of nylon rope. She quickly severed her flex cuffs on the axe, then grabbed the life ring and turned back to look for the man. Only his head was visible now. Kate flung open one of the hatches under her feet. Now there was nothing between her and the water. The wave was still rising. In moments his head would go under.

She hoped he would stay on the back side of the pier so that the jihadis on the other side of the rig couldn't see him — or shoot at him.

Then his head disappeared beneath the cross-chop on the waves.

She dropped the life ring and waited to see if he would resurface.

The wind caught the life ring and carried it past where the man had been. It was getting darker by the minute, harder for her to see him. Suddenly his head resurfaced out of the foam.

The life ring, pushed by the wind, was just out of reach. He stretched for it, his fingertips nearly grazing the ring. Stretching for the ring had stolen his concentration on maintaining his position on the big concrete strut, though, and the current caught him. He grabbed wildly for the pier, but now the current had him. It was the first time he had demonstrated anything close to fear.

Kate's heart pounded. The wind whipped at the life ring, throwing it up into the air. She lowered another loop of rope, then yanked it sharply, trying to pull the ring closer to the man. He was now scrabbling at the edge of the pier, the rising face of the wave trying to force him past the big slab of concrete. The life ring flopped wildly in the wind.

Just when Kate thought it was hopeless, the wind slackened for the briefest of moments, dropping pressure on the life ring. It plummeted, falling with an audible plastic thump on the man's head.

He grabbed it, clamping hold.

She was tempted to yell encouragement, but she didn't want to alert the jihadis as to what she was doing. Besides, Gideon Davis didn't seem to need encouragement. As soon as he reached the ring, he pulled it over his head and under his arms. The water spun him around.

Her momentary rush of pleasure at saving

the man from being swept away was replaced by concern. She was a fit woman.
But lifting a couple hundred pounds of dead
weight through fifty feet of air? There was
no way.

She pulled with all her strength. Then her
feet slipped on the wet decking and she fell,
hanging halfway off the hatch. The rope,
with all the man's weight on it, began to
slip, pulling her inexorably toward open air.

No good deed goes unpunished, she
thought. Here she was, trying to save this
guy's life, and now she was going to get
dragged into the ocean right along with
him. At the last moment, though, her feet
regained purchase, and she was able to stop.

If only she had something mechanical to
haul him up with. Then it struck her. There
was a hydraulic winch over on the other side
of the platform. All she had to do was at-
tach the rope and winch the man right up
out of the water.

She snaked the rope over a piece of pipe,
then ran over to the winch and made three
quick loops around the drive shaft. It was
going to be painfully slow, but it *should*
work.

She thumbed the large green button next
to the winch, then hit the lever again. The

shaft began to turn, slowly taking up the rope.

Through the steel mesh under her feet, she could see Gideon starting to rise into the air. He swung in a slow arc through the air, his body the weight on the end of a pendulum.

His progress upward was painfully slow. Each revolution of the shaft only pulled the rope a few inches.

Luckily the wind was pushing Gideon Davis toward the pier, so that he was not visible to the jihadis on the other platform. The darkness and driving rain, too, were working in their favor, obscuring the vision of everyone on the rig.

As he got closer to the hatch, it became impossible for her to see him anymore. She grew worried as he started getting closer to the hatch. If she pulled him too far, the inexorable power of the hydraulic winch could wedge him against the hatch frame. In which case the rope would cut him in half.

"Yell when you get to the top," she called, hoping the sound of the wind and waves would drown her voice and keep her from being heard by the jihadis.

There was a brief silence. Then she heard his voice. "Five more feet," he shouted.

300

"Three . . . two . . . okay, stop!"

She pulled back on the hydraulic lever, and the rope stopped. She searched for the *off* button, which, for some reason, was not located next to the *on* button. Finally she found it. As she turned, the man crawled from the hatch and lay down exhausted on the deck. Now that she could see his face clearly, she could see that it was definitely Gideon Davis. He was a mess, though, bleeding from his face all the way down his chest. The barnacles had sliced him up pretty nicely.

She couldn't tell if he was in the line of fire from the other part of the rig, so she grabbed him and propelled him to shelter behind the bulkhead at the center of the deck.

Gideon Davis wiped the blood and seawater from his face. "Thank you," he gasped. "You must be Kate Murphy."

"And you must be the cavalry," she said.

Gideon squinted at her, unsure whether she was being facetious. "I'm afraid so," he said wearily.

"Well, I sure hope you brought a gun." She regarded him soberly. "Because that's the only way any of us are getting off this rig alive."

Chapter Twenty-Five

Gideon recognized the woman who rescued him as the hostage he had seen on CNN. Even under these circumstances, Kate Murphy looked more beautiful in person than she had on television. But he had to focus. She was asking him what efforts were being made to rescue her crew. Gideon explained the president's plan to insert a Delta team through the eye of the hurricane eleven hours from now.

She looked at her watch. "That's cutting it close to Abu Nasir's deadline," she said, adding, "and it assumes that the eye of the hurricane passes directly overhead. Meanwhile, there's a bomb on my rig."

"I know." Gideon stood slowly on his rubbery legs. "Which is why I need to get to Abu Nasir."

"For what possible reason?"

"So I can talk some sense into him. He's my brother," Gideon said in a voice that contained equal parts shame and defiance.

"I know." She described everything that had happened until now, how she had been on the chopper deck with Abu Nasir when he targeted Gideon's approaching boat, and how the incident had distracted the jihadis long enough for her to escape.

"I'm still having a hard time believing my brother is doing this. I know him."

"Maybe not as well as you think you do. I heard him give the order to blow you out of the water!" Her voice rose to a shout. "I'm sorry, your brother told his men to kill you. I can't say it any plainer than that." The rig manager was one of those women whose beauty was only accentuated by anger. Her high cheekbones were flushed, and her green eyes flashed.

Gideon still couldn't reconcile the man who had just ordered him killed with the big brother who had always been his protector. Even when they'd fought, Tillman had always stood between Gideon and anyone who would harm him. But as much as he wanted to deny or rationalize what he'd been told, the evidence against Tillman was overwhelming. The pain of that acknowledgment was almost physical. He felt something seizing up in his chest, like a fist tightening around his heart.

As much as Gideon wanted to confront Tillman face-to-face, to at least try to figure out what was going through his mind, what tortured thinking had brought him to this terrible place, Kate Murphy was right — now was not the time for talking. As long as Tillman had the bomb, he was in control. Gideon's immediate goal was clear. Whatever it took, he had to stop his brother before any more innocent people died.

"All right then," Gideon said. "We've got to disarm that bomb." Gideon asked her, point-blank, "Do you know where they planted it?"

Kate frowned. "Even if we manage to find this bomb, would you know how to defuse it?"

"I've cleared a few land mines and IEDs over the years," Gideon said, not wanting to waste another moment talking about his experience. Kate nodded uncertainly as Gideon asked again, "So do you have any idea where this bomb might be?"

"When your brother took over the rig, he ordered his men to wheel this big metal case off the chopper."

"You think the bomb was in that case?"

"At the time I couldn't figure out what it was. But when they forced me to read their demands, I made the connection. I saw them using the crane to winch it down the drill shaft."

"Then you didn't actually see where they took it."

"Somewhere on D Deck . . ." Kate trailed off and shook her head ruefully.

"You know this rig better than anyone, where it's most vulnerable structurally." Something about Gideon's voice calmed her mind, made her feel safe. "If you wanted to take down this rig with a bomb, where would you plant it?"

Kate thought for a moment, then said, "Let me show you something." He followed her to a peculiar object cantilevered off the side of the deck. It looked like an elongated egg made of Day-Glo orange plastic, about twenty feet long and eight feet in diameter.

"What is this?" he asked.

"An escape pod. It's got a weighted keel, so it'll float in the roughest waters. The egg shape makes it ungodly tough. There's a transponder, a signal beacon, a radio, and five days' worth of food and water for fifteen people. There's also a schematic of the rig."

Attached to the wall was a schematic of the Obelisk marked with red and green arrows to show fire drill and escape plans. Kate traced one section with a slender finger. "This is the D Deck, the lowest above-water section on the rig. The struts that support the rig are made of reinforced concrete. They terminate here at D Deck, and the superstructure of the rig is held on top with a set of very large bolts. If a bomb took out those bolts, you wouldn't have to blow up the whole rig. The superstructure would shear off the struts under the pressure of the waves."

"And the rig slides into the ocean," Gideon said. She nodded grimly.

"Show me exactly where those bolts are."

Gideon scrutinized the point on the schematic that Kate indicated, a room labeled D-4. "That's on the other part of the rig, right?"

"The drilling platform, yeah."

Gideon looked at the narrow steel bridge that connected the section they stood on with the drilling platform. A steady gout of fire was still burning from the damaged gas pipe. "And that bridge is the only way for us to get to the drilling platform?"

Kate nodded. "It's also the only thing keeping the bad guys from getting over here." Beyond the fire, Gideon saw the jihadis, some of them patrolling, a clutch of them still trying to close down the gas line that was feeding the fire.

"How soon before that fire burns out?"

"Twenty minutes. Maybe sooner."

"And there's really no other way to get onto the platform except over that bridge?"

"Not unless you want to climb under it." The rig manager didn't realize the significance of what she'd said until she actually said it. She squinted into the blinding rain and frowned. "Which may not be as crazy as it sounds . . ."

"What are you talking about?"

"See how the bridge is made? It's a series of trusses with a steel deck on top. If you're willing to risk slipping in the rain, getting blown off by the wind, and falling sixty feet into those waves, we *might* be able to sneak across there without them seeing us."

Gideon looked out at the narrow bridge. Its struts extended from the side of the rig. He'd have to clamber up onto the railing, then stretch to reach the struts. The wind was blowing unmercifully now, gusting at well over fifty miles an hour. Maybe more. Far from optimal conditions to be swinging from one wet piece of steel to another. Gideon tried comforting himself with the thought that the rain would at least limit the jihadis' visibility, even as he realized that crossing beneath the bridge was his only option.

Gideon turned back to Kate, who was

shrugging out of her fluorescent yellow jumpsuit. Within seconds, she was down to a pair of nylon shorts and a bra. Her body was lean and athletic.

Gideon raised an eyebrow as he looked from the yellow jumpsuit crumpled on the deck to the woman who had been wearing it only a few moments ago.

"If I wear that, I may as well be wearing a neon sign," she said. "I'm not about to give those sons of bitches a target to shoot at."

"Maybe you should just hide in the escape pod," he said. "No point putting both of us in danger."

"Hide in some plastic egg while my crew's lives are on the line? I don't think so," she said. "Besides, you'll need my help. I know this rig better than anyone. Your words."

She was right. Even if she weren't, Gideon understood intuitively that this was not a woman who could be easily talked out of something once she'd made up her mind.

Kate balled up the jumpsuit and tossed it overboard. "You're sure you know how to defuse that bomb?"

Gideon looked back at the bridge. The gas fire was a few feet lower than it had been just moments earlier. "The fire's dying," he snapped. "We'd better get going."

"You didn't answer my question," she said.

"I know."

CHAPTER TWENTY-SIX

Gideon's father had never spoken to his sons about his military service. He had no scrapbooks full of photos of his war buddies, no framed medals hanging on the walls of his office. For a man who spent so much time around guns, it would have seemed a near certainty that he would have mentioned his time in the military at least once.

But he hadn't.

So it had come as a surprise to Gideon and Tillman when they discovered their father had requested to be buried in Arlington National Cemetery. They were sitting in a lawyer's office during the reading of his will.

"Uh . . . don't you have to be a veteran or something?" Gideon said.

Mr. Faircloth, the attorney, had looked up and raised one eyebrow. "Your father served in the United States Marine Corps for four years, son. You were aware of that, were you not?"

The boys had looked at him blankly.

Afterward Tillman and Gideon had discussed it. "Four years in the Corps and he never told us?" Gideon said.

"Maybe he got thrown out for punching an officer or something," Tillman ventured. "I mean, why wouldn't he have told us unless he did something bad?"

Gideon shook his head. "I don't know, but they wouldn't let him get buried there if he'd been dishonorably discharged."

"I don't really give a damn either way," Tillman said. "The bastard killed our mother. As far as I'm concerned, he can rot in a pauper's grave."

Although Gideon shared Tillman's anger, Tillman shared none of Gideon's curiosity. The incident in Mr. Faircloth's office had made him wonder what else their father had hidden from them.

But the two brothers never spoke about their father. From the moment Gideon had joined his brother on the front steps — the bodies of their parents lying in the house behind them — it was as if they had made some unspoken pact to draw a curtain over the past. The life they'd had before was gone, buried along with their parents.

Looking back, Gideon couldn't recall a

single conversation during which they had discussed their father. Sometimes they would reminisce about their mother, but mentioning their father was strictly off limits — what he'd done during his life, the kind of man he'd been, or the way he'd died.

And yet year after year, Gideon had held on to the box his father had kept in his safe with the words FOR MY BOYS written on top in thick block letters. Tillman had wanted to throw it away. So Gideon had kept taking it with him wherever he lived, from dorm room to apartment, but he never looked inside. Sometimes he thought he couldn't bring himself to look inside the box because he was afraid of what he'd find, some dark secret about his past he didn't want to face. Or maybe he just needed to wait until some time had passed, when he didn't feel quite so angry at the old man.

Eventually, the right moment came.

Gideon had been working at the UN for almost a year and dating Miriam Pierce for half that time. Raised on the Upper West Side of Manhattan as the only child of high-powered corporate lawyers, Miriam had forsaken the law to become a successful freelance photographer. She had been hired by Gideon's publisher to take the jacket photo for his first book. After their session,

Miriam joked that he'd been the most difficult subject she'd ever photographed, and Gideon confessed that he hated having his picture taken. Which was true. But what he didn't tell her was how distracted he'd been by her beauty. He mustered the courage to ask her to dinner, and they found themselves walking and talking through Central Park until well into the night. Their connection was instant and intense. Miriam asked questions about Gideon, direct but not invasive, and he was struck by how comfortable he felt telling her about himself. Even the hard things. And she made him laugh as she described her own colorful life as the daughter of overachievers. Because she'd been left alone as a little girl for hours at a time, her imagination had become her only companion, and she took herself around the world within the confines of her bedroom.

Six months after they'd started dating, he'd stepped into her Gramercy Park apartment. "They're sending me to Cambodia next week," he said.

"Congratulations," she said.

"One of the Tampuan guerillas has agreed to sit down with me and hash out terms for a cease-fire," he said. "Assuming he's not lying through his teeth and trying to rearm his militia, I may be able to back-channel a deal with the minister of defense."

Although she had been smiling, the corners of her slate gray eyes lowered slightly, as if pulled down by an invisible thread. It was the sad, knowing smile of a patient woman who was bracing herself for bad news she's been expecting for a long time.

"You're breaking up with me," she said.

Gideon didn't say anything for a moment. He *had* come to break up with her. He reminded her that he'd already been absent for two of the six months since they'd been seeing each other, and he wasn't sure how long he'd be away this time. Not that he hadn't warned her when they'd started seeing each other. Their first night together in Central Park, he told her bluntly that his work wasn't compatible with being in a long-term relationship, and that he'd resigned himself to living his life alone. Miriam had accepted it then, and she accepted it now, without self-pity, and with a grace that made Gideon miss her before he'd even left the apartment. Her only regret, she said, was that she had allowed herself to fall in love with him.

"Good luck trying to save the world, Gideon. You'll do great."

Trying to save the world.

Said with not even a hint of irony. As

absurd as it sounded, Gideon sincerely felt that he *was* trying to save the world. Or at least save as many lives as he could. A naive project, maybe, but one that required the freedom to leave on a moment's notice and to stay away for long periods. And so he had ended his relationship with Miriam Pierce as he had with so many other women, without any words of consolation other than to say that he was sorry.

As he left the apartment, she closed the door behind him. He heard the lock snick closed behind him.

Gideon stood for a moment, unable to move, rooted there by a sudden and deep loneliness that descended over him like a shadow. He raised his fist to knock on her door, ready to tell Miriam that he'd changed his mind, but he stopped himself. This breakup felt like more than just another casualty of Gideon's outsize ambition to save the world. Standing there, he realized that his decision to keep the people who cared about him at arm's length came at a steeper price than he'd ever acknowledged, even to himself.

Twenty minutes later, he was sitting on his neatly made bed, taking off his shoes and lying back on the hard pillow, his necktie still tight and perfectly knotted. As he lay staring at the ceiling, Gideon felt drained and vaguely restless. He looked around the room. He'd been living here for nearly two years, and yet there were no family photos on the wall, no artwork, nothing that would tell you anything about the individual who lived here. It could just as well have been a hotel room, or some rent-by-the-month apartment in a strange city.

He found himself walking to the spare bedroom and looking in the nearly empty closet. In the back of the closet lay the container with the words FOR MY BOYS written in thick marker across the top. Inside was a smaller, older box, its sides worn and creased with age. He took the box back to his bedroom and set it in the middle of the bed.

He stared at the box for a long time before he finally opened it.

Inside were several small stacks of photographs, each held together by a brittle rubber band. The first set showed his father as a boy and as a very young man. Gideon's father — only a teenager, his hair slicked back — grinning as he stood next to an early 1960s Chevy. What struck Gideon was that he'd never seen his father smile like that. A big, fat, shit-eating grin. The few times his father had smiled, it was usually hard, grudging, and slightly bitter.

The next set were photos of his father and mother. Again, they just looked so . . . *happy.* Gideon couldn't quite fathom it, his father in a tux with a cockeyed boutonniere, his mother laughing, her head thrown back, showing off her throat. Another picture showed her pressed up against his father, who held her like he was protecting her from all the ugliness of the world. He'd never seen them look happy like that. Especially not together. Not once.

The second sheaf of pictures were Marine Corps photos. On top was a young man, posing proudly in his dress uniform. It looked like it had been taken right after basic training. Behind that were more pictures from his time as a marine, one of them showing his father arm in arm with Uncle Earl, whom Gideon suddenly realized had probably taken most of these photographs. Gideon checked the inscriptions on the back as he worked his way slowly through them. Mostly early 1965. The first few were taken in the United States, then later pictures were obviously in Vietnam. But he continued to be the same grinning kid in picture after picture.

Until the last picture. Gideon barely recognized the boy. It was the same boy . . .

and yet, it wasn't. It wasn't just that he was unshaven, or that his uniform was worn and covered with mud, or that his left leg and torso were wrapped in bandages. It was something in the boy's eyes — a darkness that Gideon recognized all too well.

It was that dark, distant expression — anger buried under a hard, dead-eyed veneer. The young private carried an M-60 machine gun across his stomach, his hands cradling it with the same soft, loving familiarity that his father always used when holding his guns.

This is the man I knew, Gideon thought.

It was the last photograph in the stack. He flipped it over. 1966. In a year, he'd gone from a grinning kid to . . . *this.*

Now the bed was empty, except for a small blue rectangular case. It resembled a jeweler's case for a diamond necklace. Only, this case was embossed with the seal of the United States of America.

Gideon opened it. Inside was a small star-shaped medal attached to a pale blue ribbon.

He knew what it was, knew immediately, and yet he couldn't believe it.

Folded on top of the medal was a yellowed piece of paper. He unfolded it and read it once, then a second time, then a third.

When he was done reading, he picked up his phone and dialed the last number he had for Tillman. A man answered, but the line was so full of static that the answering voice was inaudible.

"Tillman?" Gideon said. "Tillman, can you hear me?"

The man's voice was lost in the noise, but Gideon was so excited that he couldn't wait to share with his brother what he'd found.

"I opened the box Dad left us."

There was more crackling.

"Listen to this," he said, not knowing if he was reading to his brother, to a stranger, or to an empty line. "At the top, it says 'citation.' Then it says this:

"Rank and Organization: Private First Class, U.S. Marine Corps, First Battalion, Seventh Marines, First Marine Division (Rein.). Place and Date: Thua Thien Province, Vietnam. March 10, 1966. Entered service at: Washington, D.C. Born: 13 September 1945, Staunton, Virginia. Citation: For conspicuous gallantry and courage at the risk of his life above and beyond the call of duty. In the course of a routine patrol, Pfc. Davis's platoon was ambushed by a company-sized force of NVA regulars. Eleven marines were killed and three of the five survivors wounded. Pfc. Davis ordered Pfc. Earl Parker to retreat with the surviving members of the platoon, remaining behind to lay down cover fire. A superior and judicious marksman, Pfc. Davis killed the enemy company commander, three sergeants, a machine gunner, and a mortar team before his ammunition was exhausted and his position was rushed by the remaining enemy forces. Armed with only his sidearm and a grenade, Pfc. Davis engaged in fierce hand-to-hand combat, killing all five enemy soldiers, while sustaining a bayonet wound, a gunshot wound, multiple shrapnel wounds, and a broken ankle. He then crossed two kilometers of steep and muddy terrain, eventually reaching his base at dawn. Through his efforts, Pfc. Davis saved the surviving members of his platoon from certain destruction by a well-trained and numerically superior force. Pfc. Davis's extensive injuries required nearly a year of convalescence. His courageous initiative and heroic spirit of self-sacrifice reflect the noblest traditions of the Marine Corps and the U.S. Naval Service."

"Dad won the Medal of Honor," Gideon said. "Tillman?"

There was no reply. The line was dead. Gideon wondered how long he'd been reading into the void.

He tried dialing again, but all he got was a strange busy signal.

He picked up the last two pictures and looked at them. There weren't more than twelve months separating the grinning kid on the car from the busted-up veteran in the final photo. Which one of those people was the real man? Had their father's heroic action in Vietnam twisted that sweet, grinning young man into a monster? Or had the dead-eyed killer been hiding beneath a bogus smile for the first eighteen years of his life?

Gideon closed the case, put the case back in the small box, put the small box back in the big box, and put the big box back in the closet.

Then he lay down on his bed and stared at the shadows moving on the ceiling until the sun came up.

CHAPTER TWENTY-SEVEN

Chun was looking for the woman, patrolling the stairs adjacent to the bridge, when he saw something out of the corner of his eye, a flash of motion near the base of the bridge over on the BLP side. At least he *thought* he saw something. When he looked over, he saw nothing but the rain being blown nearly sideways by the wind. Not that he could see much of anything in this weather. It was probably just rain swirling near one of the lights mounted underneath the rig.

Chun reached C Deck and found one of his men, Muammar, struggling with the handle of a huge steel valve at the edge of the bridge. They'd managed to close one of the feeder valves, but this one was stuck.

"The valve's stuck, sir," Muammar shouted, the wind whipping at his clothes.

Chun pushed the smaller man aside, gave the wheel a yank. It grabbed for a second, then broke free and turned easily. He spun the wheel hard. The flame in the middle of the bridge died to nothing, then winked out.

"Go!" Chun shouted. "Find the woman." Following his men across the bridge, Chun scanned for the woman in the yellow jumpsuit.

They'd made it only halfway across the bridge when Gideon heard the hissing jet of flame die out above them. He expected the jihadis would be crossing soon, but not this quickly. His heart thumped as he felt the vibration of their boots clattering across the bridge above them. He knew they couldn't see or hear him. But still, they were only heart-stopping inches away from him and from Kate, who continued to slither through the network of wet steel toward the far side of the bridge.

The steel was cold and slick with water, and the wind shook the bridge with every gust as they inched their way across. The trusses were about a foot and a half from top to bottom, with X-shaped rods connecting the top and bottom members. There was barely enough room for Gideon's broad shoulders to slip through the gaps. Because Kate was slimmer and more flexible than he was, she slid through without much trouble, the distance between them increasing by the minute.

Below them, the foam-capped mountains of water rose and fell. One slip and they'd be dead. Gideon knew he'd been lucky to make it up to the Obelisk after his boat was shot to pieces. If he fell now, he wouldn't get a second chance. Even if he survived the fall into the ocean, the current would drag him off in a heartbeat, leaving the waves to drown him at their leisure.

"Hurry!" Kate hissed. "Once they realize we're not over on the Bridge Linked Platform, somebody will figure out where we are."

Gideon eyed the far side of the bridge grimly. He still had a good sixty yards to go. His hands were already aching, and his shoulders were bruised from squeezing through the tight gaps in the bracing.

A white-flecked mountain of water reared up slowly from below him, threatening for a moment to overwhelm them. Like other surges so far, it finally subsided and slid away. He forced himself on, pushing through a gap, reaching out perilously far to the next strut, grasping the next piece of cold slippery metal and —

CLUNK.

A strange vibration ran through the entire rig.

"What's that?" he hissed.

"I'll explain later, just keep moving," she said. She was watching him intently now, as though she was concerned he wasn't going to make it.

Fifty yards. Forty. Thirty.

Gideon's pace was agonizingly slow. And the wind was blowing appreciably harder by the minute. The only good thing about the bad weather was that it gave them cover. Even if the jihadis looked in the right place, Kate and Gideon would be hard to see.

Gideon's arms were burning and his knees were sore. Each time he pushed through the gap between the braces, a wave of pain ran through his shoulders.

Kate was only five yards from the railing of the drilling platform, and he wasn't far behind.

Which was when Kate slipped. One moment she was there, crossing the gap from one truss to another . . . and the next she was dangling from one of the braces by the fingers of one hand.

She let out a visceral cry. Her shout was spontaneous. And loud.

Gideon was sure somebody must have heard it — even over the thunder of the waves and the howling of the wind.

She was clawing wildly with her other hand, but she was having to fight the wind. The muscles in her arm burned. As physically fit as she was, there was no way her grip would hold more than a few seconds.

Kate's face was taut with terror. In the last day she'd had several brushes with death. But only in this moment did she realize that hers wasn't as much a fear of dying as it was a fear of not having *lived*. The thought of missing her own life made her suddenly sad and angry and gave her a surge of strength, and she reached with her dangling hand, gripping the wet steel.

Gideon saw this — and also saw that the wind was blowing so hard that her grip would soon fail. He wasn't going to make it to her in time by slithering through another set of braces. In desperation he dropped his feet so that he, too, was hanging from the strutwork, holding on with both his hands. Then, like a kid on the monkey bars, he swung from rung to rung across three sets of struts, closing the five-yard gap between them faster than he would have thought possible.

Her knuckles were white as she squeezed the metal. He was close enough now that he could see her fingers starting to slide. He swung forward just as her grip gave way, catching her fall by circling her body with his legs, clamping them shut around her bare waist with the force of a bear trap. She gasped.

"Hold on," he repeated through gritted teeth. Her body felt surprisingly warm against his, but the extra weight of her body tested his grip. Gideon did a hundred pull-ups every day. On a dry bar in a dry wind-less gym, he could have hung there for a fair amount of time. But the bar was wet, and the wind was gusting faster by the minute.

He levered his legs upward, as though he were doing a hanging abdominal crunch.

"Grab it," he said.

Kate's fingers stretched toward the bar above them. Closer and closer, until only fractions of an inch separated her fingertips from the bar. But there they stopped. He couldn't raise his legs any higher, and her arms couldn't reach any farther. Waves of fire shot through his stomach muscles. Finally he had to let her back down.

"Try again," she said.

"It's not going to work," he said. "You'll have to climb."

"Climb?" Her face was only a foot below his. She looked up at him with an expression like he'd just told her to grow wings and fly.

"Listen to me," he said with a conviction that calmed her rising panic. "Grab my shoulders. Put your arms around my neck. Then I'll let go of you with my legs. Just climb me like a tree. I'll put my legs around you again, this time below your hips, and lever you up until you're close enough to grab on."

She swallowed. It meant that for a moment she would be hanging there suspended with nothing to grip on to but his wet skin.

"Hurry," Gideon said. "I see somebody on the BLP."

"Do they see us?"

"Not yet," he said. "But they will soon if you don't go."

She grabbed around his neck. He let go with his legs and she pulled herself up until finally she could circle his entire neck with her arms.

Kate's hair whipped at Gideon's face, stinging his skin as he wrapped his legs around her a second time — but this time just below her hips instead of around her waist. He pulled her up again until she was able to grab the bar. Within seconds, she had swung herself up, catching a strut with her right heel and then pulling herself onto the bridge.

Gideon followed suit, and both of them lay gasping, their bodies pressed uncomfortably together in the constricted space.

Their eyes met briefly before Kate squirmed out from under him. She pushed through the gap in the final set of braces, then glanced back at him, all the levity burned out of her face. There was one last thing to do. In order to get back onto the drilling platform, they would have to hang from the bridge and swing their feet over to the railing on the D Deck walkway, a good six feet below them. One slip and she'd be gone.

"Here goes nothing," she said. She rubbed her hands together, clenched her fists several times, then grabbed the last strut and dropped down, feet hanging over the terrible waves. Gideon felt his heart in his throat.

Kate swung her feet, caught the edge of the railing with her toes, and let go of the bridge.

That was when the bullets began thunking into the steel wall around her.

CHAPTER TWENTY-EIGHT

Chun spotted the woman from his vantage point on the top deck of the BLP. She was hanging from the bottom of the bridge, feet flailing as she swung toward the railing.

Son of a bitch, he thought. That was it. *That* was the flash of motion he'd seen earlier. The rig manager had stripped off her yellow jumpsuit so Chun and his men wouldn't see her when she crossed beneath the bridge. Whatever else you could say about her, the woman was clever. It would almost be a shame to kill her. Almost.

"There!" he shouted as he raised his AK-47, took a bead on her, and squeezed the trigger. He was a good eighty, ninety yards away. An easy shot on the range. But she was moving, and the wind was blowing so hard that he couldn't hold the weapon steady. His first shot went wide. His second went high.

A couple of his men were firing now. They

were blasting away on full auto, which was fine for fire suppression or popping somebody from across a small room, but if you wanted to hit anything farther than fifty yards, you were wasting your time. The first shot was all you got. After that, all you had was a bunch of noise and muzzle climb.

"Selective fire! Selective fire!" Chun shouted as he squeezed off another round.

But the rig manager was already diving through the gap between the ceiling and the top of the railing and disappeared somewhere onto D Deck on the drilling platform.

Finally his men stopped wasting ammo.

"Find her," he shouted. "Now."

As Kate spun in the wind and then fell away onto D Deck, Gideon weighed his options. Right now the bad guys didn't know he was still alive. From the angle they were firing, they couldn't see him. If he tried to join Kate now, they'd see him for sure. And they might even hit him. Kate had come only inches from missing the deck entirely. He realized it was pure luck that she'd gotten to the deck safely.

So he decided to wait for them to move.

He didn't have to wait long. Boots thudded back over the bridge above him toward the drilling platform.

He lowered his head below the beam that

protected him from their probing eyes, waited for the sound above him to die away, then scanned the platform for jihadis. No sign of movement.

Don't look down, he thought as he dropped his legs from the struts and hung over the water. Without thinking, he looked down. The wind was coming so hard now that the faces of the waves were almost solid sheets of white foam. It was surely the most terrifying thing he'd ever seen in his life — and yet it had a magnetic attraction. He forced himself to look toward the deck where he would be jumping. Then he swung once, swung again. And let go.

Wham. He slammed into the deck, legs buckling, rolled once, came to his feet.

Gideon found himself at the juncture of a short passage leading into the heart of the platform. He saw Kate waiting for him at the far end of the L-shaped passageway. When he reached her, he asked, "So where are we going?"

She put her index finger over her lips, then pointed to her left and held up two fingers, indicating that there were two jihadis patrolling above them. Gideon could hear the shouting of the men who were pursuing her from the BLP. "I ran up the stairs, then doubled back down on the other stairs," she whispered, her face so close to his that he could feel her breath in his ear. "The guys from the BLP think I'm up on C Deck."

Gideon gave her a tight smile.

"Room D-4, the storage room, is down that way," she whispered. "I checked it out before you jumped. They have two guards on the door."

"I'll need tools to disarm the bomb," Gideon said. "Wire cutters, strippers, screwdrivers, maybe a voltmeter and some —"

Before he could finish explaining what he needed, he heard a flash-bang grenade and saw the signature flash of light in the stairwell.

"Follow me," Kate said, yanking open a door at the end of a short hallway. Gideon followed her into the room and strained to see into the darkness. The room was no more than eight feet square, lined with shelves full of cleaning products. A mop and some brooms leaned against the wall. He shut the door. Now it wasn't semidarkness. It was absolute pitch-black.

He felt around for a light switch, flipped it up and down, but the bulb must have been dead because the room remained dark. Gideon fumbled at the door, trying to find a lock. But there was no lock, no bolt, nothing to keep the jihadis out if they started searching D Deck room by room.

"We're trapped," Gideon said.

"No, we're not," Kate said. "There's a mechanical shaft that goes from C Deck up to the top of the rig. This room is right underneath it. We can get to it by crawling up through the air-conditioning duct. Our electrician's got a workroom on A Deck. You'll find all the tools you'll need. And while we're on A Deck . . ."

"They'll search D Deck, find out you're not there, and head back up," he said, finishing her thought.

"Exactly. Then we'll come back down so you can defuse the bomb." She liked that they were on the same page.

"Hold on to this," he whispered, placing her hands on the rickety steel shelf. Her skin was ice cold. "I'm going to climb up and see if I can find the air duct that will lead into the mechanical shaft."

"Got it," she whispered. He could feel the muscles moving under her skin as she braced herself against the shelf. Outside the room another flashbang went off, followed by more shouting. "Hurry!" she hissed.

Gideon knew the jihadis would be checking each room, sweeping methodically through the maze of passages as they cleared each deck. The platform was only about the size of a very small office building. It wouldn't take them long.

Gideon climbed gingerly up onto the shelf. Despite his attempt to distribute his weight as evenly as possible, the sheet metal flexed under him. Obviously this thing was not made for holding a two-hundred-pound man. He began feeling around on the ceiling. His fingers found several small pipes or conduits, then the boxlike metal structure of a ventilation duct. Threaded thumb studs held the cover on.

He twisted the thumb studs and within a few seconds he could feel one side of the panel come free. Then the other. Dust sifted down into his eyes as he removed it.

He clawed at his stinging eyes, nearly dropping the panel.

As he pushed his head into the duct, Kate climbed up behind him. The shelf swayed and groaned. But it didn't fall. He could feel her pressed against him now, one arm encircling his hips. It had been a long time since he'd been this close to a woman. The urgency of the situation made theirs a strange intimacy.

He heard a crash behind him, followed by a muffled curse. "You okay?"

"The shelf fell," she said. He grabbed her wrist and yanked, bracing his feet against the sides of the duct.

After a moment her hips cleared the sides of the access panel and she shot forward, landing on top of him between his legs. They were so tightly wedged that Gideon could barely move. But they froze completely when a weak light suddenly burst up from the access panel.

They could hear someone moving around in the storage room below, kicking things and spitting out words in Malay that sounded like expletives. It was obvious the jihadis were as frustrated by the darkness as Gideon and Kate had been.

Gideon felt Kate's shallow breathing against his chest. Her entire wet body was trembling — whether from cold or fear he wasn't sure — as the jihadi continued to slam around in the room below them. Then the light disappeared, and the door thudded shut.

Slowly Kate's body relaxed. Her head dropped into the crook of his neck. He felt her warm breath against his shoulder, and her hair fell over his face. She smelled like soap. For a moment she molded her body around his, an impulsive gesture that kindled a warmth inside Gideon he hadn't felt in a long time. As much as he wanted to surrender to it, he knew he couldn't. Not now.

"We need to move," he said.

She stiffened, pushed herself away from him. "Yeah. Definitely. We better go."

Gideon crawled forward, pushed open the panel on the far end of the duct, and found himself at the bottom of a long shaft about four feet square and seventy-five feet high. A steel ladder ran up the side all the way to the top. Every ten feet or so there was a small access door, each one with a large letter stenciled on it to show which deck it led to. A fine mist fell on Gideon's face as he looked up, rain driven by the wind through a vent at the top of the shaft.

CLUNK.

The entire rig shook as the ominous sound echoed through the shaft.

"What *is* that noise?" he said. She hadn't answered his question the last time he'd asked her about it.

"The damping system which is supposed to keep the rig from swaying too much in heavy seas is defective. Long term, it could mess up this rig pretty seriously. But right now we've got bigger worries."

Kate began to climb past him. Gideon followed. The shaft echoed with the deep howling of the wind blowing over the top.

By the time they reached the hatch for A Deck, the noise of the wind was deafening.

They climbed into the hallway and shut the hatch, walking as swiftly and silently as they could until they reached a door at the end of the empty corridor. Gideon followed Kate inside.

"Wow," Gideon said, surveying the back wall, stacked with conduit, electrical boxes, breakers, switches. A pegboard hung from the side wall, containing every kind of tool he could think of — and a lot he'd never seen before. "You guys don't fool around."

She gave him a wry look as she slipped into a pair of grease-stained coveralls with the Trojan Energy logo on the sleeve. "When you're a hundred miles from shore on a rig with operating costs running fifty grand a day, you can't afford to shut down the rig and make a run to Home Depot just because you haven't got the right wrench. Take whatever you need."

As Gideon selected tools from the pegboard and shoved them into a canvas bag, Kate said, "So you still haven't told me — where does a guy like you learn how to defuse bombs."

"It's a long story," he said.

"We have a couple of minutes," Kate said. "They're still searching for me on D Deck, so we can't go back there just yet."

It was true: there was nothing they could do but hunker down while the jihadis scoured D Deck, looking for Kate. He might as well tell her the story while they waited. It would be something to help them both pass the time.

"You ever heard of the Tampuan?" he said.

"The what?"

"It's actually a *who* . . ."

The day after he ended his relationship with Miriam, Gideon flew to Cambodia to negotiate an end to one of those civil wars that remain unknown to most people outside the conflict zone and never make the front page of any newspapers.

Gideon explained to Kate that if you looked at a map of Southeast Asia, you'd see Cambodia in the middle of a semicircle of nations including Thailand, Myanmar, Vietnam, and Laos. Each of those countries has its own predominant ethnic group — the Khmer in Cambodia, the Laotians in Laos, the Thais in Thailand. But hunched in the middle of Southeast Asia lay a range of high, formidable mountains. And in those mountains were a host of obscure ethnic groups totally unrelated to the dominant ethnicities of each country. Cham, Kuy,

339

Rhade, Jarai, Hmong — the list was long. Cambodia alone had nearly ten ethnic minorities. And in Ratanakiri Province was one of the smallest and most isolated of these groups, the Tampuan.

There were only 25,000 in all of Southeast Asia, most of them in Cambodia.

During the hellish Pol Pot regime, the Tampuan formed a resistance movement. Once Pol Pot and his cronies got pushed out, the Tampuan Liberation Front continued to fight against the central government, dominated by Khmer out of Phnom Penh. It was what the UN termed a "low-level" conflict, which was nothing but bureaucrat-speak for a war where the people who got killed didn't own television stations or newspapers.

Eventually the Tampuan and the Cambodian government incurred enough casualties and economic damage to reach the same conclusion: their little war was not worth continuing. Under the best of circumstances, winding down a civil war is a tricky business, but the vested interests between these warring parties had created a Gordian knot that most people in the State Department thought would be impossible to untangle. That none of the representatives on either side had the authority to make any real decisions made it even more challenging.

Gideon quickly discovered that patience is a diplomat's greatest virtue. He would alternately listen and talk and then listen some more, for hours and hours, until the hours became days, and the negotiating parties went back to their superiors to redraw their respective bottom lines. During these breaks, Gideon would sometimes play soccer with the children in the village where the negotiations were taking place.

A significant factor in the negotiations was that Pol Pot had fought the Tampuan by planting mines on every road and trail and water buffalo path in Tampuan territory. As a result, northeastern Cambodia contained more mines per square mile than any place in the world. Twenty years after Pol Pot's death, the Tampuan were still being blown up almost daily. And most of the victims were children.

Children chase balls into the jungle. They go off the beaten path. They lack the caution of adults. And they paid the price, sometimes losing their limbs or their eyes or, most often, their lives.

As part of the emerging agreement he was negotiating, Gideon convinced the international community to send in teams of bomb specialists to defuse the mines. There were police from the Finnish national bomb squad, retired SAS ordnance specialists, even veterans of the many East Bloc state security forces, which were then in tatters.

A bomb disposal expert named Horst soon arrived in the village. A large ex-Spetsnaz sergeant, he turned out to be a very good bomb guy, except for the regular and substantial doses of medicinal vodka he required to steady his nerves. But the occasional by-product of his alcohol abuse were hands that trembled as if he had Parkinson's disease. Which was something of a liability in the bomb-disarming business.

One day as Gideon was waiting to hear back from Phnom Penh about some minor point of protocol, a boy ran into the village, sobbing uncontrollably. Several of the children Gideon played soccer with had chased a ball into the jungle. Normally they might not have, but this was a brand-new ball, which Gideon had given them.

Searching for the ball, the boy's younger sister had stepped on a mine. As Gideon had learned, some antipersonnel mines explode not when you step *on* them, but when you step *off* them. That particular kind of mine is called a Bouncing Betty, which is designed to pop up into the air, then detonate at head height in order to kill more people.

The little girl had heard the click of the trigger and realized that if she moved, the Bouncing Betty would blow her head off. So she froze. And now, between breathless sobs, her brother was explaining what had happened. Unless somebody could defuse the mine while she was standing on it, the girl was dead. Gideon went to get Horst, but the bomb expert's face had gone ashen, his hands were trembling like leaves. For a moment, no one spoke. Then Horst stood and said, "Gideon, you need to be my hands."

A dozen villagers followed them into the jungle, where they found the little girl standing in a clearing, remarkably composed even as her mother wailed and cried. Her khaki-colored eyes followed Gideon's movement with absolute trust as he followed Horst's instructions. Gideon lay on the ground and carefully brushed away the dusty earth surrounding the mine, so he could describe the trigger mechanism. Horst confirmed it was an M2A4 bounding mine, then proceeded to talk Gideon through the process until he'd disarmed the trigger. The girl's mother swept her up into her arms and wept, thanking Gideon through her tears.

It took another three months to finalize the agreement and end the long civil war between the Tampuan and the Cambodian government. During those months, whenever Gideon wasn't at the negotiating table, he went with Horst on de-mining missions, learning everything he could from the German about mines and munitions — from pressure plates and percussion caps to arming plugs and fuse retainer springs.

Kate listened to his story, rapt.

"So bottom line is, yeah, I think I can disarm the bomb." He looked at his watch. "We've been here ten minutes. Let's get back down to D Deck and see if the coast is clear."

Gideon slung the tool-laden canvas bag over his shoulder, then he cracked the door open and looked both ways. The corridor outside the electrician's supply room was empty. Kate suggested he follow her, since she knew the rig best, so they started moving toward the mechanical shaft hatch. Gideon heard a toilet flushing behind a door he was approaching. Kate turned at the sound, meeting Gideon's eyes, but she'd already gone past the door, which now started to open outward. As it eclipsed their view of each other, Gideon mouthed the word *Run,* but before Kate could get very far, the door banged open. Whoever was coming out would spot her immediately. Sure enough, Gideon heard the crackle of a radio and a voice on the other side of the door, shouting in a heavy Malay accent, "A Deck! She's on A Deck!"

Gideon kicked the door out of the way and tackled the man in front of him, spearing him to the floor, when he realized he'd made a mistake. The man wore a lemon yellow jumpsuit and had his wrists shackled behind him with flex cuffs, while a jihadi stood several feet in front of them, his radio raised to his mouth. Only then did Gideon realize what had happened: the jihadi had taken the hostage to relieve himself.

"What are you doing, you moron?" The hostage was a sandy-haired guy with the physique of a college wrestler, and small resentful eyes. The jihadi dropped his walkie-talkie and swung his AK toward them, but Gideon managed to grab the rifle and deflect its barrel as it spit out a volley of automatic gunfire.

Gideon drove back the jihadi — an average Mohanese weighing a good sixty pounds less than Gideon — and propelled him backward until they smashed against the exit door, which opened under their combined weight.

The rain was nearly horizontal in the hurricane wind, and Gideon's feet went out from under him on the rain-slick decking. He landed hard on his back and lay for a moment, stunned, while the panic-stricken jihadi tried desperately to free his weapon from the larger man's grasp. Gideon planted his feet on the man's hips and yanked him forward, driving his feet into the air, launching the jihadi upward, causing his hands to tear free from the rifle.

A horrible scream briefly pierced through the howling wind, then abruptly died away.

Gideon found himself alone on the walkway.

It took him a moment to understand that he had not only propelled the jihadi over his head but had also flung the man clear over the railing. Fighting the wind, Gideon stood and looked over the railing into the water. Sheets of foam sluiced down the face of the massive waves.

The jihadi was gone.

Gideon yanked open the door and was about to reenter the hallway to retrieve the hostage, when he froze. The hostage was lying dead in his own pooling blood. A jihadi holding a Makarov pistol was standing over him and now fired a second shot into the dead man's head. Then he shouted toward yet another jihadi, who was approaching from the far end of the corridor. Gideon peered around the corner. What he saw triggered a response in his nervous system that caused him to feel as if he were running a high fever. The second jihadi was shoving Kate toward the first, who now raised his Makarov to the back of her head.

They were going to execute her, too.

Only then did Gideon remember that he was holding the AK-47 of the jihadi he'd thrown over the railing. He had never shot an AK before, had never even held one. But it felt familiar and easy. His fingers knew this thing, knew what to do with it before his mind could even begin to process what his body was doing. He pressed the stock to his shoulder and sighted the target.

Gideon fired once, and the first man fell, his Makarov discharging as he dropped.

Seeing this, the second jihadi pulled Kate in front of him to use as a human shield, but a bullet from Gideon's AK drilled a hole through the bridge of his nose.

Gideon felt as if he were watching a film of a shattered mirror running backward, the pieces knitting together before his eyes, every piece in perfect alignment, his reflected image snapping into focus where only a second earlier there had been nothing but shards and glimmers and fractured glimpses.

He fired a second shot into the jihadi before he hit the ground.

Then he snatched up the tools and collected as much ammunition as he could carry from the dead jihadis. He felt Kate trembling as he wrapped his arm around her and swept her past the pile of dead men. Without a word, they made their way toward the bomb on D Deck that Tillman was threatening to detonate less than ten hours from now.

Chapter Twenty-Nine

Chun was on A Deck, reading the ID badge of the dead hostage whom Omar had let take a piss. What Chun found there was worse than he'd imagined. Aside from the hostage, Wafiq and Abbudin were also dead, and Omar was missing. Chun's voice tightened as he gave Timken a damage report, grateful that he was delivering the news over the radio instead of face-to-face. "ID says he's a diver-welder. His name's Garth Dean."

"How the hell did he get loose?" Timken asked.

"He didn't, sir. Not exactly. His cuffs are still on."

"So you're telling me that an unarmed woman and a hostage with his hands tied behind his back took out three armed men?"

"It looks that way."

Chun heard the anger in Timken's silence. What Chun didn't hear were the ball bearings rattling in Timken's pocket as he formed a simple plan.

"My men are still sweeping A Deck, sir," Chun said. "She can't have gotten far."

"Forget about that, Chun. Just meet me in B-14."

"Sir, we need to find her."

"No. She's going to come to us. Now get down to B-14."

Timken smiled to himself, pleased with his plan, as he set off for the cabin where he'd secured his high-value hostages.

Big Al Prejean was sitting on the floor of cabin B-14 when the four jihadis walked in. Two were Mohanese and two were American. One was a big guy of Asian descent, the other the bearded white guy who called himself Abu Nasir. Prejean was halfway relieved to see them. Stearns had been talking nonstop since they'd been thrown in the cabin together, and it was driving him up the wall. Not once had the ambassador expressed any remorse or sorrow over the violent murder of his press attaché. Instead, he ignored Prejean and talked nonstop to Parker, speculating that the president must surely be mounting some kind of rescue mission. After all, he and Parker were very important people. Beneath his bravado, the man was petrified.

Stearns stopped talking the moment Abu Nasir entered the cabin.

A soft clacking sound came from inside his pocket as he surveyed the room warily. His right hand was plugged into his pocket, the number 82 tattooed on his wrist. Abu Nasir looked at Parker for a moment, then at Big Al, before finally settling on Stearns, who squirmed under the icy scrutiny of the American jihadi.

"I'm glad you're here," Stearns said, his nervous voice breaking the silence. "I understand your grievances. You've got some legitimate issues with the Sultan, and I want to offer myself as an intermediary. If you let me speak to the president, I'm sure he'll be willing to listen to your demands —"

"Give me your sock," Abu Nasir said.

"Excuse me?"

"Your sock. Give it to me."

Big Al considered himself to be a pretty tough guy. But something about Abu Nasir scared the piss out of him. Apparently the Honorable Randall J. Stearns felt the same way because suddenly his face was soaked with sweat and his complexion went pasty. "Listen to me, I've got access to money. I'll give you whatever you want." He yanked off his gold Rolex Daytona, as if offering it as a down payment on his ransom.

Abu Nasir plucked the watch from Stearns's hand, dropped it on the floor, and brought down the heavy heel of his steel-toed boot. It made a sharp cracking noise.

"Give me your fucking sock. And don't make me ask you again."

Stearns didn't need any more convincing, although it took him a moment to decide which shoe to remove. His hands were shaking as he untied the laces of his right shoe and pulled it off. The stench of sweat-soaked silk filled the cabin as the ambassador peeled off his sock and handed it to Abu Nasir.

CHAPTER THIRTY

Kate's ears were still ringing. Before being shot by Gideon, the jihadi had discharged his gun inches from Kate's ear and had then fallen on top of her, knocking her to the floor. Gideon had pulled her to her feet and ushered her through the doorway and set out for D-4. Kate was about to thank him for saving her life, but she saw something in his face that stopped her from saying anything. His eyes were opaque, lost in some private thought that demanded only her respectful silence.

They moved at a fast clip toward D-4 without speaking a word. Gideon's mind kept playing back to the moment he had discovered his mother's body, the gaping wound in her chest, the empty expression on her face. He remembered piling his father's guns on the bedsheet and dragging them across the lawn toward the pond behind their house. He remembered throwing them, the splash of each handcrafted weapon as it disappeared into the water. And he remembered his oath, never to fire a gun again.

He remembered standing on the podium at the UN only two days ago, listening to the president of the United States introduce him as a man who "has dedicated himself to that ancient and most sacred cornerstone of our moral code: Thou Shalt Not Kill."

But Gideon had killed. He had killed without hesitating because he had no other choice. He had killed with ease and efficiency, shattering in a moment the core conviction that had defined him for his adult life. But rather than remorse or even confusion, he felt the bracing clarity of having finally released something he'd held on to far too tightly for far too long. What surprised Gideon most was the whispered voice he heard in his head. *Good kill, son.*

The warmth of his father's imagined approval surprised him, although it was short-lived, dispersed by a sudden burst of static that filled the corridor. Gideon and Kate stopped in their tracks as a voice boomed over the rig's public address system.

"Ladies and gentlemen, can I have your attention please?"

Kate recognized the sadistic drawl of Abu

Nasir, and looked at Gideon.

"Your brother . . ."

"My brother?" Gideon frowned and shook his head. "That's not him. That's not his voice."

Kate studied him for a moment, trying to find a way to explain his evident denial in as sympathetic a way as she could muster. "You haven't spoken to him in seven years. He's not the same person you knew." She went on to describe Abu Nasir, reminding him of the numbers she'd seen tattooed on his wrist. Gideon couldn't dispute her facts or her conviction. He had barely recognized Tillman in the photograph Uncle Earl had given him, and maybe Tillman's voice had changed just as dramatically. Could his brother really have transformed into someone who no longer resembled the man fixed in Gideon's memory?

But the man who called himself Abu Nasir was in fact Orville Timken, and he was now pacing a tight line before the public address system microphone. "I'm directing this announcement to Ms. Kate Murphy, our resourceful host on this fine rig. Wafiq and Abbudin were good soldiers. How you managed to take them out, and do whatever you did to Omar . . . well, all I can say is that I am impressed. So impressed, in fact, that I would like you to join me in cabin B-14 so we can have a little sit-down before things get more unfriendly than they need to get."

Big Al realized with relief that Kate had escaped from the jihadis. After they'd taken her the last time, he was afraid they had killed her. Somehow she had not only gotten away but had also managed to take out three of them. That's my girl, he thought to himself. He met Earl Parker's eyes with a tight nod of pride. Parker's face, however, betrayed no emotion.

"I'm here with Mr. Parker, Mr. Prejean, and the Honorable Randall J. Stearns, ambassador to the court of Sultan Ali IV, who has been kind enough to lend me one of his socks."

Ambassador Stearns looked up fearfully as Timken shoveled a fistful of ball bearings into his empty sock. "Please," Stearns said, "I'm not giving you any trouble, you don't have to do this —" Abu Nasir slapped him hard, a crisp, ringing, open-handed strike that reddened his fleshy face and shut him up.

"Ms. Murphy . . ." Timken filled the sock with more ball bearings as he continued to speak, his voice slow and clear so that the microphone could pick up every word. "I am filling the ambassador's sock with an even pound's worth of ball bearings." He funneled more of the tiny metal balls into the open sock, making a clattering sound that was audible over the speakers.

As Timkin tied the sock with a simple knot, Stearns felt a wet warmth spreading through his crotch and down his thighs and realized numbly that he was pissing himself. He stared at the sock, mesmerized, as Timken swung it back and forth like a pendulum until the momentum carried it into a full circle.

"These ball bearings are manufactured by the Timken Corporation, the world leader in ball and roller bearing technology. If I may, Ms. Murphy, I'd like to demonstrate just why the Timken ball bearing is universally recognized as the finest and most durable antifriction device on the market today."

Big Al started to stand. "Leave him alone, you sonuvabitch —" Chun gave Prejean a sharp push with the sole of his boot. Hobbled by his flex-cuffed ankles, Big Al toppled onto the ground like a felled tree.

Parker spoke softly. "Nothing you can do, Al."

Big Al knew he was right. There was not so much as a glimmer of humanity animating the man's cold black eyes. Big Al clamped his lips shut and looked away as Abu Nasir continued his macabre introduction.

"Machined to the most exacting tolerances, it is the go-to bearing for dozens of applications."

Timken was increasing the speed of the sock's orbit, which made a soft swishing noise in the air. "I'd have to say, my favorite application is how effectively it delivers an excruciatingly slow and painful death to the enemy." Suddenly Timken whipped the weighted end of the sock onto Stearns's shoulder.

Thud.

The diplomat's scream filled cabin B-14 and echoed throughout the rig. His arm went limp, hanging from his broken shoulder as he held up his remaining arm in a pathetic attempt to shield his face from the next blow. But the weighted sock folded his elbow backward against the joint at an impossible angle.

Thud.

The sickening crack of shattering bones and joints was punctuated by the ambassador's agonized cries. A third blow caved in Stearns's cheekbone and the orbit of his eye, which popped out of its socket and dangled from a cord of blood vessels and cartilage. Another to the back of his skull sent Stearns to the ground for the last time. Timken continued pummelling the ambassador's dead body, only stopping when the blood-soaked sock finally exploded, sending ball bearings flying in all directions, rattling off the portals and bouncing on the steel decking.

Timken was breathing heavily, waiting for the rolling and bouncing ball bearings to settle before he spoke. "You catch all that, Ms. Murphy?" He sighed theatrically. "Because you forced my hand. It's your fault I had to end the brief and undistinguished diplomatic career of the Honorable Randall J. Stearns. But I needed to demonstrate my resolve. I've got plenty more ball bearings, and unless you come to B-14 and surrender yourself to my tender mercies, I will take off Alphonse Prejean's sock and show him the same treatment I showed the ambassador."

"Don't listen to him, Kate!" Big Al shouted.

"You've got five minutes, Ms. Murphy. Ticktock."

Timken switched off the amplifier, then turned to Chun, who'd had to look away from the carnage in order to keep from puking.

"I feel much better now, Chun. How about you?" Chun nodded. Timken checked his watch, then looked down at the ambassador's tangled and mutilated corpse. "Clean up this mess."

Throughout the horrible broadcast of Randy Stearns's murder, Gideon held Kate tight against him, her body wracked by deep choking sobs. Then she pulled away and wiped her tears. "I have to go," she said with sudden resolve.

"No, you don't," Gideon said.

"Al Prejean is like a father to me, I can't let that monster kill him —"

"He'll kill you, too."

"No, he won't. Not as long as this storm keeps up. He's worried about the damping system. That's what we were talking about just before I got away."

"You heard what he did." Gideon's voice was etched with anger. "Kate, please don't do this."

"I appreciate your concern, but this isn't your call."

As much as he wanted to protect her, Gideon knew she was right. He was surprised by the strong and sudden connection he felt with this woman, and he found himself unable to release his grip on her shoulders, until she placed her hands reassuringly on top of his.

"You need to disarm that bomb, and you need to do it now," she said. "Since they don't know you're alive, you've got surprise on your side. Please."

He fixed her with a look. "As soon as I do, I'll come back for you."

She nodded. "I need to go."

"Wait," he said. She regarded him expectantly, but it took Gideon a moment to find the right words. "I'm glad I met you," he said finally.

Something caught like a fishhook in her gut. "Please don't say that."

"Why not?"

"It sounds like something you'd say to someone you're never going to see again."

He moved his hands from her shoulders to the sides of her face. "Be careful."

Suddenly, she stood on her tiptoes and kissed him. "You be careful, too," she said, then walked past him toward the stairway that would take her to B Deck. He watched as she opened the door and turned back to him.

"I know he's still your brother," she said. "I'm sorry."

The door closed with a flash of auburn hair, and Kate was gone, leaving Gideon in

361

a whirl of emotion. He forced himself to push aside his concern for a woman he'd met only a few hours ago and realized that he remained troubled by her insistence that it was Tillman who had murdered Ambassador Stearns. Gideon was willing to accept that his memory might no longer be the most reliable way to identify his brother. But even accounting for Tillman's altered voice and misguided ideology, he still couldn't believe that his brother would murder an unarmed hostage, especially not with the sadistic relish this man had demonstrated. Even more troubling, Gideon still couldn't accept that his brother wanted him dead.

But if the man claiming to be Tillman wasn't really Tillman, then who the hell was he and what did he want? And where was Tillman? More questions for which he had no answers. The only thing he was certain of was that he would never find those answers unless he got down to D-4 and disarmed the bomb.

CHAPTER THIRTY-ONE

Three of Timken's best men were dead because of the crazy bitch.

Before, when he ordered the rig manager to change into the yellow jumpsuit, she had eyed him like an insect, taunting him with her half-naked body. Despite his urge to tear off her bra and panties and teach her a lesson for looking at him that way, he had remained stone-faced. Timken had resisted the impulse then, and now he wanted to hog-tie her and do what he should have done before. But Parker warned Timken to leave her alone until they were sure they didn't need her any longer. She was the only one on the rig who knew about that damn clunking sound, which seemed to be happening with greater frequency — once every ten minutes or so — and with greater intensity. You could feel it through the soles of your feet. Parker promised Timken that once they were certain they didn't need her, he could do whatever he wanted with the woman.

Parker needed to make sure the rig remained standing long enough for the storm to pass, and to carry with it the obstructing cloud cover. The success of his plan depended on the Obelisk's destruction being recorded by the satellites and surveillance planes that were being deployed over the South China Sea. If Parker understood anything, it was the power of the image.

Kate stumbled as the jihadis pushed her into B-14. The first thing she noticed was the blood — on the ceilings, on the walls, on the bedsheets — streaks of it everywhere. Although the ambassador's body was nowhere to be seen, she knew where the blood must have come from.

"Dammit, Kate, why didn't you listen to me? I told you to stay away!" In the tangle of emotion in Big Al's voice, the anger quickly gave way to relief. "Thank God you're all right."

"If they hurt you . . . I couldn't have lived with myself." She looked forlornly around the blood-spattered cabin. "It's my fault he killed the ambassador."

"Bullshit." Big Al snorted. "*They* killed him. You had nothing to do with it."

"Shut up." The jihadi named Chun spoke

with an American accent, which Kate thought was strange. He pulled her arms behind her while one of the smaller jihadis secured her wrists with plastic cuffs. Chun jerked his head toward the hallway and then followed his two men silently as they exited the room.

The door closed behind him. Kate waited another minute to make sure no one was listening at the door before she whispered to Parker and Prejean. "The president is sending a Delta team to take the rig back."

"I thought the terrorists jammed the radio," Prejean said.

"They did."

"Then how do you know about this Delta team?"

"Gideon Davis."

Parker's hound dog eyes blinked, as if he hadn't heard her correctly. Then he spoke for the first time. "Gideon?"

"Yes. He's on the rig."

Keeping her eyes pinned nervously on the door, Kate explained how she had escaped from the jihadis and pulled Gideon from the sea. Prejean noticed that whenever she mentioned this man Gideon, she seemed to brighten. It was a subtle thing, but Prejean knew her well enough to pick up on it, and he allowed himself a small smile. During the nearly ten minutes it took her to get through the story, Parker listened impassively, trying not to betray his anger and concern at this unwelcome news.

"This bomb Gideon is trying to disarm . . . where is it?" Parker asked.

"There's a storage room on D Deck adjacent to the rig's most structurally vulnerable point. Even a small explosion there could take down the rig."

"Makes sense," Prejean agreed.

"And when is this Delta team coming?" Parker asked.

"The eye of the hurricane is supposed to pass over the rig before the deadline runs out. The Deltas are dropping through the eye. If Gideon can disarm the bomb before they land . . ."

"They'll have a chance of rescuing the hostages and taking back the rig from those jihadi bastards." Prejean smiled as he finished her thought. "We may get out of this alive, *chérie*. At least we have a fighting chance."

Other than his initial surprise that Gideon had survived, Parker betrayed no emotion during her explanation. Kate assumed his measured reaction was just the way he processed stressful situations. As she was about to finish her story, the noise reverberated through the rig.

CLUNK!

"There it is again," Parker asked innocently. "It keeps happening, and it seems to be getting worse."

"There's a design flaw in the rig's passive damping system. There's a forty-ton weight about sixty feet below sea level that's whacking into its housing —"

"Mr. Prejean told me what it is," Parker interrupted. "He seems to think it's serious."

"We had concerns about it when the waves were eleven feet. But with this hurricane coming in and the waves pushing thirty feet, we're in uncharted territory. Without looking at the engineer's analysis, I couldn't tell you for sure."

"Engineer's analysis?" Parker repeated.

"An engineer named Cole Ransom was supposed to come out here to assess the problem and fix it if necessary. He was scheduled to be on the same chopper as you. I think Abu Nasir killed him for his passport, so he could take his place on that flight."

Parker thought for a moment, then nodded toward Cole Ransom's notebook computer, which was sitting on a desk on the far side of the cabin. "That's the computer

Abu Nasir was carrying. If it's the engineer's computer, maybe you can find out how serious the problem is."

Prejean added. "He's right, *chérie*. We need to keep this rig standing long enough for the Delta boys to land."

The idea had only settled for a moment, when Parker coughed twice. He regarded Kate apologetically. "The damp is giving me a cold." A moment later the door opened and Chun appeared, his AK leveled at the hostages. "Mr. Parker . . . Abu Nasir wants to talk to you." One of the smaller jihadis lifted Parker by the arm and ushered him from the cabin. Before the door closed, Parker nodded to Kate, as if to confirm what they'd talked about.

Chun had been listening to their conversation inside the cabin with a stethoscope-like audio amplifier. Parker's cough had been his signal to be taken out. The first thing he did when he got outside the cabin was thrust his wrists toward Chun. "Cut these damn things off."

Gideon clutched the railing to keep from being blown off his feet as he descended the stairs to D Deck. He shifted the AK he'd slung around his shoulder into firing position as he slipped through the narrow margin of a door into a corridor. It was empty. He began working his way through the maze of passages, taking care not to make a sound.

Gideon hugged the wall around the corner from D-4 when he heard two men speaking in Malay. Gideon didn't dare peer around the corner for fear of being seen. Among the tools he'd collected from the equipment room was a mirror with a stainless-steel stem, which demolition experts use to view the inaccessible innards of a bomb. Gideon used it now to look around the corner of the adjacent corridor. Posted outside cabin D-4 were four jihadis. And one of them was walking toward his position.

Gideon pulled back and tried hiding. He pressed his back into a shallow alcove, when the approaching jihadi appeared around the corner, busily engaged in biting the cellophane wrapper off a pack of cigarettes. He had clearly walked down the hallway to take a smoke break. He was all the way around the corner before he noticed Gideon in the alcove. The jihadi froze, the cigarette pack dangling from his teeth by a thin thread of plastic.

Realizing that if he shot the man, it would alert the other three guards, Gideon smashed the wooden butt of his AK across the man's jaw. The cigarette pack flew from the man's teeth, and he dropped like a sack of bricks. Gideon hoped the howling wind outside had concealed the sound. He trained his gun at the corner and stood silently for a moment, listening.

Nothing. No sounds of alarm, no footsteps, no shooting.

He took a fresh clip from a pouch on the man's load-bearing vest. The magazine was comfortably heavy from its thirty unfired rounds. Then a pouch on the man's belt caught his eye. It contained a black cylindrical piece of metal. For a moment Gideon thought it might be some kind of impact weapon for close-quarters combat — a collapsible baton, maybe. But then he looked closer, saw the small black hole in the end, and realized what it was.

Gideon had been concerned about firing at the men in the hallway with the AK, afraid that the noise might alert everybody else on the rig, giving him very little time to defuse the bomb. Even the sound of a typhoon couldn't hide an AK-47 blasting away on full auto.

Unless you had a suppressor.

And now he did.

He slid the black cylinder from the jihadi's pouch and quietly screwed it onto the mating threads of his rifle muzzle. Five quick turns and the suppressor was firmly seated. While he was doing this, he devised a game plan. It was surgical in its efficiency. He would put a head shot into whoever was looking in his direction first, then another one into whoever was closest to him. Then he would take down the third man, who would probably be firing to cover his retreat. Three carefully aimed shots delivered in rapid sequence.

Before he could finish reviewing the mental checklist, he heard a wild shout behind him. The man on the ground had obviously regained consciousness and was warning his friends in frantic Malay.

Time to improvise.

Gideon stepped around the corner and started firing. Unfamiliar with the weapon, he hadn't noticed that the AK was set on full auto. Which was just as well. The three men in the hallway had all swung around to see what the shouting was about. Gideon swept the AK back and forth across the hallway, once, twice, a third time, fighting to keep the muzzle down.

The fusillade of 7.62mm rounds chewed the three jihadis to pieces. It took less than two seconds to burn through the magazine.

Gideon then whirled around to deal with

the jihadi he'd hit with the butt of the AK. The man was groggily clawing for his Makarov. Gideon tried to kick him in the face, but the man was quick, rolling away as he pulled the Makarov from his holster.

Gideon dove onto the man, twisting his hand around and pressing the muzzle against the man's abdomen and squeezing the trigger. It turned out that the human abdomen is roughly as effective at quieting a closed-breech weapon as a suppressor. The Makarov made some racket — but it wasn't nearly as loud as Gideon expected.

Loud enough to be heard on one of the upper decks? He hoped not. The typhoon was astonishingly noisy now — the wind howled as the waves buffeted the base of the rig, and the relentless rain knifed into the steel exterior of the rig at seventy miles an hour.

Gideon threw open the door of the storage room, flipped on the light.

At the far side of the windowless room was the large steel box Kate had described seeing winched down by the crane. She had been right. This was the place.

Stacked neatly on the floor beside the box lay an array of electronic equipment — video monitors, black boxes with switches on them. A thick bundle of cables ran from the equipment to an access panel on the wall. Gideon moved closer. What he saw on the panel's display caused him to stop breathing.

A thin LED window displayed a count-down, the seconds ticking down with frightening rapidity. It was the bomb's timer, and it was rigged to the detonator.

08:43:07 . . . 08:43:06 . . .

He looked for something to prop against the door to keep anyone from entering. Other than the big metal box and the electronics, the room was bare. On the far side of the room was a door with the words EQUIPMENT LOCKER stenciled on the front. But it was secured with a heavy padlock. He'd just have to hope that nobody showed up while he was working.

Gideon studied the tools he'd brought as he set them on the floor in a neat row. During his months in the Cambodian jungle, Horst had taught him an enormous amount, but this was going to be a lot trickier than defusing some aging Soviet antitank mine. Horst had always said that the single most important tool for disarming a bomb was your eyes. Before even touching a wire, you had to study the bomb, the trigger, the mechanism — everything. There was zero margin for error.

The detonation control equipment consisted of several black metal boxes — standard nineteen-inch rack-mount boxes of the same size as home stereo equipment. The bottom box bore two large rocker switches on the front. One read POWER and the other read ARM. Both were in the *on* position.

The next piece of equipment also had a big red rocker switch on the front. Next to that was a knob labeled FREQ. A small antenna protruded from the side. It looked exactly like the wireless router in Gideon's office at home. He guessed that it was some kind of relay that allowed the bomb to be triggered remotely — from the control room. Or even from a boat. Which meant, as he expected, that if the people who had seized the Obelisk were threatened — say by a Delta Force inserting from above — the bomb could be detonated remotely before the time ran down.

The next box was the timer with its red LED numbers and a numeric keypad like the kind found on cell phones. On top of this rested yet another black metal box with two rows of small LED lights running across it. The top lights were all white, and in the second row the lights were all green. Thin white wires ran out the back, snaking across the casing and disappearing into the access panel. He counted twenty-four. Twelve white LED lights, twelve green LED lights, twenty-four wires. One wire for each light. This was a good deal more complex than he had expected.

Significantly, there were no cables connecting the big steel box with the detonation controls.

Strange. He'd expected the detonator to be wired directly to the bomb. It could be radio controlled, of course, but that wasn't optimal. Radio was usually a secondary rather than a primary means of detonation. Radio frequencies could be jammed, sunspots could interfere with reception — any number of things could cause a problem.

He surveyed the lid of the box, checking to make sure it wasn't booby-trapped. There was a small gap, large enough to see that there were no wires or magnets or contacts inside that might signal a booby-trap circuit. The lid was, however secured with a small padlock.

He picked up the stoutest of the screwdrivers he had brought with him, slid it into the hasp, and twisted. The latch sheared off the metal box's lid.

He stared in disbelief. The box was empty.

As he slowly lowered the lid, he heard a familiar voice behind him. "Gideon."

Gideon turned, at first relieved and then confused by the sight of Parker standing inside the doorway, holding a gun at his side.

"Uncle Earl. How did you get away from them?"

Parker said nothing, but Gideon got his question answered when he saw the bearded man appear behind Parker, aiming the barrel of his AK at Gideon's chest. The number 82 was tattooed on his wrist. But he wasn't Tillman.

The harsh realization of what was happening washed over Gideon like a wave that swept over him and drew him out to sea. He felt as if he was drowning.

"I could have spared you the trouble, Gideon. You won't find the bomb in there."

CHAPTER THIRTY-TWO

Major Dale Royce Jr. had only been commanding his unit for a month now, coming into Operational Detachment Delta after a stint in Afghanistan with the 101st. He still hadn't quite gotten the rhythm of his team. Everyone always told him, "Delta is different," and sure enough they were right.

He'd led several hoo-rah units before, full of chest-pounding alpha males. But Delta *was* different. For one thing, these men were quieter. Sometimes he found their quiet intensity unnerving, but mostly it was a source of tremendous comfort. He never had to yell at them or berate them or chew their asses like he had to with other units. They always seemed to be a step ahead of him, to the point where he sometimes got the impression that they were more or less just tolerating his presence.

And here he was, being dropped right into the Big Game, his team the tip of the spear in one of the most important Spec Ops missions of the past twenty-five years. Talk about failure not being an option. *This was it,* he thought to himself as their C-17 bucked and rattled. They had reached the rough edge of the typhoon en route to the Obelisk. The pilot's voice came over the cabin speaker. She wasn't much to look at, Royce thought, but she had a soothing voice. "Sorry for the bumpy ride, gentlemen. The president is ready for you."

"Go ahead," Major Royce said.

There had been several false starts connecting the Delta team with President Diggs, but the technical difficulties were finally straightened out, and now the air force sergeant running communications nodded to the president. The screen at the front of the Situation Room lit up, showing a fuzzy, green-tinted image of a row of soldiers strapped in their seats inside the vast airplane hold. The men were bouncing around as though they were on some violent theme park ride.

"Gentlemen," the president said, "what I'm about to tell you is highly unusual for a commander in chief, but I feel strongly that you all deserve a fuller explanation than the one you've been given in your briefing packets. I wanted you to hear directly from me that the implications of your mission extend well beyond rescuing the hostages and preventing the destruction of the Obelisk. As you know, a growing insurgency is challenging the current regime in Mohan. The Sultan is an important ally who is committed to democratic reform and human rights. I believe he can prevail against these violent extremists without the intervention of our forces. Certain members of Congress disagree with my assessment and want us to fight the Sultan's war. These politicians are well intentioned, but I fear they are misinformed and misguided. So far I've been able to resist the political pressure they've generated. But if these hostages are killed and this rig is destroyed, I will have no choice but to respond. Sometimes war is necessary. But not this time. Not yet. You men know far better than any politicians the real cost of going to war. What happens from this point on will be determined by the outcome of your mission. You don't need my encouragement or my praise, but on behalf of the people who elected me to this office, please allow me to express my gratitude for your courage and dedication."

There was a pause, then Royce said, "Thank you, Mr. President. We appreciate your honesty."

"Thank *you,* Major," the president said. "At this moment, our best information is that the eye of the storm will begin to pass over the Obelisk roughly twenty minutes before the deadline the terrorists have given us."

"That's all the time we'll need, sir."

"Our prayers will be with you."

The president ran his hand across his Adam's apple, where a lump had formed in his throat, and the air force sergeant cut the connection. The screen went dark.

Only a few hours ago President Diggs had sent sixteen soldiers to their deaths at the bottom of the South China Sea. Every one of them someone's son, someone's father, someone's husband. And now he was sending another group of men to risk their lives in order to prevent tens of thousands of their fellow warriors from having to risk theirs. President Diggs saw General Ferry looking at him. He knew the general shared his sadness and dread. The odds on this mission being successful were 50 percent. At best.

"Don't bother giving me any status reports, General. I want a direct uplink on this operation in real time."

CHAPTER THIRTY-THREE

Parker's betrayal had left Gideon disoriented, lost inside some kind of black hole. As the jihadis disarmed him, he heard Parker's voice as if through a long tunnel.

"How you managed to stay alive this long is a damn miracle. Surviving that ambush outside the airport, then getting through the storm and the bullets to make it all the way out here to the rig . . ." Parker trailed off and shook his head. "But then, you always were a stubborn sumbitch."

A dozen questions clouded Gideon's mind, but one kept pushing to the front, and he finally asked, "Where's my brother?"

"We found him in Kampung Naga." Parker nodded toward the bearded man, who kept his AK leveled at Gideon. "Mr. Timken here managed to procure some aerial assets from a private contractor."

"You carpet-bombed a village."

"A nest of insurgents."

"Where is my brother?"

Parker said nothing for a few moments. Something resembling regret crossed his face, and he pulled a dog tag on a chain loop from his pocket. He tossed it to Gideon, who caught it and looked at the stainless-steel wafer. Dried blood was caked between the embossed letters:

DAVIS
TILLMAN B.
231-12-2019
A POS
NO RELIGIOUS PREF

"Mr. Timken here was forced to put him down."

A sudden anger rose up in Gideon that nearly drove him to lunge at Parker, but Timken touched his trigger, daring him to make a move. It would be suicide.

"Don't you see, Gideon? What happened to your brother . . . it's *your* fault."

Gideon squinted, tried to make sense of Parker's insane accusation. "*My* fault?"

"I sent you to the best schools, made sure you were surrounded by people who *mattered.* I paved the way for you to lead this nation toward security and prosperity. But you threw it all back in my face with your self-righeous nonsense, going around telling the world that this plague of terrorism was payback for *our* sins."

"I never said that."

"You keep trying to reason with evil! It's foolish and it's obscene. And coming from someone with your gifts, it's *dangerous.* That's why I had to bring you into this — someone had to stop you. That fool president of ours was actually starting to believe your bullshit. You can't reason with evil. The only way to stop evil is to kill it. Tillman understood that. Tillman understood what had to be done. Until you polluted his mind."

Parker's face had become a mask of pure contempt as he continued. "He actually started buying into all that bullshit you kept peddling at the UN. That insipid little book of yours became a thorn in his side. After four years in Mohan, he started doubting his mission. He said we were driving our allies toward our enemy." Parker's voice was high and mincing and sarcastic. " 'Maybe Gideon is right,' he said. Which frankly, made me want to puke."

Gideon remembered finding the bloodstained copy of his book on Tillman's nightstand in Kampung Naga. He assumed Tillman had only read the book to dismiss its contents. Instead, Gideon's words had caused Tillman to rethink his life and to realize that he didn't like the man he'd become. It must have been an agonizing process, and Gideon wished he could have been there to help him through it.

"Instead of completing his mission," Parker continued, "your brother wanted to come in from the cold and go public with every unfortunate little incident that had happened in Mohan over the years he'd been there."

"What incidents?"

"We're fighting a war! You cannot prosecute a war and expect to keep your hands clean. If you don't have the stomach to do what it takes to win, fine, step aside and let someone else do the job. Except Tillman didn't just want to quit, he wanted to air his dirty laundry . . . confess his sins. I couldn't let that happen. Especially not with the insurgency in Mohan heating up like it is. Because unless we commit ourselves to winning this war, we will lose. It may be a small country, but it's a bellwether. We let Mohan fall, the rest of Southeast Asia will fall like dominoes. We all may as well start covering our women with burqas and praying toward Mecca."

Parker's usual restraint had vanished. He

was animated in a way that Gideon had never seen, as if he was finally releasing a lifetime's worth of frustration and anger that he'd kept locked inside him.

"Senator McClatchy's got it right, but that fool president of ours has his head in the sand. Hear no evil, see no evil. No one wants to hear some gloomy old man making the same gloomy predictions about how our enemies are waiting to take us down. They all want Gideon Davis to tell them if we just reach out and give the terrorists a hug, everything will be all right."

"If you think that's what I've been saying, you haven't been listening."

"I'm not debating, Gideon. Not anymore. The clock is ticking. Eight hours and twenty-one minutes. And when the clock runs down, the people of the United States will see just how evil our enemies really are."

"Except it's not the enemy killing everyone on this rig. It's you."

"Not as far as the president of the United States and the rest of the world is concerned. For the purposes of this exercise, Mr. Timken *is* Abu Nasir, one of the most wanted insurgents in Mohan. And once this rig is destroyed, the people of the United States will wake up and realize we're still fighting a war that cannot be won just by putting up a few new scanners at the airports."

Parker sighed, his anger giving way to a kind of sadness. "I never questioned your patriotism, Gideon. Only your judgment. I know you meant well. But you need to be stopped. And now that you're here, I hope you'll find some consolation in knowing that you've sacrificed your life for your country."

"And what about you?" Gideon said. "Let me guess. You'll be the lucky one who makes it off the rig in one of those orange rescue pods."

"Someone needs to tell the story." Parker shrugged. "And having survived such a traumatic ordeal won't hurt my credibility."

Gideon nodded toward Timken. "How do you explain him?"

"According to the records at the embassy in Mohan, I brought a bodyguard with me to the rig. His name was Orville Timken. We've got pay stubs, flight records, security camera footage, endless documentation explaining his presence on the rig."

"And the rest of Timken's men? Are they just collateral damage?"

"I told you, we're done debating. The clock is ticking down, and it can't be stopped. I wish it had turned out differently. I do. I keep thinking about those two boys back in Virginia whose father was my best friend, and I feel very sad." He looked off into the distance for a moment. "You were like sons to me. Both of you." Parker's eyes welled as he looked at Gideon, as if for the last time. Then he turned to Timken and said, "Put him with the others."

CHAPTER THIRTY-FOUR

It took Kate and Big Al only a couple of minutes to access the files that Cole Ransom had created for the Obelisk. Several files contained engineering models simulating a range of scenarios involving the passive damping system. The models were complex, and Kate was unfamiliar with the programs Ransom had used.

Because they ran slowly, Kate decided to leave one of the programs running in the background while she opened a Word file titled "Obelisk Stabilization Damper Failure." She began reading. The first section outlined the conditions that would cause the passive damping system to fail. "Sustained seas in excess of twelve meters will cause the inertial module to batter the cradle, eventually causing metal fatigue at joints J-7, J-3, and J-1. Ensuing weld failure will cause catastrophic collapse of the affected limb (see Animation 1.1). J-7, J-3, and J-1 being the most heavily loaded points on the rig, force vectors as shown will cause . . ."

She scanned the rest of the report. It contained nothing that Ransom hadn't already told her over the phone. Suddenly, the engineering model that had been running popped up. ANIMATION 1.1 LOADED, the screen said.

Then a small CAD model of the Obelisk appeared on-screen. Force vectors and loads carried by various structural sections of the rig were also shown, with colors corresponding to the amount of stress carried by each structural element. Green indicated the lightest load, followed by blue, yellow, and then orange. Some of the heaviest loads were carried by the tops of the concrete piers supporting the rig. It was the reason Kate had thought the storage room on D Deck was the most destructive place for the bomb to be detonated.

But the brightest oranges, the heaviest loads, were well below the water's surface, along the seam of the cradle that held the passive damping system.

Suddenly the model on the screen began to move. Hypothetical waves and other vectors caused the skeletal rendering of the Obelisk to sway from side to side, just as the massive waves outside were doing to the real rig. As the rig flexed, the struts supporting its passive damping system changed colors, going back and forth from green to orange. The weight and stress on the various component parts of the rig shifted and redistributed, but the rig remained intact. Even at thirty-five feet, the highest predicted wave height, the Obelisk remained standing.

"If this is right," Prejean said, "if Ransom's numbers are accurate, the Obelisk will get through the storm. It'll get rough, but the rig will still be standing."

"As long as Gideon disarms the bomb," Kate said. Her relief at the rig's structural integrity under typhoon conditions was tempered by her persistent awareness of what still had to be done to save her crew. She had seen Garth and Eddie killed, and Big Al had told her about some of the others who'd been shot trying to resist. And as much as she didn't like Stearns and Tina, their deaths had shaken her. Their safety had been her responsibility, and she had failed them. She would do whatever she needed to do to save the rest of her crew. Even if it meant sacrificing her own life.

Her somber resolution was interrupted by the sound of voices in the corridor outside

the cabin. "Quick, *chérie,* put that away."
She closed the computer just as the door
opened. Kate expected Earl Parker, but her
face fell when she saw Gideon being shoved
through the doorway, his wrists and ankles
bound. Timken appeared behind him, shoving him again, harder this time. He tumbled
to the ground, barely able to catch his fall
with his cuffed hands.

Timken closed the door, ignoring Prejean's glare. Kate went to help Gideon to
his feet. Despite the ugliness of the moment,
Gideon felt an unaccountable wave of happiness at seeing Kate, who asked him what
happened.

"It's Parker . . ." He trailed off and shook
his head.

"I don't understand," Kate said.

"He's been playing us the whole time.
He's behind this." Kate and Prejean were
visibly stunned. Gideon gave them a moment to absorb this before he explained that
Parker had staged the siege of the Obelisk
and framed his brother in order to provoke
a military response from the United States.
The bearded man with the counterfeit tattoo was just some sadistic mercenary named
Orville Timken, who bore some physical
resemblance to Tillman and who had killed
him in order to assume his identity, as he

had done with Cole Ransom.

"Then you were right . . . about your brother," Kate said.

"Yeah."

"I'm sorry."

"Me, too," Gideon said, comforted by her sincere sympathy.

Prejean couldn't help but notice the connection between them. He'd sensed something in her voice before, when she had described this man Gideon, but now Prejean saw for himself that their connection was mutual. But his satisfaction was short-lived when he glanced at his watch. He reminded them that they now had less than eight hours to disarm the bomb, and that their only viable plan had just been scuttled.

"Not to make it more difficult than it already is," Gideon said, "but there was no bomb in D-4. All I saw were some fairly elaborate electronics which looked like wireless triggers. Which means it could be anywhere."

"Not anywhere," Kate said, exhaling her frustration. "Before, when I identified the weakest structural point on the rig, I only considered the section *above* the water. But the most vulnerable points are actually *under* the surface. The cradle that holds the passive damping system is more than fifty feet underwater. The piers that stabilize the rig each have vibratory nodes that sway at a certain frequency and —" Kate saw that she was losing them. "Sorry. Bottom line is this: the cradle is anchored by three big steel braces that connect to the piers. If those braces are taken out, the passive damping system will fail. There's a four-hundred-ton weight in the cradle. Once it starts moving, it won't stop until it yanks the piers apart."

"The components I saw had wires leading out of the cabin," Gideon said. "Could they feed into the ocean from D Deck?"

Kate nodded. "There's a conduit outside the cabin that runs power down to a bunch of work lights under the rig." Kate opened Ransom's computer, turned it around, hit a key, and said, "Here. Look at this."

The animation of the Obelisk appeared, wobbling back and forth. Kate hit a button that paused the simulation. "Right there. See these orange sections? They're the most vulnerable points, the link connecting the damper cradle to the pier."

Gideon studied the image, then said, "Here's what I don't get, though. I counted twenty-four wires leading out of the detonation control unit. Why so many? I could understand a few extra wires — monitor circuits, dummy circuits, redundant circuits, whatever. But twenty-four?"

"It makes sense," Kate said. "When a building is demolished, they use multiple sequenced charges to take out the most important structural members. It's almost surgical. A few small explosions properly placed can create a very dramatic structural failure. Blow out a couple of bolts and beams, and let the weight of the structure do the rest. It implodes."

Kate zoomed in on the rig, tighter and tighter. The view closed in on the cradle. Kate touched the seam between the cradle and the pier, twelve dots spaced equidistantly. "See that? Twelve bolts. Two sets of wires for each bolt. It would have been easy enough to set the charges, probably took a two-man dive team an hour, tops."

"And it would be a two-man job to disarm them," Gideon said.

"Except we can't do anything as long as we're stuck in here," Prejean said.

CLUNK!

The floor and the walls shook again. Gideon looked at Kate for an explanation. "That's the damping system I mentioned . . . the one Ransom was supposed to repair."

"How long do we have before it fails?"

"Big Al and I were just reviewing Ransom's simulations. Turns out we caught a break. If Ransom's numbers are right, the rig should actually make it through this storm."

Gideon's eyes lit up with an idea. "But Parker doesn't know that."

"As a matter of fact, no, he doesn't," Prejean said, trading a look with Kate, who was beginning to understand where Gideon was going with this.

"For Parker, this is all political theater," Gideon said, explaining Parker's intention to provoke a war. "But he needs a global audience. The last thing he wants is for the rig to come down *before* anyone can see it happen."

Kate was already working the keyboard with a flourish. "I can alter Ransom's simulation to demonstrate that the rig's gonna come apart. If we can get Parker to send us down there to fix the problem we can disarm the bombs."

The computer's disk drive light went on for at least a minute as it chugged away.

"Look at that," she said, mesmerized by the increasingly violent sway of the skeletal rig. "If you decrease the periodicity of W by fifty percent, theta zero starts to go asymptotic."

"I'm guessing there's a way of saying that

in English?" Gideon said.

"Let me just show you," she said, turning the computer around.

Gideon and Big Al watched the screen as one of the struts turned red and began to fold. Within seconds, the damper cradle had nosed over and torn away from the piers. Then an entire pier gave way. With that, the little stick-figure Obelisk slipped sideways and collapsed, a wave of red cascading upward through the rig as piece after piece failed. And then the Obelisk was gone.

"Well, that ain't good," Big Al said.

Gideon shuffled over to the cabin door and started pounding on it. A moment later, the door opened and Timken appeared.

"What the fuck do you want?" Timken said.

"Get Parker down here," Gideon said.

"Why?"

"Tell him this rig is about to come apart." The certainty in Gideon's voice unnerved Timken. But if that wasn't enough to motivate him, the cabin shook again, as if on cue. *CLUNK!* Kate tried not to betray her excitement at the lucky timing, even as she allowed herself a glimmer of hope that she might have bought her crew a second chance.

CHAPTER THIRTY-FIVE

"See for yourself," Kate said, nodding toward Ransom's computer screen. "It's all right there."

Parker slipped on a pair of reading glasses as he stood next to Timken and squinted at the screen, watching the animation of the Obelisk as it swayed back and forth until it collapsed into the ocean.

"Dammit," Timken said.

"Shut up," Parker said. He'd been on edge ever since Kate Murphy had told him about the Delta mission. And what little patience he had left was quickly being exhausted by this latest complication.

"There's a reason you feel nervous when you hear that noise," Kate said. "The situation is graver than any of us thought. This rig is about to tear itself apart. Ransom would have told you himself if you hadn't murdered him."

Timken swore again, this time under

his breath.

"How long do we have?" Parker said.

"According to this simulation, there's a ninety-five percent chance the rig will collapse in the next three hours." Kate tapped the screen. "See, this function uses the wave height and periodicity to predict structural failure. When the waves are below a certain limit, the time-to-failure function is arithmetic, basically a straight line. Over twenty-five feet, time-to-failure gets geometrically shorter —"

"Spare me the engineering lesson, and give me the bottom line."

"Cole Ransom suggested a temporary fix, but we've only got three hours to make it," Kate said. "If we don't get it done by then . . ." She looked at the screen, which was running a loop of the Obelisk model falling apart and falling into the ocean.

"Fuck it," Timken said, turning to Parker. "Let's just abandon ship and blow the rig."

Parker gave him a cold look, then ushered him away so they could talk privately. "I didn't hire you to do the thinking, Timken. Leave that to me."

"I don't trust them."

"It appears we don't have a choice."

"And I'm saying we do."

"I am not blowing this rig in the middle

of the storm where no one can see it," Parker flashed, before calming himself. "If we've learned anything from our enemy, it's that the theater of the war is what counts. A couple of buildings falling down is one thing. But having the whole world watching it again and again, millions upon millions of times . . . that's the game changer. We need to wait for the storm to pass over and the view from above is clear."

"And if that clear air gives the opening for a bunch of Navy SEALs to swarm the rig?" Timken said.

"Nothing has changed. We've planned for an assault from the very beginning. SEALs, Rangers, Delta — whatever. They're the cherry on the sundae. The rig blows as they fight bravely against the crazed terrorists. They'll be martyrs, heroes fallen in the wreckage. And we'll watch it all from inside the escape pod."

Timken grunted in grudging assent.

Parker turned back to Kate and said, "Okay, you said there's a quick fix. Tell me what needs to be done."

"Ransom's plan calls for a piece of one-inch plate to be welded over this joint." She tapped the screen with her finger. "That simple reinforcement should be enough to hold the rig together until the storm passes."

"How long will it take to weld?"

"No more than an hour. Two at the most. But every minute that passes is a minute we can't afford to lose."

Parker studied Kate for a long moment, then nodded. "All right, take whoever you need from the hostage room and get them set up to dive."

"It's not that simple," Kate said. "The hostage your man killed on A Deck a few minutes ago? His name was Garth Dean. He was my diver/welder."

"You don't have anybody else on the rig that can do it?" Parker said.

Kate opened her hands, palms up. "Me. I told you before, I paid my tuition by diving."

Timken and Parker exchanged glances.

"But it's a two-person job, so I'll need help," she said. "One-inch steel plate is extremely heavy and hard to move."

Parker furrowed his brow. "If you don't have any more divers —"

"Mr. Davis just told me he's a certified master diver." Kate looked over at Gideon.

"Uncle Earl knows that," Gideon said, looking at Parker. "He paid for my certification."

Timken shook his head. "I don't like this. I don't like this at all."

"We also need a dive tender," Kate said.

"Let me guess," Timken said. "Your dive tender's back in Mohan."

Kate smiled coldly. "That's right. But Al Prejean can handle it. He's done just about every job you can do on an oil rig."

Before Timken could level any more objections, Parker snapped, "Give them what they need and get it done. We need this rig to be standing eight hours from now."

They were surrounded by a swirling blackness, pierced only feebly by the bright floodlights aimed down at the raging sea. Kate lowered her voice to make sure she was out of earshot of the jihadis who were keeping them under constant surveillance. "Can we really pull this off?" Kate asked Gideon as they pulled on their diving gear in the howling wind of the dive control station on D Deck of the Bridge Linked Platform.

"If we can get to those explosive charges, I'll find a way." Gideon gave her a thin smile. "Either that or I'll blow us all to kingdom come."

The dive control station on the BLP was open to the air but fortunately was situated on the western side of the rig, which provided the most shelter from the rain and the driving westerly wind. Below Gideon the massive waves rose and fell, barely visible in the darkness. He tried to ignore the waves, comforting himself with the fact that once they got below the surface, it would be no different than any other diving he'd done. Simple. Nothing to it. But still — he'd been down there once already. And once was enough for a lifetime.

So he focused on suiting up. Most of the diving gear was similar to gear he'd used before — a tight neoprene dry suit, weight belt, buoyancy control device, tank harness, slate for writing messages to each other, depth gauge, and octo. Every diver carried an emergency mouthpiece known as an octopus or octo.

But some of the equipment was unfamiliar. The yellow plastic helmet, for instance.

"This is a Kirby Morgan Superlite," Big Al said, holding up a yellow plastic dive helmet. "It's the standard helmet used by our divers. It's a lot easier and safer to have your whole head pressurized, dry and protected from impact. Here's the flow valve for ventilation and defogging, and here's the auxiliary valve that controls breathing air straight through the regulator. As you start to work, your body will require more oxygen, so you can tune it to optimize the flow until you feel comfortable."

Big Al would be acting as dive tender — their topside assistant on the rig. His job was to control the winches that raised and lowered them to the correct depth, all the while making sure they had sufficient air and lines of communication. Gideon took the yellow plastic helmet from Big Al and tried it on. He'd only dived with face masks before, never with a full helmet. There was something slightly claustrophobic about it.

"This is your umbilical." Kate held up a bright red line that was just under an inch in diameter, with a handful of connectors protruding from the end. "The umbilical jacks into your helmet. It consists of a bunch of separate lines — air, twelve-volt DC, comm line, so on. It's also got a weight-bearing aluminum cable that'll clip onto your harness. If it gets crimped or tangled or caught, you're in big trouble. But the advantage of using one is that when you're blowing air from the surface, you can stay down indefinitely."

"Is it straight atmospheric?" Gideon was asking if the air they were breathing would have the same mix of nitrogen and oxygen found in normal air.

"For the depth we're going, yeah. If we

were going deeper we're set up so we can go nitrox, heliox, whatever's necessary."

Nitrox and heliox, Gideon knew, were air mixtures intended for use at great depth or during extended dives in order to alleviate the various problems, including the bends, oxygen toxicity, and nitrogen narcosis, that came as the result of gases being compressed — or decompressed — in the human body.

"We're under some major time pressure," Kate continued as Gideon adjusted his gear. "That doesn't mean we throw safety out the window. Doing something stupid and getting in trouble down there will kill us all. So be careful. We're not going super deep, but we'll be down for a good while. If you have any questions, don't guess. Ask me."

"Sure."

"We'll be diving to about twenty-five meters. The rule of thumb is that you'll be experiencing nitrogen narcosis equivalent to one martini for every ten meters you go below twenty meters. Normally it's not a big factor at the depths we'll be working, but everybody reacts differently. Pay attention to how you feel. If you start feeling like something's wrong, let me know *immediately*. Understand?"

Gideon knew about the dangers of diving

at these depths. He had dived deeper on several occasions. But not with this equipment, and not doing hard physical work. One of the hallmarks of recreational diving is that the diver intentionally conserves energy by moving slowly and deliberately. Hard work puts stresses on his body — burning more oxygen, creating more excess CO_2, and drawing more nitrogen into the tissues of the body — all of which had the potential to create problems he had never experienced before.

"Typically we have one person on the surface supporting each diver," Kate said. "Today we've only got one trained guy to superintend all the lines. And his job is going to be twice as tough because of the turbulence on the surface. If the umbilicals tangle or crimp, we'll be carrying 40s — 40 mcf bailout bottles of emergency air. It'll make it harder to work — but there's just too much likelihood of these umbilicals getting trashed by the waves."

Big Al broke in: "Normally we'd lower you in a diving basket — kind of like a little elevator. But not with these damn waves. So I'll be lowering you with a winch. You okay with all this?"

Gideon nodded. "Let's just get the show on the road," he said.

Kate reached over, attached Gideon's umbilical to his harness. Then she clipped in all the connectors — air, electrical, and communications.

"Blow some air."

Gideon found the regulator, blew some air into his mask, gave her the thumbs-up.

"Test the comm link."

"Test. Test."

Big Al said, "Can you hear me, Gideon?"

"Ready when you are."

As Big Al connected Kate, Gideon looked over the edge of the platform. The floodlights dissipated in the rainy darkness, barely illuminating the surface of the water. *Only a madman would go back into these waters,* Gideon thought as he watched the angry waves roll by.

Kate exchanged a brief glance. "I'll go first," she said.

Gideon shook his head. "Better for you to go second. If something goes wrong right out of the box, it's better that you be up here where you can do damage control."

Kate looked down at the treacherous seas.

"God, this is insane," she said.

"It's going to be fine," Gideon said, although he knew he sounded unconvincing. He looked around the dive control station. Chun stood on the far side of the station with two other jihadis. Gideon nodded his head toward them. "Can they hear us, Big Al?"

"There's a monitor over there," Big Al said. "But they aren't jacked into it. So, no, with the wind and all, they can't hear you."

"Good," Gideon said. "Because, here's the thing, Big Al. As soon as Kate's finished welding that plate, there's a good chance they're going to cut the cables and leave us down there to die."

"Not as long as I'm standing here," Big Al said.

"Just do what you can," Gideon said. "That's all I ask."

"Son," Big Al said, "Kate's like family to me. The only way she's dying down there is over my dead body."

Let's hope it doesn't come to that, Gideon thought.

Kate grabbed Gideon's arm and pointed surreptitiously toward the far side of the dive station. Timken had just arrived. He was putting on a pair of headphones, plugging their cord into a jack on the rack of dive communications equipment. He winked at Gideon. "Hey there, gang!" Timken's grating voice boomed into his ear, "I talked to my associate Sergeant Chun here. Turns out he had all kinds of dive training in the army. He's gonna come down with you two. Just to make sure you don't get into any trouble."

Chun said, "You want me to go in Mr. Davis's place?"

Timken shook his head. "Absolutely not. Keep your distance from them. I don't want your lines getting tangled up with theirs or some tool accidentally-on-purpose cutting your air hose. You just watch them like hawks."

Chun nodded.

Gideon felt a sick wave of frustration. Timken was smart. Kate had altered Cole Ransom's simulation to make it appear that the destruction of the rig was imminent. Their dive was a ruse to allow them to find the explosives and defuse them. And now Timken was guarding against just that possibility — or some other trick he hadn't anticipated.

Gideon said nothing because there was nothing to say. He just clambered over the railing and swung over the edge. There was just enough slack in the umbilical to allow him to plant his feet on the railing and lean back as if he was about to rappel into the water. Big Al hit the control handle on the winch, and Gideon jerked backward and began sliding toward the waves.

When the first wave hit him, he flipped end over end, smashing so hard into the water that he almost blacked out. Then the water closed over his head and he began sinking.

Suddenly Gideon broke free of the water again. Above him the floodlights from the rig spun crazily in the blackness. He found himself in the trough between two waves. Then the wave caught him and flipped him end over end.

He tried to breathe. But something had gone wrong.

"Air!" he shouted. "Big Al, I've got no air!"

Chapter Thirty-Six

The Situation Room was a hive of activity. But in one of those odd lulls that happens in every crowded room, it suddenly went very quiet.

In the middle of the silence, an air force major spoke to the head of SOCOM. "General Ferry, we've got an update on the weather. The typhoon seems to be changing course slightly south."

"What's that mean for the Delta drop?" President Diggs called from across the room. "Is the eye still going to pass over the rig?"

"Yes, Mr. President. On its present course it will. The problem is, since only the edge of the eye will now pass over the Obelisk, it means the window will only be open for a few minutes. And it'll come later."

"What time?"

"Roughly seven-forty-five."

"I thought you were getting them there

with an hour to spare. That only gives Delta a fifteen-minute window before the terrorists blow the rig," the president said.

"That's all the time the Deltas need," General Ferry said.

The president nodded tersely. "It better be."

As Gideon began sinking into the black water, he realized why he couldn't breathe. The air hose was shut. He reached for the regulator valve on his bailout bottle but it wasn't there. It took him a moment to figure out that he had flipped over because the umbilical had caught on his bailout bottle. Not only had it turned him upside down, but the umbilical had also stripped the bottle right off of his harness.

He had no backup.

His instincts told him to yank the umbilical free, but he knew that would only make things worse. He needed to be methodical. He had a good minute before he'd black out. If he made good use of his time —

The next wave trough reached him and suddenly there was no water for him to maneuver in. The wind whipped him around in a crazy circle as he hung in midair by his leg, looking up the long ragged slope of the next oncoming wave, which hit him hard before rolling over him.

"Pull him up, Al. Pull him up!" He heard Kate in his ear.

Gideon knew at once that it was a mistake. He needed slack on his line, not tension. But before he could respond to Kate's order, he felt a sharp jerk as the line reversed, hauling him up. The wind immediately caught him and spun him around. If he didn't get the line fixed before he cleared the next wave, the wind would slam him into the rig on the way back up and kill him.

As rapidly as he could — while upside down in churning water — Gideon worked at the umbilical. He could feel himself getting lightheaded. His vision began to narrow and darken. Suddenly the umbilical came free. Air gushed into his helmet.

"I'm clear," he shouted breathlessly. "Drop me!"

Big Al lowered the winch, and the water grabbed Gideon. This time he felt no impact at all. He simply slid into the wave as though he were slipping into a wading pool. And the world above him fell away.

Kate had said they would need to be lowered as quickly as possible for the first thirty or forty feet to get below the turbulence of the waves. If they didn't, there was a strong chance of getting spun around or dragged away, tangled in the lines and drowned.

Gideon sank uneventfully, except for the water pressure, which hit him like a pair of ice picks in his eardrums. Gideon yawned, trying to clear his ears. He kept looking toward the surface, scanning for Kate. He could make out the dim points of light that marked the floodlights on the rig, glowing then fading, glowing then fading again as the towering waves rolled slowly overhead. Other than that, there was only blackness. After only a few seconds, he saw something dark in the water — visible for a moment, then gone. A few moments later he could see that it was a person — a dark figure, arms and legs slightly splayed, like some kind of oversize doll silhouetted by the floodlights on the rig. *Kate had made it.* His relief was acute. Oddly, he realized that he'd been more worried about her than about himself.

Once he'd reached a depth of about forty feet, his descent seemed to slow — or Kate's seemed to speed up. It was hard to tell in the disorienting darkness. Seeing Kate's headlamp, he remembered that there was a light on his helmet. He thumbed the button, gratified when the arm of blue-white light appeared in front of him, illuminating Kate as she floated down to the same depth.

Together, slowly, they descended. When they reached the damper cradle, they would need to work quickly and to get lucky. They hadn't anticipated that Timken would send Chun down to watch them. As soon as they located the charges, Gideon would disarm them one at a time, getting to as many of them as he could before Chun reached them. As soon as Chun got there, Kate would have to find a way to distract him long enough for Gideon to finish the job. If he couldn't disarm all the charges, hopefully he'd get to enough of them to limit the damage of the sequenced detonations.

"You okay?" he said.

"Yeah," she said. "Although for a minute, I thought you were in trouble."

"Minor blip," he said.

After that, they didn't speak as they descended through the darkening water.

Unlike the limpid oceans he'd explored before, diving among sun-dappled reefs swimming with colorful fish, this water was dark, cold, and seething. A merciless hell. Specks of plankton and crud were visible in the shifting darkness, suspended in the green-black water. The only sound was the relentless roar of the waves passing overhead and crashing into the rig. As he and Kate sank deeper, the sound receded but didn't cease, a constant reminder of the enormous destructive forces above them. Less light reached them now. And the light that did writhed and twisted, as if it had been forced to endure some kind of torture in order to penetrate the deep.

Gideon's pulse hammered in his temples. It wasn't just an effect of the increasing pressure. It was fear. Gideon was not fearful by nature, but he felt small and fragile in the inky blackness, at the mercy of forces against which the human body was no match.

"You should be reaching final depth pretty soon." Big Al's voice was coming through the headphones. "Forty feet. Forty-five."

Gideon was able to see only a dozen feet or so in front of him, the light from his headlamp falling away into the surrounding blackness.

CLUNK!

Even though Gideon knew the rig wasn't in danger of collapsing, the great hollow boom of the 400-ton weight sounded like the crack of doom as it whacked into the edge of the cradle. The vibration rattled his chest. "Man, that sounds bad," he said.

"Yeah," she said, her voice tight. "Let's

get to work. We don't have much time."

They were suspended in blackness. No piers, beams, or damper housing were visible. Nothing at all.

"You sure we're at the right depth?" Gideon said.

Kate tapped the depth gauge on her wrist. "The current and the waves are pulling us away from the rig. We have to swim to get back to the cradle. Watch the way the bubbles are moving, and swim in the opposite direction."

Gideon followed awkwardly as she began swimming slowly through the water. As extensive as his diving experience was, this was different. Not only did he not have swim fins, but he was dragging the weight and resistance of sixty meters of cable and hose. He sure hoped she knew where she was going.

After a minute, something began to rise out of the gloom. "There's the damper," Kate said. It looked like a flying saucer from an old science fiction movie, its surface covered with mossy green algae.

Divers communicate underwater in one of two ways. If they have microphones and hard helmets, they can talk by wire. But if for whatever reason speech isn't possible, they communicate by writing on slates —

small rectangular tablets that function like old-fashioned blackboards. Even surface air divers carried them as backups in case their electronics failed. For Timken's benefit Kate kept talking about welding the plate as she pulled the writing slate off her belt and scrawled: NEED TO FIND EXPLOSIVES BEFORE CHUN GETS DOWN.

Gideon nodded.

Kate wiped the slate clean, then wrote: I'LL GO LEFT. YOU GO RIGHT. LOOK FOR DET WIRES COMING OUT OF THE CONDUIT.

Gideon gave her a thumbs-up.

They began swimming away from each other. Within seconds she had disappeared in the blackness. Gideon moved forward, looking for the point where the cradle connected to one of the three huge concrete piers holding up the rig. Beneath him was the rim of the massive steel cradle that held the motion damping system. He walked along the edge. It was like walking on a cliff that fell away into some infinite chasm.

"Big Al," Kate said. "How's that steel plate coming?"

"Donnie Rawls is working on it with the plasma cutter," Big Al said. "Should be ready in five minutes."

"Good. And the welding equipment?"

"We're rigging it right now. The welder's almost ready to drop."

The beam of Gideon's headlamp swept back and forth across the surface of the cradle. There seemed to be nothing there but algae. No bombs, no wires, no mines, no explosives.

"We're both on the cradle now." Kate continued to talk conversationally, maintaining the pretense that they were there strictly to weld the steel plate onto a weak section of the damper cradle. "You can lower the welding equipment now."

"Negative," Big Al said. "Timken wants me to send down his man first."

"The sooner we get the equipment, the sooner we can fix the rig," Kate said.

"Don't fuck with me." Timken's loud voice cut into their headsets. "I'm not letting you mess around down there without someone keeping an eye on you."

Gideon saw a big black shape looming in front of him. The first pier. He examined the joint carefully. A massive steel collar surrounded the concrete pier. A set of twelve bolts, each one the size of his wrist, secured the collar to the rim of the cradle. He carefully examined the entire joint but found no wires, no explosives, no bomb.

"I've got no apparent damage on this

joint," Gideon said, hoping Kate would understand what he meant.

"This one looks clear, too," Kate said.

"Comm test," a fourth voice said. "This is Chun, do you copy?"

"Check," Big Al said. There was a brief pause, then Big Al's voice came back on the intercom. "Diver away."

Gideon was following the rim of the cradle, doing his best to hurry and find the charges before Chun arrived at depth. But it was slow going. The algae was slippery, and the waves above them were so big that they caused the current to speed up and slow down even at this depth, making the already slick footing even more unpredictable.

Kate and Gideon reached the third pier at almost exactly the same time. Kate pointed at the big row of bolts and brought her fingers together, indicating they should meet in the middle. They slowly worked their way across the joint.

When they reached each other, Gideon shook his head and shrugged.

"Dammit," Kate said.

"What's the problem?" Timken said.

"We're scraping off algae to clean up for the weld," Gideon said. "I hit her with a tool."

Gideon searched the area. Something Kate said had triggered a memory. Scraping algae. He had noticed that a bunch of algae had been recently disturbed on the first pier. He motioned to Kate to follow him, and they moved back to the other pier as rapidly as they could.

"Okay," Big Al said. "Chun, you should be at depth soon."

"I don't see anything," Chun said.

Kate and Gideon knew that Chun had been pushed by the current and would have to swim to reach the cradle. But they weren't going to say anything. They needed as much time by themselves as possible.

The first pier loomed above them again. This time he noticed that algae on the near side had been scraped off in several places, as though a diver had kicked it off with his feet while working on something around the back side of the pier. Gideon swam around to the rear side of the pier, where he found what he'd been looking for. A bundle of white wires was secured along the pier, continuing down the side until it disappeared into the darkness.

Kate made a face as she wrote on her slate. I WAS WRONG. THEY PLACED CHARGES WHERE BRACE ATTACHES TO PIER, NOT WHERE BRACE HITS

CRADLE.

Gideon wrote back. HOW FAR DOWN?
ANOTHER THIRTY METERS.

BUT TIMKEN KNOWS OUR DEPTH,
Gideon scribbled. IF WE GO DEEPER . . .

Gideon shook his head. It was incredibly frustrating not being able to talk. But they were obviously thinking the same thing. Because Timken knew exactly where the explosives were rigged — thirty meters farther down — he hadn't worried about sending them to this depth. Ninety feet deeper — that was too far to fudge by saying they needed a little more slack in the umbilical. There was no way to reach the bomb without alerting Timken. Another thirty meters and the air mix would start to become an issue. At that depth they'd start getting narced — feeling drunk from nitrogen narcosis. Gideon also realized that placing the charges had been far more complicated than he and Kate had assumed. Timken must have subcontracted a separate dive team in a submersible well before the rig was seized — which would also explain why there were no divers among Timken's men.

"How are we doing with the welding equipment?" Kate said.

"I'm rigging it right now," Big Al said.

421

"And the plate's cut. Soon as the welder reaches the cradle, we'll send down the steel."

"Copy that," Kate said. Her voice sounded confident and in control, in stark contrast to the panic on her face. And the panic became even more acute when Gideon pointed to the dark shape resolving out of the murk. Chun was coming toward them.

Kate wiped her slate clean with her gloved hand and started to swim back around the pier toward the cradle. Gideon followed. By the time Chun reached the cradle, they were busy scraping algae off the area where Kate planned to weld the big steel plate.

"I'm with them, sir," Chun said.

"What are they doing?" Timken's said.

"Scraping green shit off the cradle."

"Feel free to help," Kate said, looking at Chun.

"I told you to keep your distance, Chun," Timken said. "Just observe. I don't want any accidents happening to you."

Chun moved backward a few feet, crossed his arms, and stood there on the cradle, swaying slightly in the current.

"All right, guys, the welder's coming down," Big Al said. "Jesus, Mary, and Joseph, it's swinging like a sumbitch in this wind. It's — Watch out!"

No sooner had Big Al begun to shout when Kate flew upward, yanked by her umbilical. She stopped suddenly after shooting upward a good twenty-five feet — almost to the level of the wave troughs.

"Kate? Are you all right?" Big Al said, the concern in his voice quickly becoming panic when she didn't answer. "The welder snagged Kate's line." Big Al repeated, "Kate!"

Still no answer.

Gideon could barely see her in the dark, turbulent water. He twisted the valve on his buoyancy control and began swimming up toward her. As he rose, she continued drifting laterally. She was motionless, her arms floating. Somehow her rapid ascent had caused her to lose consciousness.

"What's going on down there, Chun?" Timken shouted.

"Something snagged her," Chun said.

"I'm cutting the line," Big Al said.

Gideon was swimming toward Kate. Again her body jerked upward, like a marionette. This time, though, she didn't move very far. He noticed that there were no bubbles rising from her helmet. It was only then that he realized with horror that her umbilical had snapped completely. The aluminum load-bearing line had ripped free of the loop on her nylon harness. And once the load-bearing line was no longer there to support them, the weaker hoses and cables had also come undone.

Now Kate was sinking — drifting sideways and sinking. Gideon saw that not only had her umbilical snapped, but a gash had appeared in the bladder of her buoyancy control device. The BC worked by inflating or deflating the bladder with the air hose, depending on whether you wanted to float up or sink down. But her weighted belt was now pulling her downward. If she didn't regain consciousness, she'd sink slowly to the bottom, six hundred feet below. Her helmet contained valves to keep it from venting all the air in the event of a hose failure, so she wouldn't drown immediately. But eventually the oxygen would give out and she'd suffocate. Gideon immediately vented his own BC and began swimming down after her as fast as he could.

Just as his fingers were about to close around her arm, he jerked to a stop. He'd reached the end of his own umbilical. Below him Kate disappeared into the blackness as though carried by an invisible elevator.

CHAPTER THIRTY-SEVEN

"Lower me," Gideon shouted. "Lower me *now!*"

"What depth?" Big Al asked.

"Until I tell you to stop," Gideon shouted. "Kate's umbilical broke and she's dropping like a rock."

Timken's voice broke in: "Chun?"

"Just like he said, sir," Chun said. "Better drop him or you'll lose her."

Gideon felt the resistance of the umbilical give way as Big Al began paying out the umbilical with the winch.

It seemed that he was already in the dark. But as he slid deeper, the dark became an impenetrable black force. He swam as hard as he could.

"Gideon, you're already at fifty meters," Big Al said. "I'm going to have to start changing your air to heliox soon. You need to slow down so I can adjust —"

Gideon interrupted. "Just keep paying out

the umbilical."

"Sixty meters. Seventy."

The pressure in Gideon's ears was agonizing. He tried to clear them, but he couldn't blow hard enough or fast enough. He was already deeper than he'd ever been.

"Eighty meters. Gideon! Are you sure —"

"Keep going, dammit!"

The world had gone completely black. He couldn't even see a slight haze of gray above him now. And the water was cold, terribly cold. He kept looking around him, the dim white cone of light from his helmet piercing weakly into the darkness. Kate was nowhere to be seen.

But for some reason, it didn't bother him. He heard a song being hummed, some half-remembered melody he couldn't identify. Was he humming it, or was it just a voice in his head? It didn't matter. Nothing really mattered. He laughed. Suddenly he wasn't worried about anything.

"Ninety meters. Jesus Christ, Gideon!"

He realized dimly what was causing this feeling of pleasant disconnectedness. He was getting narced. Applying Martini's Law, he was seven martinis to the wind.

Focus. Gideon willed himself to concentrate.

"Gideon, there's only a hundred meters

of line."

And then he saw her — a smudge of yellow below him. It was her helmet. All he needed was another few feet.

Closer. He could see the valves on her helmet, torn straps on her harness where the umbilical had ripped free. She still had the bailout bottle, though. They'd be able to make it.

Her helmet had a large handle on top. He wasn't sure what its function was — whether for hauling divers out of the water, or for allowing an assistant to take your helmet for you. But whatever it was for, it would be perfect for him to grab hold of her.

He swam hard toward her, reaching for her with each stroke. His muscles were screaming now, and he could feel the CO_2 building up in his blood from all the exertion.

Closer. He was almost there . . .

Just as his fingers were about to close around the handle, he felt a gentle tug on his back and his body swung around. He'd gone as deep as his umbilical would allow.

Kate continued to fall. She was more buoyant at this level because of the air that remained in her helmet, so she was falling very slowly now. But still she was sinking.

Gideon rotated his body around the pivot

where the umbilical attached to his harness. He continued stroking with his hands, trying desperately to swing his feet toward her.

And then, he felt a thud against his foot. He was touching her.

He looked down, thrust his foot into the strap of her bailout bottle harness. And with that, she came to a stop.

"I got her!" he shouted. He was so narced up now that he couldn't contain himself.

"Is she all right?" Big Al said.

But Gideon didn't answer. He took a shallow breath, not wanting to move. He had a single toe looped under the strap. Just a breath of current might dislodge her. She felt light as a feather.

Big Al's questions went unanswered as Gideon pulled her slowly upward until he was able to grasp the handle on top of the helmet. Then he pulled her around so he could see her face. She wasn't moving, and her face was gray. He quickly turned the valve on the bailout bottle. He could hear the hiss as the air shot into Kate's helmet.

"Come on!" he shouted. "Breathe!"

"Gideon, talk to me!" Big Al said. "What's going on down there? Is she okay?"

"Her bailout's working. But it's straight atmospheric air. We're too deep for atmospheric. We're gonna have to deco her up to the damper as fast as we can."

"I've already started switching you to heliox," Big Al said. "Don't want you getting messed up down there, too."

"Speak English," Timken said. "I don't understand a word you're saying."

"You know what the bends are, Timken?" Big Al barked.

"Of course I know," Timken said. "The oxygen in your blood starts bubbling because you decompress too fast."

"Nitrogen, actually. But, if you don't shut up and let me do my job —"

A desperate gasp on the radio stopped him mid-sentence.

"She's breathing!" Big Al exhaled his relief when he heard Gideon's voice.

Deep below the surface, Kate's eyes blinked open. She stared at Gideon, disoriented. Her lips moved. "Where am I?"

"You're okay," Gideon said. Then, to Big Al, he said, "Look, I don't have deco tables in my head — not for dives this deep. How much decompression time will she need?"

"I don't know. We've never gone atmospheric this deep."

"Well, she's only got forty cubic feet of air in the bailout."

"What about yours?"

"My bailout got torn off when I dove

through the wave line."

"Shit," Big Al said. "Lemme check the decompression tables."

Kate was still staring at him, a moonstruck expression on her face.

"We don't have time. Just pull us to seventy and pause for five," Gideon said. "And then pull us to . . ."

And then, suddenly it came to him, how they could pull off their mission and defuse the bombs.

"Then pull us to fifty, pause for another five, then bring her to forty and pause for fifteen. I'll stay with her to make sure she's okay. Meantime, you can drop another umbilical and we'll get her hooked up to heliox before her bailout dies. Okay?"

"Got it," Big Al said. "You okay, Kate?"

"Huh?" Kate said. It was obvious that she was in trouble. But they couldn't rush her up without serious danger of the bends.

"All right, Chun," Timken said. "I want you dropping to wherever they are so you can keep an eye on them."

Big Al's voice broke in. "I can't do that. I've got to switch Gideon to heliox so he doesn't get totally narced down there. You have to adjust the mix every time they move. I can't keep on top of Chun's air mix, too. Somebody will end up dead."

"He's right," Chun said. "A lot of things can go wrong at seventy meters. With only one dive tender, we're already pushing it."

"Listen to me carefully, Gideon," Timken said. "I get even a whiff that you're doing something funky down there, we'll cut the cables and let you fall to the bottom of the fucking sea. Are we clear?"

"Crystal."

CHAPTER THIRTY-EIGHT

By the time Gideon and Kate had decompressed their way back to forty meters, Kate was still looking bleary and listless. He kept having to remind her where she was.

He swam for a while against the current until finally the piers came into view. Swimming while holding on to Kate was extremely hard work. As he had hoped, the bottoms of the cradle braces were visible just above him. He pulled himself up the umbilical until he was even with the brace, a large steel strut attached to a steel collar around the pier.

He scanned it for wires or bombs or blocks of explosive. Nothing.

He began swimming again. It took nearly five minutes before he finally reached the second pier. The cluster of white cables was the first thing he saw. It split into twelve sets of two wires.

"What are those?" Kate said vaguely.

Gideon's pulse sped up. "Just fish," Gideon said. It was nearly impossible for him to write on his slate while holding on to Kate, but he finally managed.

"Doesn't look like fish," she said, studying the explosives. Gideon slapped the slate urgently against the mask of her helmet.

PLEASE DON'T TALK! he'd written.

"Huh?" she said, then seemed to lose interest.

"Where's the umbilical?" Gideon said. "Kate's in trouble here. I think she may be hallucinating."

"I'm not hallucinating," she said, grinning at him. "That is not a fish —"

"Kate!" Gideon said. "Just relax, okay? We'll have some better air for you in a few minutes."

"Okay," she said happily.

"She's narced to the gills," Gideon said. "Hurry with the umbilical."

"On its way down," Big Al said.

Kate's bailout bottle was in the red zone by the time Gideon managed to locate the new umbilical and hook it up.

"How long you gonna stay down there?" Timken said.

"Look, she just went to a ridiculous depth. We had to bring her up way too fast," Gideon said. "I need to keep her here another ten minutes just to make sure she doesn't get up to twenty meters and then suddenly crash."

"You got five," Timken said, "then I'm pulling you both up."

Distracted by Kate's situation, Gideon had been unable to look at the explosive charges placed on the cradle strut — much less to work on defusing them.

But he finally had the chance.

Kate and Gideon were hanging suspended a few feet below the strut. Several of the explosive charges were visible now.

Kate looked at them fixedly. She still seemed to be trying to figure out what they were. Gideon swam between her and the explosive charges, then held one finger up in front of his lips.

Kate frowned in concentration. Then suddenly she blinked. "Oh!" she said. "Yeah. I'm starting to remember."

"Remember what?" Timken demanded.

There was a long pause. Gideon grabbed Kate by both arms and stared straight into her face, trying to project every ounce of urgency he could muster without saying anything.

Finally Kate nodded. "Nothing," she said. "It's okay, I got a little narced there. I'm getting straightened out, I just need a couple more minutes. When I get back to the cradle, I'll be fine. We'll get everything welded up and we'll be set."

Gideon smiled. He felt like giving her a huge hug. But there was no time.

He turned toward the nearest explosive charge and studied it. This was going to be tricky.

Kate squeezed his hand encouragingly.

Gideon nodded, trying to cover his own uncertainty, then turned to study the first charge.

Horst's most important lesson to him had boiled down to this: "Observe the bomb. See the bomb. Know the bomb. Know *everything* . . . before you cut the first wire."

So Gideon studied the bomb. There were twelve shaped charges, each attached to one of the twelve bolts that matched the ones he had seen up on the cradle. Each charge appeared to be identical, consisting of a plastic drinking cup inverted over the bolt head. Inside the drinking cup was a pound or so of plastic explosive. The base of the explosive would have been hollowed out into a cone. The cone likely contained a copper slug. When the charge was detonated, the resistance of the water, combined with the shape of the charge, would blast the superheated copper in a jet that would shoot straight through the bolt, acting like a cutting torch jet and simply dissolving the entire bolt.

By detonating all twelve charges in sequence, the bolts would disappear, and the immense weight of the cradle would twist the strut and then shear it away. And that would be the end of the rig.

Sticking out of the top of the closest drinking cup was a thin metal tube — a detonator. Two wires came out of the tube. If that had been all there was to it, the problem would have been easy. Snip the wires, the circuit would be cut, and it would be impossible for the detonator to fire.

Gideon circled around the drinking cup, looking to see if there was anything else he needed to know. If it was simply a matter of cutting the wire — well, this was a best-case scenario. Twelve quick snips with the wire cutters Big Al had on his dive belt and he'd be done. But if there was anything here that he was missing — security circuits, trap circuits, anything of that nature — one snip might blow him and Kate both to bits.

Then he traced the second set of wires, one entering through each side of the cup. It was undoubtedly some kind of security circuit — but without cutting open the cup and tracing the course of the wires millimeter by millimeter, there was no safe way of figuring out its precise function. It might be a monitor circuit to alert them up top that the detonator had been removed. It might be a redundant hidden detonator. Or it might be a decoy. There were a lot of possibilities.

If he just pulled the detonators out, there was a reasonable chance the charge would blow. If it did, the shock wave would liquefy his organs and kill him in about one ten-thousandth of a second.

There was no time to perform a full diagnostic analysis on the charge. He'd have to take a chance that simply cutting the wires would disarm the bomb.

Without hesitation, he reached out and snipped the wire.

After a moment, he realized he was still alive.

"I'm getting tired of waiting," Timken said. "I'm pulling you up to the cradle."

"Hold on," Gideon said, cutting the second wire.

"No! I'm not holding on! Pull 'em up, Prejean."

"I can only pull one of them at a time," Big Al retorted.

"Then pull Gideon first."

Gideon turned furiously toward Kate. He

pointed at the charges and made a snipping motion with the cutters, then pointed at her.

She stared back, wide-eyed.

"You'll be fine, Kate!" he said, trying to sound calm.

He tried to snip one more wire before Big Al pulled him up — but he felt a jerk and was already moving upward through the dark water before the jaws of the pliers could close.

There was nothing more he could do. He let the wire cutters drop from his grasp. They flipped end over end, their yellow rubber handles tracing an erratic path through the water, slowly disappearing from his view as the reflected light from his headlamp faded. Kate made a grab for them.

Gideon couldn't see whether she had caught them or not. She had been swallowed in the darkness.

Major Royce was gripping the console of the C-17 cockpit to keep from being thrown to the deck by the brutal buffeting of the airplane as he watched the radar monitor. The eye of the storm was going to pass over the Obelisk. But only just barely.

"What do you think?" Major Royce asked the meteorologist, who was on loan from the USS *Blue Ridge,* the navy's Seventh

Fleet command boat. "How long's our window?"

"The sweet spot, when the wind's really dropped? Maybe ten, fifteen minutes." The meteorologist was a lieutenant junior grade who had obviously never flown through a typhoon before and now looked completely terrified. He'd staggered to the head about five times already. The rest of the Deltas smiled as they heard his retching. Royce felt bad for the kid. He'd been through some rough flights over the years, but nothing like this.

Royce looked at his watch. They were set to Time Zone Golf. Local time was 07:13. "We gonna make it, Colonel?" he said to the pilot, Colonel Laurie Hills, whose unflappable demeanor and soothing voice made her a valued team member.

"We'll be there before the bomb blows. Question is, will the eye be there in time?"

Royce glanced at the meteorologist. "Where's the eye, Lieutenant?"

"Pardon me, sir," the navy man said. "I need to hit the head again."

Great, Royce thought, as the meteorologist rushed past him to puke.

Kate had been feeling more like herself. But she was far from 100 percent. Even under the best circumstances, some nitrogen narcosis occurred at this depth. And she was still feeling the residual effects of what she'd just been through.

She grabbed for the cutter, but it slid through her grip and disappeared into the blackness like some comical little sea creature, heading down to graze on shrimp corpses at the bottom of the sea.

She looked at the twelve upended drinking cups, then mustered whatever little strength she had in her shaky limbs and dove after the plunging tool.

CHAPTER THIRTY-NINE

"Sir! Sir!"

Timken turned and looked as his demolitions specialist, Rashid, burst through the door from the rig and into the dive control station.

Timken was in a foul mood. He'd been out here for thirty minutes getting rained on and blown all over the place. And every time that big clunk shuddered through the rig, he felt like he was taking one step closer to the grave. "What are you doing?" Timken said. "I told you to stay with the bomb controls."

"That's what I'm saying, sir. The alert circuits just went off." Rashid was a bespectacled young man, a chemist by training.

"What do you mean?" Timken said.

"They're cutting the wires."

"All of them?"

"Just two. So far."

"Will the bomb still take out the rig?"

"With ten charges? Yes, sir."

"Get back to the drilling platform. Stay with the detonation equipment!" Timken shouted.

"Yes, sir." Rashid ran back into the bowels of the rig.

Timken knew that Gideon had already just been pulled up to the cradle. If he was the one who had cut the two detonation circuits, then he couldn't do any more damage. But if it was Kate who had done the damage, then he needed to pull her up now. He whipped around toward Big Al. "Haul them up!" he shouted. "Haul them up now! Both of them!"

Big Al shouted into his microphone, "They're onto you, Kate. Do what you got to do and do it fast!"

Timken drew his Makarov to shoot the Cajun, who turned and tackled him onto the deck like a linebacker blitzing a quarterback. Big Al was no spring chicken — but he outweighed Timken by a good seventy-five pounds. All Timken could do was cover his face as the bigger man battered at him with fists the size of canned hams.

Then Timken growled. Leaving his face momentarily unguarded, he levered his Makarov and fired. A huge fist slammed into his face. He fired again and Big Al grunted, his face a mask of pain.

Timken kicked the bigger man away, jumped to his feet, and hit the handle on the winch again, pulling Kate upward. A display counter on the winch showed their depth. Although Gideon Davis was being pulled toward the surface, Kate Murphy was now hovering at the exact depth where his people had placed the bomb last week.

His suspicion was confirmed — this whole dive had been a ruse. Maybe the rig *was* going to fall apart. But the likelihood that the rig manager would interpret some engineer's report and predict the precise time it would fail? It had seemed plausible when he was looking at all that complicated shit and Parker had been so damn insistent. Now that he was standing here in the sobering rain, looking at the depth counter on the dive winch, he knew he'd been fooled.

"Chun, we're aborting the mission," he said. "Go ahead and kill the woman. I'll take care of Davis topside."

"Might be easier if you just cut both their umbilicals, sir," Chun said.

"Good point," Timken said. He pulled a knife from its mount on his tactical vest and sliced through Kate's umbilical. Cutting the air hose was easy, but he could see he wouldn't be able to sever the steel cable that was used to raise and lower the divers.

He looked around, saw an axe in an emergency fire box on the wall. He smashed out the glass, grabbed the axe, and with two swift blows severed Kate's and Gideon's umbilicals. The cables fell away, whipping lazily in the air, splashed into the water, and were gone.

Timken stared over the side for a moment, then smiled. He pressed the mic button on his waist and said, "Stand by, Chun. I'm hauling you up."

"You'll need to deco me so I don't get the bends," Chun said. "Take me up ten meters and leave me there for five."

"Roger that," Timken said, pulling back on the winch handle.

Gideon felt the pressure drop inside his helmet a moment before the tension went out of his line. Then he saw Kate's severed umbilical coiling and sinking beside him, like a dying serpent. He tried to breathe, but there was no air.

Rather than surfacing, he began diving toward Kate. He saw her swimming up toward him, and when he reached her, she grabbed his helmet and yanked him toward her, pressing her helmet flush against his. Only then did he realize what she was doing. With their helmets pressed together, the sound waves could pass from one helmet to the other and they could talk.

"My bailout bottle!" she shouted. Though her voice sounded compressed and muffled, he had no problem understanding her. "I still have some air left. Grab my octo!" Gideon grabbed the fluorescent pink mouthpiece on her shoulder. The problem was that the octo was only good for a few minutes of emergency oxygen.

He realized then that they only had one chance. Where was Chun? He looked around the cradle. The water around them had gone a dull gray. It was obviously dawn above them, the sun lighting the sky enough to send a few meager rays down to where they stood.

But Chun was nowhere to be seen.

There was a tiny bit of air in the helmet, but it was already going stale. Gideon's lungs were beginning to scream. He yanked his helmet off and sucked in a breath from Kate's octo.

The air coming from the bailout bottle was feeble — the pressure in the bottle barely greater than the pressure of the water around them. But it was enough for him to suck in two quick lungfuls of air to revive his strength.

Time to move. Without a word, he handed the octo to Kate, unstrapped his weight belt and propelled himself in the direction where he'd last seen Chun. His natural buoyancy at this level was quite strong, and it only took a few kicks for him to cover ten or fifteen meters, until he saw a slash of light in the darkness ahead. Closer, and he made out a dark shape, hovering. It was Chun. Gideon could tell from the direction of Chun's headlamp that he was facing away, and he tried approaching Chun from behind. But the water was so turbulent that Chun was spun around before Gideon reached him.

The big Korean's eyes widened. He was quick, unsheathing his dive knife from its scabbard. Gideon grabbed Chun's wrist with both hands. Gideon was strong — but not stronger than Chun.

The one advantage Gideon had was that he felt completely at home in the water. It was obvious to him that Chun did not.

Gideon inverted himself so that his legs were pointing skyward and wrapped them around the umbilical. By twisting one ankle over the other, he was able to put a kink in Chun's umbilical, cutting off his air. Feeling his airflow die, Chun panicked and made a grab for the umbilical, letting go of the knife.

Within seconds the water was clouded with Chun's blood. The big man's body went limp.

Gideon released the knife and fumbled with the snaps on Chun's helmet, his lungs on fire, pulled it off and settled it around his head.

Gideon blew the excess water out of the helmet and adjusted it to his head. *Air!* It had the acrid rubbery smell of hoses. But right now it smelled as fresh as the air on top of a mountain in the Rockies.

Seconds later he felt a pair of arms lock around him. It was Kate. Her eyes looked as big as plates as she stared at the now-dead Chun, his hair floating in a corona around his broad face. Gideon was wearing Chun's helmet now. That was a good first step to making it safely back to the rig. But if they were going to be hoisted to the surface, he needed the hoist cable attached to the webbing of his suit. Gideon pulled the carabiner from Chun's load-bearing harness, reattached it to his, then stabbed the bladder on Chun's BC. As the air escaped from the BC in a rush of bubbles, the big man fell away, leaving a pink trail in the water behind him.

Kate was gasping now, having exhausted the last scraps of air in her bailout. He pointed to the fluorescent pink octo on his shoulder. She tore off her helmet and began sucking in air from the octo. He wanted to ask her if she had succeeded in disarming the explosives. But there was no way for them to communicate without being heard topside by Timken. And with their arms occupied holding on to each other, it was impossible to use their slates.

Timken's voice intruded on them. "I'm pulling you up now, Chun."

"Roger," Gideon muttered, hoping that the scratchy quality of the communication link would disguise the fact that he was not Chun. Apparently it worked, because Gideon felt a tug as the winch began pulling him to the surface.

There was no time to consider what his strategy would be once they cleared the water and came into Timken's view. The good news was that Kate, Chun, and Gideon all wore identical wet suits and identical helmets. Gideon and Chun shared similar builds. With the driving rain and wind Timken would be unable to tell it wasn't Chun until Gideon was quite close to the rig.

The main problem would be that Timken would want to know why Chun was dragging Kate from the water. Gideon figured he'd have to play that one by ear.

And then they were clear of the water.

The wind slammed them like a hammer. Gideon estimated that it was blowing at well over a hundred miles an hour. The wind swept them up into the air, clawing at them, trying to strip off his mask and his vest, trying to rip Kate from his arms.

Gideon locked his arms and legs around Kate, tight as vises. *Hold on!* He wanted to scream it at the top of his lungs. But he couldn't. Not without giving himself away. *Hold on!*

Timken was working the winch, pulling Chun to the surface. The winch strained as Chun's head cleared the water. Then the wave he was in fell away and suddenly the wind caught the big man and snatched him up in the air like he was on some kind of insane amusement park thrill ride.

Within seconds, Chun was snatched a good forty feet into the air.

Timken saw a flash of auburn. *What the —* Then he realized what it was: Chun was bringing the rig manager with him! He couldn't see her face, couldn't make out whether she was alive or dead. But it was definitely her.

"What the hell are you doing, Chun?" he

shouted. "Why are you bringing her up?"

Chun was whipping in the wind now, spinning and diving crazily, but he didn't respond.

"Chun!" Timken shouted. "I can't hear you! Drop the woman!"

Timken kept winching Chun in. As Chun grew closer to the sheltering bulk of the rig, the wind lessened and he fell out of view. Within seconds, though, he reappeared. Now he was only a few yards beneath the platform. Timken's jaw dropped when he saw a pair of angry green eyes staring up at him through Chun's helmet. How in the world had Davis gotten onto Chun's umbilical?

Timken didn't belabor the question: he just wanted Kate and Gideon dead. He released the winch handle and his hand swept to the pistol on his hip when he felt his legs pulled out from beneath him.

Big Al was alive. Barely. The pain in his gut where Timken had shot him was searing. Prejean had regained consciousness only to feel the life draining painfully from his body. But he wasn't dead yet. And seeing Kate held aloft by Gideon prompted a brief but fairly miraculous reprieve.

He rolled over, grabbed both of Timken's ankles, and yanked with every ounce of his

450

waning strength. Timken hit the ground hard and his pistol flew from his hands and disappeared. Animated by a wave of anger and protectiveness, Big Al struggled to his feet and slammed down the handle of the winch.

As Kate and Gideon came closer to the deck, Timken roared and jumped to his feet. He was a somewhat smaller man than Big Al, but he knew how to fight. His fists slammed into Big Al's body. Big Al felt his vision narrowing, his blood pressure dropping, and warm wetness spreading down the front of his chest. The world receded until there was nothing but the winch handle. He pressed both his hands together, then forced his big belly onto the handle. He thought distantly, *At least I'll leave two hundred and eighty-five pounds of dead Cajun meat hanging on this goddamn handle!* It might give them just enough time to get to the rig.

Then Kate and Gideon swung toward him, Gideon grabbing hold of the railing with one hand.

Come on, chérie! Big Al tried to say. But the words wouldn't come to his lips.

And then Big Al felt a great wave of darkness rising up from the sea, hunting him, seeking him, and finally overwhelming him.

■ ■ ■ ■

Gideon practically threw Kate onto the platform. She fell over the railing, smacked onto the deck, and rolled.

Meanwhile Gideon continued to rise. Big Al Prejean was slumped over the winch controls, his chest bloodied, his eyes rolled back into his head. The winch pulled the umbilical up over a pulley on the end of a ten-foot-long crane arm that extended out over the water. Gideon rose until his neck whacked painfully into the crane arm and the winch stalled.

Gideon hung helplessly, suspended nearly ten feet out from the deck, struggling to free himself. He reached up and tried to unclasp the carabiner that attached him to the umbilical, but it had been sucked up into the pulley at the end of the crane and he couldn't get his fingers around it.

Realizing that Big Al was either unconscious or dead, Timken shoved the big man out of the way and slammed the handle up. With a sharp jerk, Gideon began descending toward the sea again. Timken was going to drop him to the water, then cut off the air and let him drown.

Kate, however, had other plans. She

hopped up, jumped on Timken's back, and sunk her teeth into the side of his neck. For the moment none of Timken's men were near the dive station. But Gideon was pretty sure Timken's roar of anger and pain would draw them soon. Timken whipped around, releasing the handle of the winch and slung Kate off his back.

Gideon had fallen about eight feet. This put him just below the railing. He swung back and forth in the wind, slammed into the railing before he managed to grab hold. There was just enough slack for him to climb the railing as Timken shoved Kate backward.

Gideon crested the railing, reached up, and disconnected the carabiner from his harness, yanked off the helmet, which was still attached to the air hose and to the comm and electrical lines.

Embedded in the railing next to one of the dive winches was the small axe Timken had used to sever their umbilicals. Gideon yanked it from the railing mount and then jumped to the deck.

Timken turned at the sound Gideon made as he landed. His eyes took in the axe in Gideon's hand. There seemed to be no fear in his expressionless eyes — just a rapid and clear appraisal of the threat. For the moment, Timken was unarmed. He was being attacked by a large and athletic man with an axe. The equation was simple. Time to retreat.

Timken was gone before Gideon could cross the five yards of deck that separated them.

Gideon turned his attention to Kate. "Are you okay?" he said, putting an arm around her shoulders.

Kate shrugged off Gideon's hand and ran to Big Al's side. "Al!" she shouted. "Stay with me!" He was nonresponsive, his pulse thready.

"We can't stay here," Gideon said. "Timken will be back with his people in about thirty seconds."

"You go," Kate said. "I have to stay with Al."

"Kate —"

"Don't worry about me. They don't care about me now. It's you they want. Go, and they'll leave me alone." Before he could object Kate grabbed his wrist. Her voice was completely calm as her green eyes locked onto his face. "Kill him, Gideon. Kill them all."

Timken's pistol lay at the far end of the dive station, half hidden under a pile of scuba gear. Gideon grabbed the gun and took off after Timken.

The rain had let up a bit, enough for Gideon to run without holding on to the railing. He'd already gone a hundred yards when he realized that he hadn't asked Kate whether she'd managed to disarm the bombs. And it was too late to go back and ask her.

He turned a corner and nearly stopped at what was the most astonishing thing he'd ever seen. A curved line of cloud extended to the horizon, like a giant white wall — and above it, pale blue sky. A brilliant orange ball of light broke over the rim of clouds, and the first bright rays of sunlight hit Gideon square in the face.

We're in the eye of the storm, he thought.

The rain had stopped and the wind had gone still. But there was no time to enjoy the extraordinary calm that surrounded him. If they were going to survive, he had to stop Timken.

CHAPTER FORTY

Major Dale Royce Jr. looked around, then turned to the pilot. "Where'd he go?"

"Who?" the pilot said.

"The meteorologist," Royce snapped. He had been making last-minute preparations with his team and he'd come to the cockpit to see how the weather was holding out.

"He's in the head," the pilot said. Royce thought to himself that the meteorologist should have emptied his stomach by now, when the plane hit a downdraft, and for a moment Royce found himself airborne. When he slammed back down on the deck, he felt something snap in his ankle, and a terrible shock ran up his leg. There was no pain, just a sensation like he'd been hit with 220 volts of AC. He knew the pain would come soon.

The pilot didn't notice what had happened — she was squinting out the windscreen into the blackness of the clouds, responding to someone on her radio.

"Copy that, SAT Seven." She looked over her shoulder at Royce. "Good news, Major," she said. "Satellite's got a visual on the Obelisk. It's in the eye. You're cleared to jump."

The pain was starting now, a sickening fire that was starting to burn its way up his leg. Royce gave the pilot a tight smile. "Outstanding," he said.

Then he turned and began limping back into the cabin, trying not to let his boys see the agony in his face.

"All right, ladies, lock and load," Major Royce shouted. "We're going in!"

CHAPTER FORTY-ONE

In the sudden eerie silence, Gideon could hear a steady thudding on the other side of the rig. He realized it was the sound of Timken's footsteps. Where was he going? Not that it mattered. If he could cut him off and kill him, the leaderless mercenaries would be easier to take out. Then all he'd have to do was find Earl Parker.

He pulled the mag of the Makarov. It was a single-stack mag, nine-shot capacity. Except for the two bullets Timken had used on Big Al, the mag was full and the chamber was loaded. He slammed it back into the Makarov and pulled back the hammer, ready to fire single action.

Timken's footsteps pounded up the stairs of the BLP and onto the bridge linking it to the drilling platform.

Gideon hoped he'd get a shot at him while he was exposed. But by the time he reached the bridge, Timken was on the other side, disappearing into the stairwell leading down to D Deck. Gideon could only figure that he was heading for the remote bomb controls in D-4. The son of a bitch was going to blow the rig!

Gideon charged across the bridge. Two mercenaries popped up on B Deck over on the drilling platform, swinging their AKs at him. He crouched behind a pipe halfway across the bridge, squeezed off a shot at the first man, caught him high in the chest. The man dropped. He squeezed off another round at the second mercenary, but the man ducked down and disappeared.

Now he was down to five rounds.

He jumped from his cover and ran toward the drilling platform. A third man stepped out from behind a bulkhead. Gideon fired as he ran, his sight picture bobbing and jiggling. The first two rounds missed, but his third shot hit the man in the face. Gideon hoped he'd be able to scoop up the man's AK on the way. But he was too late. The dying man dropped it over the side as he fell screaming to the deck, his jaw blown cockeyed and slinging blood.

Two rounds left.

Gideon hit the drilling platform, grabbed the railing, and wheeled around, taking the stairs three at a time down to D Deck.

Timken's footsteps thumped down the hallway in front of him. Gideon turned the corner in time to see Timken disappearing into the storage room where the bomb control equipment was located. Gideon blasted through the door, expecting to see Timken heading for the bomb controls. But instead he found Timken on the far side of the big steel box, standing in front of the equipment locker door, spinning the dial on the padlock. He was still unarmed. As Gideon charged into the room, Timken yanked the lock off and pulled open the door.

Behind him, Gideon heard the clank of a rifle bolt slamming home.

He froze, realizing the mistake he'd made. One of Timken's men had been standing behind the door, ready to ambush him.

Timken spun around, then grinned, his hand still resting on the knob of the half-open door behind the metal box. "Too impulsive there, chief," he said.

Gideon looked over his shoulder. A very thin, somewhat frightened-looking young man stood behind the door, eyeing Gideon through a pair of thick glasses. He wore an odd vest with a great many pockets that contained a variety of tools, bits of wire, detonators, pieces of circuit board. It occurred to Gideon that this man must be the demolitions specialist, the man who had rigged the bomb.

"Go ahead, Rashid," Timken said. "Shoot him."

Rashid hesitated. Timken was directly behind Gideon, putting him in the line of fire. To avoid shooting Timken, Rashid moved sideways. Gideon seized his opportunity. He dropped to his knees, rotating as he dropped, and squeezed off a round. It caught the bomb-maker center mass. Gideon saw in the very instant that he pressed the trigger that he'd made a mistake. The vest worn by the bomb-maker didn't carry just his tools; it also contained a large Kevlar panel. Rashid grunted and stepped backward, essentially unharmed.

Gideon raised the sight twelve inches, fired again. The shot shattered one of the lenses in the bomb-maker's glasses. He fell backward without a sound. Then Gideon turned his gun on Timken, who was jabbing his finger toward the bomb controls. "Now I'm the only one who knows how to disarm the bomb. Kill me and everybody on the rig dies."

Gideon had counted his rounds and knew his clip was empty. He kept the gun trained on Timken, hoping he wouldn't notice. No such luck. Timken's eyes flicked to the slide of Gideon's Makarov. It was locked back, the chamber open, indicating that the pistol was out of ammunition. "Damn, that's inconvenient for you, huh? Kind of levels the playing field."

Gideon noticed that the downed bomb-maker had dropped his AK-47 as he fell. It was about ten feet away, closer to Gideon than to Timken. He coiled, preparing to spring toward the weapon.

But Timken had seen it, too. As Gideon leapt, Timken leaned his shoulder against the big metal box, gave a primal scream, and heaved. The box was set on a metal frame, which in turn rested on four large rollers. The steel box began to move, heading straight toward Gideon, and slamming into him just before he could grab the AK-47. Timken propelled the box forward like a nose tackle pushing a blocking sled, pinning Gideon against the wall.

And there they stopped. Timken, though several inches shorter than Gideon, was a powerfully built man. And with his feet sprawled behind him and his shoulder against the box, he was perfectly situated to keep Gideon pinned to the wall.

Gideon struggled to free himself, but with his back against the wall, he had no leverage. If Timken let go to pounce on the AK,

Gideon would get free. The AK lay closer to Gideon than to Timken. It was a stalemate.

Timken grinned at Gideon.

Gideon had thought Timken was coming here to trigger the bomb. And yet when he entered the room, Timken had ignored the bomb controls and headed for the equipment locker on the far side of the room. Were there weapons inside? No — if there had been weapons in the equipment locker, Timken would have grabbed something from the locker instead of attacking Gideon with a clumsy metal box.

The box.

"What was in the box?" Gideon said. It occurred to Gideon that whatever they had smuggled onto the rig in the box was probably now somewhere in the equipment locker. "It obviously wasn't the bomb. So what *was* it?"

Ignoring his question, Timken said, "That bomb's ticking down. We stay here, we both die. I can disarm the bomb. But I'm not about to do it with you holding that AK to my head."

The LED on one of the bomb controls read 03:10:41. Time was running out.

Then Gideon heard a thump. It sounded

like it had come from inside the equipment locker.

"What's in the locker?" Gideon said.

Timken glanced back toward the locker again, then gave Gideon a sarcastic smile. "I realized I left my health insurance card in there," he said. "Life's so full of risk these days, I just feel naked without it."

Another thump from inside the equipment locker.

"Tell you what," Timken said, "if you put your hands up, step over here away from the AK, I'll reset the bomb. Truce, right? We'll both be unarmed, even-steven, nobody has the advantage, nobody gets hurt. Fair enough?

Gideon had no plan. But he knew a truce with this snake would go badly. "Don't think so," Gideon said.

With that, the door to the equipment locker burst open and a figure stumbled into the room. He was dressed like Timken and his men — faded, mismatched green BDUs and black combat boots. He wore a black leather holster on his hip, the same as Timken. The only difference was that his holster was empty. And unlike Timken, the man's hands were flex-cuffed behind him, and his head was covered with a black hood. A muffled, inarticulate roar erupted from the man, as though he were gagged beneath the hood.

"Shit," Timken said.

The man hurled himself toward Timken's voice, lowering his hooded head like a bull.

Timken turned to face the onrushing attacker, still bracing himself against the steel box, so that Gideon couldn't move.

Timken attempted to kick the man, who still managed to ram his hooded head into Timken's chest. The impact shifted Timken's weight just enough to give Gideon the clearance he needed to get out from behind the box.

Seeing that Gideon was about to free himself, Timken gave the box one last shove, then dove for the AK-47 lying beside the dead demolitions man.

Gideon stumbled slightly as the corner of the box caught him painfully in the left hip. It was hardly even a stumble — barely more than a stutter-step. But it was enough to slow him down. Timken reached the AK just a fraction of a second before Gideon. His right hand clamped around the grip and his left around the wooden fore end. Gideon was able to get both hands on the stock, but his leverage was no good. Timken's finger found the trigger and he began slowly forcing the barrel around.

From behind Timken the hooded man groaned. Timken glanced backward. It was just the break Gideon needed.

He reached down toward the dead man, grabbed a pair of needle-nose pliers from the bomb-maker's vest and jammed them into Timken's neck.

Timken screamed and grabbed his throat. He tried to say something, but it was lost in a fountain of blood coming out of his mouth. He stumbled backward, knocking over the box, so that it fell on top of the hooded man. Timken pulled the pliers from his neck, eyes wide with panic, then slipped in his own blood, fell on top of the box, and stopped moving.

Gideon stepped around Timken and yanked the box off the prone body of the hooded man, then pulled the hood from his face. The man's mouth was gagged with several loops of blood-smeared duct tape and his clothes and bearded face were covered with blood, obscuring his features. It took Gideon a moment to realize that it was Timken's blood, not that of the man who lay on the floor. Gideon quickly unwrapped the duct tape, the man's eyes blinking as they adjusted to the light.

"Gideon?" the man said, wincing. "Is that you?"

■ ■ ■ ■

The wind hit Major Dale Royce Jr. like a hammer as he jumped from the rear of the C-17 into the blinding sun. As he caught the slipstream, his body spun, the motion twisting his already broken ankle. He screamed. Dale Royce had played football at the academy and had gone through all of the most dangerous and painful training that the United States Army could dish out.

But never had he felt pain like this.

He spread his arms instinctively, slowing in the wind. The buffeting jiggled his ankle. But still, unaccountably, he felt a grin come across his face. Below him, stretching out to the west, was a great blue circle, surrounded by towering walls of cloud. It was surely the most amazing thing he had ever seen.

And at the edge of the circle was a tiny black dot. The Obelisk.

The drop had been pretty good. But not perfect. If they'd done a high altitude, *high* open drop, it would have been a piece of cake to land on the rig. But HALO — high altitude, *low* open drop — meant they'd fall over forty-two thousand feet before opening their chutes. Then they'd pull their ripcords at five hundred feet. A modern square ram-air chute could cover several hundred horizontal feet for every thousand feet of fall. On a HALO drop over these lethal seas, there was no room for a near miss. If you were more than a few hundred ground-feet from the rig when you pulled, you were a dead man.

So you had to steer in free fall.

Steering meant diving headfirst, extending your toes, pulling your arms to your sides, and using your feet as rudders. His team had worked out the order in which they would fall, transitioning from belly diving to head-down diving. With the greater speed and aerodynamic control of the head-down dive, they could head downward in a stack, just like a formation of fighter jets. One by one, his men assumed their positions. He followed, last.

It was only as he straightened his legs and pulled in his arms that he realized he couldn't point his left toe. In fact, when he looked down, he saw that it had been twisted backward by the force of the wind. And now the drag of his ruined foot was causing him to roll slowly over, like a plane doing a barrel roll. He tried to countersteer with his right hand. To his relief, he steadied.

Below him, though, his men were slowly drawing away from him. And, to his horror, he realized that he would be unable to steer in any meaningful way. Just keeping himself stable was going to destroy his ability to steer the dive. His men were heading in perfect formation toward the Obelisk. But he was veering slowly to the west. By the time he reached the water, he realized, he'd be as much as a mile off course.

He couldn't deploy his chute high enough to steer himself to the rig or he'd risk giving his men away. The success of any HALO jump rested on pulling so low that the enemy had no time to react. If somebody was scanning the sky and saw him deploy half a minute before his boys hit the Obelisk, the enemy would sit there and pick them right out of the sky.

It hit him with a strange shock. He was a dead man. In this orientation, he was moving at roughly 150 miles an hour, terminal velocity. He'd be airborne for nearly a minute. He wore an inflatable life vest. But so what? No one would be able to get to him to pick him up from those mammoth waves. He'd fight until he drowned or until exhaustion and hypothermia finished him off.

The men all wore comm links, but they were observing radio silence, so he couldn't even alert them to his plight. The senior

NCO, Sergeant Williams, would take command when they hit the deck. He'd do fine. Every man would do his job.

The formation of his men was drawing farther and farther away. An odd feeling of peace washed through him. *Perfect.* His boys were perfect. Royce felt a burst of pride. They'd make it. Every single man in his team would make it.

And if they hit that deck together, the bastards on that rig wouldn't stand a chance. He smiled. Well, he wouldn't make it . . . but the mission would succeed.

This was what it was all about, Royce thought. *How many men could say they'd lived a life like his? Not many. Not very damn many.*

At about twenty thousand feet, though, Royce realized he was writing his own epitaph prematurely. There was no need for him to crash into the waves. If he just splayed his legs and arms into a normal controlled descent position, he could slow his fall by nearly thirty miles an hour, allowing his men to hit the Obelisk well before he got close to the ground. Then he could pull the rip cord high enough that he should be able to pilot the nimble parafoil chute to his destination. He'd arrive late for his command. But he'd get there.

He opened his arms, and suddenly his men began to break away from him with remarkable speed.

Thirty seconds later, he saw the first parachute blossom below him. And he was still at over five thousand feet! Royce immediately pulled the ripcord, felt the massive jerk of deployment, then began gliding in a slow circle down toward the speck in the water below.

He readied his gear as the Obelisk grew closer and closer. He looked at his arm. Taped to the inside of his forearm was a photograph of the target, Tillman Davis. In the photo he wore a dress uniform, hair high and tight, black eyes staring unwaveringly at the camera. Looked like a hell of a warrior. Royce wondered where the man had gone wrong.

As the first chute blossomed, Royce spoke into his mic for the first time: "Guys, you know your orders. Every one of you has a picture of the target on your sleeve. You make a positive ID on Tillman Davis, you take him out."

A tide of emotion flooded Gideon Davis as he stared at the man on the floor. For the first time the savagery and pace of the past few days hit him, and his legs went so weak he was afraid he couldn't keep standing.

"Tillman?" The man on the floor nodded. "Earl told me you were dead."

Then, from somewhere above them they heard the sound of gunfire.

CHAPTER FORTY-TWO

Kate crouched over Big Al on the floor of the dive station as her old friend tried to breathe, a thin stream of blood running from his mouth.

He inhaled, shallow and ragged, then said, "He must have hit me in the lung."

"Don't talk, Al," she said, applying a compression bandage to his wound.

"Look," he said, pointing feebly past her to the other deck.

Kate thought maybe she was hallucinating when she turned and saw a handful of paratroopers descending onto the chopper deck. Relief coursed through her. Even from here she could see the small rectangular patches on their shoulders: the American flag had never looked so good to her in her life.

There was a brief flurry of shouting and gunfire as a gaggle of Timken's mercenaries burst onto A Deck and began shooting at the soldiers.

Big Al grabbed her sleeve. "Hey," he said, his gravelly voice now full of an ominous bubbling sound. "Listen to me, *chérie.*"

"Shh!" Kate said. "Just hang on! Help's coming."

"Listen," he said. His eyes lost focus for a moment, but then he winced and continued. "Don't let yourself die alone just because of Ben. It was bad luck, the thing that happened to him."

Kate felt the same stab of loneliness that pierced her every time she thought about Ben.

On the other platform the shooting continued furiously. The mercenaries — where she could see them — looked frightened and frantic. The American soldiers, on the other hand, seemed businesslike, making crisp hand signals to one another or shouting brief gnomic messages to one another: "Frag out! Tango down! Two in motion, flank left!" They had the unhurried competence of a well-drilled football team.

And suddenly the firing stopped. The soldiers on the other side of the rig were now disappearing inside the rig, leaving the fallen bodies of at least half a dozen of Timken's mercenaries.

"I saw the way you looked at him," Big Al

whispered. "Don't let what happened to Ben stop you from living your life."

"Help!" Kate screamed. "I need medical help over here!"

She heard several loud pops, half swallowed by the rig. Then silence.

"Over here!"

"Promise me, you'll let yourself be happy," Big Al said, his eyes closing heavily. "Promise me."

Then he took his last ragged breath, blood bubbling from his mouth.

Kate began crying quietly, in stark counterpoint to the gunfire that erupted in another part of the rig.

Gideon used his Benchmark to cut his brother's flex cuff, then pulled him to his feet.

"It's Parker," Gideon said. "He's behind everything."

"Uncle Earl?" Tillman stared, as if trying to piece together what had happened.

"Are you surprised?"

"Not really."

"He told me you'd switched sides. That you were working for the insurgents."

When Tillman finally answered, his voice cracked with regret. "I was. But only because he wanted me to stay under. I took my orders directly and exclusively from him. And my mission was to penetrate the insurgency as deeply as I could. Which meant doing some pretty bad things." He drifted off, lost in some painful memory before his eyes shifted back to Gideon. "When I told him I wanted to quit, he said he'd have me killed before he let me out. I knew he'd established enough plausible deniability that no one would have listened to me."

"I would have," Gideon said.

"I didn't think you'd understand."

"So you ran away to Kampong Naga."

Tillman nodded, then went on to explain how the village had been shelled, and how he'd been grabbed and drugged by Timken.

"He sold us out. Both of us. He used General Prang. He hired Timken to impersonate you, and a bunch of mercenaries to hijack the rig, pretending to be Islamic terrorists on some kind of suicide mission. Their plan is to blow the rig and frame you for it. When the bodies were found, yours would be among them. I imagine they were going to shoot you and make it look like you'd been killed in the assault."

"What assault?"

Gideon cocked his head at the furious gunfire above them. "That one. A Delta Force team just HALO jumped onto the rig." As soon as he spoke, the gunfire slackened. "They may need help." Gideon pulled a Makarov from the hip of the downed bomb-maker on the other side of the box, tossed it to Tillman.

"I'm still a little groggy. I got my bell rung when I hit the deck here." Tillman pulled the slide back half an inch, verifying that a round was chambered, and looked over the sights, then gave Gideon a sly smile. "But I'll do what I can."

Gideon glanced at the timer on the bomb. Just under three hours. Still enough time. If they had to, they could evacuate the hostages into the escape pods and drop into the ocean before the bomb went off. It wouldn't be a lot of fun riding in one of those pods, especially not after the eye passed and was replaced by another storm. But they'd survive.

Tillman suddenly gripped Gideon's shoulders. "Man, it's been too long." He pulled Gideon into a strong hug, which Gideon reciprocated. "I'm sorry things got so messed up between us."

"Me too." Gideon said. There were a thousand things he wanted to tell his brother, but he knew they would have to wait. "Let's go."

Tillman trailed Gideon as they charged

out into the hallway and headed for the stairs. This would all be over soon.

As they climbed the stairs, they heard gunshots on one of the upper decks and the calm assured voices of American soldiers. Gideon sprinted ahead, up the stairs to the chopper deck, where he found a handful of camo-clad soldiers.

"Thank God you're here!" Gideon shouted.

The four men turned, aiming their M-4 carbines at him. Gideon expected the men to greet him enthusiastically. Instead, their eyes went straight to his AK-47. Their faces were hard.

"Put your weapon down!" one of them shouted. "Weapon down!"

Gideon gingerly set his AK-47 down. "It's okay," he said. "I'm Gideon Davis. The president —"

"I know who you are, sir. Down on the ground! On your knees and lace your hands behind your head!" The soldier's commands were nonnegotiable.

Gideon could hear Tillman clumping slowly up the steps behind him. The effects of his drugged captivity had obviously not quite worn off: he was lagging well behind.

Suddenly Gideon noticed something. Taped to the inside of every soldier's left forearm was a photograph of Tillman. It didn't take a lot of imagination to figure out that it meant Tillman was their target.

"Wait!" Gideon shouted, as Tillman crested the stairs, brandishing the Makarov. "There's been a mistake! Don't shoot him!" Gideon flung himself in front of Tillman's body. For a moment everyone froze. Four carbines were leveled at Gideon's chest.

One of the men's eyes flicked to the photo on his arm, trying to make sure who he had authorization to kill here.

"Drop it! Put that weapon down! Do it now!"

"Don't!" Gideon shouted. "He's not the enemy here."

The soldiers hesitated, puzzled.

Then a man in a dark suit stepped out from behind a door.

"Excellent work, boys!" the man said. "I'm assistant national security advisor Earl Parker." Parker scanned the soldiers to determine which one was in command. He quickly ascertained that the ranking officer was a tall man at the back of the cluster of soldiers who was clearly favoring one leg. Parker's voice rang with parade ground military authority. "Major Royce, that man is the terrorist Tillman Davis. His brother,

Gideon Davis, was his inside man, coordinating this terrorist operation. Shoot them."

"Sir?" the Delta officer said.

"I have direct authorization from the president," Earl Parker snapped. "Your orders are to use lethal force."

Gideon continued shielding his brother with his body. "He has no such authority!" Gideon shouted. "I work directly for the president —"

"Shoot them!" Parker shouted. "These are enemies of the United States."

Gideon saw then that the Delta Force commander was badly injured. One of his feet was turned around almost backward, like a broken GI Joe doll. He was sweating profusely, and his skin was pale. "Down on the ground," the Delta Force major grunted. "Both of you. I'm taking you both into custody until I sort this out."

"On the ground!" his men echoed.

"Put the gun down, Tillman," Gideon said softly. "Put it down or they'll kill you."

Reluctantly Tillman set down the Makarov, got on his knees, and laced his fingers behind his head.

"You need to take them out, Major!" Parker shouted.

Royce shook his head. "Sir, I can't —" He grabbed the wall next to him like he was

about to lose his balance. "I can't authorize . . ."

"He's lying!" Tillman said. "He's the one
who —"

"Shut it!" An enormous blond soldier
lifted his rifle like he was going to swat
Tillman across the face.

Tillman eyed the man briefly, then decided to keep his mouth shut. He glared at
Parker.

"D Deck clear!" a voice shouted from
below.

"All decks clear!" another voice called.

"Major Royce," Earl Parker said, "you're
obviously confused about your orders, I'm
going to have the president call you directly."

"Mr. Parker, until the rig is secure I need
you to —" Parker ignored Royce, turning
his back on the soldiers and walking briskly
past Tillman and down the stairs. Under
other circumstances, the Delta commander
might have enforced his authority more
vigorously. But it was obvious he was barely
holding himself together against the pain of
his injury.

"You son of a bitch!" Tillman shouted.
"You sold me out!"

The big blond soldier backhanded Tillman, knocking him over, as the other Delta

Force operatives pinned the brothers to the ground, knees on their necks.

As Earl Parker disappeared down the stairs, it all came clear in Gideon's mind: Earl Parker was improvising an exit strategy. He would return to Washington saying that Tillman and Gideon had been in league with each other from the very beginning. Parker could be trusted to have assembled a long and detailed trail of evidence to bolster his claim that Tillman was behind the seizure of the rig. From there it wouldn't be hard to push the claim a little farther — saying that Gideon had been involved, too. Blood was thicker than water, right?

Once they got back to the States, Parker's story would seem more plausible than Gideon's. Except for Prejean, Kate, and Gideon, none of the hostages who were still alive had ever seen Parker interacting with Timken. Nor had they ever seen Timken's face. As far as everybody on the rig knew, Tillman had run the show when the bad guys seized the Obelisk. Now Timken and his men were almost certainly all dead. Gideon was pretty sure that Big Al was dying. If Big Al died, there was only one other person on the rig — other than Tillman and Gideon — who could testify directly about Parker's involvement with the plot.

Kate.

If Parker could eliminate Kate, it would be Gideon's word against Parker's.

The logical conclusion hit him with the force of a fist in the gut: Parker was going to kill Kate.

And he was going to do it now.

"Major Royce," Gideon shouted at the commanding officer of the Delta men. "You have to stop Parker. If you're going to detain me, then at least detain him, too!"

Royce's face was white. It was obvious he was in great pain from his wrecked foot. His teeth were clenched and he seemed close to losing consciousness.

"Major Royce!"

The officer sat down hard on a barrel and blinked. "Sergeant Williams," he said vaguely. "I think I need medical attention. You're gonna have to take . . . uh . . ."

"Sir?" a lean black soldier said.

Royce lost consciousness and fell over sideways, his head hitting the barrel with a hollow clang.

"Sergeant Edy," the thin black soldier barked, "you need to render assistance to the CO. I'm gonna go down and make sure the platform is clear. Sergeant Nilson, secure these individuals while I reconnoiter."

"Hold on, Sergeant Williams!" Gideon said. "You need to —"

But the lean black soldier ignored Gideon and hurried down the stairs.

The corpsman got busy working on the downed officer's foot.

"Sergeant!" Gideon called again.

"Sir, you need to be quiet right now." Nilson turned out to be the huge blond man. He was a good six foot five, and a muscular two-eighty. Gideon could see there was no arguing with him.

Gideon spotted Earl Parker in the distance. He had reached the bridge to the other half of the rig and was walking purposefully toward the BLP. A Makarov now dangled inconspicuously from his hand. He'd obviously harvested the weapon from one of Timken's dead mercenaries. Gideon saw that Parker had screwed a silencer onto the barrel.

The dive station where Gideon had left Kate and Big Al was on the far side of the BLP, out of sight of any of the small group of Delta men on the drilling platform.

"Parker is going over there to kill a woman who can testify against him," Gideon whispered to Tillman. "I need your help."

"Sir! I instructed you to be quiet. I'm not saying it again!" Sergeant Nilson loomed over Gideon, the barrel of his M-4 perilously close to Gideon's face.

It wouldn't take any time at all before Parker reached Kate. When he did, he'd just shoot her. With a silenced Makarov, no one would even hear the shot.

Parker would tell the Delta guys that he'd heard her calling, gone to help her out, and found her dead from her wounds. No one would even think twice. Just an unlucky hostage caught in the crossfire.

Gideon desperately scanned the chopper deck. Major Royce was still down, and the corpsman was still busy working on his wrecked foot.

Which meant that if they could get the huge Nilson out of the way, Gideon *might* have a chance to make it to the BLP in time to save Kate.

One of the beautiful things about family is that sometimes you barely have to say anything in order to communicate.

After their parents died, Earl Parker had paid for Tillman and Gideon to attend boarding school, where they'd both played football. Gideon had been the up-and-coming freshman quarterback, and Tillman had been the journeyman fullback. Though Tillman got the odd screen pass or off tackle running play, he had primarily been a blocking fullback. Which meant he'd spent most of his senior year getting smashed by boys who outweighed him by fifty pounds as he protected his brother.

It was just like the rest of their childhood: Tillman had protected Gideon without much apparent thought for himself. In retrospect Gideon had always wondered if Tillman had resented the attention heaped on Gideon. If he had, though, he'd never said anything about it to Gideon. He'd just unhesitatingly thrown himself between Gideon and every onrushing danger.

Now it was time to call an audible.

"Angel seven fifteen right," Gideon said.

Tillman looked at him curiously. Gideon sure as hell hoped Tillman remembered the old playbook like he did. Angel seven fifteen right had been an option play, with the left guard shifting against the right tackle and Gideon flinging himself into the gap and hitting the opposing right guard.

"I'm not telling you again!" the huge soldier Nilson shouted.

Tillman smiled thinly and winked. Then he flung himself forward without hesitation. Gideon heard the thud of his brother's tackle but he couldn't stop to watch. He jumped to his feet and leapt over the guard-rail, flailing momentarily in midair before landing hard on the deck.

Behind him he heard a loud crack, the sound of a single gunshot, and a soft grunt of pain. It was Tillman's voice.

No, he thought. *Not Tillman. Not now.*

But he couldn't stop, couldn't look back. He tore down the stairs, reaching the bridge to the BLP in seconds. A fallen mercenary lay in a pool of blood. Gideon tried to grab the man's AK, but the dead man was tangled in the sling. It would take too long, so he yanked the Makarov from the man's belt and ran across the bridge. Behind him the Delta men were yelling and coordinating to stop him.

Reaching the BLP, he sprinted to the stairs, jumped down to the landing in one bound, then onto D Deck in another bound, and turned the corner.

A flash of white — Parker's thick white hair — disappeared behind one of the orange plastic escape pods on the far corner of the rig, not fifty feet from the dive station.

Gideon cut across the open D Deck and circled around the far side of the rig so that he could confront Parker from the dive station.

It was as he had feared. Big Al lay motionless on the deck, his chest awash with blood.

Kate was crouched over him, her face in her hands, sobbing.

And Parker was approaching from the direction of the escape pods, the Makarov extended in his hands.

"Kate, look out!" Gideon shouted.

Hearing Gideon's voice, she whirled around, eyes wide.

"Behind you!"

She looked back. But it was too late for her to make a move: Parker had the drop on her.

"Don't do it, Earl!" Gideon shouted.

Parker's eyes met Gideon's. They were about forty yards apart. Gideon's front sight rested on Parker's chest. It was a long shot — but not an impossible one. Gideon's finger tightened against the trigger, but something stopped him. His hesitation was all the time Parker needed. Parker had seen the results of Gideon's shooting today and knew that he was outgunned. So instead of shooting Kate, he grabbed her hair and yanked her on to her feet. Before she could struggle, he put the gun to her head.

Still numb with grief over Big Al's death, she didn't resist. She just stood there limply, tears still running down her face.

Gideon moved slowly toward Parker.

"Not another step," Parker said. His voice

was quiet, calm, conversational. Presumably he didn't want the Delta men overhearing him.

Gideon kept moving. Parker was keeping his body firmly positioned behind Kate, his left arm under her throat. To look at him, you wouldn't have thought he was particularly agile or athletic. But Gideon knew that he'd been a marine recon officer in Vietnam, and his sixty-year-old body still contained the soul of a warrior.

"I *will* shoot her," Parker said.

But Gideon crept forward — one slow step, then another. He needed to get close enough so that he could be absolutely sure that he would hit Parker and not Kate.

Parker fired. For a moment Gideon thought she was dead. But Parker had moved the barrel just enough so that the tip of the suppressor had been lying on Kate's face, not aimed at her head. The escaping gases left a long red welt on her cheek.

"Next one goes into her brain," Parker said softly.

Gideon stopped. "Come on, Uncle Earl. You can't seriously think you'll get away with this." In truth, though, Gideon knew that if Earl Parker killed Kate, there was a pretty good chance he might get away with it. Whatever evidence he'd doctored would probably trump any claims Gideon would make.

Parker smiled an odd smile. "The clock's running out." He turned his left wrist around so he could look at his watch. Gideon saw that he was holding something in his hand, some kind of small metal cylinder. But he couldn't make out exactly what it was.

Parker backed toward the nearest escape pod, pulling Kate with him.

Gideon tracked them with his front sight. Parker was being very careful, though, to keep his body squarely behind Kate. Only a two-inch-wide slice of his head was visible. Not much of a shot from thirty yards.

"I can see you debating," Parker said. "You've got a moving target a couple of inches wide and an unfamiliar gun that may or may not shoot accurately to begin with. The only way to stop me at this range is to shoot me in the head. If you miss wide to the left, then I'll have plenty of opportunity to shoot her. If you miss wide to the right, then *you* shoot her. Either way you're thinking: 'Do I risk the shot?' "

Gideon said nothing as Parker inched back another foot or two. Unfortunately Parker was right. He had to hit a two-inch-wide moving target at over ten yards with a gun of unknown accuracy. Still, Gideon was giving it some thought. At a certain point, he had to take the risk.

"Before you take the shot, though," Parker continued, "you might want to consider one more factor." He stuck out his clenched fist and brandished the small cylinder. Gideon saw more clearly now that it had a plastic handle on the side.

"Dead man's switch," Parker said. "We had contingencies. We knew it might come down to a last-ditch situation like this. It works like this: if I let go of the handle, it sends a radio signal to the control equipment down in that little room on the drilling platform, and the bomb detonates. So forget about Kate here. If you shoot me she still dies. And so do all those heroic soldiers. And so does the entire crew of the Obelisk."

Gideon looked at Kate, but Parker answered his question before he could ask.

"She didn't disarm the bomb, if that's what you're wondering," Parker said. "I checked. There's a monitoring system down on the control equipment. If you disconnect a detonator from one of the shaped charges, a little green LED blinks off, and a little red one blinks on. You managed to defuse two of them. But the other ten are fine. I'm sure Kate will tell you that two bolts will not hold the weight of a forty-thousand-ton damper counterweight."

"Is that true, Kate?" Gideon asked.

Kate nodded.

Parker edged closer to the escape pod — close enough now that his hand was resting on the plastic door of the pod.

Gideon's eyes met Parker's. "I truly am sorry that it has to end this way," Parker said.

"Shoot him," Kate said calmly. Her eyes had gone hard as stones.

"You really want to commit suicide?" Parker said.

She laughed.

"What's so funny?"

"Do you know what the main industrial use for shaped charges is?" Kate said. Before Parker could answer, she said, "Their main industrial application is in the oil and gas industry. We use them to breach drilling pipe."

"So?" Earl Parker's voice was brittle as glass.

"So you think I don't know a shaped charge when I see one? You think I don't know with a great deal of precision how they work?"

Parker's face showed no emotion. With his left hand he was slowly opening the door to the escape pod.

"I saw two sets of wires coming out of the charges. I knew the second circuit had to be some kind of failsafe. I figured if I pulled out the detonator, it might trigger the second circuit and cause the whole thing to blow up."

"So you didn't touch them," Parker said.

"I didn't say that," she said. "See, a shaped charge is like the surgical knife of explosives. It projects its force in one direction. If the charges aren't precisely located on those bolts, they won't do squat."

Parker's hand froze on the orange door.

"So I just kicked the charges off the bolts," Kate said. "They're just dangling there in the water, fifty meters down. Oh, sure, the bomb's still armed. It'll make some noise, knock a few chunks of concrete out of one of the piers. But other than that?" She shrugged.

Parker's self-assured facade faltered. "You're lying."

"Try me."

Parker's eyes went from Kate to Gideon to Kate. And finally back to Gideon again. "Gideon, you're wrong. You've been wrong from day one. We'll never beat these people unless we show the same will, the same ruthlessness, the same —"

"Do you trust me, Gideon?" Kate said. Her green eyes bored into his. She gave him a gentle, half-smile.

"Absolutely," Gideon said.

"Then shoot him," Kate said. "Shoot the son of a bitch."

Parker swallowed and released the handle on the bomb.

For a moment nothing happened. Then a heavy thud welled up from deep underneath them. The entire rig shook slightly.

And then . . . nothing.

Gideon waited for the aftershocks, for the sound of screaming metal, waited for the rig to fail. But the soft wind continued to blow, the huge waves continued to roll under the rig.

For the first time, panic crept into Parker's eyes. His hand tightened on the grip of the Makarov. Gideon could see he was going to shoot Kate. The shock of the moment would give him time to dive into the escape pod and slap the big red button he'd been talking about.

He smiled. "You don't have the stomach, Gideon. You never did."

"Shoot him," Kate said for the third time. Then her body went limp and she dropped. As her body became dead weight, Parker was forced to let her go. His entire

494

torso was completely exposed.

Gideon pulled the trigger, felt the Makarov buck under his hand. The shot caught Parker on the bridge of his nose.

He fell without a sound.

"Drop the weapon!" a voice shouted. "Now!"

Gideon tossed the Makarov over the side and into the massive waves. "I'm done," he said. "It's over."

CHAPTER FORTY-THREE

The submarine had risen from the waves just a few hundred yards to the west of The Obelisk, water sluicing down from its conning towers. Kate touched the body bag that held Big Al Prejean until the last possible moment, when the solders lowered it down the side of the rig and into one of the zodiacs that had been launched from the sub to ferry the wounded and the dead. It surprised her that her grief was somehow tempered by the gratitude she felt for having known the crazy Cajun. She vowed silently not to forsake his last words to her, before turning to find Gideon and his brother, who were still in custody.

She found Major Royce talking on a satellite phone. The color had returned to his face as he lowered the phone and limped toward Gideon on his wrapped ankle. The Delta Force officer looked much recovered, now that he'd been worked on by his medical corpsman. "The president says you're free to go," he said, nodding to Sergeant Nilson, who removed the cuffs from Gideon's wrists.

"What about my brother?" Gideon asked.

"The president wants him transported stateside by the first available means." Major Royce pointed at the submarine. "The USS *Glenard P. Lipscomb* is the first available means."

"Everything that you were told about my brother was a lie," Gideon said. "He came here as a prisoner of the men who seized the rig. He was framed."

"I have my orders," Major Royce repeated.

"It's okay, Gideon," Tillman said. "Major Royce is just doing his job. We're all on the same team. This whole thing will be squared away as soon as you get back to Washington. You'll see."

Gideon reluctantly agreed. It wasn't as if he had much choice.

"Besides, there's a doctor on the sub," Major Royce said. "We'll get Lieutenant Davis some medical attention for his wound." Tillman was still bleeding from where Sergeant Nilson's bullet had grazed him when he ran interference for Gideon just minutes earlier.

Gideon couldn't help noting that Royce

referred to Tillman as *Lieutenant Davis.* That had to be a good sign.

"I'll be leaving half my team here to secure the rig," Royce added. "The rest will accompany me and the prisoner back to the U.S."

"I understand," Gideon said.

"Given that the typhoon is about to hit again, I wish I could evacuate everyone off this rig," Royce added. "But I can't. Not enough room on the sub. Captain Oliphant has radioed me to say that I can take back two additional individuals. Mr. Davis, Ms. Murphy — I'm offering to take you immediately to safety."

"And abandon my crew?" Kate said. "Not a chance."

Royce nodded. "Very well. Mr. Davis, if you would accompany me up to the chopper deck, I'll have my men rig you up so we can drop you in the boat. I know it looks a little scary down there but —"

Gideon cut him off. "I'm staying, too."

Royce looked at him curiously. "You're *what?*"

"You heard me. I'm staying. With Ms. Murphy."

Royce looked from Gideon to Kate and then back to Gideon again. "I'm afraid I'm going to have to insist," he said.

"Unless you want to carry me, I'm not getting on that sub," Gideon said.

Major Royce stared at Gideon.

Tillman spoke up for the first time, "Major, my brother is the most stubborn son of a bitch on the planet. So unless you plan to carry him, you might as well save your breath."

Royce finally nodded.

Gideon stepped toward his brother. They shook hands. "Don't you worry for a single minute, Tillman," Gideon said. "I'm going to get this all straightened out."

Tillman smiled broadly. "Of course you will. You can do anything. Hell, you're Tillman Davis's brother."

The two men laughed.

Suddenly Tillman reached out and grabbed Gideon, hugged him hard. "I owe you one," he whispered.

"Like hell you do," Gideon said. "You'd have done the same thing for me."

There was so much more Gideon wanted to say to him. He'd traveled halfway across the world, gone through all this craziness — and now they barely had time to speak to each other before being separated again. He wanted to say how foolish their estrangement had been, how things would never be like that again, how he'd never doubt his brother again.

But there would be time later. There would be plenty of time.

"Let's go," Major Royce said. "The storm's about to blow back in."

By the time the submarine slipped beneath the massive waves, the wind had picked up and the wall of ugly black clouds was looming over the rig again.

The entire crew of the Obelisk had gathered on the chopper deck to watch the submarine depart, so Kate took a quick head count. Her worst fears turned out not to be justified. Several crew members had been wounded by gunfire during the seizure of the rig — but other than Big Al and the diver who had been shot in front of Kate and Gideon, none had died.

With no submarine to watch, the crew began to disperse, locking down for the imminent storm.

"Looks like we're in for some weather," Gideon said.

"Could be," she said.

Gideon rubbed his eyes and sighed. "I can't remember the last time I slept," he said.

"You can get some sleep in my cabin," she said.

A ghost of a smile licked at the corners of Gideon's mouth. Then a sudden gust of wind hit them so hard that it nearly knocked them over.

"Everybody off the deck!" Kate shouted. "I don't want anybody getting blown into the sea."

Once the deck was clear, Kate and Gideon walked down to Kate's cabin. She pointed to her bed. "Perk of the job. The only double bed on the rig. Good place to ride out the storm?"

"Perfect," he said, falling onto it wearily.

"You did it," she said. "You came to get your brother, and you got him."

"Yeah," he said.

"You saved his life. You saved all of us." She brushed some stray hair from his forehead. "I'll be right back." Then she went into the bathroom, stripped off her wet clothes, and returned to her cabin, wrapped in nothing but a towel.

But by the time she'd returned, Gideon's eyes were closed.

Kate sat down next to him on the bed. For the first time since she'd met him, his face was completely peaceful. He didn't stir.

"All right then," she said. "I guess that's how it is."

She pulled the sheet over him — when his

eyes suddenly opened.

"You need to sleep," she said softly.

"I'll sleep later," he said, then kissed her as the wind outside began to howl, and the waves rolled powerfully beneath them.

ACKNOWLEDGMENTS

Writing this book has been an eye-opening education for me. Television is a famously collaborative medium, but it turns out that publishing is too. Stacy Creamer — my publisher, my editor, and now, my friend — took a chance on a rookie and remained a steadfast beacon throughout this process, and for that I will always be grateful. Stacy's energy and optimism are boundless, which is why her assistant, Lauren Spiegel, deserves special credit for keeping pace.

I am also indebted to the rest of the talented team at Touchstone, including Joy O'Meara, Michael Kwan, Mara Lurie, Kevin McCahill, and Shelly Perron, the tireless and exacting production group; and David Falk, Meredith Kernan, Marcia Burch, and Shida Carr, who've risen and continue to rise to the challenge of marketing and publicizing this book so people know it's out there; and Cherlynne Li, who designed the terrific book jacket.

My colleagues on *24* have not only inspired me over these past nine years, they've been a second family. To have been one of so many dedicated people — cast and crew, writers, directors, editors, and office staff — who all took so much pride in their work was truly a privilege.

My children, Micah, Arlo, and Capp, are the best reasons I've ever found for doing what I do, and I hope I have made them half as proud as they've made me.

Finally, I'd like to express my profound appreciation to Richard Abate, who dared me, then encouraged me to take on this challenge, and to Walter Sorrells, without whose generous help this book would never have been possible.

ABOUT THE AUTHOR

Howard Gordon is an Emmy and Golden Globe award-winning writer and producer who has worked in Hollywood for more than twenty years. He served as executive producer of the hit television show *24* for its full eight-season run, and prior to working on *24,* Gordon was a writer and executive producer for *The X-Files.* He lives with his family in Pacific Palisades, California.

www.GideonsWar.com

www.HowardMGordon.com